The GPS ar

destination."

She didn't re

those at the entrances to exclusive communities. Then, seeing the sign "Sanderson Estates," she realized that this was such a community—the one her uncle had established since her last visit.

She pulled up to the gates and stopped. A tall, well-built, very tan young man in a white Oxford shirt and jeans—a security guard—came out of a small brick building beside the drive. Clean shaven, with dark curls cropped short and strong, even features, he reminded her of the statue pictured on the cover of her high school Latin textbook. She lowered her window, and he looked in at her, examining her with direct gray eyes. He held a clipboard and had a gun tucked into his belt.

Her hands grew cold. "I'm Clare Matthews, Sally Sanderson's cousin. They know I'm coming."

He looked at the clipboard, unsmiling. "You have some identification, Miss?"

PRAISE FOR PATRICIA MCALEXANDER:

STRANGER IN THE STORM (First Place, Suspense Short, National Excellence in Story Telling)

"…A wonderful romance thriller…filled with twists, turns, and suspense…"

~Still Moments Magazine

~*~

SHADOWS OF DOUBT (Heart Awards Finalist, Oklahoma Romance Writers Guild)

"A coming-of-age novel involving the dark underworld of college drug dealing…At once chilling and literary."

~ Molly Hurley Moran, author of Finding Susan

~*~

THE STUDENT IN CLASSROOM 6

"A fast-paced romance with a dangerous edge that is easy to read and hard to put down."

~Lori Duffy Foster, author of the Lisa Jamison Mystery Series

The Last Golden Isle

by

Patricia McAlexander

This is a work of fiction. Names, characters, places, and incidents are either the product of the author's imagination or are used fictitiously, and any resemblance to actual persons living or dead, business establishments, events, or locales, is entirely coincidental.

The Last Golden Isle

COPYRIGHT © 2023 by Patricia Jewell McAlexander

All rights reserved. No part of this book may be used or reproduced in any manner whatsoever without written permission of the author or The Wild Rose Press, Inc. except in the case of brief quotations embodied in critical articles or reviews.
Contact Information: info@thewildrosepress.com

Cover Art by *Rae Monet, Inc.*

The Wild Rose Press, Inc.
PO Box 708
Adams Basin, NY 14410-0708
Visit us at www.thewildrosepress.com

Publishing History
First Edition, 2023
Trade Paperback ISBN 978-1-5092-5199-5
Digital ISBN 978-1-5092-5200-8

Published in the United States of America

Dedication

To Alexis, who introduced me to Tybee, the island that inspired the setting of this book, and, once again, to Dorothy, Jane, and Kaycee, who helped bring this book into being.

Author's Note

Nestled along the Georgia coast lie some fifteen protective barrier islands, formed between 40,000 and 4,000 years ago. The oldest of these arose before the last great continental ice sheet formed, the later ones when that ice sheet started to melt, and the sea flooded onto the land.

Treasure-seeking Spanish explorers descending upon the area more than four hundred years ago found only these beautiful islands rather than gold. Perhaps that's why they came to be called "The Golden Isles," the term most tourists now associate with four of them—Jekyll, St. Simons, Sea Island, and Little St. Simons. The main setting of this novel is a small fictional fifth Golden Isle—St. Sebastian's. I imagine it as north of those four and farther out in the ocean, not easily accessible to the public until the late 1980s, when it was linked to the coast by the longest of the island causeways. Then publicized as "The Last Golden Isle," my imaginary St. Sebastian's became a popular tourist destination.

This story takes place in the spring and summer of 2015.

Chapter One

Wednesday, May 6 - Friday, May 8, 2015

The drumbeats of dance music on the floor below pounded, pounded, almost, it seemed, in time with the pounding between her legs tearing her apart. It went on and on until at last there came another sound, faint at first, then increasing in volume—a rapping on a door. The music and pain faded, but the raps continued.

Clare Matthews woke up, her heart racing. Four years had passed, but the nightmare recurred at unexplained intervals. The door to her bedroom opened, and her mother looked in—tall, thin, dark hair graying at the temples, concern on her face. "Honey, I heard you cry out. Are you all right?"

Clare, who had always hidden the nightmares from her mother, tried to sound normal. "I'm fine. I must have been dreaming. What time is it?"

"Almost ten." Her mother entered and stood by the bed. "Maybe you're still upset about your job falling through."

Clare sat up, pulling her fallen nightgown straps up over her shoulders, pushing back her long hair. "That must have been it."

She'd planned to earn money for graduate school by working that summer as a researcher at the University of Georgia library archives, viewing old news reels, categorizing and digitizing them. After their May fourth graduation from the University, many of her classmates had headed to full time jobs in cities like Atlanta, Washington, D.C., and New York. Clare, however, looked forward to the archives' safe, self-contained, air-conditioned space all summer and to working on a master's degree in English in the fall. Then, just the day before, the library director texted her, telling her the grant had fallen through and they'd had to cut her position. "You know," her mother told her immediately after the text came in, "maybe this is for the best. You don't have to go back for a master's. It's time you went out in the world. Private schools in Athens and Atlanta are still hiring teachers with bachelor's degrees. You've focused on your studies too long, been too anti-social, ever since *that night…*"

Clare of course knew what night her mother referred to. The subject was supposed to be taboo. That forbidden reference must have brought on her nightmare.

In spite of her efforts to suppress them, something always triggered the memories of that August four years ago when she was a first-year student at the University and a new sorority pledge. Only a few days after classes started, she'd been invited with a group of "sisters" to a fraternity party at an off-campus house. Something must have been put in her drink. She didn't remember how she got upstairs to that bedroom or who took her there. She just remembered being blindfolded, then held down while three males took their turn on her.

"God, she's a virgin," she heard the first one say. Then she'd passed out completely.

Now Clare sat on the edge of her bed, thinking of

that nighttime flashback and her need of money for graduate school. Her mother put an arm around her, looking contrite. "I'm sorry your library job fell through. Yesterday, I didn't mean to mention…" Then she perked up. "Actually, I came to wake you up because I may have some good news for you."

Clare looked at her.

"Your Aunt Rose called early this morning. I've told you about the pneumonia your cousin Sally had last winter. She had to drop out of college for that semester. She's recovered, but she's still at home on St. Sebastian's Island, lonely and depressed. Rose wants you to spend the summer with them there. When she's visited us in the past, she's noticed how capable, serious, and studious you are. She says Sally needs a friend, a companion like you, until she goes back to school in the fall."

"Really?" Clare's tone was doubtful.

She wasn't sure about the invitation. Yes, she was capable enough, and no doubt mostly "serious and studious." She hadn't told any fellow students at the University about the rape, but since that night, as her mother said, she'd changed. Immersing herself in academics, she dropped out of the sorority, cancelled her social media accounts, and if any boy acted interested in her, turned him away—she could no longer bear the thought of a male touching her. Her roommates told her she was called "The Ice Princess." But serious and studious wasn't the whole story. She practiced yoga, swam at the university pool, hiked on Georgia's mountain trails, even played intramural tennis.

Also, she didn't know her cousin very well. She'd

visited St. Sebastian's only once—when she was seven. Clare remembered playing with then five-year-old Sally on the beach, the two of them scampering in and out of the waves while their mothers sat in folding chairs and talked. There were photographs taken of the cousins side by side—Sally, small and sturdy, tow-headed and blue-eyed, and herself, taller, thin, knobby-kneed, with fawn-colored hair and eyes the color of the green seaweed they clutched in their hands.

"Wouldn't you like to spend the summer with your cousin?" her mother asked. "You should get to know Sally again. You two haven't been in touch except for those little Christmas cards Rose and I make you send each other every year."

"I know. But after that visit to St. Sebastian's when I was seven, you never took me with you when you went there, and Aunt Rose never brought Sally here when she visited us. Why was that?"

"At first, I suppose it was because Sally became such a difficult child, so high strung, hyperactive. It was easier for the two of us to visit without getting you children involved. Then, when Sally was older, she was always away at boarding school and summer camps, and you had your activities too. But it sounds like this summer would be the perfect time for you and Sally to get together again."

Clare shook her head. "I need to earn money this summer."

"Well, I haven't told you everything. When I mentioned your financial situation to Rose, she said she was sorry she hadn't given you a graduation present yet, and that she'd gift you ten thousand dollars if you stay with them from now until your classes and Sally's start in August. She'd direct deposit that amount in your checking account at the end of your visit. She said that would make up for your giving up a summer job. Surely that's more than you'd have earned at the library."

Clare stared at her mother. "It is. But why would Aunt Rose do that? And would she really do it?"

"Why would she? I'm sure because she wants to give you a graduation present—and because she wants you girls to finally spend time together. Both of you are 'only children,' after all. And of course Rose would keep her promise. Your uncle Tony has made lots of money with his hotels and that gated community on St. Sebastian's. My sister may not be practical, or very worldly-wise, but she has a checkbook and credit cards, and she knows how to spend. You'd be sure to get the gift, dear, and have a wonderful summer. And then you'd have the money for that master's degree you're so determined to get."

"Would you mind if I went there for the whole summer?"

"I've gotten used to living by myself since your father died and you've been at college. You'd have been working in Athens anyway this summer if the library job had come through. St. Sebastian's is farther away, but it won't be that different for me." Her mother paused. "Rose wants you to come as soon as possible—this week, in fact."

"I have to think about it." Clare went to the bathroom off her bedroom and closed the door. She thought of her Uncle Tony's widely used promotional phrase for St. Sebastian's—"The Last Golden Isle." It was in fact the last of the currently termed "Golden

Isles" to be made accessible to and popular with the public. To her, the word "last" had always somehow made St. Sebastian's seem ominous—as if it were a place of treacherous black rocks instead of golden sand, a place of endings, even death. But this morning, as she washed her face and brushed her hair, she focused on the phrase "Golden Isle." It suggested a paradise, like the Elysian Islands of Greek mythology. After the rape, Clare had refused to see a psychiatrist or to transfer to another college, as her mother had urged her to do. She sometimes wondered if she should have followed her mother's advice. Now she wondered if spending a summer on this island might dismiss the nightmares that still haunted her.

She thought of how beautiful St. Sebastian's was, with its palm trees and sandy beaches, and what a good playmate Sally had been during her childhood visit. True, she'd thrown a couple of tantrums which Clare had watched with a kind of shock—but they'd been about childish things, over quickly. Now Sally, at age twenty and after two years of college, would be grown up, almost her contemporary. Surely, they would again have fun together. And yes, ten thousand dollars at the end of the summer would provide more than enough funds for a year of graduate school.

When Clare came back into the bedroom, her mother was leafing through the book on the table beside the bed—a Faulkner novel. She looked up at her daughter.

"How about I do a Facetime session with Sally, Mom? So we can get reacquainted."

****

That afternoon Clare sat in the wingchair in her

bedroom holding her phone. Sally's face, slightly blurry, appeared on the screen. Her cousin looked pale, but still had the shimmery gold hair of those childhood visits and the vivid blue eyes. It looked as though she wore black eyeliner, but maybe that was her natural dark lashes. "Clare?" came Sally's voice, a bit tinny on the phone. "Hi! It's been so long."

"Yes, fifteen years. We were just children."

"Mom says she's invited you to stay with us for the summer. I'd love that. If you come, we'll have a wonderful time. We can go to the beach, kayak, paddle board, hike. And we can go out on the ocean in my father's yacht."

"It does sound great. But tell me a little about yourself. My mother said you were sick but are better now."

"Oh, yes. It was a strange experience. I had to drop out of college last semester, you know. I'm tired of staying here at home, by myself at the pool or hitting tennis balls alone. I'm ready to go out and have fun again. My mother will be so happy if you stay with me this summer, and so will I. You *will* come, won't you?"

Mrs. Matthews, standing by the door, spoke up. "Can I speak to Sally?" Clare put the phone on speaker and held it up. "Hello, Sally darling! I'm so glad you're better."

Her cousin's bright voice replied, "Me, too. And I want Clare to come as soon as possible. She'll love it here."

"I know she would. I've been sorry you and she haven't visited each other all these years."

"Then it's settled?" Sally asked.

Clare thought again of her graduation "gift" and

Sally's intriguing description of the many things they could do over an idyllic summer. The visit might help her—and it seemed would help her cousin too. "It's settled," she said.

****

And so the Friday after the graduation ceremony, Clare drove her car down Interstate 16 toward Savannah, three small suitcases and a garment bag in the trunk, books and laptop in the backseat. She thought of the pictures Sally sent her when she'd agreed to come—of boats, of vivid pink sunsets over the water, of a party on a beach. In that party photo, Sally sat close to a blond young man, maybe in his twenties. His arm was around her and he was smiling, his even white teeth like those in a toothpaste ad.

Clare had texted Sally:

—Is he your boyfriend?—

—That's Jason Eldridge. He's the son of my father's partner—was Sally's reply. *—That picture was taken last summer.—*

At the time, that exchange made Clare feel a little apprehensive. On St. Sebastian's, idyllic as it might be, would she have to socialize, attend the kind of events she'd avoided the last four years? But now as she drove, listening to classical music on her radio, she began to feel more confident. After all, in this new place with her cousin, she should try at last to socialize more normally. Plus, she had her own car. If worse came to worse, she'd go home and look for another job.

That afternoon, as she drove past the exits for Savannah, she remembered the Spanish moss hanging off the trees and its beautiful squares. She stayed on I-95 South, until she came to the exit for St. Sebastian's.

Where the exit ramp joined the local highway, a sign with a picture of ocean waves and palm trees indeed proclaimed, "St. Sebastian's, The Last Golden Isle, Four Miles."

Clare soon joined the lines of cars streaming over the causeway. After reaching the island, she turned on her GPS and keyed in her uncle's address. The system's confident female voice guided her over circuitous roads until it directed her to a turn at a wide concrete road blocked with closed wrought iron gates. The GPS told her, "*You have reached your destination.*"

She didn't remember the gates. They were like those at the entrances to exclusive communities. Then, seeing the sign "Sanderson Estates," she realized that this was such a community—the one her uncle had established since her last visit.

She pulled up to the gates and stopped. A tall, well-built, very tan young man in a white Oxford shirt and jeans—a security guard—came out of a small brick building beside the drive. Clean shaven, with dark curls cropped short and strong, even features, he reminded her of the statue pictured on the cover of her high school Latin textbook. She lowered her window, and he looked in at her, examining her with direct gray eyes. He held a clipboard and had a gun tucked into his belt.

Her hands grew cold. "I'm Clare Matthews, Sally Sanderson's cousin. They know I'm coming."

He looked at the clipboard, unsmiling. "You have some identification, Miss?"

Clare did not expect this. She reached for her purse, extracted her wallet and showed him her driver's license. He glanced at it, then at her. He nodded and, holding up a black oblong device, pressed a button. The gates swung open.

"Sorry, Miss Matthews," he said. "They told me to watch for you. You didn't look the way I expected." He had a bit of an accent she couldn't place.

"Has there been some trouble?"

"Just routine." She must have looked skeptical, for he then said, "This is a private development. Residents have gate-openers, but we still have to vet all visitors." He gestured toward the now accessible drive. "Go on in. Your uncle's house is the first one on the right. You can't miss it."

"Thank you." Clare pressed the accelerator and drove through the gates. She heard a clank, and in the rearview mirror saw they had closed behind her. A little chill went down her spine. Perhaps she'd been right after all about the threating nature of the word "last."

The road went past a long stucco building on the right with four garage-like doors, and soon she saw, also on the right, a pebbled parking area. On a rise above it was an impressive two-story house of matching stucco. A set of stone steps bordered by crepe myrtles led up to the front door. To the left she could glimpse a pool with sparkling turquoise water. The young man had been right. You couldn't miss her uncle's house.

She parked beside a shiny four-door sports convertible, got out of the car, and out of habit clicked it locked. Then she climbed the steps, rang the bell, and waited. A dog inside barked. The door opened and a miniature silver poodle burst out, still barking.

Behind the poodle stood the pretty little blonde she remembered from Facetime—Sally. "Clare!" the girl cried and embraced her warmly. "I'm so glad to see you!"

Clare's fears receded. She returned the hug.

Sally pulled back and picked up the squirming poodle. "Hush, Tinsel!" The dog stopped barking and licked Sally's chin.

"What a darling dog," said Clare.

"He's my mom's dog. He stays with her most of the time. Sorry about the barking. He's not used to strangers. Where is your luggage? I'll get someone to bring it in."

"I can get it," Clare said.

But Sally pulled a cell phone from her pocket and punched in some numbers. "Jon, come up to the house for a minute when your shift is over. We need your help." She disconnected and took Clare's arm. "I've called the security guard who was at the gatehouse when you came. His shift is about over, and he'll come by to bring your things upstairs. You must be exhausted. Do you want something to drink? Lemonade, a glass of wine?"

"Lemonade sounds wonderful."

Sally turned to a buxom, mocha-skinned woman who'd come down the large entry hall. Perhaps sixty, she wore a maid's dress and matching black apron. Her dark hair, streaked with gray, was pulled back in a bun. "Maria, this is my cousin, Clare. Would you bring lemonade for her and a glass of Merlot for me? We'll be in the living room."

The woman nodded. "Glad to meet you, Miss Clare."

"Glad to meet you, Maria."

Following Sally, Clare passed a broad staircase and entered a carpeted room with a fireplace, several couches and chairs, and a grand piano in the corner. She sank into an armchair. Sally sat in another and tucked her feet under her. Tinsel jumped up and curled beside her.

The two girls looked at each other. Now Clare could see her more clearly than on Facetime: shiny, almost platinum hair cut in bangs over her forehead and falling straight to her shoulders; eyebrows professionally shaped; brilliant blue eyes outlined in black pencil. She wore shorts and a halter top that revealed her curvy figure. Although people often told Clare how pretty she was, that her eyes were striking and her slim figure like a model's, she became aware, with her basic capris and T-shirt, her lack of makeup and simple ponytail, of the contrast to her cousin. "Sally, you're so glamorous, so beautiful."

"People have told me that. But it hasn't done me much good, cooped up here for so long. Now that you've come, you can be a kind of…chaperone."

"Chaperone?" Clare laughed a little. "I feel more like a friend."

"Well, you're that, too. That's what I think you are. Of course my mother hopes you'll also be a chaperone. She'll let me go out more places if you're with me."

They were quiet as Maria brought the wine and lemonade. After she left, Clare said, "Mom told me you had to drop out of college last semester because you were sick. What was it? She said something about pneumonia."

Sally massaged Tinsel's ears. "I had a mild case and that's what we told people. But it really wasn't that. I—I had psychological problems. I don't think you'd understand."

Clare's heart went out to her cousin. "But I would,"

she said. "More than you know."

Sally looked at her. "Really? You don't seem the type. Mine were partly a reaction to…well, a drug. I wasn't myself. And I did something bad while I was home last winter—I wrecked my car. See?" She swept aside her bangs to reveal a crisscrossing of shiny pink scars on her forehead. "My parents have been over-protective of me ever since."

"Oh, Sally! Were you badly hurt?"

"They say I was lucky I wasn't killed. I didn't have my seat belt on. I had physical therapy for my back and neck, and I'm fine now. My mother says I can have cosmetic surgery to fix these scars, but they don't show under my bangs."

"No, they don't show at all."

"My father bought me a new car—you may have seen it outside. I'll take you out in it tomorrow." Sally shot a glance at Clare. "I've promised to drive carefully."

There was the sound of the front door opening. Clare looked up to see the security guard approaching the living room entrance. She couldn't help but register more fully his lean, solid physique and compelling gray eyes. The gun was no longer in his belt. Tinsel did not bark but ran to greet him.

"Jon, you met my cousin Clare Matthews at the gate, right?"

He looked briefly at Clare and nodded.

"Would you bring the luggage in Clare's car up to the first guest room?"

"You'll need my car key." Clare stood and handed him her ring of keys.

"Would you want everything brought in, Miss

Matthews?"

"I think so, yes. Thank you." Somewhat unsettled by his formality, she watched him go back to the hall. She also felt protective of her laptop. Surely, he would not drop it. But with her three suitcases and garment bag, her laptop and box of books…

"Wait a minute, Sally." She went to the outside door and looked down at the parking area. The security guard, Jon, stood over the trunk of her car, extracting its contents. He closed it, set her suitcases beside the car, the garment bag over them, and reached into the back seat for her computer and the box of books. She hurried down the steps. "I'd better take the laptop. You already have so much to carry."

He handed it to her. "Do you want me to bring in these books?"

Surely there was no way he could carry them too, not on one trip. "That's all right. I can get them later." She indicated the three suitcases and garment bag. "Can you get all these now?"

"No problem." He stacked two of the suitcases under one arm, the third and the garment bag under the other, and carried them easily up the steps. She followed him inside and watched as he climbed the stairs to the upper story of the house as if he knew exactly where he was going.

Sally jumped up from her chair, rushed to the hall, and grabbed Clare's hand. "Do you want to see your room? Come on." They went up the stairs with Tinsel prancing at their feet. A door to a room at the top of the stairs was open and Clare heard the *thunks* of her suitcases being set down inside.

Sally stopped at that door. "Here's your room, right

next to mine. They're connected. We can visit each other privately whenever we want. My parents' bedroom and my father's home office are way down at the other end of the hall."

Jon came to the door of her designated room. "Anything else you want from the car now, Miss Matthews?"

"No, that's fine. Thank you." Clare walked past him into the room and set her laptop on a desk. It was the kind of desk found in hotel suites—and as so often in such suites, the room had a balcony with sliding glass doors. Through them she could see the branches of crepe myrtles and beyond them, the pebbled parking area. Jon, suddenly appearing beside her, dropped her keys with a jangle beside her laptop. If this had been a hotel, she would have tipped him then. But although he addressed her so formally, obviously that would be inappropriate here.

He left the room. She heard his footsteps going rapidly down the stairs, Tinsel at his heels; then the front door opened and closed. She remembered that he hadn't re-locked her car after getting her laptop out. But surely it was safe in this gated estate.

"I feel like you're really here now," said Sally. "Let's go have our drinks. Maria will have dinner ready about six thirty."

****

At six thirty-five that evening, Clare sat with Sally and her parents in the dining room at a long mahogany table set for dinner with china, crystal, silver tableware, and wine glasses. Aunt Rose, at one end, was blue-eyed and blonde, like Sally, though the color of her short pixie-like hair had surely been enhanced at the beauty parlor. Her dangling hoop earrings, scoop-necked blouse, and long slit skirt were stylish and youthful. Uncle Tony, at the other end of the table, was a tall, solid man of about fifty, Clare guessed, with a ruddy complexion and thick white hair. Dark-tinted glasses hid his eyes, as if he had a sensitivity to light. He wore tan slacks and a navy sport coat over a striped shirt and had, Clare thought, the air of a successful businessman.

Both her aunt and uncle had arrived only shortly before, Rose first with an armload of packages from shopping, including two beach wraps—one turquoise, one gold. After the greetings and the hugs, she'd given Sally the turquoise one, then the gold one to Clare saying, "This one would look perfect on you, dear, with your green eyes, and it would pick up the lights in your hair."

"You shouldn't have..." Clare began, but Rose paid no attention as she showed them all her other purchases.

When Uncle Tony strode in a few minutes later, Rose had gone to him and kissed his cheek. "Look, Tony, here is my niece, Clare Matthews from Sandy Springs, come to spend the summer with Sally. I think she'll be the perfect companion for her."

He stepped forward and held out his hand. "Hello, Clare. They told me you'd grown up into a very studious, competent young lady." He cocked his head, examining her through his glasses, as if a bit uncertain about her. "You're prettier than I expected."

Now, as they all sat at the table, Maria entered with a bottle of red wine, filling the glasses at Tony and Rose's places. She paused beside Clare, who shook her head. "No, thank you."

Maria turned to go back to the kitchen when Sally spoke up. "I'd like some."

"No, dear," said Aunt Rose. "You already had a glass earlier today, didn't you?"

Sally was obviously irritated. "Why can't I have another? I'm staying in tonight."

Her father spoke up with his usual air of authority. "You know what the doctor said. No more than one."

Sally scowled but remained quiet. Maria left and soon returned to bring in the meal—a large platter of roast beef, then serving dishes of mashed potatoes and parsley-sprinkled spring carrots. "Is that your car I saw in front?" Uncle Tony asked Clare as in his turn he took the slices of beef from the platter and served his plate.

Clare nodded.

"We'll have Jon put it in the garage. You won't need it here. Sally has her own for the two of you."

A sense of unease began to rise in her again. "I can put it in the garage."

Her uncle reached for the mashed potatoes. "Don't worry about it for now."

Clare decided there was in fact no need to worry. The car keys were safe in her room.

When they'd finished the meal, Maria efficiently cleared the table and brought out chocolate mousse for dessert.

"Coffee, ma'am?" she asked Aunt Rose.

"Yes, please, for Tony and me. Sally? Clare?"

Clare shook her head. "I'd better go upstairs. I need to unpack and shower."

Aunt Rose patted her hand. "I know you're tired after that long drive. We'll see you in the morning, dear. We're so glad you're here."

"I'm going to have some decaf. I'll be up soon," Sally told her.

When Clare rose, her aunt did too and followed her to the foot of the stairs, handing her the beach wrap she'd given her. "Don't forget this. You may already have one, but you'll need another this summer." Then she lowered her voice. "Sally has to take three medicines every morning, but she's forgetful sometimes. Could you make sure she takes them?"

"Of course."

"Every morning."

"Yes, I'll make sure. Thank you again for this beautiful wrap. Good night, Aunt Rose." Clare gave her a kiss. A strange request about the medicines, she thought as she went up the stairs, but after all, now that she and Sally were almost roommates, who better to remind her? Her earlier unease about her car had long gone, and she again felt glad to be here, well-fed, secure. Surely she'd made the right decision to come.

But when she entered her room, she noticed something different. Next to her laptop and keys was the box of books she'd left in the back seat of her unlocked car. The security guard, without even checking with her, had been back.

Chapter Two

Saturday, May 9

On Saturday morning Clare woke to find Sally sitting at the foot of her bed. "I want to give you a tour of the island today," she announced. "And you came just in time for Jason Eldridge's party tonight. It will be on the beach near his father's marina, and kids who were with him back in high school and some of his college friends in the area are coming. I haven't been to a party in so long—this will be a sort of a celebration."

A party? Clare took a deep breath. *I'll be different here*. "Jason Eldridge," she said. "Isn't he the guy with you in a picture you sent me?"

"Yes." Sally jumped off the bed and opened the draperies over the sliding glass door. Sunlight poured in. "See what a beautiful day it is? Come on, let's get dressed and go down to breakfast." She skipped off through the door between their rooms.

"Have you taken your medicines?" Clare called after her.

"Yes, I have." Sally now sounded annoyed. "How did you know about that? Did my mother ask you to remind me?"

"She did mention something about it." Clare added kiddingly, "Maybe it's part of being your—chaperone."

"Oh yes, that." And to Clare's relief, Sally laughed.

Clare dressed in fresh white capris, an olive-green V-necked T-shirt, and sandals. Sally bounced back in shorts and a bare midriff shirt tied in front. The girls went downstairs together, and just like in one of those period British dramas on public broadcasting, breakfast dishes were laid out on the sideboard—scrambled eggs, bacon, toast, fresh fruit. Maria entered and poured them coffee and orange juice. Clare was quite stunned. Even if she had to attend a few parties—she would have a summer like this and be given money at the end of it?

After breakfast Sally said, "Get your purse and I'll give you the tour." As they went through the front door, Clare looked down at the parking area. The sports car she'd parked next to yesterday was there, but her own car was gone.

Her heart skipped a beat. "Where is my car?"

"Jon must have put it in the garage."

"But he didn't have my car key." Clare thought a moment. He'd taken her books from the car up to her room and put them on her desk, where he'd left her keys. He must have taken the keys, moved her car to the garage they'd mentioned, and then returned them. The uncomfortable sense of losing control returned. "I guess he found the keys in my room," she said. "Before we go, will you show me the garage? In case I need to get my car."

"Sure, we'll drive right by it." Sally skipped down the stone steps to the parking area and Clare followed. Sally indicated the sports car. "Don't you love this? Dad gave it to me for my birthday to take the place of the one I wrecked. Come on, get in."

In the front passenger seat, Clare watched Sally punch the start button, shift the gear stick on the floor between them, and wheel the car around in a fast semi-circle. Then she zipped down the driveway, passing the long stucco building near the gatehouse Clare had seen the day before. "That's the garage," Sally said. "Dad has some antique cars he keeps there—it's one of his hobbies. And he keeps a fleet of cars for his employees in there, too."

"I'd like to see where my car is parked."

"Oh, don't be a worrywart, Clare." But Sally braked and pulled over. "Okay, we'll stop and look."

"I don't even know how to get *into* the garage," said Clare, noting the four doors across the front were closed.

"There's a side entrance." Sally walked around the corner of the building, Clare behind her, and pushed open a regular door. Two rows of cars—some vintage cars dating from the 20's to the 60's, some gleaming modern limousines—stretched out before them.

"I don't see my car."

"I'll call Jon and ask him where it is." But even as Sally pulled out her cell phone, the young man suddenly appeared in the door, again in a white shirt and jeans. He must have come from the gatehouse, which was not far from the garage.

"Where did you put Clare's car?" Sally asked.

He pointed. "At the end, behind that 1960 burgundy convertible."

Clare looked down at the row of cars. "*Behind* the convertible? How can I get it out?"

"Mr. Sanderson has a machine, and I had a key to your car made. When you want it, just call the gate phone. Someone will be on duty and bring it up to the house for you."

Shock waves vibrated through Clare. "You made a key to my car?"

He opened the door to a cabinet on the wall. Inside, hanging on hooks, were all sorts of keys, with alphabetized labels under each one. "We have a key to each of these cars in the garage. We need them to bring the cars out when Mr. Sanderson or a guest or employee needs one." He must have seen her look. "That's the only time we use the keys, Miss Matthews. So like I said, just call the gate phone when you want yours."

She noted again his slight accent, his formality addressing her. "I don't know the gate phone's number."

"I'll give it to you," said Sally, tapping quickly on her phone. "There, I sent it to you. Are you satisfied? Can we leave now? Jon, go ahead and open the gates."

Seeming to note Clare's discomfort, he lingered a moment. "Your car is safer in here than left parked outside. If the weather gets bad and the wind blows branches around, or if it hails, you don't want it scratched up. We'll get it for you any time you want it."

Maybe it would work, she thought. The garage was close to the gatehouse, and apparently whoever was "on duty" would deliver the car. After all, keys were left in cars for valet service. She turned to follow Sally out. But she still felt somewhat upset. This Jon had not only gone into her room and taken her car key, but had made a copy of it, all without asking.

****

Sally drove too fast for Clare's comfort. The white ribbon of the pavement spun dizzily beneath them, the tires squealed as she rounded curves in the road, and when she had to brake, she did so only at the last moment. However, the tour of the island was fascinating. They drove through St. Sebastian City, with its shops and restaurants, little post office and police station, then passed the three hotels owned by her uncle—his first, the modest Golden Sunrise Hotel, and the newer two, The Last Golden Isle Hotel and The Golden Sands Hotel. Those two were both high-rise ocean-side complexes that included fancy restaurants, ballrooms, and conference suites. For lunch they ate low country boil—a delicious mix of shrimp, corn on the cob, sausage, red potatoes, and ham—at a restaurant called the Shrimp Shack.

In the afternoon Sally took the car past marshes, beaches, and the St. Sebastian's River, which ran through the island to the ocean. She showed Clare the marina owned by her father's partner, Kyle Eldridge, on the river's mouth. Three long piers stretched out into the water, with sailboats, outboards, and yachts parked within the U-shaped, walkway-bordered spaces all along them.

"Those spaces are called 'slips,' " Sally told her, "because boats 'slip' into them." Finally, they visited the marina clubhouse, an imposing building with a nautical-themed restaurant in one wing and a business that sold boats and boating supplies in another. "Kyle has also built a really big community pier on the beach. You'll see it tonight," Sally said.

As Clare took in these sights, she thought of the amazing arc of Uncle Tony's and Kyle Eldridge's success. The story went that in the 1980s, before the causeway connecting St. Sebastian's to the mainland had been completed and land on the island was still wild and cheap, the two of them, both then young but with family money, bought large tracts there. At the time of her childhood visit, her uncle had built only the one modest hotel, and Eldridge a small marina. There were visitors to the island, but the pace was slow. What she was seeing now—the crowds of tourists, her uncle's fancy hotels and gated community, his partner's vastly expanded marina—seemed almost the stuff of legend. The two men were now multi-millionaires.

****

Late in the afternoon they returned to the house for a snack and rest before getting ready for Jason's beach party. "Let's just have a sandwich," Sally said as they entered the kitchen. "Jason plans to have a lot of food for us."

As they ate at the kitchen counter, Aunt Rose looked in. "What time is the party?"

"It starts about eight, as the sun begins to set," Sally answered. "Then we'll have a bonfire."

"That sounds nice. Clare came just in time so you could go." The woman turned to Clare. "I wouldn't have let her go alone. This will be Sally's first party since her illness."

Clare looked at Sally's bright, happy eyes. "She seems very recovered."

"Yes, but we have to be careful still." Aunt Rose came in and poured herself a glass of wine. "Now don't socialize just with Jason tonight, Sally. There will be lots of other young men there."

Sally shrugged impatiently. "Don't worry, Mom."

After her mother left, Clare asked, "Why did your mother say not to socialize just with Jason?"

Sally blushed a bit. "He's older than I am—he's

twenty-five. Last year, before I got sick, my parents let me go out with him, and we developed…a relationship. He played guitar for me when I sang in the club rooms at my father's hotels. Did I tell you about that? I write poems that I turn into songs."

"No, you didn't tell me. That's wonderful," said Clare. "You'll have to sing for me sometime."

"I stopped writing and singing when I got sick and they wouldn't let me see Jason. They'd decided he was wild and immature for his age, but he's really special to me. Tonight will be the first time I've seen him for months." She touched Clare's hand. "So don't be too strict a chaperone."

"But I'm just your cousin and friend, remember?"

"Yes, I remember."

After eating, they went to their rooms and showered. Sally came to Clare's room afterward, wearing a turquoise bikini. "Wear the new wrap my mother gave you," Sally instructed. "Let me see your bathing suit."

Clare, still in her bathrobe, held up her suit, a lime-green one-piece, with a modest V-neck. "Yes, that will work," said Sally.

Clare turned to the bathroom to put it on. "You look like a movie star in yours."

"Thanks. You will too, except that one-piece is sort of old-fashioned."

When Clare emerged, Sally had slipped on the wrap her mother had given her, leaving the front open. "We'd better get started. Are you ready?"

Clare put on her own wrap, zipped it, and looked in the mirror. Her thick hair, now loose over her shoulders, looked shiny with gold highlights—perhaps in part due to the soft water on the island. But this was her first party and, in spite of her resolution to be more social, she felt tense when she thought about the "lots of young men" to be there. She picked up her purse and turned to find her cousin impatiently waiting.

"You look nervous," Sally said. "Is that the psychological problem you have? You're afraid of meeting new people?"

"I guess you could describe it that way," said Clare.

"Well, that's an easy one. We'll get you over that. Come on."

Downstairs, Aunt Rose, Tinsel at her feet, came to bid the girls goodbye. "You two look beautiful. Now don't stay out late. And Sally, no more than one drink. Remember, you'll be driving."

"Oh, Mom, there will be food and sodas, and the only alcoholic drink Jason will have is beer. I'll be fine."

Aunt Rose tapped Clare's shoulder. "Keep an eye on her."

In the little sports car, beach bags stowed in the trunk, the girls stopped before the closed gates. Clare could see the security guard, Jon, inside the gatekeepers' building, watching banks of screens—security camera screens, probably. Sally beeped the horn loudly. "Sometimes I feel like a prisoner here," she said. "Why can't I have my own gate opener like other residents do?"

Jon got up and came out to the car, that black box again in his hand. He leaned into the passenger side window and addressed Clare. "Can you drive that stick shift?"

Clare looked at it, then at him. “I’ve never driven a stick.”

He did not seem pleased. “I figured.” He moved away. “Okay, ladies. Be careful.” He pressed a button on the black box. The gates opened and, perhaps to express her irritation, Sally pressed hard on the accelerator and roared through.

****

As Clare and Sally walked up to the party, the scene looked like one from a movie or on television—beautiful young people in bathing suits on a sandy beach, pink and lavender clouds over the ocean, sea birds strutting along the wet sand by the waves. Farther down the beach, the St. Sebastian’s pier built by Kyle Eldridge extended out into the water, high above the waves.

As the girls neared the chattering group, a handsome blond man in bathing suit and tropical shirt turned from the others and smiled. This was definitely the person in the picture Clare had asked Sally about. He came to them and hugged Sally, lifting her off her feet as she wrapped her arms around his neck. “Hey, it’s great to see you at last. You look wonderful.”

“I’ve missed you so much,” she said.

“I’ve missed you, too.”

Sally turned to Clare. “This is Jason Eldridge. Jason, this is my cousin Clare Matthews from Sandy Springs, Georgia. She’s staying with me for the summer.”

“Glad you could come. Help yourselves,” he said, pointing to an ice-filled cooler where brown bottles of beer and cans of soda nestled. “But first you might want to go for a swim. Food will be coming out soon.”

"I'll go swimming if you come with me," Sally said.

"It's a deal. Hey!" Jason called to the group. "Better get in the water before the sun sets and the food comes out."

He took off his shirt, and Sally dropped her wrap. "Want to come, Clare?" she asked.

Clare shook her head. "I'll wait here."

As Sally and Jason ran with several other couples down the low tide stretch of sand, Clare looked after them. Jason looked like the type she'd especially avoided at college, but she had to admit he and her cousin made a good-looking couple. Then she remembered what Aunt Rose had said, that Sally should not socialize just with Jason. Maybe she should keep an eye on them—like a chaperone. She took a bottle of beer from the ice chest and sat on a bench near the food tables, watching as the pair waded into the waves, playfully splashing each other. She began to feel a little confused about her role and even, surprisingly, lonely.

"Hey, there." Someone sat beside her—a large, dark-haired young man as tan as the others at the party, wearing bathing trunks and T-shirt with "St. Sebastian's Island Marina" on the front. "You're Sally's friend?" he asked.

Clare felt glad that someone—even if male—had joined her. "I'm her cousin."

He held out a hand. "Derek Pacelli."

"Clare Matthews."

"So how do you happen to be spending time here with Sally? Just a cousinly visit?"

Clare smiled a little. "I suppose that's what it is."

"How long are you staying?"

"Until the middle of August. Then I'm going back to school."

"Where?"

"The University of Georgia. I'll begin a master's degree in English." She paused. "What about you?"

"I guess you could just describe me as a beach bum working at the marina this summer."

"What do you do there?"

"I gas, clean, and maintain boats for members, and handle reservations and check-outs." His gaze shifted to the couple in the water. "Maybe now that you're here, Sally can be out and about more. Jason says she's been like a prisoner in a tower."

"She's been sick."

"I know. But apparently, she also has very strict parents." He glanced back at Clare, perhaps aware of her also watching the couple as, side by side, they moved out into deeper water. "Want to go in, too?"

"Good idea." She unzipped and slipped off her wrap as he pulled off his T-shirt, revealing thick curly black hair on his chest. He had a good build, although he was just a bit overweight.

They went down to the water, and she waded out ahead of him, then dipped down to meet the incoming breakers. Derek appeared at her side. "You swim a lot?"

"Yes, but I haven't been to the ocean in years."

Jason, farther out, was neck deep in water now, and Sally was sitting on his shoulders. She waved at them happily. Jason tumbled her off then and she submerged, then came up laughing and shaking her head as she swam back to him. They were now face to face, treading water in the waves.

"Sally said they used to date before she got sick," Clare said.

"Jason told me that, too. But she's younger than he is. I get the feeling her parents don't trust him."

"With reason?"

Derek shrugged. "He *is* kind of a ladies' man."

"Hey, Jason," someone called from the beach. "The food's coming out."

Jason turned to the voice and waved. He and Sally swam back, stood in the knee-deep surging breakers, and clasping hands, walked to shore.

"The marina restaurant is providing the food—it should be good," Derek said. "Let's go eat."

The other young people who had gone into the water streamed back, and on shore grabbed towels, then moved toward the long tables set up on the beach. Steam trays of shrimp, fried chicken, and corn on the cob were placed side by side with platters of potato salad, sliced tomatoes, and pieces of coconut cake. Derek stayed with Clare as they took the plastic plates, filled them, and picked up bottles of beer.

"I've got a blanket over here to sit on," he said. "Come eat with me."

Clare followed him. After they'd settled, Jason and Sally came over with their food and drinks. "That was so much fun in the water!" Sally exclaimed, shaking her still-dripping hair and sitting down beside Jason.

"I'm glad you've met Derek," Jason said to Clare. "He works at the marina with me. I'm the one who recommended him for the job. He's the best of the new guys—and the most fun."

Derek laughed. "Thanks, bud." And to Clare, "You did take note of that, didn't you?"

By the time they finished eating, the sun had set and the sky over the ocean had turned a vivid rose. Shrimp boats were silhouetted black against the horizon, and the moon was rising. Jason stood. "Time to light the bonfire."

Grabbing a can of beer from the ice chest, Sally followed him to a circle of stones arranged on the beach. Jason and other boys added pieces of driftwood and set them ablaze. As darkness fell, the flames threw out flickering light. Jason brought out a guitar and began playing and singing old songs, as others joined in. Derek sat beside Clare, joining in with a surprisingly pleasant baritone.

"You have a good voice," Clare commented.

"I've done a little singing. A little guitar playing too, but I haven't mentioned that to Jason. One guitar player here is enough."

At length Jason put away his guitar, turned on an MP3 player, and along with two or three other couples, he and Sally began dancing on the sand. Clare and Derek remained sitting next to each other on the blanket.

"I've met Sally's father at the marina," Derek told her. "He and Mr. Eldridge hold a lot of meetings there. They're an impressive pair—real movers and shakers." He paused. "I guess you've known your uncle for a long time."

"Actually, I don't know him at all. He married my mother's sister—that's the only link I have with him. She visits us, but he doesn't come with her. I visited here only once before, maybe fifteen years ago. He was gone most of the time."

"Let's see, that was about ten years after the

causeway to the mainland was completed—he would have been building those two other hotels then, and Mr. Eldridge was expanding the marina."

"For someone new, you know a lot."

An intent gleam came into his eyes. "I listen. I've picked up information."

Suddenly remembering her role, Clare looked at the dancing partygoers. "Where have Sally and Jason gone?"

"I saw them walking over toward the pier."

"I should go and find them. It's getting late. Her mother told me to take care of her."

"I'll walk over there with you." Derek stood and gave her a hand up. Relieved to have his company, Clare walked beside him toward the long wooden structure that extended far into the waves. Above, it was lit by lights, but underneath, where there was still a beach, it was dark. They walked under the pier, but no one was in sight.

Clare's heart began to pound. She was supposed to take care of her cousin—and now Sally had disappeared with the young man her aunt seemed to distrust. "Sally?" Clare called, hearing a note of panic in her own voice.

A male voice with a slight accent came out of the darkness. "She's behind that support beam with Jason."

Clare turned. Jon the security guard stepped out into a ray of light and walked toward her, his white shirt now untucked and open farther at the neck, his gray eyes shadowed, sparking a bit with—was it anger? "Weren't you supposed to watch her?" Reaching them, he put a hand on Clare's shoulder. "These girls need to go home. Now."

Startled at his touch, Clare jerked away. Derek demanded, "And you are who?"

"Head security guard at the Sanderson Estates."

"Oh." Derek hesitated a moment. "Yeah, I think I've seen you at the marina with Clare's uncle."

Recognizing Jon's authority, Clare put her hand on Derek's arm. "I'd better say goodnight."

"If you're sure."

"I'm sure."

"Okay, then." Derek began to walk away but turned back. "I'll see you again, I hope."

"I hope so, too." It seemed the appropriate thing to say. She watched as he headed along the beach toward the bonfire. Then she looked at Jon, feeling defensive. "Sally and Jason just disappeared," she said. "As soon as I noticed they were gone, I started looking for them."

"Wait here."

He strode farther up under the pier, and stepped behind the beam, out of sight. She heard voices—Jon's stern and commanding, Jason's surprised and then angry, Sally's protesting. Then silence. After a few moments, the three of them emerged, Sally, wobbling as she walked, supported by the two young men, one on each side of her.

When they reached Clare, Jason said to Jon, "All right, are you satisfied?" He touched Sally's cheek. "Goodnight, girl." Then, "Goodnight—it's Clare, right?" He turned and jogged off toward the party.

Sally sagged against Jon, her hair falling over her face. He spoke to Clare. "Go get your things and meet me at my car in the parking lot. We'll leave Sally's car here. I'll pick it up tomorrow."

Hearing that, Sally roused. "I want to drive home

by myself."

"You've had enough driving for the day."

Clare noted that Sally's words were slurred. How many beers had she had? *Oh, dear, I should have paid better attention.*

Jon met her eyes and jerked his head toward the party. She went back down the beach. At the dark edges of the crowd, relieved that no one noticed her, she gathered up their beach bags, slipped on her wrap, and hurried to the parking lot. Across several rows of vehicles, she saw him, raising his arm, signaling her. She went to him.

Looking into the car, Clare saw Sally lying in the back seat covered by a blanket, her eyes closed. "Is she all right?"

"She just had too much to drink."

As Clare slid into the passenger seat, he put their things in the trunk, then got behind the wheel. They were silent as he left the parking lot and began following the road back to the Sanderson estate.

"They probably didn't tell you about Sally," he finally said.

"I know she's been sick."

"Yes. And she still needs to be taken care of. Every Monday morning her mother brings bring her to a session with a psychologist in Savannah."

Clare's eyes widened. "She still has psychological problems?"

"They hope she'll get them under control, especially with you here."

"So…that's why her mother wanted me to spend the summer with her?"

"Probably. This is her first social event since the

illness. They wouldn't have let her go alone."

"And that's why you came here tonight—you thought something bad might happen with her and I wouldn't be ready to handle it."

"I was right, wasn't I?"

"I didn't realize she'd had more than one beer."

"She drinks more than she should when she gets the chance."

"I'm sorry. I should have kept a closer watch. I will in the future." She hesitated. "I've been wondering—why did you have a gun at the gates when I first arrived?"

"Mr. Sanderson likes us to have protection."

That seems strange, Clare thought. Does he think the gatekeepers might need to shoot someone? "Does *he* have some kind of mental condition?" she asked. "Like paranoia?"

"There are people who resent him for his success, that's all. All the gatekeepers carry a weapon because they check out visitors to the estate." He paused. "I also serve your uncle as a kind of personal bodyguard when he feels he needs one."

"Is there some danger to my uncle?"

He stared ahead through the windshield. "There was a murder on the Estates last winter. Sally and her mother don't know about it."

A chill raced down Clare's spine. "What happened?"

"One of the guards at the gate tried to stop someone who shouldn't have been there from entering—someone who was angry at your uncle. The guy pulled a gun and killed the guard. Since then, all the gatekeepers have been armed."

Again a chill came over Clare—as when she'd first arrived, and the estate gates clanked shut behind her. "Oh, my God! Why was this person angry at my uncle?"

"No one knows. Probably something to do with one of his businesses."

"The police didn't catch him?"

"No. He made a U-turn, took off, and just disappeared. Tony didn't want to frighten Sally and her mother, so he didn't tell them about it. And he kept it from the media." He glanced over at Clare. "We don't think anything like that will happen again. But just in case, we're prepared. Since you're going to take care of Sally, and since you asked, I guess *you* should know."

He turned in at the Sanderson driveway, reached up, and clicked a black square attached to the sun visor. The gates opened. He waved at a man with glasses now in the gatehouse, then drove on, again clicking the remote device. The gates closed behind them.

Clare watched the process. "Why can't Sally have an opener like that?"

He drove up to the house and braked. "Because her parents want the guys working the gate to keep track of when she goes out and comes back. They've also put a GPS device on her car. They're keeping a close watch on her."

"Because of the shooting?"

"No—like I said, her mother doesn't even know about it, and Tony doesn't think Sally's in danger. They're worried about her mental condition—and they don't want her being with Jason. They want to keep them apart or at least not alone together. He was a bad influence on her in the past. Tonight, with you there and the rest of the crowd, I didn't think that would be a problem. I came because if Sally drinks, she shouldn't drive. And you couldn't drive her car tonight if she couldn't."

Clare bit her lip. "I guess I should learn how to drive a stick shift."

"That's a good idea since you're going to be going places with her."

"Maybe she can teach me."

"I think not." He looked over at her for a moment. "I can teach you."

"You?"

"I have Mondays off. While Sally and her mother are at the psychologist's this Monday, I could give you a lesson in Sally's car. They leave about eight thirty. How about you meet me in this parking area at, say, nine o'clock?"

Yes, it was a good idea, considering what he'd told her about Sally. "All right, nine o'clock. Thank you." Clare started to get out of the car, then looked back at him. "I'm glad you didn't call me *Miss Matthews* tonight."

"I'll only call you that when I'm in my employee role."

"And you weren't tonight?"

"I was acting on my own tonight."

"What about the driving lesson Monday?"

He paused a moment. "Then, too." He glanced at the prone Sally in the back seat, then up at the second story windows, dark all along the side of the house. "I'll carry her up to her room. You'll have to key in the alarm code for me—on the pad by the door: 4116125."

"Tinsel may bark."

"He stays in her parents' room at night."

Jon exited the car and gathered up the sleeping girl, wrapping her cocoon-like in the blanket. Clare went up to the door ahead of him to punch in the code. The crepe myrtle branches cast eerie shadows over the steps, and when she looked back, over Jon's face as well.

Chapter Three

Saturday, May 9 – Saturday, May 16

Back in her bright, attractive room, Clare sat on the bed for a long time, absorbing all that had happened, trying to shake off feelings of trepidation. The story of the murder at the gatehouse was shocking, but surely that was an extraordinary event, committed by some crazy person. It wouldn't happen again. As for Sally, although her parents seemed overly protective, her behavior that night was not that horrific: Young people often drank too much at parties and saw therapists for psychological problems. *I think I can take care of her now that I know what I'm supposed to do.*

At last, feeling better, she pulled off her bathing suit and stepped into the shower to wash the salt off her hair and the sand off her feet. Sally would have to wait to clean up until morning. The blanket around her would keep most of the sand out of the bed.

Clean and in her nightgown, Clare slid down between the sheets. Her thoughts turned to the two young men she had been with that night. Jon, the security guard—tall, slim, sinewy-strong. Those luminous gray eyes under thick dark brows. A glow to his tan skin. Fine features, yet a touch of ethnicity about him. Was he partly Hispanic? Native American? What exactly was his role here, anyway? He was obviously more than just a security guard.

Then Derek, with his muscular, dark-haired body and Italian last name. He said he was "a beach bum" working at the marina, but that didn't seem to be the whole story either. He wasn't as laid-back as she'd expected a beach bum would be, but sometimes rather intense—and surprisingly knowledgeable about the development of the island.

Then she realized something else. While she was still no doubt the Ice Princess, with these two she did not feel the strong aversion she'd felt with men in past years. Maybe it was the new setting, this golden isle. Maybe it was because both were unusual, different from the ones she saw most often on campus. These two did not seem threatening, but as though they would actually be protective if necessary.

Her thoughts turned then to Jason and Sally. Apparently, she was supposed to protect Sally from Jason. Yet, in spite of the negative comments about him, in spite of his resembling the frat boy type she personally avoided, Clare found herself sympathetic to the couple. Jason seemed to care for Sally, and Sally obviously idolized him. Maybe he was not as wild as her parents thought, or maybe he'd reformed. Given that Derek was Jason's friend, perhaps he and she could, platonically, double date with Sally and Jason. They could serve as chaperones—so Sally's parents would let the couple go out together.

Clare had never been in love, did not expect ever to be. But as a break from reading her English-major novels, she sometimes turned to romances and the idealized love relationships they portrayed. Such relationships, surely, were sometimes found in real life.

But she feared that because of that horrible August night years ago, a vital part of ideal love—sexual passion—was like a color on a rainbow that she herself could now never experience, never see.

****

Early the next morning when Clare tiptoed into her cousin's room, Sally opened her startlingly blue eyes. "What happened last night? Oh, my God, I'm still in my bathing suit. Where did I get this blanket?"

"You don't remember what happened?"

"The last I knew, Jason and I were walking toward the pier." She smiled dreamily and stretched. "What a wonderful party."

"You'd better get in the shower," Clare told her. "You're still covered with sand."

Sally looked down at herself and laughed. "I guess I'd better."

The two of them folded the blanket in such a way that the sand didn't spill out, and Sally ran into the bathroom adjoining her room. When Clare heard the shower turn on, she went to her own room and finished drying her hair with the electric dryer.

Sally came in shortly, wearing a bathrobe. "I must have gone to sleep or something last night. Did *you* drive me home?"

"No. Jon came in his car and took us both home."

"I hate that he did that. I only had three beers."

"You had some kind of blackout. I don't know what I would have done if Jon hadn't come. I can't drive a stick shift."

"Why didn't you just wake me up? I could have driven home."

Clare decided not to argue—or mention the driving

lessons. "He says he'll bring your car back from the beach today." She went to the balcony window, pulled aside the curtains and looked out onto the parking area. "Look, your car is out there now."

Sally came up beside her. "Jon got it there so early that my parents will think I drove home myself. That's good. I don't want my mother to get all upset and say we can't go to any more parties."

Clare sat on the bed and pulled Sally down beside her. "What is between you and Jason?"

"I tell my parents he's now just a friend."

"It didn't seem that way last night."

Sally smiled dreamily again. "No." She looked at Clare. "We hadn't seen each other in a long time. And my parents don't approve of him. Not that they don't like him. His father is my dad's business partner, after all. They just don't want us to be together too much."

"Why not?"

Sally shrugged and stood up abruptly. "Who knows? Jason's older, and you know, sexually experienced. And they think neither of us has good judgment or self-control."

Returning to her room, Clare paused and watched Sally from the doorway. Her cousin opened a bureau drawer, took out two plastic vials and shook out a pill from each. She popped the pills into her mouth and drank them down with a sip of water. Then she opened a circular foil wrapped set, punched out a pill, and likewise swallowed it.

Looking over at Clare, she said, "I'm not so good at keeping up with pills. This morning I almost forgot to take my Lithiate and Zyprene and my birth control pill. Like my mother said, you'll have to help me remember."

What were those two pills with the strange names? wondered Clare. And birth control pills? Was she taking them for menstrual cramps, as Clare herself had for the past couple of years? Or was she sexually active? Clare found herself voicing her last question. "Birth control pills? Because of Jason?"

"When I started dating him, my mother was afraid and had me get on these pills. It's true, last summer and fall, back before I got sick, he and I came close to..." She was quiet for a moment. "But for some reason he would stop, maybe because of our fathers' relationship or because he knew I never had...I think if we had dated longer..." She stopped, seeming at a loss for words.

Clare let out a silent breath of relief. If they had not already been lovers, her job as chaperone might be easier. "We should get you one of those cases with days of the week on them for those first two medicines."

"I have one." Sally held up the oblong plastic container. "I forgot to fill it."

"Let's fill it now." Clare returned to her cousin's room, thinking, as she dropped the pills into the little squares, so this is one of my duties as a "companion."

Later that morning, Clare left the breakfast table before Sally finished and went to her room. She opened her laptop and googled the first two medicines Sally was taking. Her heart sped up as she read: "Lithiate, indicated in the treatment of manic episodes of Bipolar Disorder. Maintenance therapy, reduces the frequency of and intensity of manic episodes which may occur. Zyprene, indicated for maintenance treatment of manic or mixed episodes associated with bipolar disorder. It may cause agitation or irritability. It may also cause suicidal thoughts or depression. Do not drink alcohol while taking Zyprene."

So Sally was bipolar. Clare knew it could be a dangerous condition, that it used to be called manic depression. With some forms, persons suffered from periods of extremely "up," elated, energized, sometimes crazed behavior, followed by episodes of feeling totally "down," hopeless, even suicidal. While that explained why her cousin should not drink, Jason's presence or absence obviously played a major role in triggering episodes. Her car accident last winter occurred after they were separated, and perhaps her current upbeat, boundless energy had arisen because she could now begin seeing him again. Clare now fully understood the reason Aunt Rose was giving her ten thousand dollars to spend the summer as Sally's companion and chaperone.

Later that afternoon, Clare played tennis with Sally on the Estates' tennis court. As her cousin ran exuberantly back and forth, returning balls and scoring points, she realized that the promised money was not her only reason for remaining here. Sally was like the little sister she'd wished for but never had. In fact, now that the shock had worn off, the revelation that she was bipolar made Clare more determined to stay. Besides, now Sally's medicines must be working. Her energy was unusual, but probably within normal limits.

She resolved to keep Sally from drinking. She would oversee the taking of the medicine every morning. She'd be her friend and companion. And she'd try to be a good, but sympathetic, chaperone on her dates with Jason.

****

On Monday, the day she was to meet Jon for a driving lesson, Clare got up early, made sure Sally took her pills, and ate breakfast with her and Aunt Rose. "We're sorry to leave you alone this morning, dear," her aunt said. "We're going to shop after Sally's appointment and then have lunch. We probably won't be back until after one."

"Maybe she'd like a break from me," Sally said with a laugh. "I hope I'm not wearing you out, Clare."

"Not at all. I'm having fun."

"Great! Okay, see you later." Sally gave Clare a kiss, grabbed her purse, and rushed out behind her mother. Clare heard her aunt's car start in the parking area, where someone had brought it.

After the sounds faded, she went up to her room, brushed her hair, then considered her clothes. Yes, her white pencil-slim slacks and her aqua V-necked T-shirt looked right. She went back downstairs, out to the stone steps that led to the parking area, and sat down at the bottom, waiting. She checked her phone: ten after nine. Had Jon forgotten?

Then she saw Sally's little sports car coming up the road. It made a turn into the parking area and stopped at the foot of the steps. She walked up to the passenger side. Jon, in his usual jeans and white shirt, reached over and opened the door. "Sorry I'm late," he said. "Something came up."

As she got into the car, Jon seemed all business. He sped down the driveway and opened the gates with the black remote that was now attached to the sun visor. "In case you're wondering, I've temporarily disengaged the GPS. I'm going to a parking lot that'll be empty this time of day. It will be a good place for you to practice. Watch my feet now as I drive."

She saw his left foot depress a pedal left of the brake—the clutch, she knew that much—as he shifted the central floor gear with his right hand.

He turned into a parking lot behind a mall. "Okay, give it a try." They exchanged places. "You need to depress the clutch when you brake and when you shift gears. Right now, you have your right foot pressing down on the brake, the left on the clutch, and you're in low gear. Let up on the brake with your right foot, move it over to the accelerator and synchronize letting up on the clutch as you press down on the accelerator."

She followed his directions. The car jerked forward, and the motor whined in its low gear as she sped up. "Okay, you're going fast enough," he told her. "Let up for a minute on the gas, press the clutch down, and change the gear to second."

Clare tried, but the transition was rough, and they jolted along. "I'm sorry. I'm sorry."

"That's okay, it's your first time. Speed up to about twenty-five miles an hour…Okay, shift to third."

The next hour was spent in the empty parking lot with Clare struggling over and over to brake, shift, and accelerate. Under Jon's patient direction, the transitions became smoother. "We'd better head back," he finally said. "You're doing fine. You already could manage if you had to. You won't need to go beyond third gear here on the island."

In spite of the tension of the lessons, Clare found herself wanting to spend more time with Jon. She wanted to ask him some questions. "Sally and her mother are going to shop and have lunch after her session today. They said they wouldn't be back until one. Can I buy you a soda or coffee?"

"If you can get out on the highway and drive to a coffee shop."

"I'm not sure I can do that."

"I think you can. Go on, pull out on the highway. It's clear—go!" She pressed on the gas pedal, hearing the car whine in protest from the lower gear. "Shift to second," he said.

She did. The car smoothed out nicely. Jon nodded. "Okay, now go to third." She did.

"There's a coffee shop just ahead. Pull in, stop, and put the car in reverse."

"Good job!" he said, once she followed his directions. "Now put on the hand brake, turn off the ignition, and let's go in."

In the dim interior of the shop, where several people sat working on laptops, they went over to the counter. She ordered an iced latte; he ordered black coffee. As she opened her purse, he said, "No, I'll get it." He put a credit card in the slot.

"I wanted to pay—to thank you for the lesson."

"No need. It was to keep me from having to go out and rescue you again."

They sat facing each other at a table toward the back as a waiter delivered their orders. Studying Jon's face, she was once more struck with his strong, regular features, his deeply tanned skin, those striking light gray eyes. But she needed to focus on her questions. "I want to talk with you about something besides driving."

"What's that?"

"I saw the medications Sally takes. I looked them up on Google."

"Then you learned about her condition."

Clare nodded. "Yes—she's bipolar." They were silent for a moment. Then she said, "You must be right. I'm here as a kind of special companion for her. But my aunt didn't tell me that. She just invited me for the summer as a guest."

"Sally needs a companion right now, like a high-strung thoroughbred that needs a stall mate. But she wouldn't put up with a medical professional. Your aunt knew you would be much better in that role. Sally wouldn't object to a cousin she likes staying with her."

"Well, I'm no medical professional—just a future English graduate student. But I *am* being paid. At the end of the summer my aunt will give me the amount of money I would have earned this summer at the university library if my job hadn't fallen through—actually, even more than that. She told me it would be a graduation gift."

He regarded her thoughtfully. "And your parents thought it was a good idea for you to come for the summer?"

Clare hesitated. Around them several young people remained intent on their laptop screens. A few talked quietly. A young waiter picked up cups and wiped off empty tables. Finally she answered. "My father died when I was seventeen. So it's just my mother, and yes, she wanted me to come. She thought it would be good if Sally and I got to become friends. I'm sure she didn't know Sally was bipolar, or she'd have told me. " She paused. "Sally seems to be doing well, except for that beach party Friday night. That was the first time I saw…anyway, I'll be sure to keep her from drinking from now on. But there's something else I think I'm supposed to do."

"What's that?"

"Be her chaperone when she dates, and she wants to date Jason."

He rose, frowning. "Just keep a close eye on them."

Clare rose as well. "Maybe you…Do *you* care for Sally?"

His reply was brusque. "Of course I care about her, but not the way you're thinking. I just work for her father." He tossed a bill on the table for a tip and looked at his phone. "We need to get back."

She'd thought they were becoming friends, but perhaps with her last question she'd overstepped. When they reached the car, he got behind the wheel and drove back to the estate without speaking. She sat beside him, chastened.

Once through the gates and in the Sanderson parking area, though, he turned to her. "Sally is like a child in many ways," he said. "That's why the Sandersons needed someone close to her age, but serious and capable—like you—to be with her this summer."

"You think me so serious and capable?"

"Those were the words your aunt used when she described you to me. You don't think that's accurate?"

"It makes me sound like a spinster governess in a Victorian novel."

He laughed then. "You are hardly that."

A lightness rose within her. "I think I need more practice with this stick shift."

He looked away, silent. At last he nodded. "All right. Next Monday morning. Same time."

****

That afternoon as Clare lay on the living room couch, reading her Faulkner novel, the front door burst open. Sally and her mother came in, chattering happily. "Guess what!" Sally sat next to Clare, grasping her hand. "Mom and I have some news to tell you."

"I hope you'll like it," said Aunt Rose.

"Mom said I could have a party here *next Saturday*—a mid-May party! We can have it out on the terrace. It won't be like Jason's beach party. It will be formal, more like a prom. We'll hire a band, have dinner and dancing. I'll ask all the kids who were at Jason's party. Isn't that great news?"

"Can you get a party like that together so fast?"

"Tony has a lot of connections," said Aunt Rose. "It should be no problem."

Clare smiled and returned the squeeze on Sally's hand. "It sounds like a wonderful idea."

Sally jumped up. "I'll go now and send out the evites. Mom, ask Dad about a band right away. Oh, I can't wait." She scurried up the stairs.

Aunt Rose looked at Clare. "I think this will be good for Sally, a sort of coming-out party after her illness. And I like having it here. No driving this time. I'll tell the bartenders not to serve her alcohol. I know you'll take care of her, too. She won't want me around, but I'll be right upstairs if you need me. Tony may be here as well."

"Yes, I'll watch her."

"Well, then." Aunt Rose stood and gathered the bags. "I'd better put these things away and go see about Tinsel. I'm very glad you're here this summer, Clare."

"I'm glad to be here." She watched as Aunt Rose,

too, mounted the stairs. It seemed, with all of Sally's energy, that this summer would be non-stop action.

****

Saturday night in her room, dressed for the party, Clare heard the band tuning up on the terrace below. For a moment she felt an urge to go to bed and pull the covers over her head. But, she told herself, she had to go; she had to watch over her cousin. She hoped she looked right for the occasion. She had styled her hair in loose waves that fell to her shoulders, applied mascara to thicken and darken her lashes, and agreed to wear a shimmery lime-green backless dress Sally had borrowed for her from her mother.

Her cousin's sudden excited voice startled her. "I knew that dress would bring out the color of your eyes." Sally stood in the door between their adjoining rooms. She looked almost like a young Dolly Parton with her blond hair, eye makeup, and sparkly silver dress with low neckline. "We'd better go down. I hear guests arriving."

Clare took a deep breath. "I'm ready."

The two went downstairs and to the back terrace where several young people were already milling around at the appetizer tables and bar.

"Hi, everybody!" Sally called out. "Are you getting everything you want? Dinner will be coming. You remember my cousin Clare, don't you?" She moved into the middle of a group, and soon they were all talking loudly and laughing. Clare stayed on the fringe, watching. Then she saw Derek arrive.

He came at once to her side, substantial and friendly. "Wow, you look beautiful." He looked around at the lights, the flowers, the expansive terrace. "This is quite a place. Your uncle has made a lot of money."

"I guess he has."

"But he must have needed a lot of capital in the first place for building all his hotels and this estate. Banks don't just hand out unlimited loans."

Clare laughed a little. "I wouldn't know about that." But she thought, what strange comments and questions!

White-coated caterers were soon setting up a buffet of steak and salmon, vegetables, rice, rolls, desserts. Derek plucked a stemmed glass of wine off a tray and handed it to her. "Let's go find a table."

Clare looked for Sally. She was still in the midst of the laughing group. "All right."

The guests soon settled at tables to eat. The band began to play, softly enough that people could talk. After the meal, as twilight and then full darkness settled in, lanterns glowed around the terrace and the dancing began—some fast pieces, some slow. Again Clare checked on Sally. She was at a table with Jason and several others.

A slow piece was playing when Derek rose and said to her, "This party is formal enough I need to be formal too." He bowed slightly. "May I have this dance?"

Clare hadn't danced all through her college years, but, remembering her high school ballroom lessons, she stood and placed her left hand on Derek's shoulder, her right hand into his. They began to move to the music. She felt a little stiff, a little uncertain, but she thought with surprise, I can still do this.

When the music ended, she remembered her role. "Let's find Sally and Jason."

"I guess that security guard isn't going to spoil things for them tonight like he did last week at the pier."

"He was just trying to take care of her."

Derek shrugged, skeptical. They walked over to the couple.

"Clare, isn't this the best party?" exclaimed Sally. "Or maybe I shouldn't say that because it's *my* party."

"I'll say it," said Jason. "Miss Sanderson, this is the best party." He put his arm around her. That, Clare thought, seemed innocent enough.

She and Derek stayed with the group awhile, but then he said to her, "Let's get an after-dinner drink." They walked over to the bar. There, Clare drew in a sharp breath of surprise. Behind the bar, in a black shirt and white bow tie, stood Jon, mixing drinks.

She heard Derek at her side "Well, look who's bartending! Our security guard." He laughed a little. "Guess he's keeping our drinks safe. What will you have? My advice, given my Italian heritage, is an amaretto." Clare jumped to attention and nodded. "Two amarettos," Derek called out.

Jon efficiently poured the yellow-orange liquid into crystal cordial glasses and handed them over to Derek with cocktail napkins. He gave Clare only a slight nod of acknowledgment before he turned away to mix another drink.

Slightly hurt—he must not have even noticed how she looked in this wonderful dress—Clare sipped her amaretto, danced with Derek, and talked and laughed with the other partygoers until midnight, when the band was to leave.

"Wait before you play this last set," Sally called

out, going over to the players' platform. "I want to make an announcement." She pulled the microphone down to her height. "Attention, everybody!" The talk died down. "The witching hour is almost here. The bar is now closed. This is the last dance. I want to thank you all for coming and helping me celebrate my return to health and"— she giggled—"to society. I hope you'll see lots of me this summer—and my wonderful cousin Clare." She gestured at Clare, who gave a little wave. "So enjoy this last dance. And again, thanks for coming." Sally put the microphone back up on its stand and hopped off the impromptu stage. Everyone applauded.

The band began to play soft, romantic music, but soon after Clare and Derek began to dance, she felt a little vibration under her left hand. Looking up, she saw it had come from a tap on Derek's shoulder.

Jon stood there. "Excuse me. Mr. Pacelli, isn't it? There's a phone call for you at the bar."

"For me?" Derek looked surprised, a bit annoyed. "Do you know who it is?"

"No, sir."

Derek spoke to Clare. "I'll be right back."

He walked away, but Jon remained. As other couples danced around them, he hesitated a moment, then asked, "Shall we, Miss Matthews?"

"Ah, *Miss Matthews,*" she said. "Because you're in your employee role tonight. It's your duty to dance with me."

"That's right." She looked up and saw a smile in his gray eyes. "It wouldn't be right to leave you alone on the dance floor."

She smiled back then and raised both her hands to

his shoulders. He put his together on the small of her back, warm through the thin material of her dress. This seemed more intimate than her formal dance position with Derek—and she did not mind. The stiffness she'd felt with Derek was gone. Moving to the music close to Jon, becoming part of the crowd, seemed so natural.

"I was surprised to see you bartending," she said. "You do all kinds of things here."

"And you," he said. "I saw you keeping an eye on Sally tonight."

So he'd noticed her after all, even though at the bar when he'd served Derek, he'd barely glanced her way. "Tonight was easier," she said. "Sally wasn't being served drinks."

"And I made sure no one shared any with her."

"Thank you for that."

The tempo of the music became faster, and he spun around, the colored lights whirling past. She held onto him and closed her eyes, following his lead. After what seemed only a minute later, though, he leaned down and spoke into her ear. "Your date is coming back. Good night, Clare."

She opened her eyes as he let her go and almost gallantly presented her to the arriving Derek. She watched as he returned to the bar, weaving agilely through the dancers.

"Shit," said Derek, also watching him. "He's just an employee here. He should not have danced with you."

Even as he spoke, the last strains of music faded away. They walked to the edge of the dance area while the crowd applauded the disbanding musicians. Still looking annoyed, Derek applauded only briefly.

"What was the phone call?" Clare asked.

"It was a mix-up. There was a taxi waiting outside the gates. Someone here must have called it and given this address and phone number, but the driver got the name wrong—or maybe it sounded like mine. Anyway, when no one showed up, he called the number and that *bartender* or *security guard* or whatever he is, thought he'd asked for me. I should have known. A legitimate call would've come to my cell."

Clare put her hand on his arm. "We had lots of dances together this evening anyway."

Derek smiled and pulled her against him. "That's true. Sorry, I shouldn't have gotten mad."

Yes, she thought, Derek was very nice. But a wayward thought—or maybe it was a wish—crossed her mind: could Jon have engineered that phone call so he could dance with her?

Chapter Four

Sunday, May 17 – Wednesday, May 20

On Sunday afternoon, Clare and Sally lay beside the pool and talked about last evening's party. Sally chattered happily about the good music and food and her time with Jason. "You and Derek seemed to be having a good time too," she said. "What do you think of him?"

"He's nice."

"I think so, too. I guess you know he just started working at the marina this month. You may see him next Wednesday when we go there. Did I tell you? That's the day Kyle—Jason's father—wants us to go out with him on his boat."

"I'd love that."

"He'll be meeting another boat that's bringing up some cargo from Mexico."

"What kind of boat does Kyle have?"

"Just a small yacht. It's great for watching sunsets and sunrises, water-skiing in the bays. Sometimes Kyle even takes it to various ports in Florida. This time, though, it's for that meeting out on the water."

Clare smiled and closed her eyes, feeling the sun on her face. It did seem that being Sally's companion would be more fun than work. Soon—a yacht cruise on the ocean!

But even more, she found herself looking forward to the next day, when she would see Jon for her second driving lesson.

****

On Monday Clare watched to be sure Sally took her pills, had breakfast with her and her mother, and finally waved them off as they headed to Savannah. Then she hurried upstairs to get ready for her own appointment. She wore white capris and a pink blouse, which she now tied in front to slightly bare her midriff.

She was sitting on the bottom step by the parking area when Jon drove up in Sally's car and stopped. He turned off the ignition, pulled on the hand brake, and got out, looking tan and fit in cutoffs and his usual open-necked shirt. He went around the car and got into the passenger seat. "I think you can take it from here."

She slid in behind the wheel. "It's been a week since our lesson. I hope I remember how to do this."

"You will." She sat for a moment, indecisive. He said, "Let up the hand brake, put your right foot on the brake pedal, the other on the clutch, and turn on the ignition."

"You see? I'm not ready."

"Just do what I say."

She followed his directions. The car gave a satisfied rumble. She let up the brake pedal, released the clutch as she pressed the accelerator, and drove down the driveway—reaching up to the black box now on the sun visor to open the gates.

"Who is that at the gate house?" she asked, seeing the man with glasses she'd noted there when she and Jon returned from her lesson the week before.

"Oh, that's just Bruce. He works shifts at the

gatehouse, too."

Outside the gates, she clicked the remote button to activate closure, then stopped, careful to depress both the brake and clutch.

"Turn right," Jon said. She put on the turn signal, released the brake, then gradually released the clutch as she pressed the accelerator. After she turned right, he said, "Shift to second."

She bit her lip in concentration and shifted with a fair degree of smoothness. "Speed up." She did, and without his saying anything, shifted into third. Jon gave her a look of approval. "I think you've got it, so we can just take a ride. Keep on down this road."

"Where are we going?"

"There's a place I thought I'd take you to, one most people don't know about."

The road, following the shoreline, led toward the end of the island. Along the way Clare caught glimpses of the glittering ocean beyond the trees and tall sea oats. After a few minutes Jon said, "Take the next left turn. Be careful. It's just a single lane dirt road, not well marked."

Once on the narrow road, seeing how bumpy it was, she shifted to low. They came out to a grassy area adjacent to a stretch of beach with a *No Trespassing* sign prominently displayed. "Don't worry about that sign—it's okay for me to be here. Go ahead and park." She did. "Good job. Come on."

She followed him down the footpath to the ocean. The beach was deserted, and the tide was going out. As they walked along the retreating waves, Clare collected small shells and sand dollars. "What is the hole by that mound of sand?"

"A ghost crab hole. Look—there it is." Jon pointed to a pale, insect-like creature with two antenna-like stalks sticking up from it. "They change their coloring to match their surroundings, like a chameleon. That one's an adult male—they're larger than the females. See, it has four pairs of walking legs and one pair of white claws. Look at its eyes on those stalks. They can rotate 360 degrees."

"I never saw anything like it," said Clare. "It's like a creature out of the *Star Wars* movies."

"The natural world is as fantastic as *Star Wars*."

They walked farther. He picked up a delicate tapering oval shell, its iridescent colors of pastel pink and lavender glistening like a rainbow in the sun. Clare looked at it. "How beautiful."

"It's a pen shell—see the long, pointed shape of the shell, kind of like a pen? That's how it got its name. That inner layer is mother of pearl. Native Americans used these shells to make jewelry. They're actually pretty rare now." He held it out to her. "Would you like it?"

"I'd love it." She slipped it carefully into her pocket. "Thank you."

They walked on until they came to a formation of gnarled, uprooted trees bleached to driftwood, lying like skeletons on the sand. "What happened to those trees?" she asked.

"Erosion. Decades ago, when the soil was washed away from their roots, they fell and decayed like this."

"What amazing, mysterious shapes. Like sculptures."

They sat on the beach, facing the driftwood trees and the sea beyond them. Gulls circled and sandpipers danced along the water's edge. An egret posed in the shallow water, then took off and swooped down to the water, snatching a fish. Clare looked at Jon, now lying back on his elbows beside her watching the waves. "I was surprised to see you at Sally's party Saturday."

"The party was last minute. Tony needed an extra bartender."

Clare pulled her knees to her chest and wrapped her arms around them. They were silent for a few moments. Was he thinking of their dance, as she was? After a few moments she said, "I'm glad you brought me here."

"This is the foot of the island—on this side the ocean, on the other, the marsh. I lived near here as a child and explored the whole area."

"You must have loved it."

"I did. I read that when the law got too close, pirates hid out on this part of St. Sebastian's. I used to pretend I was a pirate and built hiding places and forts. I still come to this beach whenever I can." His smile faded as he picked up a shell fragment beside him and threw it toward the waves. "I don't want to see this area developed like the rest of the island."

"Who owns it?"

"Your uncle. Years ago he put up those *No Trespassing* signs at its boundaries. He's thinking of building another hotel here. But I'd like to see this end of the island made into a nature preserve."

"That's a great idea. Have you suggested it to him?"

"I've mentioned it. But he knows a nature preserve wouldn't make money like his hotels." He was quiet for a moment. "It would be best not to mention coming here with me, Clare."

"I won't if you don't want me to." But now, as she fingered the smooth inner surface of the pen shell in her pocket, she wondered: was their friendship—if that's what it was—something her aunt and uncle would disapprove of?

Jon stood and brushed the sand from his pants. "We'd better go."

He began walking back the way they had come. Clare followed. Reaching the car, he leaned against it and waited for her as she came up. "I'll drive back."

He sped along, soon turning in at the Sanderson Estates entrance. He punched the gate opener and drove up to the house steps. There he stopped, leaving the car engine idling. "Well, you've passed the driving test."

"Do you really think I'll need to drive this car sometime?"

"You never know." He must have noted her doubtful look. Reaching over, he touched her hand. "Don't worry, you'll do fine. And you're the perfect companion for Sally."

She still didn't understand exactly all he did for her uncle, or all that was going on at the Estates, but the brief touch of his hand gave her a warm, tingling feeling. She said, "Thank you for the driving lessons—and for taking me to that beautiful beach. I think your idea about a nature preserve is wonderful."

He nodded, seeming, she thought, pleased. But then he looked away, saying nothing about seeing her again. Back in her room, she placed the shell he'd given her on her windowsill behind the curtain, in a hidden spot where the sun would find it in the morning and make its colors shine.

****

On Wednesday, the weather was perfect for the cruise on the Eldridge yacht. The spring air was clear and almost too warm. Sun glittered on the water. Dressed in their bathing suits and wraps, Clare and Sally walked along one of the marina's piers. Sally stopped by the prow of a large white yacht bobbing gently on the water. "Here it is. Kyle must be here already. And look, Jason's coming too." Smiling, she called out, "Jason!"

In shorts and a T-shirt like Derek's, emblazoned with "St. Sebastian's Marina," the young blond man looked up from the deck. As the girls walked down the little walkway beside the boat, he came to the rail, hand extended to Sally. "Hey, girl!" She took it and climbed aboard. They lingered together for a moment.

As Jason turned and offered her a hand as well, Clare wondered if her aunt and uncle knew he would be on this excursion.

"You can put your beach bags below," he told them.

Sally led her to a hatch and down narrow ladder-like stairs. Pausing at the bottom, Clare saw a small, low-ceilinged kitchen, tiny bathroom, and two narrow sets of bunks. "This boat is amazing."

Sally shrugged. "It's not that unusual. My father's yacht is a lot like this."

They went back up the steps to the deck. A man wearing a bathing suit, sleeveless nautical T-shirt, and sunhat had arrived. "Clare," Sally said, "this is Kyle Eldridge, my father's business partner. Kyle, this is my cousin Clare Matthews."

Clare studied the man. Tall and solidly built, he

had blond coloring like Jason's and small blue eyes—handsome in a rough sort of way. He, like her uncle, looked about fifty. Regarding her appreciatively, he said, "Ah, another beautiful girl. So today I'll have a pair of beauties with us. Just as I'd hoped."

Sally laughed and asked, "Are we about to leave, Kyle?"

"We're just waiting for Jon. I borrowed him from your father. He'll be our pilot today."

Clare's heart sped up. He would be on this trip? Then she saw him, walking along the pier to them—in cutoff jeans, shirtless, his T-shirt flung over one shoulder. His torso was lean and tanned, his biceps not bulging like a weightlifter's, but hard and strong.

Easy, familiar with the boat, he climbed aboard, and nodding a brief greeting to them all, headed to the cabin where the steering wheel and what looked like two computers on a sort of dashboard were located. The motor gurgled, Jason and his father untied the ropes to the pier, and the boat moved out of its slip into the river. Kyle seated himself on one of the cushioned benches in the back of the boat and leaning back, closed his eyes. Clare joined Sally and Jason at the rail as the boat passed from the mouth of the river into open water.

"So we're meeting your friend from Mexico, Dad?" Jason asked.

Kyle roused. "Yes, Manuel and I should be at about the same spot at"—he looked at his watch—"eleven o'clock. Jon is an expert navigator—he should get us there at just the right time. This gives me a chance to take a break." He lay back on the seat, tipped his hat over his face, and seemed to snooze. Jason put his arm around Sally.

Clare turned away and sat on another bench as the shoreline of St. Sebastian's receded. The wake of the boat stretched out behind them, becoming less high and foamy as the boat picked up speed. Seabirds flew overhead. She could see Jon in the cabin nonchalantly standing at the wheel in front of a high stool, his dark hair ruffled by the wind. She gave into temptation and rising, went to him.

He turned his head. "Enjoying the ride?"

"I love it." She indicated the boat's wheel and the screens on the dashboard in front of it. "So this is another of your skills?"

"Steering doesn't take much skill. Just turn the wheel. See?" He turned it and the boat arced to the right. "Want to try?" He stepped to one side. She moved next to him. "Turn it back to the left—we need to head out straight."

She turned the wheel and the boat corrected its course. "What are these screens for?"

"This one shows ocean depths and currents. And this is an ocean GPS. We have to meet Mr. Sanderson's contact at"—he pointed at a spot on the screen—"this location."

"And then what?"

"We'll pull alongside their boat and unload some cargo." He took over the wheel again. "How is your charge doing?"

"Sally? She's doing great."

"Did you find her Ambivalen?"

"Ambivalen? No. I didn't know she took that."

"Only as needed. It helps her if she can't sleep. Her mother lets her keep only a few pills at a time."

"I'll ask Sally about it."

He pushed a lever at his right then, and the boat thrust forward even faster. They stood together, his shoulder almost brushing hers, as the boat raced across the waves toward the horizon. Clare watched the GPS screen tracking their progress with a red line, then turned her eyes from the screens to his profile. "How long have you worked for my uncle?"

"Just a year—since I graduated from Savannah State."

"What did you study?"

"Marine biology and ecology. Good majors for an islander, don't you think?"

"Your parents—they live here on the island?"

He glanced over at her. "You know my mother."

"I do?"

"Maria."

"*Maria* is your mother?"

He looked back at the screens and turned the wheel slightly. "You're surprised. Yes, she is. She's from Mexico. And yes, I'm Hispanic. My last name is Figueroa. It's from the Spanish *figueira*, 'fig tree.' "

"Spanish is your native language then?"

"It's what I grew up with as a child."

That explained his slight accent. But thinking of his gray eyes and seemingly light skin under the tan, she could not help but ask: "And your father?"

He looked ahead. A muscle in his jaw twitched. "My mother doesn't speak of him."

"Your last name, Figueroa…"

"It's my mother's last name."

"I'm sorry. I didn't mean to bring up anything that…" She gathered her courage. "I just wanted to know more about you. Because I like you."

She thought she saw a flicker of reaction cross his face, but he just continued scanning the ocean ahead. And then his expression changed, grew intense. He pulled back on the throttle and the boat began to slow. "There they are."

Ahead, silhouetted against the morning sun she saw a boat similar to theirs, but larger. "The boat Mr. Eldridge is supposed to meet?"

"Yes. You'd better go tell him it's in sight."

When Clare went back, she saw that Kyle was already awake and Jason and Sally had moved apart. They all went to the rail and watched as their yacht approached the larger one. Flying from its stern was the Mexican flag with its vertical tricolors of red, white and green, in the central white stripe an image of an eagle with a serpent clutched in its beak. Several brown-skinned crew members bustled about the deck. Jon slowed the boat further as he guided it close. Then he cut off the motor and moved quickly to the rail with Kyle and Jason. The three of them threw ropes with a hook on the ends to the Mexicans, who caught them, pulled them taut, and attached them to their boat. Now the two yachts, the larger and the smaller, were linked side by side in the water.

"*Hola*!" Kyle called to them.

The men waved and lowered a large heavily loaded duffel bag down to Kyle, then another to Jon. Shouldering them, the two went to the hatch and carried them below. When they returned, two more such duffels were lowered; Jon and Kyle again carried them below. The Mexicans disconnected the grappling hooks and shoved the boats apart while Jason reeled in the ropes. Jon emerged from the hatch and went back to the steering wheel. The motor started and their boat moved away. The whole encounter took less than ten minutes.

Sally watched all this with casual interest, but Clare was amazed. The boat began to speed back toward St. Sebastian's. Kyle, too, returned to the deck. "Okay, girls, enjoy yourselves. The meeting's over. Now it's just a pleasure cruise. You can do some sunbathing. "

Jason lifted the seat of a bench on deck and from the storage area under it took out two rolled foam mats, which he laid out on the deck. Sally removed her wrap, revealing her curvy figure in the new bikini. Clare removed her own wrap and untied the straps of her bathing suit, tucking them into her bosom so she'd have an even tan on her shoulders. Both girls stretched out in the sun.

"I'll bring you up some lunch," Jason said, heading down the hatch. His father followed.

The boat slowed to a moderate speed, and everything seemed more relaxed. After a while Jason came up with a bag of sandwiches and an ice chest. He gave a sandwich to each girl and carried a third and a soda from the chest to Jon at the wheel. Sally reached in the chest and extracted a can of beer.

"Don't you want a soda instead?" Clare asked Sally.

"One beer won't hurt."

Overhearing as he returned, Jason laughed. "We'll make sure she has just one."

Clare then took a beer for herself. "Isn't your father coming up to eat with us?"

"No, he's doing some work down below. He'll eat

there."

The girls sat cross-legged on the mats, and Jason settled on a bench. Clare asked, "What was going on with that Mexican boat?"

Sally shrugged. "Kyle and my father have meetings out on the ocean like that a lot. It's some kind of business exchange."

"Today I think we picked up some electronics—parts for computers," said Jason.

After lunch, the girls lay down in the sun again, and Jason stretched out on a bench. Sally dozed, and Clare, relaxed after the beer and in the heat, drifted off as well. She wasn't sure how much time had passed, but she was jolted awake by sudden loud music coming from a stereo system in the cabin and the rough, urgent voice of Kyle, now back up on deck.

"Something's coming! I'm taking over the wheel." He strode to the cabin, put a hand on Jon's shoulder, and spoke in his ear to him as if giving an order.

A moment later, Jon walked over and pulled Clare to her feet. "Come with me—we're going below."

"Why?" she asked, still groggy. But she went with him as he hurried her to the hatch, almost stumbling as they went down the narrow steps into the dim lower depths.

Looking tense and alert, he sat on a bottom bunk and drew her down beside him. She heard another boat come up alongside, then stop. Their yacht slowed, then stopped also, drifting. All was still but for the splash of the waves. Jon pressed her hand in a warning to stay quiet. Then she heard a man's voice over what seemed to be a megaphone: "Mr. Eldridge? U.S. Coast Guard. We'd like to come aboard."

Kyle's voice yelled back over the music: "Goddammit. We're just out for a pleasure cruise."

"We have probable cause to search all boats in the area, sir."

There was a long pause, then Kyle's shouted response: "Okay, do what you have to do."

The music ceased. Feet clomped on the deck above them. Jon moved his hand to the back of her neck, massaging it in a kind of caress, as if to reassure her. She sat motionless beside him, aware of his tension, even more aware of his touch.

Then, as the steps came close over their heads, he eased Clare down on the cot and, lying over her, began kissing her—her cheeks, her neck, then her lips. Surprised, she at first instinctively resisted, but he held her, his kisses becoming deeper. She had no fear or flashbacks. Instead, another instinct took over: those warm sensations she'd felt with him, much stronger now, surged through her. She stopped resisting, stopped thinking at all.

She did not hear the hatch door from the deck lift, the heavy feet on the ladder-like steps descending. She knew only that Jon raised his head and said, "Damn, what are you doing here?" She looked up to see two men in navy blue shirts standing on the steps staring down at them.

Kyle's harsh voice came from the deck. "There is nothing down there but two consenting adults."

The men stood, indecisive a moment, but then one nodded at Jon. "Sorry, sir."

They turned and retraced their steps. The hatch closed. Jon remained over her, listening. Footsteps above them went to the side of the boat. They heard the other boat's motor, a loud roar at first, growing quieter as it departed. Their own yacht still drifted gently beneath them.

He raised himself off her, then sat on the edge of the cot, head bowed. "I'm sorry. I had to do that."

Clare sat up. "What do you mean, you *had to*?"

"The Coast Guard wanted to search the boat. Seeing us convinced them not to come down here."

Clare was stunned. "So what you did just now…was only an act?"

He was silent for a moment. Then he turned to her and gently brushed back a lock of her hair. "No."

A moment later the hatch above them opened with a loud click and Kyle called down. "All clear."

Jon stood. "We have to go."

They climbed back up the steps and into the sunny ocean air. Jason and Sally stood there with their arms around each other. It seemed they had been dancing. Grinning, Kyle came over and slapped Jon's back. "You must've been convincing down there, boy."

Jon scowled and moved away to the steering wheel. Clare stood there, her cheeks burning. The boat motor started up.

"Well, it *was* mostly a pleasure trip," Sally said. "Those men had no right to come aboard. They realized that when they saw us."

"It's not that big a deal," Jason said. "They were searching all the boats."

Clare re-tied her bathing suit straps around her neck, then put on her wrap. She pictured what the men from the Coast Guard must have seen down there on that narrow bunk—Jon's naked torso over her, her own bare shoulders and legs under his, their passionate kiss—the scene that had made them turn away in embarrassment.

A wave of anger licked up within her. She'd been used to keep those men from searching the lower cabin.

Then the anger slowly drained away. Jon may have been following Kyle's orders, but she remembered how his wonderful kiss had been—and how, when she asked him if he'd just been acting, he'd brushed back her hair so gently and said, "No."

Chapter Five

Wednesday, May 20 – Saturday, May 23

The boat moved steadily back to the marina. After retrieving the girls' bags, Jason and Kyle escorted them off the boat, leaving Jon to finish docking.

Over the next few days Clare wondered about the Coast Guard's "probable cause" for searching boats in the area, but that question was over-ridden by other, more personal thoughts.

After all these years, Jon Figueroa had been the first man to break through her barriers, the first to arouse her sexually. It proved that something inside her was not dead after all. But why him?

Perhaps in part, as she'd already realized, because of his different, almost exotic looks. His glowing skin, riveting eyes, dark eyebrows. But also his surprising, mysterious background—his mother her uncle's Mexican housekeeper, his father unknown. The fact that, except for that kiss—which *had* been ordered by Kyle— he'd never actively pursued her. True, he'd given her driving lessons, danced with her, taken her to his special place on the end of the island. But always he'd seemed to back away from anything more, as if he, too, had a wall about him.

It's up to me, she thought. Instead of retreating behind my own barrier, I must break through his.

"I wonder what's become of Jon," she asked Sally as the two lounged by the pool the following afternoon. "He wasn't at the gatehouse this morning."

"Oh, he's flown with Dad to Miami," said Sally without opening her eyes. "Dad had some meetings there. They should be back by tomorrow night."

"Does Jon live here now, on the estate?"

"Part of the time, yes—you didn't know?" Sally waved her hand vaguely toward the end of the pool. "He stays in an apartment at the back of the pool house."

Clare debated, then spoke. "He told me Maria is his mother."

Sally opened her eyes. "He told you that? Yes, she came to work for us when he was ten or so, and they stayed in some cottage on property Dad owns on that narrow south end of island. When Dad sent him away to school, Maria moved into rooms in our house. Last year, after Jon graduated from college, he came back and began working full-time for Dad. That's when Dad set up the pool house apartment for him."

"What's his job here exactly?"

"I'm not really sure. Dad started having vision problems, optic neuropathy, something like that, so he needed someone to drive him at night and on long trips, travel with him when he flies, pilot the boat. I think that's mainly what Jon was hired for at first. But he's also now in charge of the security guards at the gates, and as you saw, sometimes does other jobs—like bartending and piloting Kyle's boat." She cocked her head at Clare. "Why these questions?"

Clare stood. "I was just wondering. I think I'll swim some laps."

Later, when she climbed out of the pool, Sally was putting down her phone. "Jason just called. He and Derek want to take us paddle boarding at Fish Hook Bay tomorrow morning. I told them that would work for us. They'll pick us up at nine."

"I'd like that."

As Clare toweled off, she wondered where her relationship with Derek would go. Nice as he was, would she be able to keep on dating him and thus chaperone Sally and Jason, given her aversion to any physical relationship with men?

Except, it seemed, for Jon.

****

On Friday morning after Jason drove up in his sleek red sports sedan, he and Derek fastened Sally's two boards on a rack attached to the top of the car. As Clare and Derek climbed into the back seat, Derek told her, "Fish Hook Bay is an easy place to paddle. I think you'll take right to it."

Jason soon pulled in at a calm bay not far from the marina. On the shore, they all shed their shirts and shorts to their bathing suits underneath and put on life jackets. Derek showed Clare how to attach a Velcro strap around her ankle, like a leash, to keep the board attached to her and adjusted the height of her paddle. Then they all waded out knee deep, their paddles across the boards. "Now kneel," Derek told Clare, "like this, then stand up."

Following his instructions, she carefully got to her feet, holding her paddle before her. "Good," Derek called. "Most people fall the first time."

Although Clare enjoyed the challenge of balancing on the board and paddling around the bay, she thought she'd prefer kayaking in the marshes—the marshes that were part of the island park Jon envisioned. There was more wildlife to observe there, more variation of scenery. After about an hour, the foursome went back toward shore where they again got on their knees as the boards slid up on the sand.

"Let's go get some lunch," said Sally exuberantly, "my treat."

They discarded their life jackets, pulled their T-shirts and shorts back on over their bathing suits, and headed to the Shrimp Shack. The little restaurant was packed. They settled in a recently emptied booth as the waitress hurriedly removed used dishes and wiped the table, then took their orders. When they'd finished eating, Jason looked at Clare and said, "See how tourism here is booming? I guess you know Sally's father and my father really made this island."

"How did they happen to become partners in the first place?" Clare asked.

"They go way back. They were in the same fraternity in college, and I guess they had many adventures together. They say their island land purchases began as just another adventure."

"The land was a great investment," Derek said. "So how did they get the capital for all they've done since?"

Jason gave him a playful swat on the shoulder. "Beach bum envy, huh? Trying to plan how to make your own fortune?"

Derek laughed. "You caught me."

"Well, better ask them. I have no idea. Right now we need to get back to the marina. We were lucky to get this morning off."

"Your dad always lets *you* off," Derek said. "I

think he let me go today because he knew I was going with you to take Sally and Clare paddle boarding. But hey, next time, maybe we'll all have a night-time date. Does that sound good, Clare?"

"Sounds good." Clare smiled at Derek, but on the ride back to the Sanderson estate she leaned away slightly when he put his arm around her.

****

Late that Friday night, still dressed in the aqua T-shirt and white shorts she'd worn at dinner, Clare lay on her bed, thinking. Yes, she liked Derek, she did not feel afraid of him—but she still wanted to withdraw from any physical closeness, with that instinctive reaction to men she'd had throughout college.

Her response to Jon, though, had, strangely, been the opposite—she felt physically drawn *toward* him; she *wanted* his touch. And then that kiss on the boat! It was like the fairy tale she'd read as a child about a prince who kissed a long unconscious girl, and she awoke.

She rose, picked up the shell Jon had given her, and turned it to the overhead light. Its rainbow colors seemed like a promise. Wandering out to her balcony, she looked out at the pool, then at the beach house. Sally had said his apartment was there and that he'd be back from Miami that night. Was he there now? Back inside, she gently opened the door to Sally's adjoining room and peeked in. The girl was sound asleep, her blond hair splayed across the pillow.

Clare knew what she had to do.

She silently opened the door to the hall and went down the stairs. All was dark—everyone had gone to bed. The outside door was always locked, but she remembered the access code to get back in. She opened it, stepped out, closing it softly behind her, and walked past the pool and along the side of the beach house. Behind the building, she stopped. Yes, there was a door leading to some kind of apartment, and a light shone through the window beside it. He was back.

Even as she looked, the door opened. Jon stood there, barefoot, in his cutoff denim shorts and his usual open-necked shirt. He held a gun. "Clare, it's you!" He tossed the gun aside. "Sorry. Like I told you, Tony wants us to be careful. This begins Memorial Day weekend. There will be a lot of people coming to the island. What are you doing out there?"

"Sally's asleep. I thought I'd go for a walk…When did you get back?"

"Tonight."

"So this is where you stay." They stood facing each other. In the ensuing silence she heard the chirp of crickets, the call of katydids, the breeze rustling the palms. "Won't you invite me in?"

"If you want," he said, and stepped aside.

She walked past him through the door. The large one-room apartment was dimly lit and seemed very basic—a kitchen area with small wooden table and chairs, a couch, one upholstered chair, a narrow single bed with a table and lamp beside it. She turned to him. "You've been gone since the ride on Kyle's boat."

She thought she saw a faint flush cross his cheeks. "I apologize again for what I did below deck that day. But I told you why."

"*Was* Mr. Eldridge doing something illegal?"

"The Coast Guard crew must have suspected he might be."

"When we came up to the deck, he said you must have been 'convincing down there.' "

"I'm sorry you heard that."

She took a step toward him. "You were…very convincing."

He stood still, and his voice was apologetic. "Clare, I can't get involved with you." He must have seen the hurt in her eyes—and the question. He said, "It's better for you not to be involved with me."

She went over to the upholstered chair and sat down. "I want to tell you something. Can I?"

"Of course."

"Something happened to me when I was a freshman in college. Early in the semester, I went to a fraternity party with my girlfriends. It was my first fraternity party, and I was nervous. Someone at the house handed me a drink, and I drank it down right away. Something was in it."

He sat on the side of the bed and looked at her intently.

"I found out later there was a drug in my drink. I must have blacked out. The next thing I knew I was in one of the bedrooms upstairs. I was blindfolded, my clothes were off, and…"

"You don't need to tell me this, Clare."

"There were three of them. I was so traumatized I didn't say anything to anyone about it afterward. I went back to the dorm with my friends, showered, and went home the next morning. My mother could tell something had happened. I had to tell her. She called the police. Their exam showed I'd been raped, and blood tests showed some of the drug still in my system, but they told me no one could be charged or arrested since I couldn't identify who had done it or even describe anything unique about the bedroom. And I'd destroyed too much evidence by showering and waiting to report what had happened. The doctor gave me a morning-after pill and said I'd be all right, that I'd heal. When I went back to school a week later, I told my friends and teachers I'd had the flu. The police reported the fraternity to the university, without involving me. It was banned from holding social activities for a year."

She paused, looked away from him. "The doctor was right. I've healed physically. But I haven't been able to let any man touch me…that way…since. All through college, I didn't date. They called me the Ice Princess." She made herself look back at him. "You…you're the first I've ever *wanted* to touch me. I realized that when you kissed me."

She stood then, crossed the room to the window, pulled down the window shade with a snap, then sat down on the cot next to him. Her whisper was low, urgent. "Make love to me, Jon. I think if you do, I'll be cured. I'll be normal."

He stroked her hair but made no other move.

"Don't worry, I take birth control pills. For monthly cramps."

"I may hurt you."

"You won't. I am fine…physically."

He remained still a long moment. Then, he leaned forward and kissed her, gently at first. She clutched him to her. Side by side, they fell back on the bed. Their kisses became as deep as on the boat, then deeper still. She slid her hands under his shirt, feeling the warmth and hardness of his chest. His hands found their way to her breasts. The sensations that she'd felt with him on that bunk in the yacht rose again within her—stronger now, increasingly urgent. She arched against him. "Please. Please."

He hesitated a moment more, then in a swift, decisive motion, pulled off his shorts, reached over and turned out the light.

****

She did not go back to the house until two that morning. Upstairs in her room, she again opened the door to Sally's room and peeked in. Her cousin lay asleep on her side, hugging her pillow like a child. With a deep, relieved breath, Clare closed the door. Sitting on her bed, she undressed, one item at a time, slowly, languidly, reliving the wonderful hours before. Jon must have cured her. She'd hoped for some kind of pleasure. She'd never expected ecstasy.

As she left him, Jon had said, "That name they called you was way off. You're no Ice Princess."

****

Sally shook her awake the next morning, shattering her dream into a myriad of rainbow-colored sparkles. "Clare! Wake up! Let's go to the beach and take pictures of the sunrise."

Clare opened her eyes. The darkness of her room was pierced by the narrow white beam of Sally's phone flashlight. "What time is it?"

"Five thirty—we'll have time to get there. I have to call to get my car. And we can't go without someone letting me out." She punched numbers on her phone. "Hello, Jon! Clare and I want to go to the beach and see the sunrise. I need my car right away. And you have to open the gates." She disconnected and looked at Clare, who, upon hearing Jon's name, had sat up. "I know it's spur of the moment. But that's what makes life fun. Come on, get dressed!"

"Jon's getting your car?"

Sally giggled. "Yes. He'd just relieved the person working at the gatehouse." She ran back to her room. "I'm going to wear my bathing suit. Put on yours, too. We can go for a swim while we're there."

Clare went to the bathroom where she'd hung her suit to dry, stepped into it, tied the straps and returned to the bedroom. Sally, in her bikini now, came in and looked at her critically. "You need to get another bathing suit. One isn't enough here. When we leave the beach, we can go have brunch somewhere and then go shopping for one." Sally's energy knew no bounds.

Clare, fully awake now, put on her gold wrap. "Have you taken your pills?"

"Oh, I forgot." Sally took her three pills, gulping water down. Then, putting on her own wrap, she looked out of the window. The sky was growing lighter in the east. "I hope Jon hurries. We don't want to miss the sunrise. Come on, let's go." They picked up their phones and beach bags and went outside and down the steps.

Only a minute later they saw Sally's sports car coming up the drive. It stopped beside them. Jon, his usually neat white shirt now somewhat rumpled, got out and spoke to Sally as she ran up. "You didn't tell anyone you'd want the car this early."

Sally slid in behind the wheel. "It was just an impulse."

Clare, getting into the passenger seat, looked over at Jon, meeting his eyes for an electric moment. Then to her surprise, he opened the back door of the car and got into the seat behind them. "Go ahead," he said to Sally, "drive to the gate."

She started the car and pressed the accelerator with annoyance. "I feel like a prisoner without a remote opener of my own."

"Your parents' orders," said Jon.

She careened down the driveway. "Talk to them about it, will you? My father will listen to you."

"I don't think I can change anything."

At the gate Sally slammed on the brakes. Jon held up the remote, then pressed the button. As the gates opened, he got out of the car, the device in his hand. "Take it easy now."

"And you—talk to my father!"

****

On the Golden Sands Hotel beach, as Clare watched the morning clouds above the horizon glow pink and the red ball of sun rise through them, it seemed a new day for her in more ways than one. She felt more alive than she could remember. She and Sally took pictures and, when the sun was fully up, went into the surf. Afterward they rinsed off under the shower on the beach, then lay in the sun to dry.

"You know, you seem different somehow," Sally said.

"I do? How?"

Sally stretched and closed her eyes. "I don't know—happier, more relaxed, brighter. It must be the island and that glorious sunrise."

Clare looked at her cousin, who seemed to be drifting off to sleep. "Yes," she said. "The island and the sunrise." She closed her own eyes.

But before long she heard Sally beside her getting

to her feet. "Now for lunch and shopping."

They changed to shorts and T-shirts in a restroom in the hotel lobby and then, sitting out on the terrace, already crowded with Memorial weekend tourists, they ordered poor boy sandwiches. When they'd eaten, Sally took Clare to a little store nearby. "Here's where I found my bikini," she said. "You'd look good in one, Clare."

"I don't know," Clare began but Sally pulled her to a sale rack.

"Here's some. Come on, try them on." And she insisted, standing outside the stall as Clare hesitantly tried on the first her cousin indicated. It was a peacock blue with lime green streaks, and modest enough—though she'd need to tan her middle and the white areas on the upper swell of her breasts. Sally's voice came from outside. "Let's see!"

Clare opened the door and stood under Sally's scrutiny. Sally's pronouncement: "I like it." At the cash register, Clare insisted on buying it herself, glad for the sale price.

When they'd gotten back to the house, Sally said, "How about a game of tennis? Then you can put on your new bikini, and we can go to the pool."

Clare felt her energy flagging. It had, after all, been a late night and early morning. "I'd like to do some reading."

"Oh." Sally pouted a little. "Well, I'll go hit some balls for a while. Then I'll come get you."

"For a game of tennis?"

"If you're up to it. Or we can just go to the pool." They went to their respective rooms. Clare lay on her bed, hearing Sally rustling about in the adjoining room.

Then footsteps went down the stairs and the outside door opened and closed.

Clare must have gone to sleep, but she was awakened some time later by the click of a car door opening. She got up and went out on the balcony. Looking down over the rail, she saw Jon beside Sally's car, about to take it back to the garage. Perhaps he sensed her there, for although she'd made no sound, he looked up and beckoned to her. She hurried down the stairs, out the front door, and over to him.

He spoke quietly. "Do you think you're cured now?"

She hesitated. "Maybe I should see you again."

"Tonight?"

"If I can get away."

****

Sally had wanted to take the car and go out to meet partying friends that Saturday night, but her parents thought the island would be too full of holiday weekend traffic and tourists. "You've had Jason's party and your own. You can stay at home this weekend with Clare," her mother told her. Sally began to argue, but she accepted that verdict when her parents reminded her they'd decided she could date Jason in the future if Clare came with them.

That night Clare hoped to go to Jon the same time as the night before, around eleven. But Sally was still full of energy at ten thirty. "Let's do our nails," she said. She went to her room and returned with bottles of nail polish and paper towels. As they sat on Clare's bed in their nightgowns giving themselves manicures, Sally chattered about how she and Jason and Derek and Clare could drive up to Savannah for dinner sometime. "You do like Derek, don't you?"

"Of course I like him."

"We'll get him and Jason to go with us on our next yacht excursion." She blew on her nails. "These take forever to dry."

"Let's use my hair dryer." Clare got it from the bathroom and blew a gentle stream of hot air over their hands, then tested one of her nails. "They're done."

"I'm just not sleepy."

"But you need your rest. Do you have any sleep aids?"

"I have two Ambivalen capsules."

"Maybe you should take one."

"I think you're the one who wants to sleep." Sally got up. "But maybe you're right. I'll take one and let you rest." She gathered the nail polish equipment. "Goodnight. See you tomorrow."

"Good night." Clare watched the door between their rooms close and lay down, turning out her light. At last all was still in the adjoining room. If Sally woke up and found her gone, she'd just say she went for a walk. She silently got up and dressed. Barefoot, she padded down the stairs, this time more nervous. Tinsel might hear and bark, or someone would still be downstairs—Maria, Uncle Tony, Aunt Rose. On the bottom stair she stopped, listening. The house was quiet, as it had been the night before. She opened the front door, then closed it gently before the alarm could go off.

Outside a soft breeze blew and the pool glittered under the security lights. As she walked toward the pool house, a dark figure rose from one of the chaise lounges. Startled, her breath caught in her throat. For a fleeting moment she thought of the murder at the gates and Jon's comment about the strangers on the island over the holiday. Then she saw who it was. "Jon, you frightened me!"

"I saw Sally's lights go out."

"I thought she'd never go to bed."

As one, they turned and went to his apartment. There he closed and locked the door. The shade was already pulled.

Later, lying together, Clare smiled at him. "I would never have guessed…"

"Guessed what?"

"How amazing this is."

"So you won't be an Ice Princess with men anymore? That was why you wanted to be with me, isn't it?"

She stopped smiling. In the silence they heard the crickets outside, and the little laps of pool water against the tile edging. When she spoke, her voice cracked. "I can't imagine this with anyone but you." She leaned over the edge of the bed to pick up her shorts and T-shirt, crumpled on the floor.

"Clare." He reached out and pulled her back against him.

****

Perhaps an hour later, Jon set bowls of ice cream on his little kitchen table, and they sat down. Their relationship had changed suddenly, and both were aware of it.

"So what are we going to do?" he asked.

"I don't know."

"We'd better not keep on having night visits like this. It's better your relatives don't know about us.

You're supposed to be Sally's *serious*, *capable* chaperone. Not a good idea to be involved with the estate's head security guard." He was quiet for a moment, thinking. "But I do have Mondays off. Those mornings your aunt takes Sally to her psychologist and Tony goes to his properties. That time, I think, can be ours."

"That would be wonderful."

"We can't be together this Monday though—it's Memorial Day. Your aunt and Sally won't be going to Savannah for an appointment. I'll pick you up a week from Monday, same time as before, nine o'clock. I want to show you the cottage where my mother and I stayed our first two years on the island. It's near the beach I took you to last week. My mother lives in her apartment at the Sanderson's most of the time now, but when she gets days off she goes there. And so do I."

Clare's heart sank a little at having to wait a week to be with him, but it couldn't be helped. "I'd love to see it," she said. She set her spoon down. "You already know, I think, that Sally wants me to date Derek—to have us go places with her and Jason. That way, her parents will feel she is chaperoned."

"Damn, I guess that will be part of your job. But I don't know about that guy. There's something funny about him."

"He does ask a lot of questions. But he makes no demands on me. He's been very respectful."

"That's good. I hope he stays that way." Jon picked up the bowls and put them in his sink. "It's late. I'll watch you from here until you're back in the house. And we have a date for the Monday after next."

Clare walked out of the apartment, along the side

of the beach house, past the pool. At the steps to the Sanderson house, she glanced back, but she wasn't sure whether she saw Jon standing there or just a shadow in the distance.

Chapter Six

Sunday, May 24 – Monday, June 1

"Wake up, wake up!" Sally's happy voice intruded into Clare's sleep the next morning, along with the sound of opening drapes. "It's nine o'clock! You aren't sick, are you?"

Clare opened her eyes to see the sun pouring through the balcony's glass doors. "I'm fine."

Sally perched on Clare's bed. "I have news."

"What's that?"

"I've just talked to Dad. He said you and I can go fishing on his yacht Wednesday with Jason and Derek. That will be so much fun—just the four of us!"

"But I've never fished."

"Jason can show you how. He may have to show us all. I haven't gone fishing for years. And Derek—he hangs out on the beaches, but I don't know how much fishing or ocean boating experience he's had."

Clare sat up. "Maybe it will be a learning experience for the three of us."

"I bet they'll pick us up here at about six thirty. Jason always says the best fishing is at dawn and dusk. Oh—before I forget—Dad needs your driver's license information to get you a fishing license online. Take a photo of it and I'll text it to him." She laughed. "We don't want any more Coast Guard incidents."

Clare felt a little uneasy about this expedition. It wasn't so much that she was worried about being paired off with Derek, because he had, as she'd told Jon, been respectful. The two of them would be good chaperones for Sally and Jason. Nor was she concerned that the Coast Guard might again be stopping and searching boats. That had seemed like something out of the ordinary.

No, she felt worried because on the last excursion, Jon and Kyle had handled the yacht out on the ocean. Neither she nor Sally could, and maybe not Derek, whose work was limited to the marina. Was Jason going to pilot her uncle's boat, and could he do it as well as Jon? He did not seem as responsible somehow. But she put on her robe and went to photograph her license.

****

Wednesday morning, as the sun began to light up the horizon, Clare, in shorts and a sleeveless striped jersey, stood with Sally in front of the house steps. Jason's red sports car soon pulled up with Derek in the passenger seat.

"Hey," Jason said. "You two ready to go?"

"We are!" Sally replied. "I hope we'll have fresh fish to fry for supper tonight."

"We should. Who's that working at the gate now, anyway?"

"Wasn't it Jon?"

"No, it was someone else."

"Dad has a team of guys who work there. It must have been one of them."

Derek got out and opened the back car door for Clare, then got in beside her. As Sally took his place in the passenger seat, he again put his arm over Clare's shoulders. "How are you?"

That simple, friendly gesture didn't bother her now. She smiled at him. "Fine." He was wearing shorts, another marina T-shirt, and a sun visor. His legs looked large and muscular, as did his dark-haired arms. They buckled up, and the car headed down the driveway. Clare looked into the gate house as they passed and saw that bespectacled man, Bruce, working there.

At the marina, they gathered their things and walked down one of the piers to a yacht about the same size as Kyle's with *The Rose* painted on its hull. "It's named for my mother," said Sally.

Clare saw her uncle Tony in his dark glasses already on the boat putting bait in a container—and then by the upper cabin, someone in T-shirt and shorts setting out fishing poles. She drew in a breath. It was Jon. She saw him look up, saw his glance move to her, but they made no open acknowledgement of each other.

"I guess Tony and Jon are getting everything ready for us," Jason said. "Hi, Mr. Sanderson."

"Come aboard," the man responded.

The four climbed on to the boat.

"Are we ready?" Tony called to Jon, who was now in the cabin where, as in Kyle's yacht, the steering wheel was located.

"Yes, sir."

"Well, let's go then." He untied the ropes to the pier. The motor gurgled.

"Hey," Jason said, "you and Jon aren't coming with us, are you?"

Tony tossed down his coil of rope. "Jon will be our pilot. Did you think I'd let just you guys take out my boat? And I felt like a little fishing myself."

"I thought it was going to be the just four of us. I could handle your boat. It's like my dad's."

"Have you done much ocean fishing?"

"No, but…"

Tony laughed. "That shows I'm right to have Jon here. He's an experienced pilot and fisherman. Derek says he hasn't done much fishing, Sally hasn't since she was a kid, and I know Clare never has. I can't see well enough anymore to pilot myself, and Jon knows the best places to fish. He'll give us a great excursion."

The boat moved out from its slip. Jason turned away, muttering something under his breath to Derek. Then he shrugged and held up his hands, with a "What can we do?" look. "So where will we go?" he called out to Jon.

"To a marsh I know about farther up on the coast," Jon answered from the cabin. "It's full of spot tail and striped bass, speckled seatrout, flounder."

"What about going out deeper?" Derek asked. "Don't you go out past the twelve-mile mark on some of these trips?"

Jason laughed. "Ha, you want to fish in international waters?"

Tony responded, "We thought inshore fishing would be best this time. Maybe another time, when you've all had some experience, you can do some deep-sea fishing."

The boat headed down the river to open waters, and picking up speed, began to follow the coastline. Tony went to the wheel to stand beside Jon, and Clare leaned on the rail next to Jason and Sally. After a moment, Derek joined them. "At least it's a great day to be out on a boat."

Before long *The Rose* slowed and entered the marsh Jon had described. The sound of the motor faded. "Here we are," Tony called.

Jon left the cabin and handed out poles and nets. "The tide is right—you should get lots of bites," he said. He brought out the bait container, where live shrimp moved about in water. "Put the hook back by their tails. That way they'll swim forward and attract the fish." He reached for Clare's pole and demonstrated, then flicked Clare's line over the side of the boat and handed the pole to her.

"Ooh!" Sally grimaced and giggled as she picked up the wriggling shrimp. "I can't do it."

Jason laughed and took over the job for her, then baited his own hook. He, Sally, and Tony went to opposite side of the boat. Beside Clare, Derek baited his hook and cast his line into the water. Jon remained on Clare's other side, leaning casually on the rail. She felt her line twitch and the reel began to turn.

Jon was at once attentive. "You've got something. Wait and be sure the fish has swallowed the hook…There. Now reel it in."

"I turn this handle?"

"Right."

She turned the handle on the rod and pulled in a small, wriggling, silvery fish. She drew back, hesitant to capture it with her hands. Jon took it and removed the hook from its mouth. "A young, speckled seatrout," he said. "We'll have to throw it back. But this was a good one to start with."

He held it up to show Clare, who felt sorry as it gasped for air. Then he leaned far over the rail and gently dropped it back into the water. It stayed still for a few moments, then twitched and swam away.

Derek spoke. “Want me to bait your hook this time, Clare?”

Jon said, “You’d better watch your own pole. I think you’ve got a bite.”

Derek turned to his reel, which was beginning to spin. He held the handle, worked with it, and soon hauled in a medium-sized fish with black stripes. Proudly, he took hold of it and disengaged the hook.

“A striped bass,” said Jon. “Large enough to keep.” He indicated the large water-filled tub outside the cabin, waiting for the fish they caught. “Good job.”

Derek walked over to the tub, dropped the fish in, then stopped for two more shrimps at the bait container. Back beside Clare, he took her pole and began inserting the hook into the shrimp.

Jon watched. “Remember, put it at the back, not the head.”

Derek, obviously suppressing annoyance, changed the location of the hook and handed the pole to Clare. She cast her line, watching as her hook sank into the water. Jon stepped away from them, again leaning his elbows on the rail to watch as Derek baited his own hook and threw out his line.

“Hey, Jon, I’ve got a big one,” Tony called from the other side of the boat. Jon left and went to him. They heard splashing, then Jon’s voice, “You’ve got him.” Shortly after, Tony came over to Clare and Derek, smiling and holding up a long, thick, silver fish. “Look at this! Fish fry tonight!” He dropped the fish in the tub, calling to Jon, still on the other side of the boat, “You found us a good place to fish, boy.”

Suddenly there was an almost violent whirring noise. Clare's reel was spinning out of control. She let out a cry of surprise.

"It's a big one. Reel him in, reel him in!" Derek instructed, leaving his pole and moving to grasp hers.

Jon returned on a run, pushing Derek unceremoniously aside. "No, man, let the line go out. The fish will fight now. When it's tired, she can reel him in."

Standing behind Clare, he put an arm on each side of her and, putting his hands on the pole over hers, steadied its violent thrashing. The line ran far out. Finally the spinning of the reel and the thrashing ceased. Jon stepped away. There was a minute of quiet. "*Now* reel him in," he told her.

Turning the wheel was a struggle, but the fish finally came into sight, maybe three feet long and solid with a rosy back and a black spot on its tail.

"Wow!" whistled Derek.

She handed Jon the pole. "You'd better bring it in."

He expertly reeled, paused, reeled, paused, and when the fish was close to the boat, reached for a net, leaned over the edge and scooped it up. On deck, he lifted the fish out and, holding it firmly, removed the hook. "A red drum," he said. "Hey, Sally, quick. Clare needs her picture taken with this fish." He handed it over to Clare. It was heavy—maybe, she guessed, fifteen pounds.

Sally approached with her phone. "Look proud, Clare, you've got a prize catch."

They all watched Clare hoist the fish up and smile a little uncertainly. Once Sally had taken the photograph, Derek, obviously annoyed at Jon's taking over, stepped up with a proprietary manner. He took it and put it in the tub with the others.

Later that morning Sally and Jason each caught a flounder—"but not as large as Clare's drum," Jason commented. "Beginner's luck!"

Around eleven Tony announced, "Time for lunch." They all replaced their poles against the side of the boat. Jon went to the lower cabin where the kitchen was located. Jason followed. Tony went to a folding table fastened to the wall, unhooked it, and set it up on the deck, then set up six folding chairs. The boat drifted along the marsh channels as Jon and Jason appeared with a picnic basket and ice chest. They set paper plates on the table, then sandwiches, cookies, and cold cans of beer. Everyone sat down.

"This morning was great!" Sally exclaimed. "So exciting. I can't wait for our fish supper."

"So who's going to clean the fish?" Derek asked grouchily.

Jon smiled faintly. "I do the dirty work."

"But the marina chef will *cook* the fish," Jason said. "Let's all meet at the marina restaurant at six to eat. My father will probably bring the latest woman he's dating. Tony, will Rose come?"

"She wouldn't miss it."

Sally spoke up. "Thank you for this expedition, Daddy. Thank you, Jon! These sandwiches are delicious. I want another beer."

She began to reach into the ice chest, but Clare gently took her wrist. "I saw some bottled water down in there too."

"Is my beer limit still one?" Sally pouted, but she seemed happy, and her pout was not fully genuine. She pulled out a bottle of water.

Derek put his hand on Clare's shoulder. "You want to go look at your champion catch again? Come on."

"Yes, go and gloat," Sally said.

Clare and Derek went to the tub outside the cabin door and looked down at the fish. She didn't really enjoy seeing them there in the water, their gills still opening and closing, their eyes round and expressionless, the fish she had caught dominating them all. "You're soft-hearted," Derek said. "Will you be able to enjoy eating fish tonight?"

"I hope so."

Then, to Clare's surprise, he leaned over and gently kissed her. "I like soft-hearted women."

Although she did not feel any magic, Derek's light kiss, like his arm behind her shoulders earlier, did not frighten or repel her as it once might have. She heard some metallic clatter, and he drew back. Jon had passed them as he entered the cabin to take the wheel. The motor again gurgled. The boat swung around and headed back to the marina.

When they arrived, Jon stayed on board, but the others walked up the pier to the marina office door. There, Derek told her, "I have to get to work. I'll see you at supper." Tony went inside to talk to Kyle. Jason and Sally sat on a bench outside in the sun, talking and laughing, waiting to thank Tony again before leaving.

Clare felt sure Jon had seen Derek kiss her. When they'd disembarked, he'd jumped up on the pier, the proper "captain," first helping Sally as she climbed off the boat. She was next. When he grasped her hand, she said, "It was a great trip." His reply seemed cool, business-like. "Glad you liked it." Then he'd busied himself with the boat as Derek, Jason, and Uncle Tony climbed off.

Walking away, she looked back, but he paid her no heed. "I left my hair brush down below on the boat," Clare told Jason and Sally. "I need to get it. I'll be right back."

She walked down the pier to *The Rose*. Jon stood at the table on the deck, plying a knife with some force into a fish and tossing the offal into a bucket. She stepped onto the boat and walked over to him. His hands, slightly bloody, stilled. He looked up.

"What am I going to do?" she asked.

"About what?"

She glanced around. No one was in sight. She put her hand on his. "This situation with Derek."

He moved it from her. "You'd better not touch me. This is a messy job."

"I don't care if it's messy."

He thrust the knife downward and below the gills. "Maybe now you *can* have relationships with other men."

"No."

"Then maybe we should stop hiding our relationship."

"What do you think my aunt and uncle would do?"

He grimaced. "Probably send you home." He crossed to the deck, passing the spot where the fish tub had been earlier, where he surely had seen her with Derek. She followed. In the cabin, Jon rinsed his hands in a pan of water. She walked over to him. He put his arms around her and kissed her—no light, simple kiss like Derek's. Her lips parted, and she pressed close against him.

****

For dinner at the marina that night, crispy fried fish fillets were served along with coleslaw and home fries, then strawberry pie. Jon didn't come, but Aunt Rose and Kyle Eldridge joined them. Jason asked his father, "You didn't invite that woman you've been going out with?"

"Kitty?" Kyle responded. "Naw, I'll see her later."

Drinking several beers during dinner, the two older men became jovial and talkative. "Tony and I had great times when we were your age," Kyle told the two young couples. "Jason here is a lot like we were back then."

"You mean like going to wild fraternity parties and stuff in college?" Sally asked. Clare's stomach contracted as she thought of fraternity parties and wondered what her uncle and Kyle had been like.

Tony tipped up his glass of beer, his dark glasses glinting in the overhead light "Ah, yes, the parties got pretty wild."

"And remember our trips to Mexico?" asked Kyle. "That first one—spring break, 1984, our sophomore year. It was so much fun we went back every year for a while, even after we graduated." The two men laughed.

Sally asked, "How about you, Mom? What were you like in college?"

"I wasn't wild like them," said Aunt Rose. "But I had fun. I went to a Golden Isle—usually Jekyll or St. Simon's—with my girlfriends every spring break. But I didn't meet your father until 1991, the summer after I graduated. I worked as a hostess at his first hotel on St. Sebastian's. He was so handsome and impressive."

Kyle spoke up. "I was already married and envying

Tony's bachelor life, but he gave it up for Rose that very summer. I got him to go with me on one last trip to Mexico, but that was it. They got engaged when we got back."

"Yeah, Rose agreed to marry me and live on the island," Tony said. He smiled at his wife. "We both love it here. Maybe that's one reason she and I are still together, unlike my pal here and his ex-wife."

"Divorce was the best thing for Jane and me," Kyle said. "She was a big city girl. And, okay, I wasn't the best of husbands. But we had Jason, and he stayed with me in the summers. And it's great to have him living with me now that he's finally graduated from college—at age twenty-five." He squeezed his son's shoulder. "People tell me he's a chip off the old block."

"What does that mean?" Sally asked a bit sharply.

Jason laughed a little. "Don't ask." He stood up. "It's time to call it a night. I'll be right back—I'm going to the men's room."

"Wait for me," said Derek, pushing back his chair.

When the waiter came to clear the table, Clare asked for a take-home container. "We can bring some of this food to Jon," she told Sally. "After all, he took us to that fishing spot and cleaned the fish."

"We invited him to come tonight," Sally said. "I don't know why he didn't."

As Clare filled the container, Derek and Jason returned. "Let's go," Jason said to the girls. "So long, Dad, Mr. Sanderson, Mrs. Sanderson."

The two couples went to Jason's car. After he pulled through the estate gates and stopped in the usual place at the house, he gave Sally a quick kiss. Derek, to Clare's relief, kissed her in the same way. The girls got out and watched from the lower step as Jason's car roared off.

Clare looked over toward the pool house. "I'll bring this food to Jon right now if his light is on."

"Good idea. I'll come with you."

Disappointed, Clare agreed, though she knew she couldn't have stayed with him—Sally would have been waiting for her to return. The two walked to his apartment. The light shone through the window. When they knocked, Jon opened the door, in shorts, his shirt unbuttoned. Clare stepped forward and held out the container. "We brought you some food from dinner."

He took it. "Thank you."

"Why didn't you come and eat with us?" Sally demanded.

He shrugged and smiled faintly. "I didn't want to make it an odd number."

****

Now that she had this relationship with Jon, Clare worried less in the following week about her role on the island, its mysteries, or its possible dangers. She drank in its beauty, enjoyed her activities with Sally, and counted the days until Monday, the first of June, when she and Jon could be together again. When that morning came, she watched her cousin and aunt leave for their Savannah appointment, then dashed upstairs to change to shorts and a halter top. She grabbed her beach bag, which contained the new bikini and a towel, and ran out just as Jon pulled up. She threw the bag in the back seat, jumped in, and they were off.

"How long do we have?" he asked.

"They won't get back until one or later. After the appointment they're going to have their hair done and then have lunch."

"Great. At least three hours. When we get to the cottage, I want to take you out in my boat. The tide will be right."

"You have a boat?"

"Just an outboard." He turned on to that narrow one-lane dirt road he'd shown her before, but this time took a spur, and followed it to a small, white-shingled cottage overlooking the beach on one side, the marsh on the other. "That's the cottage where my mother and I lived our first years on the island. I'll take you inside another time." He switched off the ignition, picked up her beach bag, and led her down the weedy pebbled walk to the cottage porch.

"I visited Sally on the island the summer she was five and I was seven. I guess you hadn't come yet."

"No, we moved here about two years later. And two years after that, when I was twelve, Tony sent me to boarding school. But I came back here every summer and worked for him—during middle and high school washing his cars, doing yard work, later waiting tables in his restaurants. And sometimes I worked for Kyle too, at the marina with the boats. When I was in college Tony gave me more responsibilities—at different times put me in charge of restaurant landscaping, of the cleaning crews at the hotels, even of the gates at the estate."

Clare looked at him, impressed. "You were pretty young for those jobs."

"He trusted me, I guess. And he liked that I was bilingual." Jon dropped her bag on the porch step and led her down the foot path to the marsh. On the grassy edge at a wooden dock, a boat was tied—gleaming white, with a large black motor at the back. They climbed in. He pushed out with a paddle, then climbed over to the front seat at the wheel and turned the ignition key. Clare sat beside him. The boat moved slowly out around the foot of the island into the open ocean. There Jon sped up. Clare held on to the sides of the boat, excited, her hair blowing back.

They went past more marshes along the coast, and he turned into one of them, maneuvering skillfully through a maze of channels bordered by waving grasses. Birds flew about them. He slowed down, and raising her phone, Clare took pictures. Then he sped up again, curving along through the channel cuts.

Back out on the ocean, he pointed: "There's a dolphin." She saw its black pointed fin make brief appearances. Jon pulled out his phone and, tapping the screen, began to play a pop rock piece. "Now they'll follow us." And before long several dolphins' fins indeed appeared in the wake, then alongside the boat, their rounded bodies periodically emerging, arching gracefully to the music, then submerging again, like synchronized swimmers.

Back near the St. Sebastian's marsh, Jon turned off the phone, and their dolphin escorts disappeared. The motor quieted to a soft buzz as the boat glided into the grasses and up to the dock. Clare, still thrilled, exclaimed, "That was wonderful!"

"Do you see why I want this part of the island to be a nature preserve? If I were in charge, I'd make trails for tourists through the woods here and along the marsh for hiking, give boat rides like this, and lecture on the history and ecology of the island."

"They'd love it. You'd be perfect."

Jon tied up the boat and checked the time. "We have another hour. How about a swim? You can change on the cottage porch. Then follow the footpath that goes the opposite way—down to the ocean. I'll meet you on the beach."

Clare agreed. In her new bikini, feeling shy, she wrapped her towel around herself as she walked down the path to the private beach. Jon had pulled off his T-shirt and stood there waiting. When she came up to him, he took the towel from her. His eyes drank her in, and embarrassed, she ran into the surf. He followed and captured her in his arms. They made love on the wet sand as waves slid in and out under them.

Later, he spread a towel on the upper beach among the sea oats. As they lay beside each other, she remembered how he'd looked, naked in the wave-foam, his skin where the sun had not tanned him almost as light as her own. She asked softly, "Do you ever wonder about your father?"

"Of course I do."

"He must have been white," she said. "And tall, maybe with blue or gray eyes. Your mother never speaks of him?"

"No. When I ask her about him, she doesn't answer. I used to think about it a lot. It must have been someone in Cancún while she was living there and working as a maid for a rich Anglo family. But I don't know much about her life in Mexico. I was born in Texas. My earliest memories are of living in El Paso in a big, rambling house with two or three other Spanish-speaking families."

"And when you were older?"

"We lived in the same house the whole time we

were there. I didn't learn English until grade school. The Mexican kids in the school used to make fun of my lighter skin and my eyes. Of course, the white English-speaking kids didn't like me either."

"That must have been hard."

"It didn't last too long. I learned to fight, and when they saw I was good in those grade school sports, everyone pretty much accepted me. Once we came here, I didn't have to choose between Anglo and Hispanic—I could just be myself."

"How did you and your mother come to live here on St. Sebastian's?"

"When I was in fourth grade, she suddenly packed up and took me on the train to Savannah. Probably through some kind of employment agency there, your uncle hired her as a housekeeper. She and I lived in that cottage I showed you for two years. I went by bus to fifth and sixth grade on the mainland. Then, when Tony sent me away to boarding school in seventh grade, she moved into the apartment in his house. That was more convenient. The cottage is still ours to stay in when we want, though." He again checked the time on his phone. "We have to go."

They rinsed off the sand at an outdoor spigot by the cottage and dressed. On the way back to the Sanderson Estates, Clare said, "Uncle Tony has been generous to you and your mother, hasn't he?"

"Because of paying for my schooling? I suppose. But I paid part of my college expenses. I had scholarships and part-time jobs on campus, and like I said, I worked for him here every summer for just a minimum wage." He glanced over at her. "But you're right—and he hired my mother even though she was undocumented. He even somehow got her a forged green card. When I graduated from college last year, his eyesight was failing, and he asked me to come here and work for him full-time as security guard, chauffeur, and boat pilot—for a good salary."

"How long do you think you'll work here for him?"

"We haven't discussed a time frame."

"Do you like what you do?"

A shadow crossed his face. He hesitated, then he said, "I'd like work that relates to my degree. But I love living here on the island."

As they went through the estate gates, she scanned the drive ahead. "I hope Uncle Tony doesn't see us together and guess—about us."

"He won't be here now." He stopped the car at the steps.

She looked at the clock on his dash. It was almost one. "But my aunt and Sally will be back. I've got to get in." She grabbed her beach bag, rushed up the steps, tapped out the alarm code to enter. Inside, she ran up to her room and hung her damp towel and bikini in the bathroom. Then she looked out of the balcony windows. Jon's car was gone, and her aunt's car had just come into the parking area.

Within minutes Sally burst into her room. "Hi!" She looked at Clare. "You've been in the sun!"

Clare did not like to lie, but as Jon had said, it was best to keep their relationship a secret. "Yes, I—I went out to the pool for a while. I wanted to tan in the white areas that showed in my bikini."

"That was a good idea."

That night at dinner, Aunt Rose said, "I'm sorry

we're having to leave you these Monday mornings, Clare."

Sally chattered away happily. "She doesn't mind. This morning she sat out at the pool in her new bikini."

Maria was placing a platter of sliced ham on the table. Her hands froze for a moment, and she looked at Clare, who had a flash of insight. *Maria was here this morning. She knows I wasn't at the pool.*

That night as she lay in bed, Clare determined that she would talk with Maria. But when? Except for those Monday mornings, Sally, her beloved, happy, exuberant cousin and charge, seemed ever-present.

Chapter Seven

Tuesday, June 2 – Sunday, June 7

The next morning, while Clare went out to the terrace to eat breakfast, Sally stopped in her mother's room for a moment. As usual, Uncle Tony had already eaten, then gone somewhere for work.

When Maria came out to pick up his dishes, Clare realized this was her opportunity. "Maria," she said, "I'm getting to know your son. I like him."

The woman regarded her with her penetrating brown eyes. Except for the color, they looked very much like Jon's. Clare noted the fine wrinkles in her face, the gray strands in her hair. She looked to be in her sixties; she must have had Jon when she was in her forties. If she was surprised that Clare knew Jon was her son, she didn't reveal it. "Thank you, Miss."

"He showed me your cottage yesterday."

Maria was turning to leave, but now she turned back. "Did he?"

"I haven't told anyone but you."

"The women Jon sees are usually from the mainland. He doesn't bring them here to the island."

"He sees…women from the mainland?"

"Savannah, Brunswick. But he's had little time for women." She left quickly, moving through the sliding glass door.

Clare felt as if a rock had fallen upon her heart. Of course Jon, handsome and sexy as he was, would have had women. Did she think just because she was new to sexual experiences, he was as well?

She forced a smile as Sally ran out onto the terrace with a sheet of paper in her hand. "Now that I can see Jason, I've started writing song-poems again. You're an English major. Will you look at one I've just written?"

"Of course."

Sally stood over her as she read it. The poem told the story of a young girl walking on an ocean beach one morning, waiting for her lover. But though he'd promised to meet her, the sun rose higher and higher, then began the descent toward the west. Finally she realized he was not going to come, that the relationship was over. Her sorrow reflected Clare's sudden fear that the relationship with Jon would not last.

"This is beautiful," Clare said. "And so sad."

"I felt that way when I was sick and couldn't see Jason." Sally took the paper back and began to sing in her clear soprano: *"The waves tell me, 'He's left you, he's gone./ Lie on the beach, close your eyes./ The sun is your lover now.' "*

Then her usual happy excitement returned. She grabbed hold of Clare's hand. "I've just talked with my mother, and now I can tell you. There's a talent contest in Savannah this Saturday. I'd applied for a spot last fall and sent them a video—but they wrote that all the spots had been filled and put me on a waiting list. They emailed me yesterday that there was a last-minute cancellation, and I was next on the list—so I can be in the contest. I want to go and sing this song. I told you how, before I got sick, Jason would play his guitar when I sang. He said he would accompany me for this contest. Mom just told me that she and Dad will let me go with Jason—*if* you come with us, of course."

"You know I will. I want to hear you sing and Jason play."

"Derek can come too and be *your* date."

"Maybe…" Clare hesitated. She did not want Jon to go to the coast for other women. "Wouldn't it be easier to ask Jon to go as my date?"

"Jon will be driving my parents there. Like I told you, he chauffeurs my father for long trips and at night. So it has to be Derek." Sally whirled about, hugging herself. "I'm so happy! I can't wait!"

Jason and Sally practiced for the contest all that week, with Sally at the piano in the living room and Jason beside her in a straight chair with his guitar. Apparently, he came and went from his work at the marina as he wished—an advantage of being the owner's son. Since Aunt Rose wanted Clare to remain in the living room with them while they practiced, she sat in an armchair, alternately reading a book or listening to them. They performed not only that first song but also a second in case they made it to the finals—another "poem" Sally had written, this one about a lover returning on a moonlit night. Clare thought both songs were quite good and felt moved by the couple's performance.

On Saturday evening, Clare helped Sally dress in an off-the-shoulder blouse, long skirt, and dangling hoop earrings. Then she styled her cousin's hair. Sally watched in the dressing table mirror, chattering excitedly. "Before I got sick, my parents weren't so opposed to Jason. We never entered any contests, but the audiences at the night clubs in my father's hotels liked us. We were not very serious then—we just had fun."

"Performing *should* be fun," Clare said, brushing and curling Sally's long hair. She surveyed her handiwork. "You look beautiful." She herself wore a wrap-around skirt and scoop-necked green jersey and had tied her hair back with a simple matching ribbon.

When they went downstairs, Aunt Rose and Uncle Tony stood at the bottom, waiting. They would leave with Jon later—the performers had to get to the theater early and go in the stage door. Sally had gotten passes for Derek and Clare, her parents, Jon, and Jason's father and his date to get into the theater before the doors opened to the general public.

They all went outside when Jason drove up with Derek. Aunt Rose looked at the young men, both wearing a jacket and tie. "You two look great. We don't see you dressed up like that very often."

"Good luck, baby," Tony said, kissing Sally. As she got in the passenger seat, he looked into the car at Jason, serious now. "Be good."

"Of course, sir."

"We'll be cheering for you, honey," said her mother. And then she spoke to Clare as she got into the back seat with Derek, "Take care of them."

The drive to Savannah was full of excitement as Sally sang her lines again and again to them. "Which way sounds better?" Then, "Do you really think so?"

At the auditorium, Jason parked in a lot reserved for performers and staff. "There are long lines out in front of the theater," Clare said.

Derek looked over at them. "I guess the doors

haven't opened yet."

The two couples entered the theater through a door at the back of the building. "I'm sorry, there isn't room for friends and family backstage," a staff member told Derek and Clare. "We have tables in front of the stage reserved for them. You can get there from here—go through that door and down the steps."

Following the directions, she and Derek saw several round tables near the stage, each for eight people. They selected a table and sat down. People who had early passes, apparently also "friends and family" of performers, filtered in from the front entrance and took seats at nearby tables. Seeing Clare intent, watching them arrive, Derek asked, "Who are you looking for?"

"Sally's parents and Mr. Eldridge and Jon," Clare answered.

"Jon? Is he coming?"

"He's driving the Sandersons."

Derek scowled a little.

Kyle, with a tall blonde date in a lowcut blouse, soon joined them. "Meet Kitty Garner," he said. "Kitty, this is Clare Matthews, Tony's niece. You know Derek."

"Hello, Clare. My, aren't you pretty! Is Derek your date?"

Aunt Rose and Uncle Tony arrived, greeted everyone, and took two more of the seats. They said Jon was parking the car. It seemed a long time before he came through the door, handsome in a white sport coat and red tie.

"Sit down, boy," Kyle boomed heartily.

Jon sat in one of the two empty places across from

Clare. She removed her hand from Derek's. A waiter came by and everyone ordered drinks. An auburn-haired girl stopped behind the last empty chair and asked in a hesitant voice, "Is this seat taken?"

"No, sit down," said Kyle.

"My brother is performing," the girl said, sitting in the empty chair beside Jon.

The doors must have opened for the general public. A raucous crowd began to enter from the front. Clare could not hear, but only watch as the girl spoke into Jon's ear and he responded. She pointed at something. He looked and they laughed. Something pinched in her heart. *The women Jon associates with are usually from the coast…Brunswick, Savannah.*

When Derek reclaimed her hand, Clare did not move it away.

The tables throughout the auditorium were now filled. The lights dimmed. A man in a tuxedo stepped out into a spotlight. "Welcome to Savannah Talent Search. We have many great contestants lined up tonight. Remember that the applause meters will register the volume of your approval for each one, and three judges will also score them. The top three acts will then perform again to determine their final ranking."

The lights dimmed and the performances began. First, a trio of girls in shorts and cowboy hats, The Dixie Belles, came out and sang a western ballad. Next a ballet dancer performed, then Jason and Sally, with her song "The Lost Lover."

Jason stayed in the background, strumming chords on his guitar, his jacket and tie now off to look more in beach attire, while Sally, in the spotlight, sang mournfully and sweetly, gazing out at the audience. At the end of the song, she stared downward, and extended her hands as if feeling the waves. She is an actress too, thought Clare. As Sally rose, bowed, and held her hand out to Jason, who joined her in the spotlight, the applause meter reached an eight, then wavered on to a nine. An intermission followed, during which more drinks were served.

"Sally was great!" exclaimed Clare.

"She has real talent," said Derek. "I didn't expect her to be so good."

The lights dimmed as the contest resumed. A soprano named Renee DeGaro sang "Musetta's Waltz" from *La Boheme,* and the applause meter also reached a nine. The final performances followed, including the auburn-haired girl's brother singing "Danny Boy." After a short break, the announcer came out with the results. The top three acts chosen by the judges and the audience were the soprano, the cowgirl trio—and Sally and Jason.

Their table applauded wildly. The auburn-haired girl gamely congratulated them. The three finalists would perform encores after one more break. Waiters hurried from table to table, refilling drinks. Clare took a second wine but noted that Jon kept to his seltzer. Derek was drinking scotch neat. Was this his fourth? Maybe his fifth.

The lights dimmed. The Dixie Belles sang a western-themed medley. Sally sang her second love song, the one with the happy ending, after which Jason came forward and kissed her, as if it were part of the story. Last, the soprano sang the excerpts from "The Habanera," the dramatic, sexy aria from *Carmen.* After a brief break, the master of ceremonies appeared with the final winners: "Number three, The Dixie Belles. Number two: Sally Sanderson and Jason Eldridge. And number one—our opera soprano, Rene DeGaro!"

The audience applauded, and though Clare was sorry Sally and Jason were not number one, she had to admit the opera singer was amazing—and to be in second place in this contest, especially as a last-minute entrant, was quite something. The winners came out, received their trophies and prize checks, and the show was over.

The waiters took orders for the last round of drinks. Sally and Jason, flushed and smiling, came out to the table, Jason with his guitar case strapped over his shoulder. Hugs were exchanged all around.

"I have to go to the rest room," Sally told them. "Jason is taking his guitar to the car."

Before long, the crowd thinned out. "Guess we'd better go on home, Kitty." Kyle said, throwing back the last of his drink. "The party's over." He leaned closer to her and winked. "Let's go have our own private party." They made their farewells and everyone at the table watched them leave.

"I'll get the car and pick you up in front," Jon said to Aunt Rose and Uncle Tony. "Good night, Derek, Clare." He walked to the front entrance among the remaining few stragglers.

Aunt Rose finished her drink. "We'd better go wait for him by the door." She and Uncle Tony left.

Derek and Clare were the only ones at the table, now littered with napkins and empty glasses. "I hope Jason and Sally haven't forgotten us," Derek said, his words a little slurred. "Let's go check the car."

In the now almost empty parking lot outside the stage door, they saw the red sports car, its windows partially open. "Did you forget us?" Clare called over, laughing.

Then, coming closer, she smelled the acrid odor of burned marijuana and saw Sally and Jason lying on the back seat locked in an embrace. Her heart turned over. She had failed as chaperone. Panicked, she looked up to see Jon driving the Sanderson limo to the main road. He glanced in their direction and must have seen her stricken look.

He pulled the limo over to an empty parking space, turned off the ignition, and ran over. "Anything wrong?" He looked into the back seat of Jason's car. Though Sally and Jason had separated physically, Clare saw Jon's recognition of what they'd been smoking. He jerked open the back car door and pulled Sally out. "She can't take pot, Eldridge! Have you no memory of that, man?"

"We were celebrating," Jason mumbled.

Sally, in Jon's grip, began to cry. Clare went to her, arms extended, and Jon handed the sobbing girl into them. But even as he did so, Derek shouted, "You should mind your own fucking business!" and to everyone's shock, took a swing at him.

Jon ducked, then raised his fists to defend himself. The two young men began pushing and slugging each other. Jon was the more agile, avoiding most of Derek's punches and scoring some of his own. Derek, though clumsy with drink, was larger and heavier, and some of his punches did connect.

"Stop!" Clare cried. Intent on each other, the two paid no heed.

Uncle Tony suddenly appeared, looking tall and solid. He grabbed Jon and pulled him back from Derek. "What is this?"

Jon, breathing heavily, glanced at Jason, still in the back seat of his car. Tony followed his gaze, then leaned into the back seat shouting, "I can smell it. Jason, you've been warned. By God, this is the last you time you'll see my daughter. Take Derek and get the hell out of here." Letting go of Jon, he pushed Derek around to the other side of the car and into the passenger seat.

"But Mr. Sanderson—" Jason began, getting out of the back seat.

"No *buts*. Go!"

A subdued Jason handed Sally her purse, then got behind the wheel, turned on the ignition, and drove off. Aunt Rose hurried over, a little wobbly in high heels, and put her arm around Sally too. "Oh, darling, don't cry."

Tony reached out and turned Jon's face to the parking lot light, checking for injuries. "Are you all right to drive?"

Clare spotted blood at the corner of Jon's mouth and angry red marks on his jawline, but he said, "Yes, sir."

"We'll have extra passengers tonight." Tony put his hand on the young man's shoulder and walked with him to the Sanderson limousine. Clare and Aunt Rose, their arms around Sally, followed.

"You women get in back. I'll sit up front with Jon." Tony took Sally and put her in the back seat of his limo. Aunt Rose slid in from one side, Clare from the other. Jon drove the car out onto the highway. Sally, quiet now between them, slumped against her mother.

She remained that way until they'd returned to the island and the car was parked at the Sanderson house. "Let's get you cleaned up," Tony said to Jon. "Come on to your apartment." The men walked off together while Aunt Rose, holding Sally's arm, led her inside. Clare hesitated at the door.

"Don't worry about Jon," Aunt Rose told her. "Tony will look after him. I'll put Sally to bed. Then I'd like to talk a little with you. Would you wait for me in the living room?"

"Of course." Clare walked into the living room and sat down, concerned about Jon and afraid Aunt Rose would be angry at her, blame her for what had happened. But when her aunt came back down the stairs and settled on the couch, she merely said, "I gave Sally two Ambivalen capsules and she's going to sleep. She told me about smoking marijuana tonight. She must not have had time to smoke much, but in the past, it really affected her. It was what started her…sickness through the winter and most of this spring."

"It wasn't pneumonia?"

"Well, it was that too—both together. The pneumonia made her physically ill—but we think the marijuana put her over the edge mentally. Once the pneumonia was cured, we investigated sending her to a residential treatment center, but she said she'd hate it—she'd run away."

"Aunt Rose, I looked up her medicines. I know she's bipolar."

Rose looked at her in surprise. "That's what I wanted to tell you about, dear. She was diagnosed later in the winter. I'm sorry I didn't tell you—or your mother. At first, I thought the diagnosis might be a mistake. Then, after she started taking the medicine, she seemed to be doing better. I was afraid if you heard she was bipolar, you might not come this summer. It was selfish of me, but she needed a companion like you so much."

"I understand. I'm sorry I didn't prevent what happened tonight. I should never have let her go to the rest room alone."

"I'm not blaming you. I blame Jason."

"What exactly is her relationship with him?"

"She's had a tremendous crush on him for years—even when she was a little girl, then a pre-teen and she'd see him at the marina. Jason's good-looking, but quite a ladies' man, and as Sally got older—well, he began to notice her, too. Last summer they began dating and doing their little singing act together. Kyle thought that was great, but Tony and I worried. She's impulsive—she'd be so susceptible to anything Jason wanted. Tony talked to him about the relationship, and he promised to respect her. But I didn't trust him. I got her on birth control pills just in case. Once her fall semester at Georgia Southern started, they saw each on the weekends when she came back to visit us, and I guess sometimes he went over to Georgia Southern to see her. I don't know if they slept together, but we later learned they drank, and he introduced her to marijuana—I hope nothing stronger. During that semester her crazy behavior kept getting worse, and during Christmas vacation here at home, she had a major episode. When we realized what she'd been doing with Jason—the alcohol and pot, we said they couldn't see each other again."

Rose stood and paced to the window. "Then Sally went into a deep depression. She tried to commit suicide—took her car and drove off on a wild ride around the island, finally crashing on the causeway. The car was totaled. Luckily, she got away with only a concussion, some back pain, and cuts on her face—her bangs and makeup hide the scars pretty well. But her injuries and mental breakdown—not her mild case of pneumonia—are what kept her out of school for the spring semester. After that suicide attempt, we took her to a psychiatrist for testing, and she was diagnosed with Bipolar Two Disorder. He prescribed the medicines you've seen, and she started having these Monday morning sessions with a psychologist. Finally by April, when she seemed better, they both suggested a compromise about Jason, given how strongly she felt about him. They said if the two of them promised to stay away from marijuana or any other illicit drugs and were only together with a chaperone of some kind, we might, as an experiment, let them begin to see each other again. So it seemed you could be the perfect solution as her companion. It worked for a little while. She's been so happy. But now, this."

"What are you going to do?" Clare asked.

"I don't know. I heard Tony tell Jason he'd never let him see her again. But given how she reacted before when they were separated, we'll have to think about it. Maybe I'll ask the psychiatrist to adjust her meds or give her a different one." Aunt Rose took Clare's hand. "I apologize again for not telling you about Sally's condition. I'd hoped I wouldn't need to."

"Jon tries to take care of Sally, too."

"Yes, he saw what happened to her last winter."

"He seems to have a pretty important role here."

"I don't know what we'd do without him." Then Aunt Rose gave her a look and asked, "Why do you say that about his role here?"

"I could just see it. On a couple of Mondays while you and Sally were in Savannah, he taught me to how to use the stick shift on Sally's car in case I needed to drive it when she and I were out together. I thought that was such a smart, insightful thing for him to do."

"That *was* smart of him. Tony should never have gotten her that new sports car. But he dotes on her so." She kissed Clare's cheek. "Thank you for everything, dear. I'm going to bed. You should too. We'll leave on the lights for Tony. He should be back before long."

The two went up the stairs together. Clare entered her room and soon heard her aunt's bedroom door close. She silently opened the door to Sally's adjoining room and saw the outline of her cousin's body under the sheets. The Ambivalen must have taken effect. Relieved, she went back into her own room and walked out to the balcony. The night air and the sound of the crickets were comforting. Her uncle's car was still parked below.

Then she heard a noise like running footsteps, and looking toward it, saw a small female figure in a white nightgown rushing down the road toward the garage. Clare ran back to Sally's room and drew back the bed sheet. The mound that had looked like Sally was only pillows. Panicked, Clare ran down the stairs, out the front door, and to the garage. The white night-gowned figure was now nowhere to be seen. Then one of the front garage doors opened, and Sally's sports car burst out, a grim-faced Sally behind the wheel.

"Sally!" Clare cried, jumping aside.

As Sally braked in front of the gates, Clare ran over to the passenger door and tugged at the door handle. Sally clicked open the lock and Clare jumped in. "*What are you doing*?"

Sally's eyes were glazed, and she did not answer.

"The security guard won't let you out the gates."

"I took the opener out of my father's car." Sally held it up, clicking the button, and the gates opened.

The bespectacled man working there, Bruce, looked out in shock as Sally pressed the accelerator and roared onto the main road, not bothering to close the gates behind her. The car began beeping the fasten-seat-belt warning. Clare clicked hers on, but Sally did not, and the frantic beeping increased. Sally cried out over the sound, "I'm going to Jason."

"No—please go back home, Sally."

But Sally continued down the curving two-lane road toward the marina, the speedometer at fifty, then sixty. A car came from the other direction, its headlights illuminating her crazed expression. She swerved aside, then suddenly pulled over to the shoulder and braked. "I can't stand this beeping." She clicked on her seat belt. The sound ceased, but she continued to sit there. "I have to see Jason." Her voice was slurred.

"I'll talk with your parents tomorrow, Sally. I'll tell them I'll keep going places with you and Jason and be much more careful as a chaperone if they let you go out with him again. I think I can talk them into it. Let's go home."

Sally was silent for long moments. Then she pulled on the handbrake, unbuckled the seat belt, and got out.

Leaning on the car, she staggered around to the passenger side. Clare followed and helped her in. Then, remembering her driving lessons with Jon, she went to the driver's seat, released the brake, and drove carefully along the road to the estate. Sally leaned her head back and seemed to sleep.

At the gates, Clare pressed the opener button and drove through. Bruce rushed out to the car. "Miss Matthews! I was about to alert Mr. Sanderson and the police."

"Everything's all right now," said Clare. "Please don't tell anyone about this. I'm taking Sally to the house. Will you get her car and put it away in about five minutes?"

"I sure will, Miss."

Clare parked the car beside Tony's and replaced the gate opener on his sun visor. Then she shook Sally. "Wake up, honey. I'll help you to your room."

Sally allowed Clare to lead her up the steps, into the house, and to her bed. Clare breathed a sigh of relief when, a few minutes later, she heard Sally's car start up and go down the road to the garage. Tony returned to the house from Jon's apartment a few minutes after that.

****

Sunday morning Clare woke up with a foreboding. It was nine o'clock and all was quiet. How would Sally be after the debacle of the night before? How was Jon?

She got up and opened the door to Sally's room. Her cousin lay in bed, her eyes closed, her face pale. Clare advanced into the room. "Sally?" There was no response. Clare touched her shoulder. "Do you remember last night?"

Sally moaned and opened her eyes. "I don't know." She sat up and rubbed her forehead, then spoke slowly. "Oh, yes—Jason and I won second place! Then one of the performers gave Jason some marijuana in a little baggie, and Jason had some wrappers, so he and I smoked in his car. I'd promised Mom and Dad never to do that again, but it just seemed a great way to celebrate our second-place win." She looked at Clare, recognition dawning, her speech becoming more normal. "Oh—then you and Derek found us, and Jon came and pulled me out of the car and yelled at Jason. Why was he so angry?"

"He knows marijuana has had a bad effect on you."

"Jason and I only had time for one joint." Sally hesitated, thinking. "Now I remember Derek and Jon fighting. I went home in Dad's car in the back seat with you and Mom, and Jon was driving. What happened to Jason and Derek?"

"They left in Jason's car. Your father didn't see you and Jason together in the back seat the way I did, but he's really angry about you smoking that marijuana."

"Oh, God, now I remember. He yelled at Jason, something like, 'This is the last you time you'll see Sally.' And when we got home, my mother gave me sleeping pills. They must have put me to sleep until just now, when you waked me up." Sally's voice choked. "Clare, if my parents keep me from seeing Jason the way they did before, I don't know what I might do. I might do something crazy like I did last time with my car."

Clare looked closely at her cousin. Sally must have had another blackout, this time due to the marijuana and the sleeping pills. She obviously had no memory of taking her car the night before. Maybe that was a good thing. She would surely tell the psychologist about her strong feelings for Jason and her fears of another breakdown, so she would get the needed treatment anyway.

Clare sat on the bed and put her arms around her cousin. Sally rested her head on Clare's shoulder. "Please help me with my parents."

"There are lots of other guys for you to meet. Is Jason really that important to you?"

"Yes, oh, yes."

"All right, I'll talk with them. I think I can convince them to let you see him again. But you and he must not sneak away from me like you did last night. And this time you must keep your promise to never, ever smoke marijuana again." Clare stroked Sally's hand. "I know about your…condition."

"You know I'm bipolar?"

"Yes, I'd googled what your medicine was for, and then your mother told me herself last night."

"I'm glad you know. Okay, as long as I can see Jason, I promise to be sure you're always with us—and never to smoke pot again."

Chapter Eight

Monday, June 8 – Sunday, June 14

The next day, Monday, was rainy and windy. Sally and Aunt Rose, aware this would be an important session with the psychologist, were unusually serious as they left for their appointment. Clare knew they would discuss Sally and Jason's smoking pot Saturday night, her father's renewed threat to keep her from seeing Jason, and Sally's emotional reaction to that threat. She also knew her aunt was going to set up an appointment with the psychiatrist and ask him about adjusting Sally's meds. She looked after them, hoping that not telling Sally's parents, at least so far, about the car episode had been the right thing.

Shortly after her aunt's car had disappeared down the drive, Clare's heard a ding on her phone and opened Jon's text:

—I want to take you to the cottage today. Is it clear to pick you up at nine?—

She tapped out a simple

—Yes.—

When he came, she ran out, swathed in a plastic poncho. Looking over at him as he drove down the driveway and on to the main road, she noted the now purple bruises on his jaw. "I have so much to tell you, and I've been so worried about you."

"I texted you that I was okay."

"But I wanted to see you for myself. You look better than you did after that fight with Derek Saturday night."

He laughed a little. "Do I?"

"I don't understand why he attacked you like that. He'd had a lot to drink, but—"

"He probably thought he was protecting Sally. I guess I was rough when I pulled her out of the car. But I was angry. Jason got her smoking marijuana last fall. It took her months to come out of the reaction. Her brain was really messed up. And there he was, doing it again. He should have known better. He doesn't think. He just wants to have a good time. He's used to older, more experienced women. Sally's parents know that. But Kyle wants them to date, and you know how crazy she is about Jason."

"I talked with Aunt Rose when we got home Friday night. She told me when Sally crashed her car last winter, she was trying to kill herself because they wouldn't let her see him again."

"She told you about that? Then you see why they're afraid to keep the two of them totally apart. That's where you come in, I guess. How is Sally?"

"That's what I wanted to talk to you about—in person. Her mother gave her two Ambivalen tablets when we got home Saturday night, but later she got up, took my uncle's gate opener out of his car, went to the garage, and drove her car out of the gates. I don't know how she got the garage door open."

"Your uncle's gate opener works on the garage doors, too."

"Oh, that's how, Anyway, I ran after her and

jumped into the car at the gate. She told me she was going to see Jason and drove fast for a few minutes, but pretty soon she pulled over and let me drive her home. Thank God you gave me those driving lessons. Sunday morning she had no memory of any of that. I haven't told her parents about it yet. I guess I should tell them before they see the psychiatrist."

Jon grimaced. "It might make matters worse for her if you do. Sally was probably sleepwalking when she took the car. Sometimes Ambivalen has that effect. Google it on your phone."

Clare typed "Ambivalen" into the Google box and read the answer aloud: "Ambivalen is a sedative used to treat insomnia. People who take it may experience side effects such as memory loss and episodes of sleepwalking or perform activities like driving that they later forget." She looked over at Jon. "You're right."

"Why don't you just tell her parents you saw her sleepwalking one night and suggest they ask her psychiatrist for a different sleeping med? And I'll make sure she can't take her car like that again. I'll tell the gatekeepers to park it behind other cars."

Clare breathed a sigh of relief. "That should work." She was quiet for a moment, then said, "I hope things can go back the way they were, but her parents might decide it's better for her not to see Jason at all. Then they might tell me to go home, that I am no longer needed."

"She would still need a friend, maybe more than before."

"I have to go back to school in mid-August anyway. The University's classes start August seventeenth. Sally's at Georgia Southern start shortly after that. If her new meds work, it would be good for her to go back." Clare hesitated a moment, then asked, "Will you come to see me when I'm in Athens?"

He seemed not to hear, for he was concentrating on making the turn into the little dirt road, then onto the spur that led to the cottage. He parked, and they ran through the rain to the door. On the porch, she removed her poncho and shook off the water, and once they were inside, he hung it in the shower in the bathroom. She looked around at the modest rooms with their slight smell of mildew, typical of a little-used beach dwelling. Jon leaned against a door jamb, watching her. "So this is it," he said. "Quite different from the big house."

"The big house is *too* big."

"It's a good morning to stay inside," he said. He walked away and opened a door to a bedroom. "This has been my room since we came here." She saw a double bed, desk, and a bedside stand made of driftwood. There was a bookcase filled with books—mostly scientific ones. On the walls were framed photographs of sea birds, the beach, the marsh. Seashells lined the windowsill. She slowly made her way in, examining the pictures, touching the bleached driftwood, the seashells as she moved.

"I collected those shells the first year I came here. Those are photographs I've taken."

"I love all these things. I love this room." She could think now only of making the most of their brief time together. She reached up as if to unbutton his shirt. "Shall we spend some time in it today?"

Later, they sat at the kitchen table eating sandwiches—they'd found bread in the freezer, peanut butter in the cupboard. Clare said, "You never answered my question about visiting me at the University of Georgia."

"I don't have an answer."

"What do you mean?" She hesitated, and a slight edge came into her voice, unbidden. "Maybe it's easier for you to visit those girls from the coast your mother said you—associate with."

"You talked with my mother? What did she tell you?"

"She said you didn't bring *your women* to the island."

"My women?" He laughed, then sobered. "Yes, I've gone out with women in Savannah and Brunswick, but you are the only one from anywhere that I've ever taken to this part of the island and to this cottage. You're the only one I've wanted to take. But…it won't be easy for me to visit you in Athens, Clare."

"You went to Florida a few days ago."

"I went with Tony. It was part of my job."

She frowned in thought. "Do you think you might get another job sometime? One that gives you more freedom—maybe one that relates more to your degree?"

"I can't leave Tony."

"Why not? You're not an indentured servant. I know he's done a lot for you and your mother, but he can't keep you working here if you don't want to."

"As a matter of fact, he can." She looked at him in surprise. He pushed back his chair and stood up. "Your uncle's a good guy in many ways, but he's ruthless to get what he wants—like those hotels and that gated community."

"But what has that to do with you?"

"I've gotten involved with him and his other money-making business, that's all."

"What other money-making business?"

"I can't talk about that."

Warnings flashed in her brain—Derek's questions about how her uncle made his money, the Coast Guard searching Kyle's boat, the murder at the Sanderson Estates gatehouse. But she stood also and put her arms around him. "I don't know what's between you and my uncle, but how could it change anything between us?" He held her for a moment, his embrace warm in the chill of the room.

****

When they arrived back at the estate, Jon raised his hand to the opener, then lowered it without hitting the button. "That's Jason's car."

The red sports car was parked at the side of the road in front of the gates. They watched as Jason got out from behind the wheel, ran through the rain to Jon's car, and climbed into the back seat, water dripping from his hair and jacket. He glared at Jon. "You really messed things up for me Saturday night."

"You messed them up for yourself. You knew what marijuana does to Sally."

"Are her parents going to try and keep us apart again?"

"I don't know."

"Shit. My father's going to be fucking mad. I think he wants me to marry her—you know, combine the two financial kingdoms. I'm not ready for marriage, and she's too much of a little girl for me anyway, but hell, I should at least keep dating her this summer to please him. Will you put in a word to Tony for me, man?"

"You'll need to talk to him yourself. Right now I have to get Clare back to the house."

Jason turned his head to her, and a canny look came to his face. "I could tell him about you and Clare, you know."

"Get out of my car, Jason."

Jason made an angry gesture, opened the car door, and got out. Jon pressed the opener button, drove through the entrance, and closed the gates behind him.

Clare looked back, stunned. "What if he tells my uncle about us?"

"I don't know. Tony doesn't like his estate employees to get involved socially on the island. But he trusts me. Maybe he wouldn't mind that much, as long as I'm doing my job and you're doing yours. And he wouldn't tell your aunt or Sally. There are a lot of things he doesn't tell them." He pulled up by the house. "Hurry, now, go inside."

****

On Wednesday, the weather cleared. Sally and both her parents went to Savannah for that special conference with the psychiatrist. That afternoon Clare, now used to her new bikini, lay in the sun on a chaise lounge at the side of the Sanderson pool, her eyes closed. Apparently, Jason had said nothing to her uncle about her relationship with Jon, but other worrisome thoughts coursed through her mind. She still wondered if she had done the right thing by not telling Aunt Rose about Sally's taking her car out Saturday night. She reminded herself that doing so might have made matters worse, and that with Jon's precautions, her cousin couldn't do anything like that again. And she *had* told her aunt that Sally had been sleepwalking and suggested they ask the psychiatrist for a sleeping aid other than Ambivalen.

But the problems were clear. If Sally continued to see Jason, there was the possibility of a sexual relationship and illegal drugs. If they were kept apart, she might again have some kind of suicidal breakdown. After what Jason had said about Sally being "too much of a little girl" for him, Clare was beginning to fear the relationship would not have a happy ending. Perhaps, she thought, as Sally's companion and chaperone the rest of the summer, I can try to convince her not to be so intense about Jason. But will she listen? Will her parents even want me to stay here?

And she wondered again what power her uncle had over Jon and what Jon had meant by his comment that her uncle was ruthless. Did some kind of dark secret lie behind the Sanderson's glamorous life on The Last Golden Isle?

Feeling hot in the sun and upset by her thoughts, she got up and dove into the pool. As she swam back to the edge, she saw two dark-haired masculine legs planted there. She looked up to discover Derek standing above her.

"Hi," he said. "The gatekeeper let me in—he remembered me. Can we talk?"

She laughed a little. "The gatekeeper must not have been Jon."

Derek reached down a hand and helped her up onto the tile. "No, it wasn't. I wanted to apologize to you about Saturday night. I've been under a lot of stress lately. I drank too much. It was stupid of me to start that fight. Sure, Sally and Jason shouldn't have been smoking weed, but Jon just made me mad, pulling her out of the car like that."

Clare sat on the edge of her chaise lounge and put her towel around her shoulders. "You don't know the whole story. I can't give details, but she's had some problems because of Jason, and so her parents want Jon and me to watch out for her."

He sat on the chair next to her. "You and *Jon*?"

"Mostly me."

For long moments Derek looked thoughtful. Then he said, "I really like you, Clare. I'd like to take you out sometime, just the two of us, with no outside obligations for either of us."

"I like you too, Derek. You're a good friend."

"A good friend? Well, I suppose we've hardly had a chance…We need more time together. Then we can see what develops, can't we?"

Clare heard the Sanderson limousine pulling up to the house and turned to see it parking next to another car there—it must have been Derek's. When she turned back to him, he answered his own question. "Yes, we'll see."

Car doors slammed. As Sally and her parents walked up the steps to the house, they looked over toward the pool. Derek called to them, "Hello! I stopped to see Clare. I was just leaving."

They waved at him, and Sally called, "I'll see you soon, Derek." She seemed happier than she had in days.

He looked at Clare and spoke in a dry tone. "She's smiling. We may soon at least have a double date with her and Jason."

After he'd driven away, Aunt Rose motioned to her. "Go change and come back down to the living room. We need to have a family conference."

Oh, no, Clare thought, what could that mean? When, a few minutes later, she nervously joined the three Sandersons in the living room, her uncle began speaking as if he were at the head of an important board meeting, but mostly, it seemed, directing his comments to her.

"We had a good session with the psychiatrist. He has changed two of Sally's medicines—the Ambivalen and the Zyprene—and we're hoping the new ones will be better for her. Rose and I have also decided to give Sally one more chance with Jason, but she must follow the rules—no marijuana or any other illegal drugs, no spending time alone with him. I phoned him after the session—he understands and agrees. So we'll try to go back to the way things were before Saturday. We'll need your help, Clare. Are you willing to stay on with Sally for the rest of the summer—until your classes start?"

"Yes," she said. "Yes, I'm willing to stay."

****

Since Clare and Jon had begun texting occasionally, she always deleted what they wrote for fear Sally might pick up her phone, somehow get through the password, and see what was there. But she hadn't the heart to delete the photos she'd taken of the marshes during her boat rides with him or one of Jon on the beach after a swim—his hard, tanned body, his shoulders glistening with ocean water, his dark hair ruffled in the breeze.

Sally, excited about her relationship with Jason continuing, even with restrictions, returned to being her happy, hyper self. Clare began to feel fairly confident there would be no more sleepwalking and no more episodes with Jason like the one after the concert. And she was not surprised when the two announced they'd set up a singing gig for the very next Saturday at her father's fancy Golden Sands Hotel and scheduled her and Derek to go with them.

"We expect you to come back to the house right after the show," Uncle Tony told Jason on that Saturday night before the four left for the Golden Sands Hotel.

"Yes, sir, we will," Jason said.

The couple's performance went well, and afterward Jason indeed drove directly to the Sanderson Estates, through the opening gates, and to the house. "I'll walk you to the door, like a gentleman," he told Sally.

"I'll stay here with Clare a minute," said Derek, putting a hand on her arm as she, too, started to get out of the back seat and follow them up the steps.

When she turned to him, he put a hand under her chin and lifted her lips to his. The action seemed non-threatening, and she let him kiss her—again, an affectionate, gentle kiss. But before it could become more, she moved away and began to open the car door. "Thank you for coming tonight," she said.

He must have recognized the dismissal in her response. "Am I still just a date so you can be Sally's chaperone?"

"I don't like to think of it that way."

"But you do." He regarded her. "Is there someone else? It's not Jon, is it? If so, you've made a bad choice." He looked out of the car window at Jason, coming back down the steps. "I need to talk to you about him sometime. How about tomorrow? Are you and Sally going to the beach?"

Clare hesitated. Maybe he could throw some light

on her uncle's relationship with Jon—and that mysterious "other business" he'd mentioned. "I'm sure we are," she said.

"Let me know about the time. I think I can take a break from my work at the marina. You need to hear what I have to say."

****

On Sunday, as Clare lay beside Sally on the beach and felt the sun move toward the west, she knew four o'clock, their arranged meeting time with Derek and Jason, was at hand. "Hey, there," she heard Jason's voice, and opened her eyes to see them standing nearby in bathing suits. "We can't stay long," Jason said. "So Sally, want to go in for a quick swim?"

"Sure." Sally jumped up. "Are you two coming?"

"I'm good right here," said Derek, stretching out beside Clare and setting a water bottle beside him. They watched the blond couple run to the surf. "Okay, I need to talk fast," said Derek. "You know I've been working at the marina since May. I've noticed some things. Jon and either Tony or Kyle go out on the ocean in one of their yachts pretty often and come back with loaded duffel bags they put in a closet at the back of the marina office. I think they meet a Mexican boat and pick up cocaine in those bags. And once in a while a Mexican boat comes into the marina. They unload the same kind of duffel bags."

He sat up and looked at her. "Are you listening, Clare? I think there's a drug trafficking operation going on involving Kyle, your uncle, and your friend Jon."

Shock rippled through her. "Have you seen what's inside the duffel bags?"

"No, that marina closet is kept locked. But cocaine

comes up from Peru through Mexico. Mexican cartel boats can easily come around Florida, up the coast, meet either your uncle's or Kyle's boat out on international water, and pass off the drugs. I believe for years Tony and Kyle have been arranging the transport of cocaine to Atlanta and other parts of the Southeast. And now Jon's part of the system. There's a lot of money to be made in this work. Surely, you've heard of the I-95 corridor as a trafficking route."

Clare sat up too and faced him. "You're just guessing about all this."

"It's an educated guess—based on observation. I have some knowledge of these things."

"I was on Kyle's yacht once when they met a Mexican boat. Jason said they were picking up electronics."

"Jason doesn't know what they're doing. His father doesn't involve him."

Clare was silent, absorbing what he'd said. Finally she asked, "What are you going to do about your *observations*?"

"I haven't any hard evidence of the trafficking yet. But if you're getting involved with Jon, I want to warn you about him now. He, your uncle, and Kyle could get sent up for years."

She turned away.

"Clare." Derek put his hands on her shoulders. "I'm only telling you for your own good. You don't want to get involved with Jon. And…you don't want to be suspected as an accessory."

She looked back at him with startled eyes. He drank a swig from his water bottle. "Now listen, this is important. I'd be in trouble if any of them knew I suspect what's going on. So I'm counting on you not telling anyone what I just told you."

"I won't say anything about this conversation."

Derek seemed to want to say more, but Jason and Sally were returning, laughing and dripping.

"Hey, Clare, what's the matter?" asked Sally. "You look like you've seen a ghost. Derek, what did you do to her?"

"I was telling her about stinging jellyfish," said Derek.

"There's none here today," said Jason, grabbing a towel and blotting his chest. "Don't let him scare you, girl! Okay, Derek, we need to get back—you took just enough break time."

Derek rose heavily from the blanket. "Sorry I told you about those jellyfish, Clare," he said. "Just keep a lookout for them."

****

On the way home, Clare told Sally, "I don't feel very well. I think I'll just skip supper and go to bed."

"Please don't get sick," said Sally.

"I'm sure I'll feel better tomorrow. Do you have an appointment with your psychologist in the morning?"

"Yes. We considered cancelling after having those double sessions last week, but Mom decided we should check in with him and discuss what's happened since. I'm so glad we'll have a good report for him."

In bed that evening, Clare went over and over what Derek had told her. Was drug trafficking the way her uncle and his partner had made enough money to expand and complete their island enterprises through the 1990s? If Tony was organizing drug distribution in the Southeast, was that the purpose of the fleet of cars in his garage? Was that behind the murder at the gatehouse?

And Jon—how involved had he been since he came back from college to work for her uncle? He sometimes carried a gun. On that cruise with Kyle, he'd caught two of the duffel bags thrown from the Mexican boat, the duffels Derek said contained cocaine, and stored them below, as if it were routine. He'd helped thwart the Coast Guard's search of *The Rose,* and he'd accompanied her uncle to some kind of meeting in Miami after that boat trip, the place in movies where kingpins sometimes met with their U.S. contacts. Derek's theory also could explain Jon's reluctance to have a relationship with her at first, and now to make any commitment to a longer-term one.

Yes, Derek's suspicions were more than credible. So what should she do? Go home before Derek found "hard evidence" and got them arrested?

As it grew dark, she heard Sally return to her room. Finally all was quiet. Clare got up and took her suitcases out of the closet. As she began to lay clothes in them, she remembered Jon carrying all three at once, plus her garment bag, up the stairs to her room, how he had brought her books up to her room later, taken her keys, moved her car—and how even then she had been very aware of him.

She thought of how close they had become in so short a time. She opened her phone. Scrolling to the picture of herself with that big fish, she remembered how Jon helped her land it, his arms around her, his hands on hers. She went on to the picture she had taken of Jon on the beach, lingering long over the image. Pulling aside her window curtain, she picked up the shell he had given her. She tipped it to show its rainbow colors in the overhead light, thinking of their hours together, his love for the island, his dreams of creating a nature preserve.

Then in her mind she re-played the conversation she'd had with Jon the week before. She'd said of her uncle, "He can't keep you working for him if you don't want to." He'd replied, "Yes, as a matter of fact, he can...In some ways he's ruthless to get what he wants—like the hotels and that gated community he built here."

She didn't want to believe her uncle and his partner were involved in drug trafficking, but even more she didn't want to believe that Jon, too, was involved.

She regarded her partially packed suitcases. She needed to know more about Derek's charges before making any decision. Anyway, how could she leave when Sally needed her?

Chapter Nine

Monday June 15 - Wednesday, June 24

In Jon's car the next morning on their way to the cottage, she looked at him and wondered how to ask him about Derek's charges. But before she could speak, he asked, "Did Sally and Jason's show Saturday night go all right?"

"Yes, they performed well together."

"Did you and Derek have a good time?"

"He asked if I were involved with someone—and wondered if it was you."

"And what did you say?"

"He didn't give me a chance to answer."

Jon laughed. "And you charge me with being evasive." The mention of being evasive would have been a perfect lead-in to a question about his trafficking drugs. Then her chance was lost. Once he'd turned onto the dirt road and the cottage came into sight, he turned serious. "My mother's car is here."

He pulled up beside it and they got out. Maria came out onto the porch. Jon said, "*Mamá*, you know Clare."

Remembering her high school Spanish, Clare said, "*Hola,* Maria."

The woman looked perturbed. "Hello, Miss Clare. Could I ask a favor of you? I need to talk to my son alone for a few minutes."

"Of course," she replied. "I'll walk down to the beach."

"No," said Jon. "You can sit on the porch. My mother and I will go inside."

He escorted her up the steps. She sat in a wicker rocking chair while he and Maria went inside, closing the door behind them. She heard them through the thin walls. Clearly his mother was upset about something, but Clare could not discern the words. Soon Jon came back out to the porch and down the steps to Maria's car. He now seemed perturbed as well. Opening the trunk, he took out a heavy duffel bag—like the ones they'd picked up on Kyle's boat. He put it on his shoulder and carried it up the steps, then returned for another.

"My mother needs to store these here," he told her as he took the second one inside.

Clare continued to rock in the chair while thumping sounds came from inside the cottage. Eventually, Jon and his mother came out. "I have to get back," Maria told her.

"Maybe next time, we can have more of a visit," Clare replied.

Jon walked his mother to her car, opened the door for her, then closed it and spoke to her through the open window before she turned on the ignition, turned the car around, and drove up the narrow drive.

He came back up the steps to Clare. "I'm glad you'd talked to my mother about us so she wasn't shocked to find you here with me. She's had enough surprises today."

"What were the other surprises?"

"Just some problems at the big house. It would take

too long to explain."

Clare gathered her courage. "What's in those duffel bags?"

"Some cargo your uncle and Jason's father stored at the marina. They decided to store it here instead. They had my mother get it and bring it over."

It must be drugs, Claire thought. She burst out, "I'm thinking of moving back to Sandy Springs early."

He sat in the chair next to her. "Why?"

"The murder at the gatehouse. Your gun, the Mexican boat, those duffel bags. My uncle's 'other business' that you mentioned. All the money he's made." She took a breath and plunged. "I've heard about drugs coming into the States from Mexico. I think Kyle, my uncle, and you, are trafficking cocaine."

She saw the color draining from his face under the tan. He looked away for a long moment, then turned back and placed his hand on hers. "Clare, I promise you, all that is about to end. There will be no more guns or duffel bags or Mexican boats."

She stared at him. He'd as good as admitted what Derek had suspected. "How can you promise that?"

"Tony and Kyle don't need that money anymore. Your uncle has wanted to pull out of the business for a while now. Kyle didn't want to at first, but he's finally agreed."

Clare heard the anguish in her own voice. "Why did *you* get involved?"

"You know some of the story. My mother is in the country illegally. She came to Texas to have me so I'd be an American citizen, and she lived under the radar in El Paso for ten years. After she came to Savannah with me, your uncle hired her and brought her here to the island. He kept her safe from the authorities and paid for my education."

He stood, paced to the window, and looked out toward the ocean. "When I graduated from college and he asked me to work for him as his driver and boat pilot, I felt I owed it to him to accept. He was going to pay me a very generous salary—too generous, I thought. Then I learned why. My work would be related to drug trafficking. I was shocked. All those years here, I'd never known about that. When I told him I wouldn't get involved, he threatened to turn my mother over to ICE."

Horrified, Clare joined him at the window. "My uncle said he'd report your mother as an illegal immigrant if you didn't work for him?"

"He was angry when I refused his job offer. He said, 'After all I've done for you—sent you to school, given your mother work, kept her from ICE'—and then he looked at me. Even with his dark glasses, I'll never forget that look. He said, 'I could still turn her in, you know.' "

Clare found her voice came out only in a whisper. "So you *had* to work for him." She, too, looked out at the ocean. "But if the Coast Guard is boarding and searching yachts in the area, they must be getting suspicious about the trafficking."

"Yes, they seem to be, after all these years. The day the Coast Guard came to search Kyle's boat was a close call. But Tony and Kyle have always covered their tracks well. And now, like I said, Kyle and your uncle have decided to quit the business. The last cocaine shipment is here at the cottage. We need to get it out of here as soon as possible. We'll return it to the cartel the next time one of their boats comes. It's almost over." He turned to her. "But I understand if you want to go back to Sandy Springs."

"No," she said, and then more decisively, "No. If that business is going to be over, I want to stay here. With Sally. With you."

****

Something awakened Clare that night—or rather, someone. Opening her eyes, she saw a dark female figure standing silently beside her bed, holding a flashlight with a red beam aimed at the floor. It was not Sally.

"Hush, Miss. Be still." Maria's accent was unmistakable. "Will you come with me to my apartment for a few minutes? Jon is waiting for us. I'll explain when we get there."

Mystified, Clare threw off the cover and stood up, reaching for her robe. She followed the woman silently, tying her belt as she went. She had never been to Maria's apartment, didn't even know where it was. She followed the woman downstairs and along a narrow hall behind the kitchen. When Maria opened a door at the end and stood aside, Clare stepped into a room that was dark except for a flickering candle on a central table. Jon sat on one side.

Maria followed her in and closed the door. "I am going to consult my spiritual guide tonight. I wanted you and Jon to be with me." At Clare's puzzled look, she went on, "Cecelia lives in Cancún, Mexico, where I'm from. She has advised me for years. She's reliable, she always understands my situation, she predicts the future. Tonight, we will all consult with her."

Jon indicated the chair next to him, and Clare sat in

it. Maria took a seat across from them. She picked up her phone, tapped out some numbers, then placed it in a little stand on the table, the screen facing toward her. They heard two rings on the other end—it was on speaker phone—then a click and a voice: "*Buenas noches*, Maria."

"*Buenas noches.* Can we speak in English tonight? We have an Anglo with us."

"I know—she is sitting beside your son. Let me see them." Maria turned the screen around. The face of a wrinkled, dark-skinned woman filled it. "Ah, yes. Your handsome son is with a young woman. They have become close, perhaps too close. I need to ask her some questions." The black eyes looked directly at Clare. "What is your birthday, my dear?"

"January 26, 1993."

"Where were you born?"

"Atlanta, Georgia."

"Your favorite color?"

"Blue."

"Your favorite sound?"

Clare hesitated. "The ocean waves."

"May I see the palm of your right hand?"

Clare held it up to the screen. The woman looked at it for several seconds. "You suffered severe trauma several years ago. You are only now getting over it. Someone here has helped you—yes, the young man beside you." She was quiet for a moment, then called out, "Jon."

"Yes?"

"The relationship with this woman could be both good and bad for you. Think before you go further with it—for both your sakes. Now let me see you, Maria.

You have several questions tonight."

Maria turned the screen back toward her and stared at it intently. "Yes, I do."

"I cannot answer them all. Tonight I can only tell you someone new to the island is a threat." Clare drew in a breath. The woman continued, "I cannot see who the person is or exactly the nature of the threat. I only sense it. I also see plans for change, plans that will create danger for yourself, for your son, for Tony. You may lose someone close to you. Be prepared." There was a crackle of static. When it stopped, she said, "That is all I can say tonight. Stay alert, Jon and Maria. Plan carefully to avoid danger." The screen went dark.

There was a moment of silence. Then Jon got up and flicked on the lights. Clare blinked in the sudden brightness. She now saw the table they'd been sitting at was a wooden kitchen table beside a small sink, microwave, and refrigerator. Adjacent to this kitchen area was a little sitting room with a couch, chair, and television. Another door led to what must have been a bedroom and bath.

"How much did you pay Cecelia for that session?" Jon asked, snuffing out the candle on the table with an abrupt motion.

"You know she does not charge. You do not like what she said, and you wish she'd been more specific. But she has always been accurate with her visions and advice. Remember, it was Cecelia who told me to go with you to Savannah thirteen years ago—she knew I'd find a place here."

Jon nodded, then said, "I think Clare had better get back to her room."

Still shaken, Clare stood. "Goodnight, Maria."

"Thank you for coming. I wanted Cecelia to see you."

"Does she think I'm the threat to Jon?"

"She did not say that, but you are new here, and a woman can always be a danger to a man, can she not?"

Jon steered Clare toward the door. "No more than a man can be to a woman. I'll take Clare as far as the Sanderson kitchen. Goodnight, Mamá." Jon opened the door and closed it behind them.

They paused there in the narrow hall. Clare looked up at him. "She did seem to know what happened to me."

"She is very insightful. I cannot explain it."

"She said you, your mother, and Tony are in danger because of 'planned changes.' It must be because you and my uncle are getting out of…the business."

"She also said to plan carefully. I will."

"I may be the new person who is a danger to you."

"I don't think so."

Then Clare wondered: did Cecelia somehow know about Derek and his suspicions about the trafficking? He, too, was new to the island.

****

In the following days, life went on in a seemingly normal way. By day she and Sally kept up a rigorous schedule of swimming, biking, kayaking, tennis. She and Derek, the "chaperones," went with Jason and Sally to that dinner in Savannah and to some parties on the island. The evenings that Sally and Jason rehearsed at the "big house," Clare was in attendance. They seemed not to mind her being there and often asked her opinion. When they sang in one of her uncle's hotels, Clare continued to go with them and sit in the audience. Sometimes her aunt came with her, sometimes Derek, sometimes both.

"Can I see you sometime alone?" Derek asked her one Friday evening in mid-June at the club in The Golden Sands hotel as they waited for Sally and Jason's act. Her aunt, who had also come that night, had left them to go to the ladies' room.

"I have almost no free time," said Clare. She did not mention her Monday mornings.

"There has to be some way," said Derek. "You can't be with Sally constantly. She's supposed to go back to college in August too, isn't she? Then she won't have you or anyone else in the family to oversee her."

"I know. I worry about that."

"And you need a break." He lowered his voice further. "Have you been able to avoid Jon?"

Images of those wonderful mornings with him, on the beach, in his boat, in the cottage bedroom, came to her mind. "He's been no problem."

When Aunt Rose returned, Derek said, "Mrs. Sanderson, would you mind if Clare and I walk out on the terrace? We'll get back before Sally's performance."

Aunt Rose looked at Clare, then back to Derek. "Of course not."

As they walked through the crowd toward the French doors, he said, "First we could go backstage and check on Sally and Jason."

"We aren't allowed there."

"They know you're Sanderson's niece. Let's give it a try." He veered, steering her to the stairs to the stage, then through the door at the top. When they opened it, a young boy stepped over to them. “Members of the audience can’t go backstage, sir.”

Derek spoke with a kind of authority, enhanced by his deep voice and large frame. “This is Clare Matthews, Mr. Sanderson’s niece and Sally Sanderson’s cousin. She just got a text from Sally wanting to see her. Show him your phone, Clare.”

“Oh, that’s all right, sir, no need. She and Jason are over there.” He gestured. Sally was sitting on a high stool, and Jason was standing beside her, chatting. Other performers and crew milled around them.

“They’re okay,” Clare said quietly.

“All right,” said Derek. “Let’s go. I don’t want to be intrusive like Jon.”

Clare did not respond to that. She turned to go back through the door. “Thank you,” she said to the boy’s questioning look. “She’s busy now and just waved me on. I can see her after the show.”

“And now to the terrace.” Derek led her outside into the warm summer air.

“You acted so sure of yourself—like a television detective—with that stagehand,” said Clare. “I don’t know what I would have done if he’d asked to see my phone.”

Derek leaned on the rail, looking out at the ocean and the rising crescent moon. “I figured he wouldn’t ask. But on the other issue I’ve told you about—the one involving Jon, your uncle, and Kyle, I’ve been watching. There have been no more boat runs, no more deliveries.”

“Then maybe your suspicions are wrong.”

“I don’t think so. They’re just being careful.

Maybe they suspect they're being watched."

"Well, maybe they're getting out of the business."

"You don't just *get out* of that kind of business, Clare. Those cartels take care of defectors."

Something in his tone struck Clare. She stared at him. "You're not just a beach bum."

He turned to her, hesitated, then spoke. "I guess I should tell you. No, I'm not just a beach bum with a summer job at the marina. I'm an undercover agent with the Federal Drug Enforcement Administration." He looked around the terrace, saw it was empty, then pulled off his shoe. He lifted the insole and pulled out a laminated identification license. "My real name is Derek Ruggeri. I'm based in Savannah." He held the license out to her. It had his photo with the Ruggeri name on it, along with "special agent," the label "DEA," and a badge image and number. Hot amazement flooded Clare's face.

He replaced the license under the insole and put his shoe back on. "I've been on the force a couple of years, but this is my first undercover assignment. I was the right age, had spent a lot of time on the beaches here, and my supervisors thought I could play a beach bum type, one that would fit in at the Eldridge marina. So they gave me a new name and the necessary documents, and I started going to the bars where Jason hung out. Pretty soon I became one of his drinking buddies. When I told him I needed a job, he got me one at the marina—a perfect place to observe what was going on." He paused. "I've broken all kinds of rules telling you this. But now that you know what I am, maybe you'll help me. I need to get into that marina closet where they store those duffel bags. It has an expensive pick-resistant lock on it. I have to get a key."

Clare could hardly believe where the conversation was heading. "Is that legal?"

"Not technically. I couldn't use what I saw there as evidence in court. But the home office is suggesting I've been on this job long enough, even that we may have been wrong about the trafficking through the marina. So I need to take a look in that closet to prove to them we're not. You could help me get a key."

"How could I do that?"

"Get another fishing trip set up on your uncle's yacht—with you and me, Sally and Jason, and Jon as pilot. I've noticed Jon has a set of keys he takes with him when he goes out on the boats. I'm sure one is a key to that closet—he unlocks it when he brings in the duffel bags and stores them there. On our fishing trip I saw he put those keys somewhere down below. I've checked the lock on that marina closet and know the kind of key it takes. You keep Jon distracted, and I'll go down, find the key, make a tracing of it, and return it—it will only take a couple of minutes. Then I can get a copy made and check out that closet."

Clare bit her lip. Since Maria had brought the latest duffel bags from the marina closet to the cottage, Derek wouldn't find anything there. So if he got in, perhaps he and his supervisors would decide their suspicions were groundless and drop the investigation. It might actually help Jon if she did what Derek asked. And then, with the trafficking ending, perhaps all could be well.

"What do you think, Clare?"

"All right," she said.

"Great." Derek took her hand. "So on that fishing trip with Jon as pilot, I'll give you a sign at the right time. Then, you keep him occupied while I go down below and find his keys." He smiled a little, wryly. "I think you can do that."

A click of heels on the terrace stones—Aunt Rose was walking toward them. "You two had better come on. Sally and Jason are about to perform."

"Oh, thank you, Aunt Rose."

She and Derek followed her into the club room.

****

Although Clare felt apprehensive about suggesting a second fishing trip, it had been easy. Sally was enthusiastic when she suggested it, and Uncle Tony set up just the kind of excursion Derek had described for the following Wednesday. This time neither her uncle nor Kyle would be with them. She would be paired with Derek, Jason with Sally, and Jon would be in charge of the boat.

The morning of the excursion Derek was standing on the pier as the girls walked up to the boat. He greeted them as they climbed aboard, giving Clare an extra smile and hand squeeze. Jason was on the deck. Jon, in shorts and a sleeveless fishing vest, soon came up from below and went directly to the pilot's space in the upper cabin. Jason and Derek untied the ropes, Jon started the motor, and the boat moved away from the pier.

"He'll stick to the marshes along the coast again," Jason told them. "The radar shows a storm out deeper."

Sally pranced to the front to talk to Jon. Was she going to try to get him to change his mind about where to fish? Remind him about getting her father to give her a gate opener? Clare sat on the cushioned bench seat by the rail and watched the retreating shore of St.

Sebastian's island. Derek came and sat beside her. "I think the best time for me to get the key will be while we're just beginning to fish," he said quietly. "I'll say I need to use the bathroom. Get Jon to help you bait your hook while I'm gone."

She nodded, not meeting his eyes. Sally came back and sat beside Jason. Jon was taking the boat along the edge of the coastal marshes, moving quite fast. Clare suddenly began to have misgivings about what she was doing. She remembered Cecelia saying to Jon, *This woman is both good and bad for you.* "I need to speak to Jon for a moment," she told Derek. She went to the cabin and stood beside him.

He glanced sideways at her. "Abandoning Derek?"

"I have to ask you something."

"What is it?"

"Is anything left in the closet at the marina? The one your mother took the duffel bags from?"

"Why do you want to know?"

"I was just wondering."

"Jason's father put some equipment in it."

"Marina equipment?"

He turned to look fully at her. "Yes."

"That's all?"

"That's all."

She began to move away but he caught her arm. "Why do you ask?"

She raised her eyes to meet his, hoping her own showed nothing. "I just wondered."

He scrutinized her for a minute, then let her arm go. "Ready to fish?" he called out and turned the wheel sharply toward the marshes.

"I think we all are," she said and returned to stand

closer to Derek.

Jon maneuvered the boat into one of the channels and turned off the motor. "Get your poles."

The two couples went to the side of the cabin where the poles were leaning. Jon stood by the wheel watching them, his gray eyes strangely luminous. "Bait is in the pail."

Jason picked up two poles and handed one to Sally, plucked a shrimp out of the pail, and baited her hook. He then took his own pole and baited it. They walked to the back deck. Jon remained by the wheel, watching Derek.

"I have to go to the head," Derek said. "You can start fishing, Clare." He handed her a pole, then went toward the hatch. She heard him clambering down and glanced at Jon, who remained unmoving, not looking at her, seeming to listen. She went to the bait pail and with a grimace, picked up a shrimp, then turned toward him to ask for help baiting the hook, as Derek had instructed.

But Jon abruptly moved away from the wheel and dashed toward the hatch. Clare set her pole aside, dropped the shrimp back into the pail, and hurried to the back deck. Jon had already descended. Sally and Jason, at the rail, their lines cast, were looking to the hatch opening in surprise.

They heard Jon shout, "Hold it right there!" Then thumps and grunts came from below. After a moment, there was the sound of steps coming up. Derek emerged, looking a little disheveled, with Jon right behind.

"Don't tell me you two are fighting again," Sally cried.

Jon shoved Derek against the rail. “Don’t let me catch you going through my things again.”

Derek, big and bear-like, raised his arms in a peace-making gesture. “I wasn’t going through your things. I was looking for a match, man. Do you need to ask me why? When I’d just used your head?”

Sally and Jason began to laugh. Jason said, “I think it’s okay, Jon.”

Jon spoke to Derek with no change of expression. “The rule for you from now on during any excursion I’m on is no going below without me. Understand?”

Derek gave a slight nod. “Sorry, man.”

“Okay, go do your fishing.” Jon stepped back and watched as Derek left to pick up a pole. Then he too left and went into the cabin.

Jason, looking after them, was no longer laughing. “Does Jon know something about Derek we don’t?”

“What, for heaven’s sake?” asked Sally. “Do you know, Clare?”

Clare shook her head. Inside she was quaking. Jon must have caught Derek looking around down below. Would he think she’d known about that? And would Derek be angry with her for failing to distract Jon? She walked slowly to Derek, surprised when he turned to her and smiled almost apologetically. “I’ve baited my hook. Come watch me cast—give me advice,” he said.

She went to his side and watched him raise his pole and fling the line outward. “That looks good to me,” she said. She glanced back at the cabin and saw Jon intently scrutinizing the screens on the dashboard. “What’s Jon doing?”

“Avoiding us.” Derek lowered his voice. “It’s all right, Clare. You tried. I can figure out another way to get into that closet."

"I really don't think you'll find anything there."

"We'll see. But if it comes to raids, I'll let the law know you aren't involved."

"Raids?" She looked at him fearfully.

Jon came out of the cabin at that moment. "Hey," he called out. "I just checked the weather. The storm has veered and is heading inland. We have to go back. Pull in your lines."

"Oh, no," came Sally's voice.

"How much time do we have?" Jason asked.

"Enough to get to the marina." Jon collected their poles, making no comment on Clare's, still leaning against the wall, and put them away. Then he went to the cabin and started the engine. As they headed back, Clare felt the waves getting somewhat rougher, and looking at the sky, saw gray feathery clouds gathering.

The boat was soon safe in its slip at the pier. Jon, tying it up, said, "You all go on. I need to get the canvas over the boat before the storm."

"Can we schedule another day to fish?" Sally asked, lingering beside him after Derek and Jason had stepped up onto the pier.

"You're the boss," said Jon. "You and your father."

"I don't know," said Sally. "Sometimes you seem like a boss too." She took Jason's offered hand and climbed from the boat. When Jason held his hand out to Clare, she looked back at Jon, but he paid no attention. He looked grim and angry, busy with the ropes attaching the boat to the pier.

****

Rain of the late June storm lashed at the windows of the Shrimp Shack as the two couples had lunch.

Then Jason drove to the Sanderson estate. The same bespectacled gate keeper, Bruce, let them in, and Jason drove off as the girls ran though the rain to the house.

"I know what you're going to say—that this will be a good afternoon for you to read," said Sally. "So maybe I'll work on a new song."

"That's a good idea." Clare stared out at the rain. Yes, Jon must have realized she had a role in Derek's looking through his things. In spite of her promise to Derek, she had somehow to explain her actions to Jon.

That night as the storm blew stronger and the household slept, she put her plastic poncho, then went down the stairs and out the front door. The rain slashed against her. Ducking her head in the poncho hood, she ran past the pool house and around to the apartment door. The window was dark. Afraid to knock too loudly, she hesitated by the door. "Jon!' she called softly. Then a little louder, "Jon."

She breathed a sigh of relief as the light came on. He opened the door a crack, then, seeing her, opened it a little wider. She went in. He stood there in his shorts and T-shirt, his hair ruffled, his gray eyes cold.

"I had to talk to you. Everyone in the house is asleep."

He did not move. "What was Derek up to on the boat today?"

"He suspects about the drugs coming up from Mexico and wants to find evidence to give to the police. He thinks they're stored in that marina closet. He asked me to set up that fishing excursion so he could go below on the yacht to find your key to the closet and make a copy. He wanted me to distract you while he looked for the key. I agreed because it might be good if he did find it—when he checked that closet, he'd see nothing there. Then he might give up his idea."

Jon thought for a moment, absorbing what she said. Then he reached over and lifted the dripping poncho from her. "Better take that off," he said,

"After you stopped him, he told me he'd get into that marina closet another way."

"The only drugs on the island now are the ones in the cottage closet. Does he know about the cottage?"

"No."

"The Mexicans are coming back for those soon. So—is Derek just playing an undercover detective? Or is he one?" He looked at her expression. "He *is* one."

"I don't want him hurt."

"Don't worry, he won't be. I won't tell anyone. Besides, he's no danger to us. Our trafficking is over. If he gets into the marina closet, he won't find anything."

"He mentioned a raid."

"That was just big talk. Maybe to impress you." He paused. "I'll get a towel." He went to the bathroom and emerged with one over his arm. "Sit down." He began to dry her hair. "That poncho didn't work very well, did it?" He kissed her briefly. "I think the rain is stopping now. You'd better get back."

Chapter Ten

Thursday, June 25 – Monday, August 10

Jon had said there would be no raid, that he, Tony, and Kyle had nothing to worry about. Yet as June turned to July, Clare sensed a rising tension in her aunt and uncle. As she went down to breakfast one morning, she heard their voices raised in an argument, though they quieted when she appeared. At dinner one night, Maria dropped a platter of fish she was serving, incurring Tony's anger. When the family went to the marina to watch the Fourth of July fireworks over the water, Aunt Rose said she had a headache and went home early.

And while it probably had nothing to do with the situation, Jason suddenly left the island without a word to anyone. No one heard from him, not even Sally or his father, though both repeatedly emailed, texted, and called him.

Sally went into another deep depression. The psychiatrist adjusted her medication, but neither that nor the next two appointments with the psychologist helped. On those Monday mornings, when everyone was away, Jon and Clare continued to see each other. He took her on boat rides in his outboard and on tours of the island. He pointed out the new restaurants and shops, commented on her uncle's more recent fancy high-rise hotels, and noted why the junction of the river and ocean was the perfect place for the marina. They went on walks on the land he dreamed of making a nature preserve. He described the trails he hoped to make, the best locales for bird watching, the observation tower he would build by the marsh. They made love—sometimes in the bedroom of the cottage, sometimes in the surf or in the sea oats on their private beach.

But anxiety underlay Clare's happiness. Of course she worried about Jon. "Are you being careful the way Cecelia told you to?" she asked.

"Everything will be all right," he'd answered.

"Derek said you don't just *get out* of working with drug cartels."

She saw muscles in Jon's jaw tighten.

She also worried about Sally. There were no longer tennis matches, bicycle rides, and beach visits. Her cousin slept much of the time, and when awake, lay about the house or by the pool, seeming to have lost her enthusiasm for everything. "Why don't you write some more songs?" Clare suggested.

"I don't feel like it if Jason isn't here to play for me."

"Maybe you could get another guitarist."

"I want Jason!"

Clare tried another tack. "You might make him jealous by finding one."

Tears rolled down Sally's cheeks. "No one would be as good as Jason. I wonder where he is and what he's doing. He must have gone away because my parents wouldn't let me be a real girlfriend to him. He's found someone else. If it weren't for you, Clare, I don't know what I'd do."

Derek came by to visit one afternoon in mid-July as she and Sally sat listlessly at the pool. "I don't get to see you two now that Jason's gone," he said, sitting down in one of the pool's lounge chairs.

The girls were quiet.

"So you aren't singing anymore?" he asked Sally.

"I can't sing without Jason to play the guitar. Clare says I should find someone else, but…" She sighed and shrugged.

Derek bit a fingernail and was silent for a moment. Then he said, "I play the guitar—just for fun. I sing a little, too—just for fun."

Sally eyed him. "You do?"

"I could audition for you."

Clare spoke up. "That's a great idea. When could you do that?"

"My schedule's pretty tight at the marina by day."

Sally sighed. "I'm here all the time now. I guess we could try a standard cover together."

"I could come by tomorrow night around nine."

"I'll be here."

"I haven't played in a while, but I'll get out my guitar and see you then."

Clare walked with Derek to his car. "Have you heard anything from Jason?"

"He's MIA," said Derek. "Missing in action, or maybe I should say AWOL, away without leave. Anyway, I guess, from what his father says, this is typical for him. He disappears for periods of time. Maybe he got tired of playing in the shows and the restrictions with Sally. But at least I've realized—he's definitely not part of the drug trafficking ring."

"But you don't know *for sure* there's really such a ring, do you?" Clare waited a moment, and when he did not answer, went on, "Anyway, I'm glad you offered to play the guitar for Sally. I've been so worried about her."

"I feel sorry for her. She's a good singer. She's what made them a winner in that contest. And playing for her will have advantages for me too. "

"How?"

"It would get me into the Sanderson house. That could help with my investigation."

Clare's heart skipped a beat. "I didn't think of that. I thought you just wanted to help Sally."

"I do. Like I said, she's really good, and I feel sorry for her. So I'll be here tomorrow."

"Just focus on her—forget your investigation."

****

Though Clare was uneasy about Derek's coming to the house, he turned out to be a good match, musically, for Sally. He played the guitar well—better than Jason, thought Clare— and with his rich baritone voice, he could join her in singing. Once they'd done some standard favorites together, Sally was sold. He came on Monday, Wednesday, and Friday evenings for those last two weeks of July. They sang her songs; she wrote verses for each of them, and then they joined together in the choruses. Her mood improved. "I don't feel romantic about Derek," she told Clare, "but you know what? He's a really good guitar player. And I think his singing with me makes an even better act."

Derek made himself more at home there each time he came. He'd go to the kitchen to get them snacks and then hang out after their sessions, sometimes with a visiting Tinsel on his lap. But most of their time was spent rehearsing. Before long they actually performed at The Golden Sands, and the audience applauded their performance more enthusiastically than when Jason played.

But Clare felt sure those evenings when Derek came, he was also keeping his eyes open, checking out the house and the areas around it. "Clare," he said quietly to her one evening as Sally stood at the piano sounding out a new tune, "does Tony have an office here in the house?"

"No snooping around, Derek," she replied.

Another time he said, "Sally tells me Jon has an apartment behind the pool house."

"That's right," said Clare. "And he has a gun."

"Thanks for that information," he said.

One night Clare left the two at the piano and went upstairs to get a novel. Outside of her room she heard a jingle of dog tags and hurried footsteps. She opened the door a crack and saw Tinsel trotting down the hall, followed closely by Derek. The little dog stopped in front of the door to Tony's office and scratched at it. Derek pushed it open. "Oh, sorry, Mr. Sanderson. I didn't know this was your office. Tinsel was restless so I followed him to see what he wanted." He picked the dog up and stepped inside the door. Clare heard him continue, "I thought he needed to go out, but I guess he just wanted to see you."

Tony chuckled. "Yeah, he probably wants *me* to take him out."

"I'd be glad to do it if you're busy. Sally and I were just taking a break."

"Actually, I need a break, too." Tony and Derek

came out of the office, and Tony shut the office door firmly behind him. The two went down the stairs together. Clare looked at their retreating backs. Yes, in spite of her warnings, Derek was taking advantage of every opportunity to check out the house. She reminded herself that Jon had said there was nothing to be afraid of—that the trafficking was over.

When Jon picked her up on the last Monday in July, she saw a new glow in his eyes. "Your uncle decided a nature preserve at the end of the island is a good idea and promised once we've wrapped up the last of the other business, he'll put me in charge of developing it."

"That's wonderful!"

"It will be exactly the kind of life I want here on the island."

****

The first Monday in August, when Jon arrived to pick Clare up, he was not in his car but in hers, and he looked worried. "We need to keep your battery going," he told her. "I've started it a few times, but you haven't driven it since you came here. And you may need to."

"Yes, I don't want a dead battery." She glanced at him. "You say I may need to drive it?"

"You might want to get out of here sooner than you'd originally planned."

"Has Cecelia told you something new?"

"She said what Derek told you—that you don't get out of a drug cartel."

"What did she say they will do?"

"She didn't say. Maybe they won't do anything. But I'm staying alert for Tony's sake—and doing what she said. I'm making plans."

Clare began to have trouble sleeping at night. She remembered a news story about a drug organization coming to a Mexican family's house for vengeance and murdering everyone there—women and children too. When she did sleep, she had nightmares of cars ramming down the estate gates, Spanish-speaking men killing Jon and the gatekeepers, then rushing to the house, shooting out locks, killing her aunt, uncle, and Maria, and then pounding up the stairs to Sally's bedroom and hers.

At that point she would wake up feeling as traumatized as she had after those now almost forgotten rape nightmares. She told herself something like that surely wouldn't happen. But given her freshman year experience, she knew horrible things could occur suddenly, at any time—and change everything.

The next Monday morning, only a week before her classes at the University of Georgia were scheduled to begin, Sally and her mother left as usual for Savannah, and Jon picked her up, again driving her car. "Didn't you think my battery was charged enough?" she asked as he drove it through the gates.

"I thought I'd leave your car in the house parking area when we get back. I know this is last minute, but I want you to leave for Sandy Springs early tomorrow morning and take Sally and your aunt with you for a visit. UGA classes start next Monday on the seventeenth, don't they?"

"Yes, but I don't need to get home *tomorrow*. I was thinking maybe I could even wait to leave until that Monday afternoon. I'm pre-registered and could miss my first day of classes." Her voice lowered. "I want to be with you one more morning." She looked at him then and noted his grim expression. "Is something wrong?"

He shook his head. "Just trust me on this, Clare. Promise me you'll leave tomorrow and take Sally and your aunt with you. You can talk them into it. Someone on the staff here can go to Sandy Springs in a few days and take them home."

"I'll promise—if you promise to come to Sandy Springs while Sally and Aunt Rose are still there. You can meet my mother. And then you can be the one to take them home."

He put his hand over hers. "I will if I can." He removed his hand and turned onto the familiar dirt road. She quieted as he negotiated the bumps. She could ask more later.

But when he drew up to the cottage, she saw her uncle's limousine parked by the steps and the cottage door wide open. A man wearing dark glasses slumped against the limo—my God, it was Uncle Tony, his white hair bloodied, his hands and ankles fastened with zip ties. As shock swept over her, she heard footsteps coming down the porch steps. A short, solid, brown-skinned Mexican approached, carrying a gun. He went to her uncle and yanked him upright. At the same time another Mexican came up the path from the marsh. Her premonitions had come true: members of the cartel had come.

She looked to Jon. But he suddenly seemed hard and cold, like a different person. He turned off the ignition, opened the glove compartment, took out a gun he must have put there, then tucked it into his belt. Without a word, he got out of the car and came around to her side. "Get out." Grasping her arm, he spoke in

Spanish to the man holding her uncle. Clare's high school study of the language allowed her to at least partially follow the exchange.

"Manuel! You weren't supposed to come here until tomorrow afternoon."

"Plans changed. We got dropped off at the marina this morning. Señor Eldridge was very helpful. He took us to get Sanderson and his limo and gave us directions to your cottage. He said to pick up that last drug shipment you had here and get it back to our boat before the law found it."

Jon glanced toward the open cottage door. "Did you find it?"

The man nodded. "We loaded those duffels onto your outboard. We were going to take them out to our boat, unload them, and set your boat adrift. But now that you're back, you can take us."

Jon indicated Tony. "What are you going to do with him?"

"What we do to all traitors."

Clare let out an inadvertent gasp, and her uncle, who had seemed only semi-conscious, perhaps because of the blow that had bloodied his head, now seemed to become aware. He struggled at his ties and cried out, in broken Spanish, "I'm no traitor. I just wanted to get out of the business."

Manuel slapped her uncle's face, knocking off his glasses. "Shut up! You must be the one who got the law checking for us."

"My glasses! I can't see!"

"You won't need to."

"I swear I didn't set the law on you. Someone else must have."

Jon stooped and picked up Tony's glasses. "Let him have these." He held them out to Manuel. "Let him see what's going to happen to him."

The man took them with a bark of a laugh. "Good idea." He placed them back on Tony's face. Tony slumped again, gasping with harsh, uneven breaths. Manuel had a bruise on his face. Tony must have struggled before they subdued him.

The man now indicated Clare. "Who is she?"

"A friend."

He looked at Clare and smirked. "A friend for pleasure?"

"You could say that."

"Too bad we got here so soon." Manuel turned to the man who'd come up from the marsh. "José, take Sanderson to the woods over there. You know what to do."

Terrified, Clare saw Jon standing still—tough, expressionless, part of this gang. So he'd been secretly working with the Mexican drug dealers after all—keeping those duffel bags for *them.* He'd known they were coming. That was why he'd wanted her to go back to Sandy Springs early—at least he wanted her, Aunt Rose, and Sally out of the way. But he'd miscalculated.

Manuel, who seemed to be in charge, waved his gun at her. "Now we'll have to kill her too."

Clare's breath left her. Jon's hold on her arm tightened. "Why?"

"There's no choice. She's a witness. We'll take her with us out to our boat—make it look like an accident, a drowning."

Jon was silent.

"Sorry, Jon. There will be other women."

"Let me give her something to sedate her first."

Manuel laughed. "You still have a soft spot for her."

"It will just make it easier for everyone. But another thing. If the cops find a body in our woods, they'll question me and Maria. Bring Sanderson out to your boat and take care of him the same way you do her."

Manuel studied him. "You think too much." Finally he said, "But you may be right. We'll do it that way."

"I have tranquilizers in the cottage." Jon half pushed, half dragged Clare toward the porch, the muzzle of his gun against her back. Her legs felt like rubber, and her vision began to go black. Inside, Jon lowered her to a chair.

Her vision cleared and she could see him again. Away from the Mexicans, anger surged over her like a tsunami. "So you're still working with those drug dealers after all?" Her voice broke. "And I'm just a *friend for pleasure*?" She raised her hand in an effort to hit his face, and he caught her wrist.

He shook his head as if in warning, his lips tight. "Good—act angry."

Suddenly she understood, if not everything, enough. He had not stayed with the cartel. He was pretending to do so, deceiving the Mexicans. Surely, he would somehow keep them from killing her—or her uncle. So she nodded and then cried out, loud enough for them to hear, "You bastard!"

He pulled her to the door. She fought him as convincingly as she could while he called out to the men, "The meds will take effect in a few minutes. The two of you take Sanderson and the duffels on out to your yacht. That will be enough of a load anyway. Then, Manuel, you come back for me and the girl. She'll be unconscious by then."

Manuel turned to José. "*Vamos*."

The two men went down the footpath to the marsh where the outboard waited, José leading, Tony, handicapped by the zip ties around his ankles, shuffling in the middle, and Manuel, holding the gun, in the rear. When they'd disappeared from sight, Clare stopped struggling. Presently they heard the growl of the outboard motor. It faded to a hum as the boat left the marsh and headed out to sea.

Jon released Clare. "God, Clare, I'm sorry. Do you understand what happened? The Mexicans were supposed to get here tomorrow and pick up the last cocaine shipment at the cottage. But they docked at Eldridge's marina this morning instead. Manuel and José stayed while the rest of the crew took their yacht back out to sea. Kyle must have lied to us when he agreed to leave the cartel. He dropped those two off at the Sanderson Estates to get Tony and come here. He knew what they were going to do to Tony after they took back the drugs."

Clare grasped his arm. "Can you save my uncle?"

"I don't think they'll have time to kill him. I'd alerted the Coast Guard to be on the lookout for a Mexican yacht on the coast at the beginning of the week." He pulled out his phone, tapped in some numbers, and spoke. "It's Figueroa. The Mexican boat I told you about came this morning. Did you spot it? Good. There's an outboard heading to it right now with two Mexicans and a cocaine load in it, and they have

Tony Sanderson at gunpoint. They left the marsh behind my cottage a few minutes ago…There is? Great!"

Jon disconnected. "A couple of Coast Guard helicopters and one of their boats are in the area." He grabbed a pair of binoculars, and she followed him outside and down the path to the ocean-side beach. They watched the outboard speeding over the waves.

"Didn't the Mexicans think *you* wanted to get out of the business too?" Clare asked.

"Like Maria said, I made plans. I contacted Manuel and agreed Tony was a traitor. I told him I wanted to stay with the cartel, that I could pilot the pickup boats and help with distribution. I thought if they accepted me—and they did—I could help Tony if any of them came for him. And the way Manuel talked, I was afraid they would."

"How did they get into the cottage? It was locked."

"Maybe they picked the lock. It was a cheap one, one that would be child's play to these guys. Or maybe my mother gave Kyle a key and he gave it to them."

"Maria? Is she involved?"

His jaw muscles twitched, and he looked away. "She must have always been involved. When I came back after college and began to work full-time for Tony, she got really angry. She told me to leave, to get away. I realized then she knew what he was doing and what I would be doing. I told her I made my own decisions."

Before either of them could say anything more, the sound of choppers came over the waves. Two red helicopters, *US Coast Guard* painted on the side, appeared and circled above Jon's little boat. They heard faint shots over the water, and from one of the helicopters, a megaphone calling out indecipherable words. The hum of the outboard motor ceased; the boat drifted on the waves. Taking turns with the binoculars, Clare and Jon saw the Mexicans, apparently covered from above, throw their guns down and put up their hands. A cable dropped from each of the helicopters, lowering a uniformed Coast Guard wearing a life jacket. Deposited into the little boat, the two men seemed to be handcuffing the Mexicans, then untying her uncle and handcuffing him. One of them then sat at the outboard's steering wheel. The motor sputtered and started up again. Escorted by a hovering helicopter, the boat made a U-turn and headed back toward shore. The other helicopter flew out to the deeper waters where the Mexican yacht waited. On the horizon Clare and Jon saw a Coast Guard boat moving in the same direction.

"It's over," said Jon. "And the Coast Guard now has the authority to seize their yacht."

He and Clare walked back up the path and into the cottage. They stood, emotionally drained, in the kitchen. She put her arms around him and felt that he was trembling. "What will happen now?"

"The Coast Guard has those duffel bags—enough evidence of the trafficking to arrest your uncle, Eldridge...and me. They'll probably extradite the Mexicans. St Sebastian's won't be a distribution point anymore."

They heard a police car, siren shrieking, careening down the dirt road. The siren stopped with a bleep as it braked by the cottage. There was a pounding on the cottage door, and in burst two uniformed officers, their guns drawn. Derek stood close behind. Jon and Clare turned to face them. One of the officers gestured at Jon with his gun. "Is he one?"

Derek nodded in assent. "That's Jon Figueroa."

The officer stepped forward, pulled Jon's arms behind him and handcuffed him, as the other perfunctorily read him the Miranda rights.

"But he was the one who called the Coast Guard," Clare cried.

Derek stepped to her side and spoke to the officers. "She's a Sanderson relative, but she's not involved. I'll take care of her."

"We need to get her back to the estate."

Clare moved away from Derek. "My car is outside. I'll get myself there."

He spoke to the officers. "She's upset. I'd better drive her."

"No, I don't want to leave. Jon's boat is coming back with my uncle and the Mexicans."

"We know that, Miss," said one of the officers. "We've been in touch with the Coast Guard. Backup is coming—we'll have a team down there to meet them. Best for you just to get out of here." He spoke to Derek. "Okay, take her car and drive her to the Sanderson Estates. Some officers will still be there—you can go back to headquarters with them. Some DEA representatives will be waiting there."

The squad car was parked by the porch steps, its red light flashing. The officer who had handcuffed Jon took him down the steps to it, pushed his head down, and put him in the back seat. Clare and Derek followed. As she stopped by the still open police car door, Derek took her arm. "Come on," he said.

Jon looked out at her. "Go with him, Clare."

Yes, he meant it. Reluctantly, she let Derek lead her to her car.

"Do you have the evidence to arrest Jon and my uncle?" she asked as he drove up the road.

"We have enough, and I'm sure we'll find more. By now the estate has been searched. I'd located your uncle's office and Jon's apartment those evenings with Sally so the team could be pretty efficient. They've also arrested Eldridge, if you're wondering."

"Anyone else?"

"I'm sure some of those gate house guys will be arrested. I don't think anyone else." He glanced over at her. "You're worried about Figueroa."

"Of course I am. We…I care about him."

"I warned you not to get involved with him."

"You're wrong about him, Derek. He's not a criminal."

"You think he wasn't involved in the drug dealing?"

She could not tell him why he'd had to be involved. Doing so would expose Maria as an illegal immigrant. She said only, "He alerted the Coast Guard."

He shrugged. "I don't know anything about that."

When they pulled up to the estate, the gates were wide open. Several police cars were parked there, and officers were milling about, some in the road, some by the gates, others outside the big house. Derek drove to its parking area. "The search should be over by now."

He got out and escorted her to the door. There they met an official-looking man in coat and tie on his way out of the house, carrying some bundles. Derek held up an ID. "Detective Peters, I'm Derek Ruggeri, Federal

Drug Enforcement Administration. I've been working undercover on this case. This is Clare Matthews, Mrs. Sanderson's niece. She was spending the summer here. She's not involved."

"All right." The detective turned to her. "Do you know where Mrs. Sanderson is? And her daughter?"

"Sally and her mother went to Savannah for a doctor's appointment. They should be back any time."

"They aren't involved either," Derek said.

The detective looked at his notes. "Okay, we'll wait for them by the gatehouse. You, Miss, can go on in." As she started to open the door, he added, "Since you're a relative, I can tell you that Sanderson, Eldridge, and Figueroa will be held in the Chatham County jail."

Clare could only nod.

Derek laid his hand comfortingly on her shoulder. "I'll be in touch." He and the detective left, and she watched them walk down the drive and speak to the officers at the gate. Numerous police cars started up, Derek in one of them. The parking area by the house became empty except for her car, and only one squad car remained, waiting by the gatehouse. Clare entered the house, closed the door, then ran to the kitchen and down the hall to Maria's apartment. She knocked on the door. "Maria—it's Clare."

The door slowly opened. Maria stood there not in her usual housekeeping dress, but in flats, a navy skirt, and a peasant blouse.

Clare breathed deeply, trying to stay calm. "Most of the police have left."

Maria opened the door wider. "You better come in." Once Clare entered, Maria shut the door. "I told them I was just the housekeeper. They asked a few questions, and I showed them the ID Tony got for me. They searched my apartment but didn't find anything. They weren't interested in me."

Clare noted a packed suitcase on the couch, the lid still open. "Are you going somewhere?"

"I'm going to call a taxi to take me to the Savannah airport. I'll fly to Atlanta and then see if I can get a standby to El Paso."

"Why?"

"Cecelia has advised me to go back there. Once I get to El Paso, I can cross the border and find my relatives in Cancún."

"What about Jon?"

"I don't think he'd want to come with me even if he could. He's lived on St. Sebastian's since he was a child."

Clare took her hand. "Maria, now you can tell me. Who is Jon's father? Is it Tony?"

"Child, I cannot tell you who Jon's father is. I do not know. Clearly Jon has Anglo blood. It could be Tony. It could be Kyle. They both were with me in Cancún about the time Jon was conceived—Kyle even though he was married with a one-year-old son. But many other Anglos were with me during that time period also. I was forty-two and had never had a child—I thought I never could. The doctors told me I was sterile."

The realization dawned on Clare. "You weren't a *maid* in Cancún, were you?"

"No. What I did paid much more."

Chapter Eleven

Monday, August 10 – Tuesday, August 11

"Perhaps you should sit down," Maria said. "I'll tell you the rest."

Feeling weak, Clare sank down onto the couch beside the suitcase.

"When I realized I was pregnant," Maria continued, "I did not want to abort. I left everything—my money, family, possessions—and found a coyote to smuggle me across the border to El Paso. I wanted to give birth there so my child would be a U.S. citizen. I named him Jonathan Alejandro—Jonathan meaning God's gift, for I felt he was truly miraculous, and Alejandro, which means defender. After he was born, I had my tubes tied and continued my work in El Paso, living with friends who took care of him while I was with…clients. But my health and looks were not what they had been, and I no longer made much money. When Jon was ten, I was afraid he would realize what I was doing—and I knew I was getting too old for that kind of work. That's when Cecelia told me to take Jon and go to Savannah."

"Did you know Tony and Kyle were living in the area?"

"Yes, she told me they were. They'd come to me many times when they were hormone-driven little college boys traveling to Cancún for their wild vacations. They even came to me a few times after they graduated. I taught them a lot and we actually, in a way, became friends. So even though years had passed, I thought one of them might help me. Tony did."

Clare tried to absorb the story. But there was no time for further details and there was something else she needed to ask. "Were you involved in the drug trafficking?"

Without answering, Maria lifted her cell phone, punched in a number, and spoke into the receiver. "Please send a taxi to the Sanderson Estates. I'll be waiting outside the gate."

She put down the phone and looked at Clare. "I was not directly involved. But when I decided to come here, one of my Mexican clients learned where I was going and gave me a message to give Tony and Kyle when I found them. He knew they were developing St. Sebastian's and wanted more money than the banks would lend them. They responded to his message. That's how the trafficking began. They started just as distributors but worked their way up to higher positions and much bigger profits. So yes, I've known about the drug trafficking from the beginning."

She closed the suitcase and lifted it to the floor. "After I arrived in Savannah and contacted Tony and Kyle, Tony offered me a job as his housekeeper. That's the only relationship we've had here; his wife has no idea of our past. He was generous. He gave me steady employment, good pay, a cottage to live in, later this apartment as well. The work was not hard, and he did more than I'd ever hoped for my son, sent him to boarding school and helped pay for his college. All that time Jon never knew about the trafficking."

Her mouth twisted. "The last thing I expected once he graduated with so many honors was that your uncle would make him part of the drug business. But Tony needed help because his vision was failing, and both he and Kyle recognized how strong, capable, and smart Jon was. When they were going to pay him such a generous salary, I knew what kind of job they'd offered him. In spite of all my advice, all my pleading, Jon accepted their offer. I was so disappointed, so angry at him, but he was immoveable."

Clare spoke softly, urgently. "Don't you know that Jon agreed to work for them only to protect you? Tony threatened to turn you over to U.S. Immigration and Customs if he didn't."

Maria stared at Clare. Her eyes turned to black ice. "No, I did not know that. Oh, my poor son." She sat heavily in a chair and stared at the floor for a long minute. Then she picked up her phone and punched in a number. "Cancel that taxi."

****

Later that afternoon, when Clare went to the front hall and looked out of the windows, she saw her aunt's car at the gate. One of the remaining two police officers was leaning in at its windows, talking. After several minutes, the officer waved them on, and Aunt Rose drove to the parking area and stopped next to Clare's car. Clare ran out to meet them.

"This is terrible," Sally wailed. "What can we do?"

Aunt Rose's voice shook when she spoke. "There must be some mistake. That officer asked us a lot of questions. I told them Sally and I didn't know anything about drugs. They seemed to believe us and told us we could go on to the house. But he said they've arrested Tony, Jon, and Kyle."

Clare tried to sound strong. "I'm sure Tony's called his attorney. The lawyer will know what to do."

Aunt Rose took a tissue from her purse and wiped her eyes. "And things were going so well. Today the psychologist talked with Sally alone. When they finished, he came out and told me how much better he thinks Sally is now that she's singing with Derek."

"I *was* better," Sally said as they walked to the house, "until this."

Her aunt looked back at the parking area. "Why is your car here, Clare?"

"I took it for a drive—to keep the battery charged," said Clare. "Jon said I should."

They went inside and sat in the living room as Maria entered, now dressed in her housekeeper's black dress and apron. "I'm so sorry about all this, ma'am. Is there anything I can do?"

"Thank you, Maria, no. We'll all just have to wait. I hope Tony and his lawyer will straighten everything out."

The rest of the day and most of the next were agonizing. Then, late Tuesday afternoon, Clare saw a limousine come up the road. It pulled into the parking area and stopped beside her car which was still in the parking area beside Aunt Rose's. No one seemed to be working at the gate house. She stood at the window, watching a silver-haired man in jacket and tie get out and open the passenger-side door. To her surprise, Tony emerged, as usual wearing his dark glasses. His face was bruised and scabbed from the Mexicans' beating.

She opened the house door. "Oh, Uncle Tony, I'm

so glad you're home. Are you hurt badly?"

"They had a doctor check me over. He said these injuries will heal. Clare, this is my lawyer, David Jefferson. David, my niece, Clare Matthews." They shook hands. "This guy is great," Tony told her. "He got me out on bond. I had to pay a small fortune, and I'm still under house arrest, with an ankle monitor, but it was worth it."

"We were lucky," the lawyer told her. "Drug defendants are usually held without any bond."

"They'll set a date for my hearing within thirty days," Tony said. "I don't know what's happened to Jon and Kyle. I'm sure they're extraditing the Mexicans—their country will handle them. Thank God Rose and Sally were away when those two cartel guys came."

"Aunt Rose has mostly stayed in bed since Monday," said Clare. "She's there now."

"Where's Sally?"

"She's in her room. Both of them think your arrest must be a mistake."

Tony turned to his lawyer. "I really do appreciate everything. When will I see you again?"

"I'll come by tomorrow. Go talk to your wife and daughter." They shook hands, and the lawyer went back down the steps to his car.

Tony now scrutinized Clare. "You were at the cottage yesterday. You saw what happened."

"Yes."

"What were you doing there? "

"Jon and I were going to walk on the beach while Sally and Aunt Rose were in Savannah. He didn't know the Mexicans would be there."

Anger darkened Tony's face. "Jon—that traitor!" He took a deep breath. "How much do you know about all this?"

She realized she had to tell him. "I know you were trafficking cocaine and but decided you wanted out—and that was why the Mexicans came after you."

Tony shook his head. When he spoke next, his voice was bitter. "So I was wrong about you, too. I thought you'd be just a plain, out-of-it, studious type who would take care of Sally—and not get friendly with my employees. You'd be like my wife and daughter, never questioning, never figuring anything out." He paused, and when he spoke, was calmer. "Have you told Rose and Sally anything?"

"No."

"Well, thank you for that. I'll talk to them now."

Clare watched as he went up the stairs. She heard Sally cry out a greeting to her father, and their footsteps going down the hall to the bedroom where her aunt lay. Then all was still.

What kind of man was her uncle? He had been generous to Maria and Jon for years. Surely, he was not a killer like those Mexicans. But he was willing to traffic cocaine for the money and to exert his power over Maria to coerce Jon into working with him. And he'd hidden all that side of his life from his wife and daughter.

Now she had to find out what had happened to Jon. She picked up her phone and called the Chatham County jail. When she said she was a member of the family he worked for, the responding officer told her only that he'd been released. She guessed where he was.

Certain she wasn't needed or even wanted at the house, she rushed out to her car and drove to the cottage. Its parking area was empty—of course, Jon's car was still in the estate garage and the police had taken her uncle's. She ran up the porch steps and knocked. No answer. She opened the kitchen door and looked in. He'd been there—a plate with crumbs on it was still on the table. She went back down the steps and followed the footpath to the beach. There he was, sitting on the sand, looking out at the horizon, a two-day's growth of dark whiskers on his face.

She walked over and quietly sat down beside him. He turned to her. "You found me."

"I called the jail; they told me you'd been released. I knew you'd be here." She took his hand. "Did someone post your bail?"

He shook his head, twining his fingers through hers. "I was released on personal recognizance, probably because I was new to the trafficking business. Plus, it helped my case that I'd alerted the Coast Guard to that Mexican boat and agreed to testify at Kyle and Tony's trials. But I can't leave the island, not that I'd want to. An officer drove me here."

"My uncle's lawyer got him out on bond. But he's under house arrest." She hesitated a moment. "Tony thinks you betrayed him."

"He would think that—when the Mexicans were here, it looked like I'd stayed with the cartel. I guess in another way, I really did betray him—by alerting the Coast Guard to the cartel boat. But I had to do that. If I hadn't, the Mexicans would've killed him."

"You did the right thing—for many reasons." After a moment, she said, "I'd better get back to the house.

Do you want to come with me?"

"Yes. I need to explain to Tony. And see my mother."

"I've talked with your mother. She told me how angry she'd been when you agreed to work with Tony after you graduated. Then, I couldn't stop myself—I told her that Tony threatened to turn her in to immigration authorities if you didn't."

"You told her about that?" He stared out again at the ocean for a long moment, then said, "Maybe it's a good thing she knows."

"She was thinking of going back to Texas and then Mexico, but she changed her mind."

He withdrew his hand from hers and stood. "I need to get there."

****

When Clare pulled up into the house parking area with Jon, Tony burst out the door and ran down the front steps. Fists clenched at his sides, he confronted Jon as he got out of the car. "You hypocrite—you stayed with the cartel after all. At the cottage, you were going to let those Mexicans kill me."

"No, Tony! I'd told them I wanted to stay on, but I was lying. I was afraid of what they might do to you for quitting. I hoped that way, I'd have a chance to stop them. I guess I was thinking of myself as your bodyguard."

As Tony's fists began to relax, Jon went on, "*Kyle* was the one who betrayed you. He really did stay with the cartel. Didn't you hear Manuel say that 'Señor Eldridge' brought him and Jose to your estate? He knew what they planned to do to you."

The wind seemed to go out of her uncle. "No, I

didn't catch that. So that's how it happened—Kyle brought them to my house to get me. Good God—my partner, my fraternity brother, my friend since freshman year in college." Overcome, he took off his dark glasses and turned away. After a moment, he replaced them and turned back. "Those two Mexicans must have been hiding in his car, and the gatekeeper thought nothing of it when he came through early that morning. My car was already out waiting for me. When Kyle left, they got in it and crouched on the floor of the backseat. Once I was out driving on the road, they jumped me."

"So that's how they did it. Tony, I have to tell you—I was the one who alerted the Coast Guard about the Mexican yacht and the drugs. That's why two helicopters were in the area, and how they got to my outboard so fast. I thought it was better for you to be arrested than dead. And the trafficking had to stop."

Her uncle was silent for a moment, then nodded. "The law was finally getting suspicious anyway. It was just a matter of time. All those years I'd never let myself think beyond that drug money—so I could develop the island the way I wanted to." He paused, then continued, "I told Rose and Sally that the arrest was a mistake, that I just got a little roughed up when I resisted arrest. But they'll have to know the real story sooner or later. My lawyer says the government may confiscate the last two of my hotels because I paid for them with drug money. But Rose will be all right if I'm sent to prison. I'd put the Sanderson Estates in her name." He turned then to Jon. "You weren't as involved in the trafficking as I was. I'll tell the truth—that basically all you did was pilot the pickup boats and serve as my chauffeur and head security guard."

"I'll testify about you and Kyle trafficking. You know that."

"Hell, yeah, plus since you also alerted the Coast Guard, your lawyer can probably get you off with a short sentence, maybe just probation. Okay, that's fair. And like you said, the trafficking needed to stop. I suppose I deserve whatever I get."

Shoulders sagging, Tony began to walk toward the steps to the house.

"Wait," Jon said. "What about my mother?"

"I don't see why she can't stay on here working for Rose when I'm gone, if she wants."

"Will the law find out about her status?"

"Not from me."

"When I came back after college, you told me if I didn't work for you, you'd turn her in to ICE."

"I guess I did suggest something like that. But…I wouldn't really have turned her in—not because I was worried she would tell the law about the trafficking. I just couldn't do that to your mother."

"She wants to go back to Cancún now," said Clare.

"She does?" Tony thought a moment. "If Maria gets safely back there, Jon, I can testify that I'd threatened you with turning her in. It shouldn't get me in any more trouble than I'm in already, and it will help you. They'll see you as working with me under duress—which was the case."

He spoke then, just to Jon. "There's something else I might as well tell you now, boy. Years ago, I'd put the cottage and the property on the foot of the island in your name. So the land you want to turn into a preserve is all yours. And I've set up a fund in your name to pay for developing it."

Jon looked at Tony, stunned, then said, his voice husky. "Thank you, sir. If everything works out, I'll do my best with it."

****

Dinner that night was a solemn affair, with Maria serving expressionlessly and Sally and Aunt Rose treating Tony like an injured hero. Clare stayed silent. After dinner, she went to her room. She thought the family needed some time alone together. Surely that night Tony would tell them the real story behind his arrest. But once in bed, she couldn't sleep. It was wonderful that Jon would probably get off lightly and would be given the land and money for the park, but still horrifying that her uncle had trafficked a harmful illegal drug for years and now would go to prison.

A tap sounded on her balcony door. She rose and, after a moment's hesitation, pulled the drapes open. Silhouetted outside the glass panes was the tall, straight figure she would recognize anywhere. She opened the sliding door and felt Jon's warm arms encircle her.

"How did you get up here?"

"I climbed up on the crepe myrtle below your balcony."

"We can't let them catch you here in my room."

"I came to see my mother. I just wanted to see you for a minute." He stepped away. "I'll take the back stairs down to her apartment."

"Will you tell her what Tony said today—about giving you the land and money to develop a park?"

"Yes, I plan to. Are they still downstairs—Sally, Tony, your Aunt Rose?"

"They must be."

"I wonder if my mother has gone to her

apartment."

"She usually cleans up the kitchen, but she should be done by now. Do you want me to check?"

"Yes—let me know what's going on."

Clare put on her robe and opened the door to the hall. Once downstairs, she saw the three family members in the living room. Both Sally and her aunt were crying. Her uncle must have finally told them what he'd done.

She hurried on to the kitchen. It was clean, gleaming—and empty. She went down the narrow hall behind it to the apartment and knocked. Maria answered the door, still in her maid's dress. "Jon is upstairs," Clare told her. "He wants to see you. He asked me to check that you were here. I'll tell him to come down." But as she turned to go back toward the kitchen, Tony entered the far end of the hall.

Maria saw him. Her voice was tense. "Clare, wait. Don't get Jon. I need to talk to Mr. Sanderson—alone."

Clare stepped aside as her uncle came up to them. He said quietly, "Hello, Maria."

He entered the apartment, and Maria closed the door. Clare stood there a moment. Then, when she was halfway back to the kitchen, she heard Tony cry out, "God, no!" There were banging sounds, then a metallic clatter. Clare rushed back and pushed open the door.

Tony was holding his arm, blood gushing down his sleeve. A large, red-stained butcher knife lay on the floor. He must have knocked it out of Maria's hands, for she faced him, pale under her mocha skin, her hands splattered with blood, her eyes wide and crazed.

"I want to kill you!" she screamed. "You *made* my son work with your dope trafficking and threatened to turn me in to ICE if he didn't."

"I did say something like that to him, but I wouldn't have really done it, I swear."

"He thought you would—that's what counts. That's why he worked for you. You've ruined his life!"

Clare rushed over. "This could have ruined your life and Jon's." She picked up the knife and threw it into the sink in the adjoining kitchen.

At that moment Jon burst in. "I heard shouts." He looked at Tony's bleeding arm, at Maria's bloody hands. "*Dios mio*, what have you done?"

Clare said, "Tony needs help."

Jon reached out to her. "Give me your bathrobe belt."

She untied it and handed it to him. Maria watched, frozen, as Tony sank into a kitchen chair. The young man tied the belt around his arm, snatched a wooden spoon with a long handle from a container on the counter, attached its handle to the belt and turned it like a corkscrew until the blood flow stopped. Maria began to sob.

Tony said, "It was an accident."

Clare said, "He needs to go to a hospital."

"There's an urgent care office here on the island. I can take him there." Jon seated Maria in another kitchen chair. "Clare, will you stay here with my mother?"

"Of course."

Maria looked up at Jon. "You will help him in spite of everything?"

"He's done a lot for us both."

"But he threatened to turn me in if you didn't work for him in that trafficking business. So you did, and now you've been arrested. He's destroyed your life, my son."

Clare put her hand on Maria's shoulder. "Jon's life isn't destroyed. He was not as involved in the trafficking as Tony and Kyle. He may just be let off on probation. And Tony's given Jon the cottage and the land it's on."

Silent now, Maria watched Jon help Tony to his feet and guide him out of the apartment and down the corridor. At its end, the door to the Sanderson kitchen opened with a flash of light, then closed. As Clare shut the apartment door, Maria moaned and swayed in the chair. "I guess I went crazy. But Cecelia said I might lose someone close to me. I thought it was going to be my son."

"You will not lose him."

"Then who did she mean?"

"Perhaps Tony. He's someone close to you, in a way. He will probably go to prison."

Maria sat still for a moment, then nodded. "And Kyle? Will he go to prison too?"

"Yes."

"He was the leader in all those college escapades, buying my services in Mexico, and I'm sure setting up the drug trafficking here. I should never have delivered that message to them when I first came. I didn't fully understand, then, what it meant or what it would lead to."

Clare sat in a chair beside her. "Tony said this house is in my Aunt Rose's name, so it won't be seized by the government. He said you could stay on as housekeeper here if you want."

"I don't want to stay. I lived here for Jon, but now

he's a man, and you say he will be all right." She looked down at her still blood-splashed hands. "Tony has given me some extra money over the years. But after what I just did, how can I keep it?"

"What happened here tonight—I'm sure we all can consider it an accident. And don't you agree that Tony, in many ways, has been good to you and Jon?"

"Yes, but he was trafficking drugs all that time—drugs that harmed people." She paused. "I played a part in that. I knew but never said anything. All I did was work here to live near my son."

Clare could think of no reply.

Maria stirred on the chair. "You and Jon, will you stay together after all this?"

"I hope so."

"You love him—as a woman loves a man?"

"Yes," Clare said. "Yes, I do."

At last a small smile came to Maria's lips.

****

Tony and Jon returned after about two hours, Tony with his arm heavily bandaged. He told Maria he understood why she'd been so angry. They all agreed to tell Sally and her mother that she had accidentally fallen against Tony with the knife in her hand.

"Clare said you were thinking of going back to Mexico," Tony said. "But we need you here right now, Maria. Would you stay a little longer, until this legal stuff gets settled and Rose can find a new housekeeper? Maybe you'll even change your mind about leaving."

"I won't change my mind. But if you wish it, I will stay on a little longer."

"*Gracias,* Maria."

Jon put his arm around his mother. "If you stay,

maybe we can begin the process of making you a United States citizen."

Maria only shook her head.

Later, as Clare walked with Jon out to the parking area, she found she could hold back no longer. "I've been thinking of something, Jon. I don't know whether I should tell you or not."

"You can tell me anything."

"All right." Clare took a deep breath. "In many ways Tony's treated you like a son—sending you to boarding school and college, wanting you so much to stay and work for him after you graduated, leaving you the cottage and the land. I looked at his eyes this afternoon when he took off his glasses. They were blue, but they might have had a little gray in them. Your eyes are gray. Have you…have you thought Tony could be your father?"

He stopped walking. "Yes, I have sometimes thought of that. I know he and Kyle went to Cancún—where my mother lived—for vacations. They might have been there nine months before I was born."

"You could ask Tony to take a paternity test."

"I've also thought of that. But I've come to realize it would be too crazy, too improbable that my mother ever met Tony and Kyle in Cancún—a city of almost a hundred thousand people. Their circles would not have overlapped. She's much older than they are, and she was working full-time as a maid for a large, rich Anglo family. It's more likely my father was a member of the family, maybe somebody who was married, somebody she's protected all these years and who doesn't even know about me. To Tony, I am just a sort of substitute son, brought here by chance. And I've seen his eyes.

They're not the color of mine. That was just your imagination. No, there's not enough reason to ask him to take one of those tests."

He took her hand and began walking again, slowly. "I've also thought of taking a DNA test to see if I could find my biological father through the testing site. But I've finally decided, Clare, that some things are better left unknown. That must be what my mother thinks, why whenever I questioned her about my father, she wouldn't talk about it. I should respect her wishes."

She stroked his palm gently. "Maybe you're right. Some things are better left unknown."

Chapter Twelve

Wednesday, August 12 – Saturday, September 5

The next morning, Clare called her mother. "Mom, I'm fine, don't worry, but I have something to tell you about Uncle Tony—something that hasn't made the news yet."

"This sounds like something bad," her mother said.

"It is." When Clare told her about Tony's arrest for drug trafficking, she was shocked. "I never knew him very well, but I still can't believe it! Poor Rose! I'm sure she had no idea. Should I come down to be with her? I can stay for as long as she wants."

"I know that would mean a lot to her," Clare said. "But there's something else, some good news too. I want you to meet someone here."

"Who is that?"

"His name is Jon Figueroa—Jonathan Alejandro Figueroa. He worked for Uncle Tony."

"He worked for Tony? Has he been arrested, too?"

"Yes, but I think he'll be let off on probation. He wasn't fully involved with the trafficking—he actually didn't want to be involved at all. It's a long story. I'll tell you when you get here. Tony has given him land on the island where he's going to develop a nature preserve. Jon is great. You'll see when you get here. And because of him, Mom, I've gotten over what was wrong with me. You know—when I was the Ice Princess."

"Ah, there was something in your voice when you said his name, something I'd never heard before." Her mother paused. "I should have guessed then."

****

That afternoon the doorbell chimed. Clare answered the door. Derek stood there, looking shy and guilty. "Are you speaking to me?" he asked Clare. "The last time you saw me, I was part of the team arresting Jon."

"You were just doing your job."

"When we came to that cottage and I saw you and him together, I realized how it was between you two. And now I've learned that he wasn't as involved with the trafficking as I thought he was. Maybe I was biased against him. Hell, I admit it—I was jealous. I'm sorry, Clare."

"I understand why you thought what you did. What I don't like was that you sang with Sally to get into this house and find evidence against him and my uncle."

"I wasn't singing with Sally just for that. I like her. I liked singing with her."

"Then I'll leave it up to you to tell her what you really are."

"She doesn't know?"

"No, and Tony doesn't either."

"So I can see her?"

Clare stepped aside. "She's in the living room."

Derek walked to it, Clare following at a distance. Sally was at the piano, slowly fingering keys and tentatively singing while looking at a piece of paper. She looked up as Derek entered. "Derek! I've written a new song. Come here, I'll show you."

He walked over and sat at the piano bench beside her. She showed him the sheet of paper where her lyrics were written. "Wow," he said, looking it over, "this one is a zinger."

"I wrote it after I learned something I didn't know about my father. Listen." She hit some keys and began tentatively to sing—a song about illusions and learning the truth. When she finished, she asked, "What do you think?"

He cleared his throat. "It's great."

She looked at him in pleased wonder. "It did affect you, didn't it?"

After a moment, his voice now normal, he said, "I do have one suggestion. Maybe…what if the refrain melody went more like this?" He hit some keys and hummed in his pleasant baritone.

Sally listened, tilting her head. "Yes, I like that."

Clare quietly left the room. Sally didn't need a chaperone with Derek the way she had with Jason. For now, though, she thought, this relationship seemed good for them both. But if it continued, Derek needed to tell Sally his real occupation, and Sally would have to tell him about her psychological condition. Some things did need to be known.

As she reached the hall, the doorbell chimed again. To her shock, Jason stood in the doorway, leaning casually against the jamb. "Well, hello, Miss Clare," he said. "Is Sally here?"

"You're back. You played a good disappearing game."

"I needed a break. But my father's lawyer tracked me down. He told me what was going on and said I'd better get my ass home. So…the law's caught my father and your uncle at last. And your friend Jon, I'm sure."

Clare's voice was sharp. "Maybe the law should have caught you, too."

"Me, no. Not for what they were doing. I did help unload cargo once in a while. They never told me what it was. I admit I suspected—but that's not enough to incriminate me. Of course I've indulged in weed a little—as you well know. But that's a whole different ball game."

"Your father may lose the marina."

Jason shrugged. "He won't need it where he's going. And that's no problem for me. The marina was a lot of work. I wouldn't mind if someone else took it over. I don't need money—my father set up a trust fund for me long ago. So, where's Sally?" He heard the piano down the hall. "Ah, there she is." He advanced into the house. Then he heard the two voices singing, the baritone and the soprano. "Who's that with her?"

"Your friend from the marina. Derek."

Jason's mouth fell open, and then he laughed. "Derek sings?"

"Yes. He also plays the guitar. Better than you do."

Jason laughed again. "Maybe, but I'm sure I could do some things for Sally far better than he can."

Clare blocked his advance toward the living room. "I don't think this is a good time for you to see her."

He brushed her aside and strolled into the room, clapping loudly. "*Bravo* and *brava*! You two going to win some contests?"

The music stopped and they both looked up. "Jason!" said Sally. "What are you doing here?"

"Is that any way to greet your long lost…friend?"

Jason walked to the piano bench and bent over to kiss her. Sally turned her head away.

"And hello to you, Derek," Jason continued. "Why aren't you working at the marina?"

"I quit."

"You what?"

"Actually, I have another job."

"You do?" said Sally. "You didn't tell me that. What is it?"

"It's complicated. I'll explain to you some time." Derek stood up and looked down at Sally still on the bench. "Do you want me to leave?"

"No. I want Jason to leave."

"I thought you'd come for a ride with me," Jason said. "Just the two of us for once."

"You left without a word and never answered my emails or texts or phone calls. This time you had no excuse—I wasn't sick, and my parents were letting me see you. And now you know what? I've kind of got used to you not being here."

"You'll get used to me being here again. And now maybe things can be different."

"I don't think so," Sally said. "I've been doing a lot of thinking, and my psychologist has helped me see some things I refused to see before. Now will you leave nicely, or do I need to call my father?"

"My, you've become feisty." Jason glanced at Derek standing there like a bulwark beside Sally. "Okay, you don't need to call your father. I'll go *nicely*. But I'll check with you later. You'll change your mind." He turned and sauntered out. As he passed Clare, he patted her cheek. "So long, sweetheart."

Clare looked after him. At the beginning of

summer she'd thought he and Sally were an ideal couple. She should have known better. But she hadn't known Jason very well back then—and perhaps hadn't had a good idea of what love really was.

****

After Tony told his wife and daughter the whole story, Clare thought he and Aunt Rose seemed in some ways closer than they had been when he was so often away. And Sally grew calmer and more subdued, perhaps because of what had happened to her father, or because she had freed herself from Jason's influence, or because that new combination of meds her psychiatrist had prescribed was taking effect—or maybe all three.

As for Clare, her time to leave the island for graduate school and her master's degree work was fast approaching. Somehow those plans seemed to belong to another person, the old Ice Princess Clare, yet she knew she had to face them.

"Maria," Clare said, coming to her in the Sanderson kitchen Thursday morning, "Could I consult with Cecelia again the next time you speak with her?"

Maria turned from loading the dishwasher. "You have something you wish to ask her?"

Clare nodded. "I'm supposed to go back to school in three days. I want to know what advice Cecelia will give me."

"About you and my son."

"Yes."

"I am scheduled to talk with her tonight. Can you come to my apartment at ten?"

"I can. Thank you, Maria."

That night, with Sally asleep in her room and her aunt and uncle in theirs, Clare went downstairs and to the narrow corridor behind the kitchen. When she knocked on the apartment door, Maria, in bathrobe and slippers, answered. "Come in."

Clare saw the phone on a stand in the middle of the table, as it had been that night when they'd all consulted a few weeks before. She sat down before its blank face and could not suppress a shiver.

Maria took a seat beside Clare. "Do not be afraid. Tonight Cecelia will call us. She's due any minute now." The two looked at the phone as if mesmerized. Then the screen lit up as the phone jingled softly. Maria picked it up and slid the circular green icon to answer. "*Hola*, Cecelia. Let us speak in English. I have Jon's friend Clare here with me again tonight. She wishes to consult with you also. Is that possible?"

She pressed the speaker phone button and Clare heard the Spanish-accented, "Yes, let me talk to her."

Maria handed the phone to Clare. The dark face in the screen looked out at her. "Good evening, *Señorita*. You wish my counsel?"

"Yes."

The woman closed her eyes for a few moments, then opened them and regarded Clare. "Sometimes we change, and then our plans for the future must change. You must be confident in forming your new plans. Only then will the future work out as you wish." The eyes then moved to Maria, beside Clare. "The same is true of you, Maria."

"Yes, my situation has changed. I've worked here thirteen years to be near my son. But he has become a man. I can now return to Mexico."

"That is one of your options. But you could continue working there and study to become a citizen."

"I do not wish to do that. I have some money. I would like to go home and spend my last years there."

"Then you should follow that plan."

"Will Jon be all right if I leave?"

"Yes. He loves St. Sebastian's Island. It is his home now. But do not fear that you will never see him again. You will—many times."

Clare leaned closer to Maria and looked into the phone. "Cecelia, can you tell me what my options are?"

"That is something I believe you can determine yourself. I send you both my blessings. Goodnight, dear ones." And the screen went black.

That night Clare composed an email to the University of Georgia English department withdrawing from the graduate program. She would have it ready if she decided to hit "send."

****

Now that Jon was not working for Tony as he had been, he had more free time. She texted him early the next day telling him that Sally and her mother had gone to Savannah to shop for Sally's college clothes and that she'd declined going with them. "Could we meet at the cottage beach this morning? I need to talk to you."

He texted back, "Yes, there's someone to work at the gates. I need to talk to you, too."

That Friday morning, as they lay on the beach side by side, she turned to look at him. "Everything is about to change. My mother's coming tomorrow. She'll stay here for a while with my aunt. Sally will leave for Georgia Southern next week…and I'm supposed to go back to Athens this Sunday."

"I know. To start work on your master's degree."

"Yes. Sally is better. I think she's ready to go back

to college."

"I do too. I guess you'll get those ten thousand dollars from your aunt."

"That doesn't matter so much to me anymore."

"You'll need it for school."

"School doesn't matter so much to me anymore."

"You should go back, Clare." His voice lowered. "You—you can find someone at the University of Georgia now."

"I don't want to go back. I don't want to find anyone else. I talked to Cecelia last night. She said—I remember her exact words—'Sometimes we change, and then our plans for the future must change. You must be confident in forming your plans.' When I was afraid of men, I'd escape to my books, my studies. I suppose that's the main reason I wanted to go to graduate school. But this summer, because of you, I *have* changed. And I've come to love this island the way you do. I don't want to leave it…I don't want to leave you."

"Clare, I wish I could ask you to stay here with me. But I can't. Who knows what a judge or jury will decide to do with me? I may have to serve time. I don't know what my future will be."

Her voice was confident. "I believe that considering what you did with the Coast Guard, and with Uncle Tony testifying you worked with him under duress, you'll just get probation. Then you can create The Last Golden Isle nature preserve just as you wanted. I could help you. And when it's ready, I could set up a web site, work as a tour guide—anything you need. You can teach me what I need to know…I'm a good learner, aren't I?"

"Yes, you are."

"We could live together in the cottage."

"It's kind of in bad shape right now."

"We'd fix it up, make it beautiful. I can use the money from my aunt. We won't have just Monday mornings anymore. We could sleep together there every night, listening to the waves."

He turned away from her. She lay still, waiting, afraid she'd once again overstepped. The waves she hoped they'd listen to together surged up on the wet sand, over and over, and gulls called as they flew overhead.

It seemed a long time before he turned back to her. "You really want to stay here with me?"

"I do."

"You really believe I'll just get probation?"

"I really believe that."

"If we live together here in the cottage and develop the nature preserve together..." He took her hands in his. "We should get married."

Her eyes glowed warm with relief and love. "Yes."

He lowered his lips to hers and they kissed, not so much in passion this time, but to seal a plan and a promise. "You know something?" he said, when they drew apart. "You say I've healed you, Ice Princess. But you've healed me, too. You've given me confidence in my future."

That afternoon Clare returned to her room, opened her laptop to the email she had composed to the English Department, and hit "send." And then she called her mother, telling her she'd decided not to go back for the master's degree after all.

****

They decided to have a simple ceremony before the hearings and announce their marriage plans once her mother arrived. On Saturday Clare and the Sandersons had just finished a late lunch when they heard the expected car turn into the parking area. "My mother!" Clare exclaimed.

She, Aunt Rose, and Sally rushed out and embraced her. When the four came into the house, Tony greeted his sister-in-law, then went upstairs to his office to give the women time alone together. "I'll be down later," he told them. "You all need some time to talk."

Clare and Sally sat in upholstered chairs in the living room while the sisters, Rose and Helen, settled together on the couch, hands clasped. "I'm so sorry about what's happened," Helen said.

Rose's voice now trembled. "It's been a terrible shock. Tony has a good lawyer, but he'll probably have to go to prison for years. With Sally going back to school, and Maria to Mexico, I'll feel so alone."

"I'll come and stay with you here for long visits."

"Oh, that would be a wonderful help." Rose smiled a little, tearfully. "It will be like when we were little girls."

"And I'll visit you as often as I can," Sally said.

"Thank you, darling. But I'm just glad you're well enough to go back to college." Rose wiped her eyes and looked at Clare. "That's in part thanks to you. You have done so much for Sally this summer."

Helen spoke then. "Something else good—something totally unexpected—has come out of Clare's being here. She tells me she has met a man she seriously cares for."

Surprise replaced the sadness on Rose's face. "You hadn't told *us* that, Clare. Is it Derek?"

Embarrassed, Clare glanced at Sally. "Derek and I are just friends." She hesitated for a moment. "It's Jon."

"Our Jon Figueroa?" Aunt Rose's mouth dropped open. "When did you…? How did you…? I wasn't aware you and he really even knew each other that well."

Sally spoke up. "I knew you liked him, but you certainly kept any relationship a secret."

"We didn't know if you'd approve. But at the beginning of the summer he taught me how to use the stick shift on Sally's car in case I needed to drive it sometime—"

Sally laughed. "That shows how much he trusted my driving."

Aunt Rose said, "But you must have done more than take those lessons from him."

"He gave me lessons twice while you two had your Monday morning appointments in Savannah. Then, after that, it just seemed natural to get together on those mornings."

"And here I was worried you'd get bored while we were gone," Sally exclaimed. "But you never let on. You didn't tell even me."

"You did tell me about the driving lessons," Rose noted. "But I didn't realize…Well, he's a fine young man."

"He's supposed to come by this afternoon to meet you, Mom. I'll text him that you're here." Clare took out her phone even as she spoke.

Sally bounced in her chair. "Oh, this is exciting!" It did not seem long until she cocked her head. "I think I hear his car." She dashed to the door. They heard her open it and call, "Jon! Come in."

In a minute he appeared following Sally, tall, lithe, good-looking as always, but not quite his usual at-ease self. "Mom, this is Jon Figueroa," said Clare, standing and going to him. "Jon, this is my mother."

Jon held out his hand. "I'm glad to meet you."

Clare's mother stood and took it. "And I'm glad to meet you." She perused him closely, then seemed to realize what she was doing and stepped back. "I knew you had to be someone quite special."

Clare leaned close against him. "He is," she said.

That night she knocked lightly on the door between her room and Sally's. Looking in, she saw her cousin at her computer typing—probably another song-poem. "I hope you understand why I didn't tell you about Jon and me," Clare said.

Sally swiveled around in her chair. "I do. Back then I would have been jealous—and want my relationship with Jason to be like yours with Jon must have been. I would've expected you to be my ally more than a chaperone. And my parents might have sent you home if they knew."

"I felt like a hypocrite."

"But it was the right thing. If you hadn't been such a good friend, and always with Jason and me, playing your proper role, I might have done anything he wanted me to do—the way I did before my breakdown. And this summer he wanted a real sexual relationship. He would whisper in my ear, trying to talk me into running away with him to the Coast, where we could do anything we wanted. Because of you, I said no. Now I see what kind of person he is and why my parents were so worried." She rose and put her arms around Clare. "But Jon is a great guy. He'll come through this legal stuff all right, I know. I'm happy for you."

"And you—you're excited about going back to school?"

Sally nodded and laughed a little. "My psychiatrist thinks we must finally have found the right medical cocktail. Thank heavens—I don't want to give my mother any more to worry about." She hesitated a moment. "Derek says maybe we can still do some singing together even after I go back to college. Georgia Southern isn't that far from Savannah."

"That would be wonderful. You and he are good together—singing, I mean."

"He's so different from Jason."

"He is."

"But we're just friends."

Clare smiled at that old familiar phrase, sometimes true, sometimes not. And sometimes true at first, but eventually growing into something more.

****

Clare and Jon's wedding was held at sunset on the beach below the cottage on September fifth, the Saturday before Labor Day. A Unitarian minister from Savannah performed the ceremony. The guests were few: Clare's mother, Maria, Sally, home for the weekend from Georgia Southern, Aunt Rose, Uncle Tony, who'd been given special permission to attend, and Derek, the only non-family member, who'd driven down to the island from Savannah.

The wedding party stood on the beach as the clouds in the eastern sky turned pink, reflecting the setting sun. The foaming breakers surged close to their feet. Jon wore blue trousers and his signature open-necked white shirt, Clare a simple white dress, flowers in her hair, and a beautiful rainbow-tinted seashell on a chain around her neck. The minister read the words of the wedding vows, and the couple repeated them and kissed. Afterward, everyone had cake and wine. In spite of the difficulties soon to be faced, there was a sense of happiness and of faith in the couple's future.

Night came on, the moon rose, and lights twinkled from the ships still out on the ocean. Jon and Clare bade the guests goodnight, and hand in hand, followed the footpath up to the cottage—not a fancy place like the suites at the Golden Sands Hotel, but perfect for the honeymoon both of them wanted.

A word about the author...

Patricia McAlexander earned a bachelor's degree from The University of New York at Albany, a master's from Columbia University, and a doctorate from The University of Wisconsin, Madison, all in English. After moving with her husband to Athens, Georgia, she taught composition and literature at The University of Georgia. Now retired, she enjoys hiking, travel, and photography. But most of all, she enjoys writing novels. https://patriciamcalexander.weebly.com

Thank you for purchasing
this publication of The Wild Rose Press, Inc.

For questions or more information
contact us at
info@thewildrosepress.com.

The Wild Rose Press, Inc.
www.thewildrosepress.com

Printed in the USA
CPSIA information can be obtained
at www.ICGtesting.com
CBHW051417111223
2557CB00008B/496

12-LESSON STUDY GUIDE

THE BOOK OF

HEBREWS

LIVING FAITH

BroadStreet
PUBLISHING

BroadStreet Publishing® Group, LLC
Savage, Minnesota, USA
BroadStreetPublishing.com

TPT: The Book of Hebrews: 12-Lesson Bible Study Guide
Copyright © 2021 BroadStreet Publishing Group

978-1-4245-6262-6 (softcover)
978-1-4245-6263-3 (e-book)

All rights reserved. No part of this book may be reproduced in any form, except for brief quotations in printed reviews, without permission in writing from the publisher.

All Scripture quotations are from The Passion Translation®, copyright © 2017, 2018, 2020 by Passion & Fire Ministries, Inc. Used by permission. All rights reserved. Scripture quotations marked NLT are taken from the Holy Bible, New Living Translation, copyright © 1996, 2004, 2015 by Tyndale House Foundation. Used by permission of Tyndale House Publishers, a Division of Tyndale House Ministries, Carol Stream, Illinois 60188. All rights reserved. Scripture quotations marked NASB are taken from the New American Standard Bible® (NASB), copyright © 1960, 1962, 1963, 1968, 1971, 1972, 1973, 1975, 1977, 1995, 2020 by The Lockman Foundation. Used by permission. www.Lockman.org. Scripture quotations marked KJV are taken from the Holy Bible, King James Version, in public domain.

Stock or custom editions of BroadStreet Publishing titles may be purchased in bulk for educational, business, ministry, fundraising, or sales promotional use. For information, please email orders@broadstreetpublishing.com.

General editor: Dr. Brian Simmons
Managing editor: William D. Watkins
Writer: Jeremy Bouma

Cover and interior by Garborg Design Works at GarborgDesign.com

Printed in the United States of America

21 22 23 24 25 5 4 3 2 1

Contents

From God's Heart to Yours

"God is love," says the apostle John, and "Everyone who loves is fathered by God and experiences an intimate knowledge of him" (1 John 4:7). The life of a Christ-follower is, at its core, a life of love—God's love of us, our love of him, and our love of others and ourselves because of God's love for us.

And this divine love is reliable, trustworthy, unconditional, other-centered, majestic, forgiving, redemptive, patient, kind, and more precious than anything else we can ever receive or give. It characterizes each person of the Trinity—Father, Son, and Holy Spirit—and so is as unlimited as they are. They love one another with this eternal love, and they reach beyond themselves to us, created in their image with this love.

How do we know such incredible truths? Through the primary source of all else we know about the one God—his Word, the Bible. Of course, God reveals who he is through other sources as well, such as the natural world, miracles, our inner life, our relationships (especially with him), those who minister on his behalf, and those who proclaim him to us and others. But the fullest and most comprehensive revelation we have of God and from him is what he has given us in the thirty-nine books of the Hebrew Scriptures (the Old Testament) and the twenty-seven books of the Christian Scriptures (the New Testament). Together, these sixty-six books present a compelling and telling portrait of God and his dealings with us.

It is these Scriptures that *The Passionate Life Bible Study Series* is all about. Through these study guides, we—the editors and writers of this series—seek to provide you with a unique and welcoming opportunity to delve more deeply into God's precious Word, encountering there his loving heart for you and all the others he loves. God wants you to know him more deeply, to love him more devoutly, and to share his heart with others more frequently and freely. To accomplish this, we have based this study guide series on The Passion Translation of the Bible, which strives to "unlock the passion of [God's] heart." It is "a heart-level translation, from the passion of God's heart to the passion of your heart," created to "kindle in you a burning desire for him and his heart, while impacting the church for years to come."[1]

In each study guide, you will find an introduction to the Bible book it covers. There you will gain information about that Bible book's authorship, date of composition, first recipients, setting, purpose, central message, and key themes. Each lesson following the introduction will take a portion of that Bible book and walk you through it so you will learn its content better while experiencing and applying God's heart for your own life and encountering ways you can share his heart with others. Along the way, you will come across a number of features we have created that provide opportunities for more life application and growth in biblical understanding:

Experience God's Heart

This feature focuses questions on personal application. It will help you live out God's Word, to bring the Bible into your world in fresh, exciting, and relevant ways.

Share God's Heart

This feature will help you grow in your ability to share with other people what you learn and apply in a given lesson. It provides guidance on how the lesson relates to growing closer to others, to enriching your fellowship with others. It also points the way to enabling you to better listen to the stories of others so you can bridge the biblical story with their stories.

The Backstory

This feature provides ancient historical and cultural background that illuminates Bible passages and teachings. It deals with then-pertinent religious groups, communities, leaders, disputes, business trades, travel routes, customs, nations, political factions, ancient measurements and currency…in short, anything historical or cultural that will help you better understand what Scripture says and means. You may also find maps and charts that will help you reimagine these groups, places, and activities. Finally, in this feature you will find references to additional Bible texts that will further illuminate the Scripture you are studying.

Word Wealth

This feature provides definitions and other illuminating information about key terms, names, and concepts, and how different ancient languages have influenced the biblical text. It also provides insight into the different literary forms in the Bible, such as prophecy, poetry, narrative history, parables, and letters, and how knowing the form of a text can help you better interpret and apply it. Finally, this feature highlights the most significant passages in a Bible book. You may be encouraged to memorize these verses or keep them before you in some way so you can actively hide God's Word in your heart.

Digging Deeper

This feature explains the theological significance of a text or the controversial issues that arise and mentions resources you can use to help you arrive at your own conclusions. Another way to dig deeper into the Word is by looking into the life of a biblical character or another person from church history, showing how that man or woman incarnated a biblical truth or passage. For instance, Jonathan Edwards was well known for his missions work among native American Indians and for his intellectual prowess in articulating the Christian faith; Florence Nightingale for the reforms she brought about in healthcare; Irenaeus for his fight against heresy; Billy Graham for his work in evangelism; Moses for the strength God gave him to lead the Hebrews and receive and communicate the law; Deborah for her work as a judge in Israel. This feature introduces to you figures from the past who model what it looks like to experience God's heart and share his heart with others.

The Extra Mile

While The Passion Translation's notes are extensive, sometimes students of Scripture like to explore more on their own. In this feature, we provide you with opportunities to glean more information from a Bible dictionary, a Bible encyclopedia, a reliable Bible online tool, another ancient text, and the like. Here you will learn how you can go the extra mile on a Bible lesson. And not just in study either. Reflection, prayer, discussion, and applying a passage in new ways provide even more opportunities to go the extra mile. Here you will find questions to answer and applications to make that will require more time and energy from you—if and when you have them to give.

As you can see above, each of these features has a corresponding icon so you can quickly and easily identify them.

You will find other helps and guidance through the lessons of these study guides, including thoughtful questions, application suggestions, and spaces for you to record your own reflections, answers, and action steps. Of course, you can also write in your own journal, notebook, computer, or other resource, but we have provided you with space for your convenience.

Also, each lesson will direct you into the introductory material and numerous notes provided in The Passion Translation. There each Bible book contains a number of aids supplied to help you better grasp God's words and his incredible love, power, knowledge, plans, and so much more. We want you to get the most out of your Bible study, especially using it to draw you closer to the One who loves you most.

Finally, at the end of each lesson you'll find a section called "Talking It Out." This contains questions and exercises for application that you can share, answer, and apply with your spouse, a friend, a coworker, a Bible study group, or any other individuals or groups who would like to walk with you through this material. As Christians, we gather together to serve, study, worship, sing, evangelize, and a host of other activities. We grow together, not just on our own. This section will give you ample opportunities to engage others with the content of each lesson so you can work it out in community.

We offer all of this to support you in becoming an even more faithful and loving disciple of Jesus Christ. A disciple in the ancient world was a student of her teacher, a follower of his master. Students study and followers follow. Jesus' disciples are to sit at his feet and listen and learn and then do what he tells them and shows them to do. We have created *The Passionate Life Bible Study Series* to help you do what a disciple of Jesus is called to do.

So go.

Read God's words.

Hear what he has to say in them and through them.

Meditate on them.

Hide them in your heart.

Display their truths in your life.

Share their truths with others.

Let them ignite Jesus' passion and light in all you say and do.

Use them to help you fulfill what Jesus called his disciples to do: "Now go in my authority and make disciples of all nations, baptizing them in the name of the Father, the Son, and the Holy Spirit. And teach them to faithfully follow all that I have commanded you. And never forget that I am with you every day, even to the completion of this age" (Matthew 28:19–20).

And through all of this, let Jesus' love nourish your heart and allow that love to overflow into your relationships with others (John 15:9–13). For it was for love that Jesus came, served, died, rose from the dead, and ascended into heaven. This love he gives us. And this love he wants us to pass along to others.

Why I Love the Book of Hebrews

Hebrews—there is nothing in the New Testament like this book. What makes it different?

Well, unlike Paul's other books (yes, despite the theories of some modern scholars, I do believe Paul was the human author), Hebrews is written to Jewish believers, to Christian Jews, instead of gentile believers. Hebrews shows us that Jesus makes sense against the background of the Jewish Scriptures. Every page of this book drips with truths about Jesus. Paul declares that Jesus is better than angels and everyone else in this universe. I really think the theme of Hebrews could be described as "Jesus is *greater than everything*!"

Hebrews also reveals that Jesus is the fulfillment of the Old Testament. His sacrifice is better, more enduring, than any sacrificial lamb offered in the Temple. Jesus' life and power are better, more enduring, than any priest who ever served or any king who ever reigned or any prophet who ever spoke. Jesus is greater than all! No other book gives us such a long list of reasons why Jesus is superior to religion, to Moses, to Joshua, to the sacrificial system, and to the priesthood. Jesus is the One who opened up a living access to the Father by the blood of his cross. Why do I love Hebrews? Because it helps me "look away...onto Jesus" (Hebrews 12:2) and focus my attention on him.

Hebrews presents a Jesus who is both gloriously divine (1:1–3) and wonderfully human (2:5–9; 5:7–10; 12:2–3). Most of Hebrews develops Christ's human achievements. As a man, Jesus restored dominion over the earth to humanity (2:5–9). He has regained for the human race what Adam lost in the Fall. Hebrews describes a Jesus who is everything we are supposed to be as bearers of God's image. Hebrews presents a Jesus who was able to do in his humanity what we could never do in our sinful condition:

he conquered sin, Satan, and death to restore us to God that we might rule with him in the world to come (2:14–18).

Some of my favorite verses (and chapters) in the Bible are found in Hebrews. I learn that Jesus is the same yesterday, today, and forever (13:8) and that faith trusts in unseen realities (11:1). I discover that we have already come into Zion's glory, the New Jerusalem (12:22), and, like a cloud, are surrounded by a myriad of holy witnesses (12:1). I find my soul-rest in Hebrews 4, an anchor for my soul in Hebrews 5, and reasons advancing past the elementary aspects of our faith in Hebrews 6. I love this book because it pushes me onward into the great inheritance we share in Christ.

Many scholars believe Hebrews was first written as a sermon (or series of sermons) to a congregation. Wouldn't you love to hear a sermon like the book of Hebrews? This could explain why there is no formal introduction to this letter like the ones we see in every other New Testament epistle.

Even so, this epistle is, I believe, one of God's greatest gifts to his church: an expository look at the person, life, covenant, sacrifice, and ministry of the Lord Jesus Christ, who is indeed greater than all others.

But perhaps the one theme that Hebrews is most famous for is *faith*. Who isn't stirred when reading through the "Hall of Faith" in chapter 11 and seeing all our faith-heroes as overcomers who won the victory? Some of them lived to see victory while others laid down their lives in martyrdom, but all of them were overcomers. Every man and woman can be thrilled to see that faith is the victory that overcomes the world.

Living and believing the truths of Hebrews will change your life.

- If you want to learn how to interpret the Old Testament, read Hebrews.

- If you want to see Jesus and be saturated with glory and power, read Hebrews.

- If you want your faith enlarged, stretched, and made stronger, read Hebrews.

Yes, I love this book, for it stirs me to remain faithful to God when I feel misunderstood or persecuted. It contains the radiance of Jesus to brighten my path and encourage my heart. It always contains warnings to cling tightly to Jesus, so much the more as we approach the end of the age.

Enjoy your journey through the spiritual lens given to you in the book of Hebrews.

> Wrap your heart tightly around the hope that lives within us, knowing that God always keeps his promises! Discover creative ways to encourage others and to motivate them toward acts of compassion, doing beautiful works as expressions of love. This is not the time to pull away and neglect meeting together, as some have formed the habit of doing. In fact, we should come together even more frequently, eager to encourage and urge each other onward as we anticipate that day dawning. (10:23–25)

Dr. Brian Simmons
General Editor

LESSON 1

Jesus Is Better Than...

The great Scottish minister William Barclay once said, "When we come to read the Letter to the Hebrews we come to read what is, for the person of today, the most difficult book in the whole New Testament."[2] Good to know we're in good company when it comes to approaching this rather enigmatic book!

Chances are you probably have heard very few sermons on Hebrews and probably have had few chances to engage the book yourself, either in a group or personal study. This is understandable as the letter is filled with obscure names like Melchizedek and ancient customs related to temple sacrifice. Yet the message this book bears is ripe for the church today, offering modern Christians revelation-insight into the very heart of God, for it unveils a remarkable unfolding of his revolutionary rescue plan for all the world through Jesus Christ.

The book of Hebrews presents the magnificent Jesus on every page, showing how he is better than everything that had come before and that would come after him. Hebrews is written for every believer today, for we have passed from darkness to light, from shadows to substance, and from doubt to the reality of faith. What once was a sign has now become substance; all the pictures and symbols of the Old Testament have found their fulfillment in Jesus.[3]

Hebrews is a divinely inspired composition given to show us the magnificence of Jesus as our glorious High Priest, better than the merely human high priest. He is better than the law, the angels, the system of temple worship, and greater than any high priest or religious structure. Because our royal Priest gave his sacred blood for us, we now have unrestricted access to the holiest place of all. With no veil and nothing hindering our intimacy with God, we can come with an unbelievable boldness to his mercy-throne where we encounter enough grace and mercy to empower us through every difficulty. We find our true life in his presence.[4]

Engage heaven's words that are now before you, reading them with spiritual hunger and a passion to embrace their truth, exploring the glory and grandeur of Jesus they describe, and living them out by his grace.

Authorship

Though Hebrews' authorship is debated today, many of the earliest church fathers taught that the apostle Paul wrote the letter to and for Jewish Christians.

In the Western church, ancient church historian Eusebius (CE 260–339) refers to an even earlier church father, Clement of Alexandria (CE 150–211), who confirms without question that Paul wrote Hebrews in the Hebrew language for the Hebrew people. Clement also thought that Luke then translated the book into Greek. Apologist and theologian Tertullian (160–215) attributed the book to Barnabas, while Bible scholar Jerome (345–419) and theologian Augustine (345–430) believed that Paul wrote Hebrews. Meanwhile, the Eastern church had all along accepted the letter as one of Paul's, and after Augustine, so did the Western church.

Paul's authorship of Hebrews then went unquestioned until the Protestant Reformation when Martin Luther, John Calvin, and others began to challenge it and propose different authors, such as Apollos or Clement of Rome. Along with Barnabas, Apollos, and Clement of Rome as possible authors, more contemporary scholars have suggested Priscilla, Luke, or another one of Paul's close associates.[5]

The bottom line is that Pauline authorship has never been

disproved, the early church accepted the book of Hebrews as God's inspired Word, and the truth of its message has stood the test of time. If Paul did not write the letter, the Spirit still inspired it, and God's people still embraced it as divine revelation.

Date of Composition

The book of Hebrews was most likely written sometime around CE 50–68, within two to three decades of Jesus' death and resurrection, and to a community of believers who had been Christians for a while. It had to have been written prior to Clement of Rome citing it as inspired Scripture (CE 95) and before the Roman war that destroyed the Jerusalem temple in 70 because the major themes in the book point to a group of Jewish Christians who may have been getting cold feet, wondering if the old temple system of worship and sacrifice was still relevant.[6] However, if the temple had already been destroyed, there wouldn't have been anything for these early believers to go back to. In fact, the writer assumes that the temple and the practices conducted in it are still taking place because he refers to them in the present tense (Hebrews 8:4–5, 13; 10:8–11; 13:10–11). As Bible commentator Philip Hughes says:

> Had the Jerusalem temple been in ruins and its ministry abruptly ended, the use of the past tense would have been expected throughout [the book of Hebrews]. Moreover, it would be incredible that the author should not then insistently have drawn his readers' attention to the striking fact that both temple and priesthood now belonged to past history, since this would have clinched his argument with visible proof that the former covenant had given way to the new, the Aaronic order to that of Melchizedek.[7]

- *What do you suppose may have been the draw to Jewish Christians to return to the religious system centered around the Jerusalem temple?*

- *Do you think you need to be in a building or have certain religious symbols nearby for you to worship God? Why or why not?*

Recipients of Hebrews

The inscription placed on the original document is "To the Hebrews," and its major themes point to a group of Jewish Christians who may have been tempted to return to Judaism. This sermon-letter is steeped in ancient Jewish practices—practices that would have been quite familiar to Jews who had converted from Judaism to Christianity. And yet, the letter still speaks to us today, whether we are converted Jews or gentiles, showing us why we can rest assured that by faith in Jesus Christ, we have entered into a new and better covenant with the one God through Jesus Christ.[8]

- *How familiar are you with the ancient Jewish practices and teachings that form the background of the book? Very familiar? Somewhat familiar? Or about as unfamiliar as one can be?*

- *What questions do you have about the connection between Judaism and Jewish practices and Jesus' fulfillment of them?*

- *As you come to the book of Hebrews, what are you hoping to get out of your study of it?*

THE BACKSTORY

Although this New Testament epistle was "To the Hebrews," who were the Hebrews during the first century, during the time of Jesus and the apostles? There were several Hebrew groups at this time, namely the Pharisees, Sadducees, Zealots, Sicarii, Herodians, and Essenes.

The Pharisees were distinguished by their strict observance of the Jewish law, whether it had to do with the Sabbath, food, or ritual cleansing practices. They also worked against priestly control of Judaism and moved several ceremonies from the temple and placed them in Jewish homes. This group held the spiritual high ground among the Jewish populace, exercising the greatest influence over congregations and "all acts of public worship, prayers, and sacrifices."[9]

The Sadducees were similar to the Pharisees, but they were far more political. The Sadducees were an aristocratic class that controlled the temple, and many of them were members of the Sanhedrin, the Jewish ruling body. They accepted only the written law of the Torah as binding while rejecting Jewish oral tradition. They also denied the resurrection of the dead and the existence of angels. They found favor with Roman authorities while frequently bowing to the Pharisees because of their great influence on the populace.

The Zealots were revolutionary and patriotic Jews with an active zeal for Jewish tradition. They wanted to use force to overthrow the Roman occupation of Palestine. According to scholar H. Wayne House, the Zealots "refused to pay taxes and terrorized their political opponents and Roman rulers."[10]

The Sicarii were an extreme Zealot group. They not only opposed Roman rule but also would linger in large crowds and use daggers to kill individuals who were friendly to Rome. Their name comes from the Greek word for "daggerman." They led the Jewish uprising against Rome in 66 CE, which ended with the destruction of the Jerusalem temple, their flight to Masada, and their deaths in 73.

The Herodians were Hellenistic Jews who derived their name from their political support of Herod and who wanted to restore the kingdom of David. They tended to be wealthy and had a good deal of political influence. They were not a religious group.

Finally, the Essenes, some of which may have lived at Qumran (the location of the Dead Sea Scrolls discoveries), rejected the worship at the temple as polluted, had more rigid Sabbath-law requirements than the Pharisees did, and strictly observed ceremonial washings, daily prayers, and the continuous study of the Old Testament. They believed in communal property and generally refrained from marriage.[11]

- *Just as there were a variety of Hebrew groups in Jesus' day, so there is a diversity of Christian groups today. What are some of these, and what are some of the differences you see between them?*

- *What are some of the beliefs and practices these Christian groups share?*

- *What are some of the core beliefs and practices that define your Christian faith?*

- *Do you believe they are essential for all Christian believers? Why or why not?*

Setting and Purpose

The purpose of Hebrews becomes more evident the further you read through it: the author is trying to prevent its recipients from abandoning their Christian faith and returning to Judaism. Along the way, the author teaches them—and us—about the superiority of Christ above the religious institutions of Moses and the Old Testament. Hebrews is filled with references to the old sacrificial system and priesthood of ancient Israel and explains how Jesus' death has replaced this old religious system, making it the perfect book to understand how Jesus' story fulfills Israel's story.[12]

- *Have you ever felt the pull to abandon your Christian faith and return to your way of living or believing before you met Christ? If so, what do you suppose led to this temptation? If not, what has prevented you from leaving your faith behind?*

Key Themes

The book of Hebrews connects several themes together that explore the better-than revelation of Jesus Christ, including a deep dive into the person and work of Christ; the relationship of the new covenant to the old covenant; warnings against turning away from Christ in rebellion and unbelief; the reality of heaven, where God keeps his throne and where our ultimate redemption and atonement took place; and the significance of faith and what it means to persevere in it.

One of the central areas of study in Christian theology is what is called *Christology*. This is the study of Jesus Christ's person and work. The letter of Hebrews is a full-on course in Christology. The revelation of Jesus fills the pages of Hebrews, and absorbing it and applying it to your life will set you free.[13]

As you read through the sampling of passages below, list some key christological concepts you find and what they reveal about who Jesus is and what he has done for us.

1:1–3

2:14–15

4:14–15

10:11–14

The Core Message

In many ways, the central message of the book of Hebrews comes to us from the start, in the very first few verses: "Throughout our history God has spoken to our ancestors by his prophets in many different ways. The revelation he gave them was only a fragment at a time, building one truth upon another. But to us living in these last days, God now speaks to us openly in the language of a Son, the appointed Heir of everything, for through him God created the panorama of all things and all time" (1:1–2).

EXPERIENCE GOD'S HEART

- *Re-read these first few verses of Hebrews. How has God spoken to you personally about himself through the "language of a Son, the appointed Heir of everything," Jesus Christ? What has God said to you about himself through Jesus' life, death, and resurrection?*

- *Now read verse 6 of chapter 8 and verse 40 of chapter 11, which carries forward this revelation-truth that what God communicates to us through Jesus is "better than." In what ways have you personally experienced the truth that Jesus is better than what you had before you met him?*

SHARE GOD'S HEART

- *Part of what it means to be a Christian is to be available and faithful vessels through which God speaks to others about himself—just as the author of Hebrews was in writing down God's revelation-insight into the person and work of Christ. In what ways can you similarly share with those you know what God has spoken to us about himself through Jesus?*

- *Jesus Christ is the better-than revelation of God—better than the old religious systems of ritual and regulation, better than the worldly systems of power and pleasure, better than the personal systems of accumulation and self-actualization. How might it look in your life to share this aspect of the heart of God with others?*

Talking It Out

Since Christians grow in community, not just in solitude, here are some questions you may want to discuss with another person or in a group. Each "Talking It Out" section is designed with this purpose in mind.

1. Read through the entire book of Hebrews in one sitting. As you approach studying this letter, what are your biggest questions based on what you read? What most confuses you? Pray for guidance in the coming weeks that God would impart his revelation-insight from his Word to your heart.

2. The New Testament scholar N. T. Wright explains, "Jesus exploded into the life of ancient Israel—the life of the whole world, in fact—not as a teacher of timeless truths, nor as a great moral example, but as the one through whose life, death, and resurrection God's rescue operation was put into effect, and the cosmos turned its great corner at last."[14] Hebrews illustrates in bright, bold colors the truth that Jesus defies our expectations of God's operation in the world. Discuss what has surprised you about God's work in your life, in your church, and in your culture?

3. The book of Hebrews presents Jesus as both fully human (yet without sin) and fully God. When you reflect on what Jesus has accomplished, what about his humanity made this possible and what about his divinity paved the way? For instance, God is invisible (Colossians 1:15; 1 Timothy 1:17), but Jesus was not during his life on earth. And yet, as a human prophet and as the One through whom creation came, he uniquely and more fully revealed God and his truth to us (Hebrews 1:1–3; cf. John 1:14–18). How do you think Jesus' humanity and also his deity made this achievement possible? (This will give you a taste of the work theologians do when they consider the doctrine of Christology.)

4. The theme of faith and persevering in faith is an important one in the book of Hebrews. In what specific ways do we need persevering faith in our day and age? Now pray for the Spirit's strength "to run life's marathon race with passion and determination" (Hebrews 12:1).

LESSON 2

Jesus, God's Message to Us

(1:1–2:18)

There was a time when the latest and greatest way to send a message across long distances was tapping out a code through electrical signals over a wire strung between two telegraph stations, then writing it down and translating it before delivering the original message to the recipient. Today, you would text out that same message on a device in your pocket that would have seemed futuristic not that long ago. And if you're in a hurry, you might swap emojis for words and call it good. Same message, different and better transmission.

The book of Hebrews opens with the glorious revelation-insight that God has spoken his same message of love and salvation to the world but in a new and better way. No longer through the old covenant of laws and sacrifices, God's heart has been unveiled before us through a new covenant forged in a person—God's own Son!

Jesus Christ was born a real live human being, sharing in our very flesh and blood, to rule with justice and righteousness in ways not evident before. Although he lived for a short time lower than the angels, he was crowned with glory and honor after suffering for our sins on the cross, serving as a true pioneer for our ultimate salvation—and broadcasting God's message of love loud and clear. Perhaps the greatest revelation-message God could unfold through Jesus is the reality that through his life and death, we can be made children of God, fully embraced as Christ's brothers and sisters. What's more: as our very human King-Priest who suffered the same temptations in this life, he is able to help us in our own times of need.

Jesus is God's message to us, which is far better than how he communicated to us in the past. So listen with open ears and a welcoming heart to what he has to say to you this day!

Jesus, the Language of God

The New Testament was originally written in Greek. This original in Hebrews 1:1 is "God spoke in different times in different parts." That is, he reveals one piece and then another, like pieces of a puzzle, with one piece complementing the other. The Aramaic, another language spoken in Jesus' day, can be translated, "God spoke to our ancestors by all methods and at any price" or "in every way, shape, and form." In other words, "by sample and by example God reveals his ways progressively, building on previous understandings, leading us into Christ's fullness."[15] Verse 2 makes clear God changed his language: he has spoken through a Son. We speak in different human languages, such as English, Spanish, French, and German. God has used human languages to reveal his written word, such as Hebrew and Greek. But the fullest and most magnificent speech from God is his very Son, Jesus Christ. Jesus is God's own language. The Sonship of Jesus is the language he now uses to speak to us rather than simply by his prophets.[16]

- *Make a list of all the ways God spoke to his people in the past before the coming of Christ.*

- *What difference has the Word made flesh made in God's communication to us? Consider how one's personal presence and face-to-face speech differs from one's written communication in emails, letters, articles, and books. What would you notice about that person when you met face-to-face that you may not have realized through these other forms of communication? Now put yourself in the shoes of Jesus' disciples. What do you imagine they experienced and finally understood about God when they came face-to-face with his Son?*

DIGGING DEEPER

The opening verses of Hebrews supports an important aspect of Christian belief: Jesus is God. The Nicene Creed, recited by Christians from ages past and around the world, reminds us of this foundational belief:

> We believe in one God, the Father Almighty, the maker of heaven and earth, of all things visible and invisible.
> And in one Lord Jesus Christ, the Son of God, the begotten of God the Father, the Only-begotten, that is of the essence of the Father. God of God, Light of Light, true God of true God, begotten and not made; of the very same nature of the Father, by Whom all things came into being, in heaven and on earth, visible and invisible.

Hebrews 1:3 teaches this exact truth: "The Son is the dazzling radiance of God's splendor, the exact expression of God's true nature—his mirror image!" This basic Christian teaching is known as the *incarnation*—the historical reality that the Son of God assumed our human nature and became a man in the person of Jesus. As the apostle John explains, "the Living Expression became a man and lived among us!" (John 1:14).

- *Why do you suppose it is crucial to our faith that we uphold the truth that Jesus is truly God, that the Son assumed our human nature while remaining fully divine?*

- *What does it mean to you that God was incarnated, living this same earthly life that you live?*

God's Answer to Our Sin Problem

Part of the message God has spoken to us through the language of Jesus is the reality that "He accomplished for us the complete cleansing of sins" (Hebrews 1:3). It isn't that we no longer sin, for the Holy Spirit continues to enable us to work out our salvation through the process of sanctification. It's that we have a complete forgiveness that's permanent. Through his Son, God has told us that he has accomplished our purification from sins and has opened the door into his presence. Another word for this is *atonement*. This is a very Jewish concept, coming from the old covenant where an atoning sacrifice would be offered in place of the people of God, its blood given in their place to pay the price for their sins, purifying them and paving the way for their forgiveness. This old covenant provision foreshadowed the better things to come in Christ's own atoning sacrifice on the cross—an act that secured God's new covenant with us.

- *What sins has Jesus cleansed for all human beings? Are there any exceptions?*

- *What about the ones in your own personal life, the ones you continue to struggle with and the ones from past memory? Has Jesus' death handled those too?*

- *Now spend time in prayer thanking him for this cleansing from sin.*

Jesus, Greater Than the Angels

After telling us that Jesus is the better-than revelation from God, the writer of Hebrews makes the case that Jesus is greater than God's spiritual messengers, the angels. Why the writer makes this argument has been a matter of speculation. Some commentators think that the audience of Hebrews was tempted by some form of angel worship or thought Christ to be a subordinate spiritual being to the angels. In Paul's letter to the Colossians, he certainly addresses a problem that was threatening his readers—namely, resisting those who were tempting the new Christians to engage in "angel worship" (Colossians 2:18), which is why Paul says earlier in his letter that all that was created "both in the heavenly realm and on the earth...was all created through [the Son] and for his purpose" (1:16). Angels came through the Son, not the Son through angels, making the Son higher than the angels.

Another possibility for the first readers of Hebrews is that they needed to understand that Jesus' role as Creator and Revealer showed he was greater than the angels and their role as deliverers of God's earlier revelation:

> The giving of the [Mosaic] law...was held by the Jews to be the greatest inspiration of the old revelation and it came through a twofold mediation. Moses, who received the law and passed it on to the people, had it delivered to him by an angel or angels (cf. Acts vii. 53; Gal. iii. 19; Heb. ii. 2). It is possible that these angelic bodies were looked upon as the highest of God's creatures. It was necessary, therefore, to show that the revelation through them was inferior to the revelation in Christ. This the writer does by bringing out the surpassing dignity of the Son while at the same time showing that the angels were merely servants. He further

> points to the kingship of Christ and to the angels as subservient. He is the Creator while they are His creatures sent forth to serve the heirs of salvation.[17]

Regardless of the author's reason for showing Jesus' superiority to the angels, the case that he makes provides a number of important contrasts between the angels and Jesus, the Son of God.

- *Complete a chart to sketch the differences this writer establishes in Hebrews 1:5–14. In the left column, record what the writer says about Jesus, the Son. In the right column, record what the writer says about angels.*

- *After completing this chart, consider what the writer says about Jesus' greater-than stature. Why is Jesus greater than the angels? What is it about who and what Jesus is and his relationship to the Father that makes him greater than angelic beings?*

Hebrews 1:4 reminds us that Jesus "is infinitely greater than angels, for he inherited a rank and a Name far greater than theirs." Angels are celestial beings who serve God, having been created by him to perform the work of God, often as messengers. They are of a higher order than humans, with greater power and might. Yet Jesus is higher and greater than these spiritual beings, with a higher "rank" and "Name" than they have. This word for "Name" is *Ha-Shem*, "in the Aramaic, the common title for God. This elevates the meaning of the passage much clearer than in the Greek, for Jesus is now given the 'Name,' that is, he has the title of God (*Ha-Shem*, the Name)."[18]

Jesus receives several names/titles in the New Testament. Look up the passages that follow and jot down the names/titles of Jesus that you find and research what they mean.

Matthew 1:21

Matthew 1:23

Matthew 16:16

Mark 8:31

Luke 24:46

John 1:1, 14

John 1:29

John 1:30

John 1:41

Philippians 2:11

Titus 1:3

- *Which of the above names are most significant to you? Why?*

"But you are 'I am,'" Hebrews 1:12 says of Jesus' personhood, his identity as the better-than Name far greater than the angels. This *'I am'* identity as presented is translated from the Aramaic, which is literally "you are as you are." This is a variation of the name of God revealed to Moses in Exodus 3:14, "I am who I am" (NLT). There is an obvious connection here to that incident and endorses the truth that the preincarnate Christ was the One who appeared to Moses in the burning bush.[19]

Jesus references this same truth about himself in John 8:58, saying, "I give you this eternal truth: I have existed long before Abraham was born, for I am!" Clearly, Jesus identifies himself with the "I am that I am" of Exodus 3:14 (KJV).

- *Read John 8:54–59 and Exodus 3:11–15, then read the commentary on these passages from https://www.bibleref.com/Exodus/3/Exodus-3-14.html. What insight does this commentary and the previous passages provide that helps you better understand Hebrews 1:12 and who Jesus is?*

A Warning Not to Drift from Truth

At the beginning of Hebrews 2, there is a clear warning and exhortation to engage and attend to the deep truths of the Christian faith "so that we do not drift off course" and "despise the very truths that give us life" (vv. 1, 3). Some of the deep truths covered in the book of Hebrews are the divinity of Jesus, his full humanity, the necessity of his suffering and death, the sufficiency of his sacrifice to cover our sins, and the perseverance of faith.

- *What are some of the manifestations of people drifting from and despising "the very truths that give us life"?*

- *Why do you think the truths of Christ face such opposition today? Be as specific as you can.*

- *What do you think you can do to support Christ's truths in your home, workplace, and other areas of influence? List at least two steps you can take and consider how you can begin to implement them in the next few weeks.*

SHARE GOD'S HEART

Sometimes there are people in our own lives—a son or sister, a friend or fellow believer—who drift off course from the fundamental truths of the Christian faith and from Christ himself.

- *Do you know anyone who has drifted off course or despised the truth of Christ? If so, who? What was their story? Why did they drift or despise?*

- *How might it look to walk with someone you know through seasons of drifting in order to warn them against despising "the very truths that give us life"?*

- *Pray for them now, and commit to sharing with them with grace God's truthful heart.*

Miracles and Gifts

The author of Hebrews tells us that God validated the ministry of the apostles "who heard [the Lord] firsthand [and] confirmed their accuracy…with signs, astonishing wonders, all kinds of powerful miracles, and by the gifts of the Holy Spirit, which he distributed as he desired" (2:3–4). Signs, wonders, and miracles were components of the ministries of the New Testament believer to confirm the truths of Christ. "There is no place in Scripture to indicate that any of the works of Jesus or his apostles should not be seen today."[20] And the Greek word for "distribution" is "often used for dividing an inheritance. The word *gifts* is implied in the text and made explicit" in The Passion Translation.[21]

- *What sort of signs, wonders, and miracles were these—particularly as we find them exercised in the book of Acts? (See Acts 3:1–10; 5:12–16; and 12:1–18 for examples.)*

- *What are the gifts the Holy Spirit continues to distribute as he desires in order to validate the ministry and testimony of his followers in these last days (see Romans 12:6–8 and 1 Corinthians 12:1–11)?*

Jesus Brings Many Sons to Glory

The writer of Hebrews continues his exploration of our Savior's better-than identity by discussing Jesus' *incarnation*—the doctrine that God became man. Before shifting to Christ's ministry on earth, "[experiencing] death's bitterness on behalf of everyone" (Hebrews 2:9), the writer begins with his heavenly exaltation, declaring: "For you have placed everything under his authority," and "we see Jesus, *who as a man*, lived for a short time lower than the angels and has now been crowned with glorious honor because of what he suffered in his death" (vv. 8–9).

- *What does it mean that everything has been put under Jesus' authority? What all does this include?*

EXPERIENCE GOD'S HEART

Read Hebrews 2:11 again: "Jesus, the Holy One, makes us holy. And as sons and daughters, we now belong to his same Father, so he is not ashamed or embarrassed to introduce us as his brothers and sisters!" Wow! Consider the revelation-truth that Jesus is not ashamed or embarrassed to embrace, name, and *announce* you as his brother or sister.

- *What does this embracing tell you about the heart of God?*

- *What does this mean to you personally, that Jesus embraces you as his brother or sister?*

Jesus, One of Us

This passage in the book of Hebrews reminds us that Jesus was a real live human being, becoming human "to fully identify with us...[taking] hold of our humanity in every way" to the point of taking on "flesh and blood" like his children. Now, this may sound self-evident, that Jesus was a real live human being, but for some early Christians it was an incredibly controversial belief. You see, certain people known as *Docetists* believed Jesus wasn't really a human, wasn't a *physical* human being. They taught he only *looked* like one, appearing in a spiritual sense. They couldn't wrap their minds around the fact that the second person of the Trinity would stoop so low as to become one of us—and yet he did, sharing in our flesh and blood by assuming our human nature.

- *In what ways did Jesus fully identify with us? List those ways here.*

- *Why do you suppose it was necessary that he identified fully with our humanity? Check out Hebrews 2:14–18 for some insight on this.*

- *One of the ways Jesus identified with us was that he "endured every test and temptation" (2:18). What sorts of temptations do you suppose he endured? Why did he endure them, for what purpose?*

Let's Get Personal

Sending messages to one another today is so much easier and faster than it was in the past. And yet, an electronic message does not compare to the more personally delivered face-to-face message, especially when it comes from family and friends. The God of the universe has sent us the most personal message of all, and he did it through his own Son, Jesus of Nazareth, Jesus the Messiah. Through Jesus and those who knew him best—the apostles—God has unfolded the fullness of his heart for us and for all others who are willing to listen.

- *How have you embraced and applied the message of Jesus and his apostles in your own life?*

Talking It Out

1. Hebrews 1:2 tells us, "To us living in these last days, God now speaks to us openly in the language of a Son, the appointed Heir of everything, for through him God created the panorama of all things and all time." Share with your group how God has specifically unfolded his heart to you through the message of his Son.

2. What does it mean to you personally that Jesus Christ accomplished for you "the complete cleansing of sins" (1:3)?

3. Have you ever found yourself drifting off course from the truths of Christ or perhaps struggling with certain truths that give us life? Which truths, and what was that experience like? How can you come alongside a fellow believer who may be struggling with one or more of Christianity's core truths?

4. What does it mean to you that Christ was a real live human being?

5. Given what Hebrews 2:14–18 reveal about why the Son became human, how can you use these truths to help others understand why the Son became like us?

LESSON 3

Jesus, Our Faithful Example

(3:1–4:13)

In one of his classic books on Christian discipleship, the late pastor and author Eugene Peterson describes our journey with Christ as a "long obedience in the same direction." One aspect of the disciple-life with Jesus is *faithful* obedience, which is the idea of perseverance. However, as Peterson writes:

> Perseverance is not the result of *our* determination, it is the result of God's faithfulness. We survive in the way of faith not because we have extraordinary stamina but because God is righteous, because God sticks with us. Christian discipleship is a process of…making a map of the faithfulness of God, not charting the rise of our enthusiasm. It is out of such a reality that we acquire perseverance.[22]

The writer of Hebrews offers us a spectrum of faithfulness and perseverance in the faith that culminates in chapter 11, but it largely begins here in chapter 3, starting with Jesus and then pivoting to a remarkable example of unfaithfulness with the children of Israel. Jesus is our faithful example, and we are called to fasten our thoughts fully onto him because he was "faithful to the Father who appointed him, in the same way that Moses was a model of faithfulness in what was entrusted to him" (3:2). But while Moses was a faithful servant as a *part* of God's people, Jesus was a faithful Son *over* God's people, enduring temptation and suffering the cross's shame as our Apostle and King-Priest.

Our own faithfulness arises when we fix our eyes on Jesus' example by turning toward and responding to the living God rather than being led astray by sin and unbelief. Our twenty-first century life flies by in texts and tweets, in instant news and posts. May we heed Hebrews' words: "Fasten your thoughts fully onto Jesus," taking the long view in our walk with Christ by entering into his faith-life this day and every day.

Jesus, Greater Than Moses

The book of Hebrews reveals that "each of you is invited to the feast of your heavenly calling" (3:1). The Greek phrase "heavenly calling" implies "an invitation to a celestial feast. It could also be translated 'you are called to share the life of heaven.' This calling originates in heaven and draws us into heaven." In the Aramaic, this phrase can be translated "called with a calling [from heaven]," which is the Aramaic title of Leviticus, and there "refers to the calling of the Levites as priests."[23]

- *Think back to your own invitation to enter into the life God promises in Jesus, when you accepted it and were fully embraced by the heart of God into his forever family. What is that story of personal invitation?*

Under the old covenant, Moses, the Torah, and the prophets that followed were God's voice and through them believers affixed their attention to Yahweh. But under the new covenant, we have the more complete revelation of Yahweh in Jesus. Jesus is God incarnate, the fullness of his majesty, truth, and goodness. The written Word points to him, is fulfilled in him, is alive with him. The very Center of history and the very Heart of divine revelation has arrived forevermore, and his name is Jesus. He is the One on whom believers are now called to fasten their eyes. He is the One who has made us holy, and we embrace him as our Apostle and King-Priest.

- *Why do you suppose it is vital that we fasten our thoughts fully onto Jesus?*

- *How does this look practically?*

Commenting on Jesus' titles of Apostle and King-Priest in Hebrews 3:1, Bible translator Brian Simmons says: "God joins the apostolic and priestly ministries together in Christ. An apostle will always release God's people into their priestly calling of entering into the holy of holies without going through a system, a church or a person."[24]

Furthermore, the Messiah's fulfillment of the offices of King and Priest was predicted in Zechariah 6:12–13 (NASB):

> "The Lord of armies says this: 'Behold, there is a Man whose name is Branch, for He will branch out from where He is; and He will build the temple of the Lord. Yes, it is He who will build the temple of the Lord, and He who will bear the majesty and sit and rule on His throne. So He will be a priest on His throne, and the counsel of peace will be between the two offices.'"

The Branch is the Messiah who still was to come, and he will be both King (ruling from his throne) and Priest (on his throne), thereby bringing together the two offices in harmony.

- *In what way are the ministries of apostle and king-priest joined in Christ? How was he faithful to the Father who appointed him as our Apostle and King-Priest (see vv. 2–6)?*

The word "King-Priest" is from the Aramaic, which uses a word for "a priest not of the Levitical order" (see lesson 6 for background on the Levites). Jesus could not be a "High Priest" according to the Mosaic law, for he was not a descendant of Aaron. It was from Aaron's line that the Hebrew priesthood came (Exodus

28:1). Jesus was, however, of the tribe of Judah, the same tribe from which Israel's King David originated (Matthew 1:2–6, 16–17). So the word here for "priest" is not *cohen* but the Aramaic word *kumrea*, the word used for Jethro (Exodus 3:1) and Melchizedek (Genesis 14:18), both of whom were priests before the Mosaic law was revealed and enacted. Jesus becomes a priest but not under the requirements of the law. His priesthood is pre-law. And he was born through the line of David—the line from which the Messiah, the Savior, was prophesied to come (2 Samuel 7:8–16; Psalm 89:20–29; Isaiah 9:6–7; Matthew 1:1; Luke 1:26–35).[25]

- *Look up and read at least three or four of the passages listed in the above paragraph. Then jot down below what you learned from them, especially anything that concerns Jesus and his messianic roles as king and priest.*

The writer of Hebrews reveals that "Moses served God faithfully in all he gave him to do" (3:5), and this work served as a prophetic illustration for the things that were to come in Christ. "That is, Moses saw and believed that the [wilderness] tabernacle and all its furnishings were an illustration of something greater that God would unveil later on" in history.[26] For Christ was more than a servant; he was the Father's faithful Son.

- *What are some differences between a servant and a son?*

- *Now consider what you know about Moses and what you know about Jesus. In what ways did Moses show he was God's servant? In what ways did Jesus show that he was God's Son?*

Secrets from Psalm 95

Read through all of Psalm 95, which the writer of Hebrews quotes in 3:11–14. Make a list of observations from this psalm to prepare for studying the part where it is quoted in Hebrews.

- *The psalmist implores the reader to "listen" to Yahweh's voice. How do you think it looks to assume this posture? What practical steps can you take to "listen" to his voice in your life?*

- *Hardness of heart is something that makes God angry, the psalmist reveals. What does it mean to be hard-hearted? Have you ever experienced this yourself or seen its evidence in others? How did you deal with it?*

- *The psalmist references "days of their rebellion, when they were tested in the wilderness." What is this referring to in Israel's history? What led to this wilderness wandering? See, for example, Exodus 17:1–7; Numbers 14; 32:6–13.*

Even though the people of God were wandering in the wilderness as discipline for their rebellion, they saw Yahweh's miracle-working power at work in their lives. Look up the following passages and list some of the specific miracles God performed on behalf of his people. What do his actions reveal about his heart?

Exodus 15:22–27

Exodus 16:1–21

Exodus 19–20

Exodus 24

Numbers 9:15–23

The writer of Hebrews reveals that Yahweh's heart "grieved" over his people's sinful rebellion because they refused to listen and learn his ways. The Greek word *orge* that appears in both 3:11 and 4:3 is "used for any emotion of extreme passion, usually anger."[27]

- *Consider how you have "grieved" the heart of God in your refusal to listen through your own sinful rebellion. What does our refusal to learn God's ways and our rebellion reveal about this aspect of God's character, that he would be "grieved" over what we do and how we act?*

EXPERIENCE GOD'S HEART

Hebrews 3:12 exhorts, "search your hearts every day, my brothers and sisters, and make sure that none of you has evil or unbelief hiding within you. For it will lead you astray, and make you unresponsive to the living God."

- *How do you go about doing this each and every day—searching your heart, making sure you don't have any evil or unbelief hiding within you? How might you be able to more fully enter into such searching?*

- *Explain how having evil or unbelief hiding within you will lead you astray, making you unresponsive to sin. How are the two connected—harboring evil or unbelief within and being led astray? Have you seen the truth of this played out in your own experience of God's heart or the lives of others? Explain.*

SHARE GOD'S HEART

"This is the time to encourage each other to never be stubborn or hardened by sin's deceitfulness," the writer says in 3:13.

- *How can we go about living this exhortation practically with one another, encouraging one another not to be stubborn or become hardened? If you know anyone in your life who needs this encouragement, pray for them now, asking the Lord for wisdom to come alongside them in their spiritual walk with Christ.*

Hebrews 4:3 reveals that "God's works have all been completed from the foundation of the world." Another way of saying this is "God's works have been completed, even though the world has fallen."

> The Greek word *katabole* means "to fall down," "to throw down." It is most often used for "laying down a foundation," but it can imply the fall of humanity through sin. Even though the world has fallen, God's works have already been accomplished, unhindered by the sin of man. God's finished works supersede the brokenness of our planet.[28]

- *How can God's works be completed when the Bible is clear that Christ will come again, establish his kingdom, and judge each person for what he has done (see the book of Revelation, for example)? Hint: It has to do with God's power, knowledge, and sovereignty. See Psalm 33:11; 135:6; Proverbs 16:9, 33; Daniel 4:34–35.*

- *What are some specific works of God that have been completed in history so far? Why is it so significant that they are complete?*

The Faith-Rest Life

The story of Israel is bound up with their captivity in Egypt, laboring under the yoke of slavery until Yahweh acted as their Redeemer and freed them from bondage, leading them out of captivity as slaves and into freedom as his children. However, the book of Hebrews explains that those who first heard the good news of God's deliverance (the gospel, if you will), "failed to enter into the realm of faith's rest because of their unbelieving hearts" (Hebrews 4:6). There were those who were excluded from God's promised rest in the promised land on the grounds of their disobedience. You can find more about that story in Numbers 13 and 14.

- *After reading those chapters in Numbers, identify the people who led the way against following God's call into the promised land.*

- *Why did they make the report that they did, and what influence did they have on others?*

The thing about this backstory is that it is still *our* story in this day and age. People continue to fail to enter into the realm of faith's rest because of their unbelief. And yet, there is amazing revelation-insight that offers each of us a promise straight from the heart of God!

- *What does it tell you about God's heart that, despite our failure to enter faith's rest, people "still have the opportunity to enter into the faith-rest life and experience the fulfillment of the promise" (Hebrews 4:6)?*

- *What do you suppose it means that God's appointed day to enter into this rest is called "Today"? Why might it be called "Today," and what is implied in this name? What should this mean for us, for others?*

- *How do you suppose it looks to be eager to enter into this rest? Why should we be eager for it?*

- *Read 4:12 again: "For we have the living Word of God, which is full of energy, like a two-mouthed sword. It will even penetrate to the very core of our being where soul and spirit, bone and marrow meet! It interprets and reveals the true thoughts and secret motives of our hearts." What a rich description of God's Word in our lives! What all do we learn about the Bible and how it operates as it is applied to our hearts?*

EXPERIENCE GOD'S HEART

"Soul and spirit are the immaterial parts of every person that make us who we are," and "joint and bone marrow are the physical aspects of our existence. All of this combined forms our humanity."[29] God's Word has the ability to uncover our hidden aspects and make them known, which is a gracious gift straight from the heart of God to our own hearts.

- *How have you experienced this application of his powerful Word in your life?*

- *How has its application shaped your experience of God's heart?*

Hebrews 4:13 reminds us, "There is not one person who can hide their thoughts from God, for nothing that we do remains a secret, and nothing created is concealed." And yet we all follow in the footsteps of our ancient ancestors, Adam and Eve, hiding in the bushes when God's heart seeks to approach us in the garden of life.

- *Do you tend to hide from God? Do you try to hide some of your thoughts or motives or even certain sins? Explain.*

- *How have you experienced his heart on the other side when those thoughts, motives, and sinful secrets have been exposed?*

- *The rest of verse 13 says, "everything is exposed and defenseless before his eyes, to whom we must render an account." How should this impact our walk with God, knowing that all our thoughts, motives, and sins are exposed before his eyes?*

- *Furthermore, what should it mean to you and your daily walk with Christ that each of us must one day give an account for everything we do (Romans 2:5–11; 2 Corinthians 5:10)?*

The Long View

It's no secret that we live in a fast-paced world, ruled by social media, hot takes, and cable news sound bites. Taking the long view of life and eschewing immediate gratification by cultivating a long-distance, well-paced faith seems out of place in a world of instant news and Instagram. Yet this lesson challenges every believer to take the long view, fixing our eyes on our example of a "long obedience in the same direction" in order to experience the life-giving faith-rest our Savior offers, Today. For he is our better-than faithful example!

Talking It Out

1. What barriers to living a life of faithful obedience do you find in our world? What barriers to embracing a "long obedience in the same direction" do you find in your own life?

2. In what specific areas of your life do you need to more fully fix your eyes on Christ? Perhaps it is trusting the Lord with your finances, thinking more honestly of yourself, facing and repenting from secret sins, or resting more in God's love and goodness. Whatever it is, consider reaching out to a fellow Christian for counsel, accountability, and support. Also offer those areas to the Lord and commit to fixing your thoughts on Christ in order to live more faithfully.

3. When was a time when you tested the Lord, rebelling and hardening your heart against him? What was that like, and what happened? How can you more fully be encouraged and encourage others to never be stubborn or hardened by sin's deceitfulness?

4. Have you entered into the Lord's promised salvation-rest "Today"? If so, when was that day, and what was that like? If not, what's holding you back from embracing Christ's call to experience his faith-rest for yourself?

5. Name something specific that was uncovered in your heart and life, something that the powerful living Word of God in your life revealed to you. Describe what that experience was like.

LESSON 4

Jesus, Our Compassionate King-Priest

(4:14–5:10)

It is utterly remarkable, when you think about it, that the Creator of the universe sought out a relationship with his crowning-achievement creatures from the start. Even when Adam and Eve rebelled against God, ruining all of the created order and wrecking the intimate connection between us and him, God returned to his creation—but in the most unexpected way: becoming the ultimate King-Priest, chosen from among his creatures, one who actually understands the ongoing fallout from that initial rebellion.

One of the most unexpected things our lesson reveals about this better-than King-Priest is that God understands what we go through in this life. Whether joblessness or homelessness, loneliness or sickness—God understands! But it's more than that: because not only does Jesus, the God of the universe, our very Creator, understand our frailty, he *sympathizes with it.* Not only does he sympathize with the sin we experience in life at the hands of others, but he also sympathizes with the sins we continue to struggle with personally.

The reason why is that the appointment of Jesus Christ as our better-than King-Priest mirrored the earthly high priest under the old covenant in an important way: he was chosen from among the people. Because God called and glorified him, not from self-appointment but from divine appointment, Jesus experienced everything life has to offer through all his suffering, and he learned to listen to and obey his Father. Proving himself perfect in all his ways, he became "the source of eternal salvation to all those who listen to him and obey" (Hebrews 5:9).

All of what we discover in today's reading gives us great hope and great reason to listen and believe and obey—especially given the revelation-insight that the writer offers: "Draw near freely and boldly to where grace is enthroned, to receive mercy's kiss and discover the grace we urgently need to strengthen us in our time of weakness" (4:16).

Our Approachable King-Priest

The front end of our lesson acts as a crossroads for the rest of book, a sort of rest stop before carrying on with the theologically rich exploration of Jesus Christ's High Priesthood. Here, the author steeps us in the revelation depths of Jesus' sonship, the importance of faith, and a consideration of our sin and weakness. And he does so with the exhortation *krateo*: "hold fast" or "cling" to all that we know to be true about our faith.

- *What is it that you know to be true about such realities as God, the gospel, and our life with Christ? List some of those things here.*

- *Why do you suppose it is vital to our experience of God's heart and our life with our compassionate King-Priest to cling, which carries with it the connotation of "commitment to something" and "remaining true to someone"?*

EXPERIENCE GOD'S HEART

Now consider the next revelation-insight the writer unfolds before us, exposing an unbelievable aspect of God's heart: the Creator of the universe "sympathizes with us in our frailty." Another word for "frailty" is "weakness," which refers to anything in this life on the other side of the fall that has been ruined by human rebellion. We do not live in a world that operates in the way it's supposed to be—from sickness to emotional struggle to moral weakness through temptation. And Jesus feels the suffering you're going through. He bears an unplumbable depth of compassion for what it is like to experience all of this fallen life—having endured the same sort of frailty and experienced the same sorts of temptation.

- *How does Jesus our King-Priest understand the frailty of our humanity? What sorts of temptations do you suppose Jesus endured and suffered?*

- *What does this truth mean to you personally, to know that God's heart reaches out to you with understanding in the midst of your own frailty?*

- *How should this revelation-insight impact our understanding of the heart of God, that our King-Priest understands the fullness of our humanity?*

A King-Priest Like Melchizedek

Launching the main exploration of Jesus' role as our better-than King-Priest, stretching from chapter 5 through the middle of chapter 10, the writer of Hebrews first addresses the office of high priest that we find in the Old Testament. He lists four main qualifications for this office, originating under the terms of the old covenant. The person chosen for this office should:

1. Come from among the people;
2. Represent the people before God with gifts and sacrifices;
3. Deal gently with the people because of his own weaknesses, requiring sacrifices for his and the people's sins; and
4. Be appointed to the honor by God himself.

- *Explain how Jesus Christ fulfills each of these four qualifications as the better-than King-Priest. Or if there's an aspect that is different between him and the merely human high priest, explain that as well.*

THE BACKSTORY

According to the Old Testament, the high priest shared in the responsibilities that general priests performed in the tabernacle, from leading worship to offering various sacrifices, except for the sacrifices on the Day of Atonement. It is understandable that when many people study this material in the book of Hebrews, they find it difficult to understand, given how removed we are from the original covenant. However, it is vital to keep in mind the specific tasks and roles from the old covenant assigned to the earthly high priests in order to gain the full impact of the challenge from the author of Hebrews to his readers.

- *To get a sense of these responsibilities, read through Exodus 29 and Leviticus chapters 1–6 and 16. List these responsibilities from the backstory forming the context to this passage, as well as anything else you note.*

- *In light of this original priesthood and sacrificial system, what were these gifts and offerings mentioned here in Hebrews 5:2?*

- *Why were these gifts and offerings necessary?*

- *For what reason did the high priest offer sin offerings for others as well as for himself?*

- *Read Matthew 3:13–17 about Jesus' baptism, mission, and appointment for ministry. What do you learn from this to help you better understand the truth Hebrews reveals that "Christ was not self-appointed and did not glorify himself by becoming a high priest, but God called and glorified him" (Hebrews 5:5)?*

One of the crucial aspects to this lesson is the identification of Christ with the Old Testament priest from Genesis 14 known as Melchizedek. There are varying viewpoints on the identity of Melchizedek. Some scholars view him as merely a type or picture of Christ. Others think he was a Canaanite royal priest. Some Bible scholars believe he was a Christophany—a pre-incarnate appearance of Christ as both a priest of the Most High God and King of Salem (peace).

What's fascinating about his story is that he appeared out of nowhere in Abraham's narrative, with no genealogy or pedigree other than being a king-priest. Two of the Dead Sea scrolls, which date back to at least the first century BCE, state that Melchizedek was a divine being and was given the Hebrew title "Elohim." These documents maintain that Melchizedek proclaims the Day of Atonement still to come—a day when one will atone for the sins of the people and will be their supernatural deliverer and judge. In John 8:56, Jesus said that "'Abraham...foresaw me coming and was filled with delight.'" In other words, "Abraham saw the day of Jesus as Melchizedek came out to meet him with bread and wine."[30]

What's clear is that the writer of Hebrews explains both continuity and discontinuity between the old covenant and the new, between Melchizedek and Christ.

- *Read Hebrews 5:5–6 and TPT study note "i" for verse 5. How does Jesus' commissioning as a non-Levitical priest by the Father compare to Melchizedek's?*

The author explains that while Christ was on earth, "he pleaded with God, praying with passion and with tearful agony that God would spare him from death" (5:7). What death? This seems to reveal that Jesus prayed in the garden to be spared from death *that night* and live long enough to die on the cross rather than die prematurely in the garden: "'If possible, take away this cup of suffering'" (Matthew 26:39),[31] he said in the garden.

> Most expositors believe this was the "cup" of God's wrath that was the sin payment. Yet it is possible that the cup he was asking God to let pass from him was the cup of premature death in the garden, not the death he would experience the next day on the cross. He had already sweat drops of blood, but the prophecies [about Jesus being pierced on a cross for our transgressions] had to be fulfilled.[32]

God answered his cry: Jesus lived through the agony of Gethsemane so that he could be our sacrifice for sin on Calvary. His courage and commitment were extraordinary!

- *Knowing this background, what does this tell you about the heart of Christ, that he went through with his death on the cross for you and for the world?*

- *The writer of Hebrews teaches that "because of his perfect devotion his prayer was answered and he was delivered" (Hebrews 5:7). To what was Jesus devoted, and how was he delivered?*

- *Why might this be important to our own experience of the heart of God?*

The Greek word for "obedience," *hupakoe*, means "to hearken" or "to listen for the knock on the door" or "to pay attention." As the study note says, "Jesus' sufferings were seen as lessons of listening to and obeying God."[33]

- *What have you learned from some of your own experience of suffering, especially as it relates to God?*

Because of Jesus' obedience unto death through the cross and deliverance from death through the resurrection, he is "the source of eternal salvation to all who listen to him and obey" (5:9). Far from being a works-based salvation, our obedience is connected to Christ's own obedience. Another way to understand the "obedience" of *hupakoe* is the sense of submitting our will, understanding, conduct, and allegiance to the will of another—in our case God. This submission manifests itself initially in faith as converts and later as perseverance in the faith as believers, where we have fully submitted ourselves to God and his divine will.

- *Consider those four aspects of hupakoe: will, understanding, conduct, and allegiance. How are you at obeying God in these four areas? This is not about giving yourself a letter grade or rating yourself on a scale of 1 to 10. It's about taking stock of yourself and your relationship to God. So do that now in the quietness of your heart—just between you and the Lord.*

Hebrews 5:10, as translated from the Aramaic in The Passion Translation, says: "For God has designated him as the King-Priest who is over the priestly order of Melchizedek." Jesus, our magnificent King-Priest, has "made us kings and priests that serve him and extend his kingdom on the earth."[34] As 1 Peter 2:9 reminds us: "But you are God's chosen treasure—priests who are kings, a spiritual 'nation' set apart as God's devoted ones."

- *What does it mean to you that you have been made a king and priest to serve him and extend his kingdom on earth?*

SHARE GOD'S HEART

- *As our magnificent King-Priest ruling over the priestly order of Melchizedek, how do you suppose he wants you to live out your own kingly and priestly role in your individual life and world?*

Bold Honesty

Remarkably, the God of the universe understands your life. Not only that, he *sympathizes* with your frailty in all its forms. That's because he lived your life, experiencing the full measure of this broken, busted world, including the temptation to sin and the heartache of suffering. Because our King-Priest was taken from among humanity as God in the flesh, he is precisely qualified to be our compassionate High Priest. And because of this reality, we can come before the throne of God with not only access but *boldness*—communing directly with God in frank conversation about our lives and honest confession of our sins.

Take time to do that now: Draw near to him without fear and in total freedom "to receive mercy's kiss and discover the grace [you] urgently need to strengthen [you] in [your] time of need" (Hebrews 4:16).

Talking It Out

1. How have you personally experienced the truth of God's sympathy with and Christ's understanding for your weakness? Explore one of those moments, explaining what happened and what it was like to experience God's sympathizing, understanding heart.

2. One of the crucial aspects of Christ's King-Priesthood is that, like all other priests, he was chosen from among the people, being clothed in weakness and humility. It is because of this that he shows "compassion to those who are ignorant of God's ways and stray from them" (5:2). Share some of the ways in which Jesus Christ has shown compassion to you, whether in your ignorance of God and his ways before you were saved or in how you have strayed from those ways even now.

3. What does it mean to you that, even though Jesus pleaded with his Father "with passion and tearful agony" for him to remove the cup of wrath and death from him, he "learned to listen and obey through his suffering?" What should we learn from this for our own walk with God?

4. Pick one way our magnificent King-Priest has called you to reign as a king and priest, sharing and explaining how you can do that this week.

LESSON 5

Jesus, Source of Our Maturity and Truth

(5:11–6:20)

For some time, religious leaders have warned of the danger of moral relativism, where right and wrong actions were decided at the whim of every individual in whatever circumstance they found themselves in. That fear has fully manifested itself, where what's important is not *the* truth but *my* truth and *your* truth, leading to many ways of living in response to those many "truths"—both inside and outside the church of Christ.

However, our reading today confronts us with a radically different, better-than perspective rooted in spiritual maturity, and a sobering warning about falling away from the faith—while offering a dose of encouragement at the end in our struggle to hold fast to the truths of Christ. It is a topic that has caused uncertainty and confusion over the years, but one we hope is clarified in this lesson that carries important revelation-insight.

The writer begins by taking certain believers to task for their spiritual immaturity, exhorting them to grow beyond the milk of their faith and into consuming the full-on feast of spiritual maturity so they can discern between "what is truly excellent and what is evil and harmful" (Hebrews 5:14). Such maturity comes from growing beyond the elementary teachings of our faith and fully grasping and embracing the deeper truths of God, leading not merely to believing rightly but also to living rightly. For the danger in remaining in kindergarten when you should be in college manifests itself in the second warning: falling away from the faith entirely.

Here is where it gets controversial, the sobering warning that "it is impossible to restore an apostate" (6:4) to relationship with God when they have abandoned their faith and rejected Christ. We will explore this more fully shortly. For now, suffice it to say that the writer of Hebrews expresses a dire warning in order to wake believers up to the possibility of becoming so confused in our beliefs and hardened in our sin and in our heart toward God that we ultimately abandon our faith.

And yet, we do not have to wring our hands with worry at every relapse into sin, wondering whether we are still saved or whether we have finally committed the unpardonable sin that has exhausted God's grace. For not only does the writer have the deepest confidence in his hearers' commitment to the Lord, but he also is fully confident in the promises and hope flowing from the heart of God—urging believers to "run into his heart to hide ourselves in his faithfulness" where his strength and comfort empower us "to seize what has already been established ahead of time—an unshakeable hope" (6:18).

As we continue to explore the better-than promises of Christ, may we have eyes to examine our hearts and ears to hear the warnings the Spirit offers us—resting in the anchor-hope of Christ along the way.

Moving on to Full Maturity

The writer of Hebrews takes a short break from the deep discussion of Christ as our King-Priest in the order of Melchizedek, mostly because his audience has become spiritually hard of hearing. Where they should understand the deeper things of their faith, they seem to need a review of the basics—like a high schooler in algebra needing to review the basics of elementary math.

- *Read Hebrews 5:11–14. From these verses, what would you say it means to "become too dull and sluggish to understand" the essential elements of God's revelation?*

- *Can you think of a comparable analogy that would convey the same basic idea that the writer of Hebrews makes here? What would that analogy be?*

- *How do you suppose we as believers might remain immature, like children, in our understanding and application of divine teaching?*

- *What would that immaturity look like in a person's daily faith walk?*

The writer suggests that his audience still needed to be taught the basics of their faith, the milk of their faith, rather than moving on to more advanced aspects of their faith—the solid food of Christian beliefs.

- *Below, list what some of the basic beliefs of the Christian faith are in comparison to more advanced aspects of the faith. One example might be belief in the existence of one God (basic, milk-level belief) versus belief in the tri-unity (or trinity) of that God (advanced, solid food-level belief). What might be some other examples?*

The Greek word *nepios* for "like children" in 5:12 means "still unfit to bear arms," that is, unprepared for battle.[35]

- *In what ways can Christians still be unfit to bear arms and unprepared for battle in their daily walk with Christ because of their "diet," whether simple milk or solid food? How about in your own life?*

- *When it comes to your own level of consumption (from milk to solid food) in your walk with Christ, where do you land? Why do you suppose that is? Is it because of your level of understanding or confusion regarding certain aspects of the faith? Or are their practical reasons, such as not having enough time to study or having no access to resources?*

- *What are some resources (for example, Bible scholars, theologians, pastors, sermons, commentaries, systematic theologies, websites, blogs) you may have used that have helped you learn the basics of the Christian faith and perhaps even move beyond some of those basics?*

If you are not sure where to find help, doing Bible studies like you are now is one way to further your understanding. Also consult with your pastor, more mature believers in your church, professors at a local Bible-teaching college, and the like. It's even wise to find someone much more mature in the faith than you who will commit to discipling you. All of us can grow in the faith, but each of us needs to take some responsibility for our own growth by seeking out individuals, groups, and other resources that can take us to where we need to go in our grasp and application of God's truths.

- *Why do you suppose it is necessary to "progress beyond the basic message of Christ and advance into perfection" (6:1)? What happens to our spiritual life when we do not progress and advance? What do we become and gain when we do grow deeper in the faith?*

A Warning to Never Turn Away

Hebrews 6:4–12 is one of the most controversial and disputed passages in the book of Hebrews as well in the entire New Testament. Given how strong the exhortation seems to be for turning away from Christ, one can appreciate why. Some scholars believe that the hypothetical apostate was a believer who had received Christ and then rejected him, thus coming into the graces of God in Christ and then falling away, never able to return to Christ again. Others contend that the hypothetical person was never a believer to begin with, only trying out the Christian faith, so to speak, without having fully partaken and believed. Either way, the writer offers a stern warning for people who have heard the gospel and participated at some level in the faith, in many ways intending to put some level of fear into their hearts so that they do not drift.

- *The Passion Translation uses the term "an apostate" in 6:4 to describe the believer who has been enlightened and tasted the fruits of the gospel. What is an apostate?*

- *Why do you suppose such people leave the faith? What are the reasons you have heard for people walking away from Christianity?*

The writer says, "It is impossible to restore an apostate" (v. 4). That's strong language! To say it is impossible does not mean that the all-powerful God cannot bring them to repentance but that he chooses to leave them in their hardened state, much like Pharaoh who hardened his heart to God (see Exodus 4–15). The Aramaic is very clear: apostates "cannot be renewed to conversion."[36]

- *Why do you suppose this is the case for such a person who has apostatized from the faith? Why do you suppose they cannot be renewed to conversion, or why does it seem God chooses to leave them in their hardened state?*

- *Do you know anyone who has or might be on the verge of apostatizing from the faith? What might it look like to come alongside them in the faith in order to preserve or restore them in their relationship with God?*

There are five qualities listed in this passage describing a person who can become an apostate. Take some time to see what you can learn about each one and then write down what you discover:

Come into God's light (Hebrews 6:4; see also 10:32; John 1:9, 12–13; 1 John 2:9–11)
Tasted the gifts of the heavenly realm (Hebrews 6:4; see also Psalm 34:8–10; John 6:31–35; 1 Peter 2:1–3)

Received the Holy Spirit (Hebrews 6:4; see also 2:4; 1 Corinthians 12)
Feasted on the good Word of God (Hebrews 6:5; see also Isaiah 40:8; 2 Timothy 3:16–17)
Entered into the power of the age (Hebrews 6:5; see also 2:2–4; 9:26)

- *Put into your own words what it is this person has enjoyed in their experience of God's heart.*

- *Now consider a person who had these qualities and yet chose to abandon his faith (6:6). What do you think that person's life would eventually look like? Put another way, what would be some telltale signs of apostasy?*

The writer explains that the reason there is no use trying to lead an apostate to repentance is because "By their sin of apostasy they re-crucify the Son of God, and have publicly repudiated him" (6:6). In other words, they have denied their repentance and have thus rejected Christ. Again, this is strong language, because instead of being blessed by repenting and finding acceptance in the crucified Christ, they are standing with those who mocked and disparaged Christ on the cross.

- *Why do you suppose this is, that an apostate re-crucifies and repudiates the Son of God in their denial after having embraced him as Lord and Savior? How do you feel about such repudiation?*

- *The writer of Hebrews compares the hearts of people like the soil, some yielding crops and some not. Now read the Parable of the Sower in Matthew 13:1–23. After reading this parable, make a list of all the "soils" of people's hearts that Jesus mentions, jotting down notes on what he says about each soil type. Then relate this important teaching of Jesus to what the writer of Hebrews reveals in 6:7–8.*

Following the writer's warning about apostasy, he offers an encouraging word: "Even though we speak like this, beloved, we are fully convinced that there are more beautiful and excellent things, which flow from your salvation" (6:9).

- *What can you glean from Hebrews about the initial readers that gave the writer confidence in their faith?*

- *What can you point to in your life that gives you confidence in the genuineness of your personal relationship with God?*

The writer continues his exhortation and warning but with a softer hammer: "Don't allow your hearts to grow dull or lose your enthusiasm, but follow the example of those who fully received what God has promised because of their strong faith and patient endurance" (6:12).

- *How can you ensure that your heart doesn't "grow dull" or that you don't "lose your enthusiasm" as you daily experience God's heart? Make a list of spiritual disciplines or practices (see the endnote for information on these),*[37] *and then commit to one or two in order to maintain and cultivate your understanding and experience of God's truths and heart.*

- *Consider the "examples of those who fully received what God has promised because of their strong faith and patient endurance"—whether in the Bible or church history. Which believers in or outside of the Bible do you identify with most when it comes to drawing inspiration for your development and commitment to a strong and enduring faith? Why?*

God's Faithful Promise

In this final part to our lesson on this section of Hebrews, the writer reminds us of God's faithfulness to make good on his promises (Hebrews 6:13–18). We find the original promise to Abraham in Genesis 12:1–4, and then it is reaffirmed in 22:15–18, which the writer of Hebrews quotes.

- *What did God originally promise Abraham?*

- *What did God do to fulfill it?*

- *What does this tell you about the heart of God when it comes to his own promises for our lives?*

This section (Hebrews 6:13–20) is an exposition on hope, connecting what we have in Christ to what God promises on a surefire oath. If we are to remain loyal to Christ in a day of increasing persecution and apostasy, surely hope is the foundation for that perseverance! If the previous section places the spotlight on our own efforts at remaining faithful (vv. 4–12), the current section throws it back on God and his own faithfulness toward us.

- *According to the writer, what is the anchor that can keep us from blowing off course in the midst of temptation, trials, and persecution? What does this anchor offer us?*

EXPERIENCE GOD'S HEART

The writer reminds us of a crucial truth: "We have run into his heart to hide ourselves in his faithfulness. This is where we find his strength and comfort, for he empowers us to seize what has already been established ahead of time—an unshakeable hope!" (6:18).

- *When was a time when you endured temptation, trials, or persecution by running into God's heart to hide yourself? How did the faithfulness of God shine through?*

- *Why do you suppose we can find strength and comfort from God's faithfulness? What about it enables such strength and comfort in the midst of life's storms?*

Hold On

The threat of apostasy is real, and it seems to start when people become dull and sluggish in their understanding and remain content to feed on the basic elements of the Christian faith instead of maturing into the deeper, solid-food truths of Christ. So don't lose your enthusiasm—but also don't lose heart! For in Christ we are secure (Hebrews 7:25). It is in him and the faithfulness of God that we find our strength, an anchor-hope for our faith, fastened to the mercy seat and he who has gone on before us to the very throne room of God as our King-Priest!

Talking It Out

1. What are some of the basic truths of the Christian faith that you have either grasped and settled in your mind or that you might still struggle with? How about the more advanced ones: What solid-food truths have you accepted and understood, or which do you find hard to understand or believe?

2. Do you think apostasy is a problem in the twenty-first century church? Explain. How can we guard against it in order to guard our experience of God's heart?

3. Who have you known who has "fully received what God has promised because of their strong faith and patient endurance" (6:12)? How might they be an example for you in ensuring your heart doesn't grow dull or you don't lose your enthusiasm? Share who that is and why they are an example to you.

4. When was a time in your life when the anchor-hope of Christ was crucial for you getting through temptations, trials, or persecution? What was so vital about it? How did it get you through and help you persevere?

LESSON 6

Jesus, Our King-Priest Forever

(7:1–28)

During the sixteenth century, the Renaissance scientific community was rocked when Nicolaus Copernicus published a work that challenged the prevailing models of how our solar system works. His model launched what was later called the Copernican Revolution. It completely changed the way we understood how our solar system works. Copernicus challenged the long-standing geocentric Ptolemaic model that described the cosmos as revolving around a stationary earth. Copernicus proposed a heliocentric model, in which the sun was at the center of the solar system and the planets, including earth, revolved around it.

Revolutions do that—whether the American Revolution that was the downfall of British imperialism or the personal computer revolution that opened access to digital tools for average people and families. Revolutions change how we relate to our world and how we define our place in it. They create shifts from one paradigm to another, thereby opening the door to new ways of interpreting the world that impact how we are living inside it. The same could be said of what happened in Christ when a Jewish orientation toward the Mosaic law and the promises of God were reinterpreted in light of the death and resurrection of Jesus.

All along, the writer of Hebrews has been arguing that Jesus is better than the old covenant. However, what we will discover in this lesson is that this new better-than revelation was also in continuity with the old, fulfilling what God had promised long before and completing what he had been doing all along. This exploration may seem a bit "in the weeds" when it comes to Old Testament theology and practice, but it's worth the journey. The writer offers us a matchless portrayal that far exceeds a mere theological treatise, instead presenting a relational theology that plumbs the depths of the heart of God.

The Melchizedek Priesthood

Key to Hebrews 7 is an enigmatic figure from the Old Testament, a man named Melchizedek. We need to go all the way back to Genesis to learn about this figure in order to grasp what Hebrews says about Jesus in chapter 7.

Genesis 14 gives the account of a war between kings that led to the victors capturing "all the possessions and all the food of Sodom and Gomorrah" as well as to their taking "Lot, Abram's nephew who had been living in Sodom,...and all his possessions" (14:11–12). Abram heard of what happened to Lot (v. 13). He then mobilized more than three hundred men and set out to find Lot and free him from the invaders, all of which he accomplished and more (vv. 14–16). As he was returning with Lot and his family and possessions and fellow captives, Abram was met by the king of Sodom and a priest and king named Melchizedek (vv. 17–18).

Read Genesis 14.

- *Now focus in on verses 17–20, which tell us about Melchizedek and how Abram responded to him. What do these verses tell you about Melchizedek? Who was he? From where did he come? What were his titles and offices?*

- *Summarize the blessing that Melchizedek spoke over Abram. What did his blessing acknowledge about God? What did it acknowledge about Abram?*

- *What was Abram's response to Melchizedek and his blessing?*

WORD WEALTH

The name Melchizedek alludes to the Hebrew words for "king" and "righteousness": *melek* and *sedeq*. Further, he is a king of "Salem," which means *peace* in Hebrew.[38] Moreover, as Don Richardson explains: "The Canaanite name of that very city [Salem]...would later give rise to the very meaningful Hebrew greeting *Shalom* and also its Arabic equivalent *Salaam*. Salem would later contribute its five letters to form the last part of the name Jerusalem—'the foundation of peace.' For Salem stood precisely on the original site of Jerusalem!"[39] The writer of Hebrews explains that Jesus Christ is a priest in the order of Melchizedek, this "king of righteousness" who presided over "peace."

- *Why are the terms "king of righteousness" and "peace" appropriate for one who prefigures the Messiah? In what way does the writer of Hebrews suggest that Melchizedek is a picture of the Son of God (Hebrews 7:3)?*

- *Read 7:4–12. What "proofs" does the writer of Hebrews offer for how great Melchizedek is? The Passion Translation lists six specific proofs, so list them here.*

Blessing is a crucial issue in the book of Genesis, from which the writer of Hebrews takes this account, as well as an important function of what later became the Levitical priesthood. And the Genesis account shows the Canaanite gentile king-priest Melchizedek blessing Abram, the founding father of the Jewish faith! The writer of Hebrews explains, "no one could deny the fact that the one who has the power to impart a blessing is superior to the one who receives it" (v. 7). So at this time in history, Melchizedek was greater than Abram, although Abram was the one who had originally received the promise of blessing from Yahweh in Genesis 12—a blessing that would abound to all the world's peoples, not just to those who would later make up the nation of Israel. Notice that the Messiah would be a priest according to the priestly order of Melchizedek (gentile) while also being a descendant of Abram (the father of the Jews) who would fulfill what Yahweh promised Abram, namely, that through him "all the families of the earth" would be blessed (Genesis 12:3). Jesus the Messiah is the long-awaited King-Priest of both Jews and gentiles, the One through whom "all the families of the earth" would be blessed. In him, all peoples—Jew and gentile alike—have a Redeemer, a King, a Priest, and a Reconciler.

The issue of tithe-paying is also important to the argument of Hebrews that Jesus is a better-than King-Priest. The tithe was an important component of the Levitical priesthood. The Levites would live off of 10 percent of the Israelites' bounty.

- *Hebrews 7:8–10 focus on tithing in relationship to the Levitical priests. What do you learn there about this 10 percent offering and how the writer of Hebrews uses it to advance his case that the Melchizedek order is greater than the Levitical one?*

The writer of Hebrews makes some curious statements about Melchizedek still living (v. 8), having "no father or mother," and never being born or dying (v. 3). The key to unlocking the meaning of these statements is found in some words sandwiched among these comments: that there was "no record of any of his [Melchizedek's] ancestors" (v. 3). Bible scholar Merrill F. Unger explains that the record referred to here concerns the genealogical records of the priests who served under the old covenant: "Melchizedek is not found on the register of the only line of legitimate priests; his father's name is not recorded, nor his mother's; no evidence points out his line of descent from Aaron. It is not affirmed that he had no father or that he was not born at any time or died on any day; but these facts were nowhere found on the register of the Levitical priesthood."[40]

Essential in Genesis are genealogical accounts of numerous individuals and families that came from Adam and Eve, Noah, and Abraham, to name but a few. In fact, genealogical lists appear throughout the book (Genesis 4:17–26; 5:1–32; 10:1–32; 11:10–32; 25:12–34; 30:1–13; 35:23–36:43; 46:8–27). But no such list is connected to Melchizedek who makes his appearance in Genesis.

Also, the known genealogy of a priest from the giving of the Mosaic law onward was critical to establishing his legitimacy; he had to be from the line of Levi.[41] This was so important that when the Jews started returning to Israel after their exile in Babylon, the priests among them had to have their families' names in the genealogical records that would show they were from the priestly line. For those priests whose needed genealogical line could not be determined, "they were disqualified from serving as priests" (Nehemiah 7:64 NLT).

Melchizedek had no genealogical record that showed his priestly line, much less his family line. As a gentile priest who lived before Moses received the law from God that established the Levitical priesthood (Numbers 3:1–39; 8:14–19), Melchizedek had no need to prove his priestly right to Abraham. Furthermore, Genesis' silence on Melchizedek's genealogy and time of birth and death leads the writer of Hebrews to see in this ancient king-priest a type of the deity of Christ. For Christ as God has no beginning or end, no birth or death, no mother or father, no human genealogy. He is eternal and immortal (Colossians 1:16–17; 1 Timothy 1:17; 6:16; Hebrews 1:10–12).

Jesus and the Priesthood of Melchizedek

Another critical aspect of Jesus' priesthood has to do with his tribal relation in Israel. Jesus is from the tribe of Judah, not the tribe of Levi. To understand the significance of this, we have to journey to the book of Numbers to pick up the backstory.

Numbers 3–4 recounts the story when the tribe of Levi was chosen as the special priestly tribe of Israel. Yahweh deliberately set them apart as his in order to first assist Aaron the priest with his duties and then to act as priests by nature of their ancestry. The Levites had the wonderful privilege of serving God in his presence. Their inheritance was not a piece of land, like the other tribes, but the privileges of intimate worship. The tribe of Judah, on the other hand, was designated as a ruling tribe, where the son of Jacob was blessed in Genesis 49:8–12. Judah was to become the source of leadership in Israel, the source of the Davidic dynasty. And it would be from David's line that the Messiah, Jesus of Nazareth, would come (Matthew 1:1–17).

- *Why do you suppose it matters that Jesus came from the tribe of Judah rather than the tribe of Levi?*

Hebrews 7:16 reveals that the King-Priest Jesus "did not arise because of a genealogical right under the law to be a priest, but by the power of an indestructible, resurrection life!"

The Greek word for "indestructible" is *akatalutos*, a rare word that occurs in the New Testament only here in Hebrews 7:16. It comes from a word that means "tied together in unity," that is, "a united life" (or "union with God"). Resurrection life is implied, for the priestly ministry of Jesus began *after* he was raised from the dead. The Aramaic can be translated "He has life-giving power that has no beginning."[42]

- *The writer reveals here that in Jesus, the appointment to his office did not come from ancestry, as it had with the Levitical priesthood under the old system. Under what basis does Jesus' ministry of Priest and King flow instead? Why might it be important for the argument the writer makes about Jesus' better-than priesthood?*

- *Hebrews 7:18 explains, "The old order of priesthood has been set aside as weak and powerless." What was the old order unable to do (v. 19)?*

- *What is the new order able to do (v. 19)?*

- *Who is the guarantee of this new order, and why can we be sure that the new order is permanent and will never pass away (vv. 20–24)?*

WORD WEALTH

The writer of Hebrews says Jesus himself is the "guarantor" (in the Greek, *egguos*) of the better-than, superior covenant. It is the only place in the New Testament where this term occurs. The guarantor "guaranteed that a legal obligation would be carried out. This could lead even to risking his life for another."[43] When this term is used in Hebrews, the guarantor is Jesus, and he pledges himself, thereby guaranteeing that the new covenant he inaugurated is permanent and will never fail. Bible scholar Robert Gromacki explains how Jesus did this:

> Christ, both by His person and work, is the divine personification of the promise of God to man. He is the one who established the better covenant, the new covenant, through the shedding of His blood. The church ordinance of Communion remembers that significance (Luke 22:20). Christ's return to the earth will finalize the blessings of the new covenant promised to Israel (Jer. 31:31–37; Rom. 11:26–27). His resurrection life and position of advocacy before the Father in heaven can give the believer assurance that he will fully inherit all of the divine promises given to him.[44]

This is what Jesus has done for us.

SHARE GOD'S HEART

The world needs the matchless message that Jesus Christ saves—not partly but fully; not only now in this life but for all eternity, as Hebrews 7:25 explains.

- *Why is this such good news for our world?*

- *Who in your life do you know who needs to hear this message—that every ounce of them can be saved fully, "from now and through all eternity"? Commit to sharing this good news with that person sometime soon.*

EXPERIENCE GOD'S HEART

- *In what ways does our better-than High Priest perfectly fit our needs, as 7:26 reveals?*

- *How has he met your own needs as you have experienced the heart of God?*

- *In 7:27–28, the writer presents a contrast between "the former high priests" and Jesus Christ in two ways. What are those ways, and why do you suppose they are significant to his argument that Jesus is better than the old system?*

Our Far Better Hope

This lesson offers us tremendous insight into the relational revolution our heavenly Father underwent through appointing our King-Priest Jesus to fulfill what he had begun with his people. Here we see God initiating this relationship, bringing us into "a far better hope which gives us confidence to experience intimacy with God" (v. 19); paying the price for this relationship as the "guarantor" and securing it forever (vv. 22–24); satisfying the requirements for salvation as "the High Priest who perfectly fits our need—holy, without a trace of evil, without the ability to deceive, incapable of sin, and exalted beyond the heavens" (v. 26); meeting our needs by saving us "fully from now throughout eternity" (v. 25) through forgiveness, sanctification, and the consummation to come; and maintaining this relationship through the intercession of his Son, who "lives to pray continually for [us]" (v. 25).

Talking It Out

1. How would you summarize and explain the writer's argument that the old system under Moses and the Levitical priesthood has been superseded by a new and much better covenant—an approach that can now truly rescue us from sin and death and restore us to God forever?

2. Given that "the old order of priesthood has been set aside as weak and powerless," what should this say about the continued reliance on religious ritual and priestly mediators? If we have in our King-Priest Jesus "a far better hope which gives us confidence to experience intimacy with God," then how should we view such orders and systems of ritual today?

3. How should the fact that Jesus Christ acts as a guarantor of the superior covenant for your salvation impact the way you experience the heart of God—when it comes to your security, your gratitude, your worship, and your overall relationship with him?

4. Who is it you identified above as needing to hear the matchless message that Jesus "is able to save fully from now throughout eternity" (v. 25)? How can you share the heart of God with them this coming week? Spend time praying for them, and then look for an open door to share this good news with them.

5. Hebrews 7:26–28 summarizes much of the writer's argument, but it also anticipates the one he makes later in 10:1–18, that Jesus' sacrifice was final. "Unlike the former high priests," Jesus "is not compelled to offer daily sacrifices" (7:27). What does it mean for your salvation, and to you personally, that Jesus no longer offers sacrifices for sins?

LESSON 7

Jesus, Infinitely Greater Than the Old

(8:1–9:10)

One of the most striking developments of the last two decades of the twentieth century was the sweeping change in the relationship between citizens and their governments. Several former communist countries became democracies, and while their citizens may have held on to some of their old ways of relating to the state, they had to relearn a new and better way that was rooted in individual liberty, rule of law, and limited government. The same relearning could be said for how believers in the earliest decades of the church had to rethink relating to God.

Many of these early believers were Jews who had related to Yahweh under an older relational regime that was rooted in the old covenant of priests and temples and sacrifices. However, in Christ, an entirely new way of relating to God was revealed. This new way is infinitely greater than the old way; it is a better-than way offered by a King-Priest who ministers on our behalf at the very right hand of God himself!

We discover that it's not so much that the old way was bad, but rather it anticipated the better-than way of relating to God. The writer calls this old way "a copy" and "a shadow of the reality" anticipated in Christ's priesthood (8:5). No longer would God's laws be codes of external conduct but instead would be embedded within his children's thoughts and fastened onto their hearts by his Spirit. The old offerings and animal sacrifices could not ultimately cleanse our consciences, which required the new offering of Christ. And the old way of worship through rituals and rules was replaced by a new pattern of worship through heart-restoration. In the end, the place and blood and eternality of Christ's better-than way of relating to God is fully unveiled in this lesson.

Part of the reason why the book of Hebrews can be a challenge, and probably why more people haven't engaged it for themselves, is that it harkens back to a former way of relating to God that is foreign. May you more fully appreciate and understand the depths of the heart of God by understanding the nature of the old covenant and all that Jesus fulfilled in order to establish a much better covenant.

Our Better Covenant

This lesson opens with "the crowning point of what we are saying" as a way to summarize what has come before in order to drive home the point, like any good preacher (8:1).

- *What is this "crowning point" that the writer of Hebrews has been making so far?*

- *Now, why is this point so significant to the major argument the writer is making—namely, that Jesus Christ is better than the old covenant and priestly system (vv. 2–4)?*

The writer of Hebrews reveals that "every high priest is appointed to offer both gifts and sacrifices" (v. 3). These rituals included:

- *Burnt offerings* as acts of worship, to atone for unintentional sin, and as expressions of devotion to God (Leviticus 1; 6:8–13; 8:18–21; 16:24).

- *Grain offerings* as acts of worship, recognizing God's goodness and provisions, and expressing devotion to God (2; 6:14–23).

- *Peace offerings* as acts of worship, thanksgiving, and fellowship (3; 7:11–34).

- *Sin offerings* as mandatory atonement for specific unintentional sins, to confess sin, to secure forgiveness of sin, and to be purified from defilement (4:1–5:13; 6:24–30; 8:14–17; 16:3–22).

- *Guilt offerings* for the mandatory atonement of unintentional sin requiring restitution, for purification from defilement, to make restitution, and to pay a 20 percent fine (5:14–6:7; 7:1–6).

- *What did the better-than High Priest Jesus offer instead of all of the above (Hebrews 8:4)?*

The writer says that the priests of the old order served in an earthly sanctuary (Hebrews 8:3–5). In Exodus 8:5, Yahweh implored Moses to make everything that was part of the old tabernacle in accordance with a pattern Yahweh himself showed him on the mountainside. As divinely directed as it was, it was still only an imperfect copy. Not only because it was built by humans but also because it only mimicked the greater reality of heaven.

- *What does it tell you about this system that it belonged "on earth" and that it was a "shadow of the reality" and not the reality itself?*

- *How should this impact our experience of God's heart when it comes to religious trappings, whether inside or outside the church?*

- *Why was Jesus the Messiah's priestly ministry far surpassing that of the old earthly priests? In what ways was it better than the old (Hebrews 8:6–13)?*

- *Read Jeremiah 31:31–34, which the writer quotes in his explanation of the new covenant and which showcases the "far more wonderful promises" the writer of Hebrews signals in 8:6. What were those promises? Make a list of what you can identify from the passage.*

- *The writer of Hebrews argues that the original, first covenant was faulty, that it needed a second one to replace it because something had happened with the first one. According to the Jeremiah passage, why did the first covenant fail?*

- *Jeremiah and the writer of Hebrews remind the reader that Israel failed to remain faithful to Yahweh's covenant, that is the Sinai covenant he made with them and Moses after he had rescued them from Egypt. In what ways did they break this covenant (Jeremiah 11:1–13)? List some of them.*

- *The reality is that we still remain unfaithful to the relationship God has established. In what ways do people reject the Lord in this day?*

One of the remarkable things about this passage from Jeremiah 31 is its promise of a future relationship with God that is new in quality. It speaks of a future new covenant unlike the old, established at Sinai, and based on people's outward obedience to God's laws. Unlike the old system, in which the Lord's laws were written on external stone tablets and scroll parchments, with this new one Yahweh "will embed my laws within their thoughts and fasten them onto their hearts" (Hebrews 8:10). The new covenant imparts a new heart and empowers one to fulfill God's desires. God gives a new, faithful heart to follow him. The Sinai covenant required perfect obedience to an external law, while the new covenant extends perfect forgiveness and removes the guilt, stain, and power of sin, embedding his law on our hearts. The first was written on stones; the second on tender hearts.

- *Apart from external codes of conduct, how are we now established in the ways of God and knowledge of them? What are the types of "laws" or ways of Yahweh that are established on our hearts so that the content of God's desires for how we live are known (Hebrews 8:10–12)?*

- *By establishing the new covenant, "the first is now obsolete" (v. 13). What of the old covenant is now obsolete? All of it? If just some of it, what is still in effect, and how do you know?*

The Old Pattern of Worship

- *Read through Exodus 25–26. Based on that description, as well as the one found here in Hebrews 9:1–7, draw a picture of the "sanctuary on earth" that Israel used to worship in, including labels for the sections and objects within.*

- *What purposes did each of the elements serve in worship?*

- *What do all of these elements tell you about how much God values worship?*

- *Now, how does the Holy Spirit use the symbols of the old pattern of worship to reveal God's new plan for our experience of his heart and for our salvation (see Hebrews 9:8–10)?*

EXPERIENCE GOD'S HEART

The writer speaks of the old system under the old covenant failing "to perfectly cleanse the conscience of the worshiper" (9:9). You see, it is our internal conscience, the seat of our moral awareness of good and evil, that ultimately keeps us from experiencing the heart of God in intimacy.

- *In what ways are people's own consciences holding them back from having a relationship with God in our day and age?*

DIGGING DEEPER

Because our breach in intimacy with God is ultimately an internal issue of the heart, we needed something more than external regulations to make experiencing God in relationship possible; those regulations were always meant to be provisions until the "appointed time," as the writer explains. He lists food, drink, and cleansing laws as some of those provisions.

- *Referencing Leviticus 11–15, explain what some of those laws were.*

- *Although food, drink, and cleansing laws are no longer practiced in churches, sometimes there is a tendency to add rituals and regulations on top of our relationship with God. What are some of those in our own day?*

- *How have you experienced the pressure to perform externally in order to maintain your relationship with God?*

WORD WEALTH

Hebrews says that the old patterns of worship were only meant to be used until an "appointed time of heart restoration" (9:10). The Greek word for this timing of things is *diothosis*, used only here in Hebrews 9:10 in all the New Testament. It means "to set things right" or "to snap a broken bone back into place." When applied to the divine-human relationship, the thrust of the word is to bring *restoration*.[45] The old covenant highlighted the need for a deeper, more permanent, and more personal restoration of our relationship with God.

- *When was the "appointed time" that Hebrews refers to, and what happened when it came?*

SHARE GOD'S HEART

Unfortunately, there are many people who still think that religious ritual regulates their relationship and access to God. But this lesson reminds us that Jesus is infinitely greater, that he is better than the old way Yahweh instituted as a provisional means to experiencing the heart of God. The doors into his presence have been thrown open in Christ, for the appointed time has arrived!

- *How might it look in your own life, whether as a believer or in church leadership, to share this aspect of God's heart with those you know?*

Jesus All in All

The Bible commentator Matthew Henry offers an apt concluding thought to the lesson:

> We must not dare to approach God, or to present any thing to him, but in and through Christ, depending upon his merits and mediation; for we are accepted only in the Beloved. In all obedience and worship, we should keep close to God's word, which is the only and perfect standard. Christ is the substance and end of the law of righteousness. But the covenant here referred to, was that made with Israel as a nation, securing temporal benefits to them. The promises of all spiritual blessings, and of eternal life, revealed in the gospel, and made sure through Christ, are of infinitely greater value. Let us bless God that we have a High Priest that suits our helpless condition.[46]

Do just that: Take a moment to bless God for all that you have received from him.

Talking It Out

1. Although this lesson teaches the fulfillment of the Jewish story in Jesus Christ, that the old covenantal system is no longer active in light of the priestly ministry of our King-Priest Jesus, we must be careful not to marginalize Judaism and Jews, as Paul so cogently argues in Romans 9–11. How

can we guard against this while also expressing Christ's fulfillment of the old covenant?

2. What does it mean to you and how does it make you feel to know your relationship with God is no longer regulated by external rules and rituals but instead internally through the work of his Spirit and the cleansing of your conscience?

3. Although external rituals and rules in our relationship with God have been set aside, the truth still stands that God is holy and should be worshiped in holiness. How can we guard against cavalierly approaching God in communion, fellowship, and worship, while also doing so in freedom?

4. Hebrews 9:10 capstones our exploration of the "appointed time of heart restoration" when the old system of relating to God was replaced with the new one in Christ. How did this truth become actualized in your own life? When did that appointed time occur in your own heart? What has been your experience of the heart-restoring power of God?

LESSON 8

Jesus, Our Infinitely Greater Covenant

(9:11–10:18)

Imagine it is the tenth day of the seventh month, the Day of Atonement. You and thousands of your countrymen are standing at the base of Solomon's Temple. Inside, the High Priest has taken the blood of a slaughtered bull and sprinkled it on the front of the atonement cover and then seven times again. He's done the same with the blood of a slaughtered goat and then again with both its blood and the blood of the bull on the horns of the altar—cleansing and consecrating the Most Holy Place from the uncleanness of the Israelites. Afterwards, the same priest brings forward a live goat and confesses over its head the rebellious sins and wickedness of God's people. Finishing, he sends it into the wilderness, carrying upon itself their sins.

What's interesting is that this ritual will happen again the next year and then the year after that. In fact, every day priests will continue to ritually offer the same sacrifices again and again, day after day—sacrifices that can never completely take away sin's guilt. That is, until the better-than Priest offered the one supreme sacrifice for sin for all time on those wretched boards of execution that served as the final altar! For "by his one perfect sacrifice he made us perfectly holy and complete for all time!" (Hebrews 10:14).

Today's lesson deepens the theme the writer of Hebrews has

been making from the beginning: Jesus Christ is *better than*. And in this case, better than the former covenant and its requirements that regulated and maintained the relationship between God and humanity. In today's reading, you will see how Jesus serves in a better-than tabernacle, one not made with hands. He offered a better-than sacrifice, now freeing us from dead works. He has enacted the better-than covenant, paving the way for a new relationship with God. Ultimately, he is the better-than High Priest, offering the ultimate sacrifice that could finally accomplish what the earthly high priests could not: taking away sin's guilt permanently.

Keep exploring this better-than sacrifice of this better-than Priest who has brought us into an infinitely greater covenant, a sacrifice confirmed with his "It is finished, my bride" (John 19:30) declaration from the cross!

The Heavenly Pattern of Worship

The nineteenth-century preacher Charles Spurgeon offers some insightful commentary that sets the stage for this section of our lesson:

> We should shudder to think of the guilt of sin and its terrible penalty, which Jesus, the Sin-bearer, endured. Blood is all the more priceless when it flows from Immanuel's side. The blood of Jesus sealed God's covenant of grace, guaranteeing it forever. Covenants of old were struck by sacrifice, and this everlasting covenant was ratified in the same manner. Oh, the delight of being saved upon the sure foundation of God's divine agreements that cannot be dishonored. Salvation by works of the law is a frail and leaky boat whose shipwreck is certain, but the ship of the covenant fears no storms, for Jesus' blood ensures it from stem to stern.[47]

- *Read Hebrews 9:11–10:18. Now that you are familiar with this section of Scripture, create a chart that will help you compare and contrast the blood of the original covenant with the blood of the new. Mark the heading for one column "Blood in the Old Covenant" and the heading for the other column "Blood in the New Covenant." Then in separate rows, list the following under the appropriate heading: who offered the blood, what was offered in shedding it, where it was offered, why it was offered, when it was offered, and what it accomplished.*

- *Now review your chart. What do you notice about these contrasting covenants? Jot down your observations and conclusions here.*

- *The writer of Hebrews explains that the original covenant forged in the blood of sacrificed animals was meant to cleanse the children of Israel outwardly, in a ceremonial way. What were the ceremonial impurities that the children of Israel needed to be cleansed from?*

Our exploration into the efficacy of Christ's blood moves on from merely cleansing outward defilement to an inward cleansing of our very conscience from the guilt and shame of sin. "Yet how much more will the sacred blood of the Messiah thoroughly cleanse our consciences" (9:14) in comparison to merely making one religiously clean on the outside—achieving what the old sacrificial system could not.

- *Consider how your own conscience has been cleansed—which relates to our entire being in relationship to God and all that stood in the way and disqualified us from experiencing the heart of God. In what ways have you experienced this cleansing in light of the blood of Christ in your own conscience?*

- *Jesus "died to release us from the guilt of the violations committed under the first covenant" (9:15). What was this first covenant? What were the violations that led to your own guilt? Use the Ten Commandments as your guide (Exodus 20:1–17). Which ones did you violate? Which ones did you obey?*

DIGGING DEEPER

The theological term for Christ's sacrificial work is *atonement*, and there are a variety of views when it comes to its meaning. The *ransom theory* says Jesus Christ paid a ransom to Satan to buy us sinners back. Another view, *Christus Victor*, explains Jesus' death as a conquering victory over Satan's rule and reign. *Recapitulation* views both Jesus' life and death as undoing humanity's collective sins against God. The *satisfaction theory* sees the meaning of Jesus' death as the point where God's justice was satisfied. Others see the cross as the highest and purest expression of love, whether God's love for us (*moral influence theory*) or merely a human display of love (*moral example*). Finally, *substitutionary* atonement views Jesus' death as paying the penalty for our sins in our place, exchanging his life and taking upon himself God's wrath in place of humanity.[48]

Many non-Christians and even Christians have asked why Jesus needed to die in the first place. After all, if God wanted to forgive the sins of the world, why sacrifice his Son? Some people have even labeled the idea of atonement "divine child abuse," as if God the Father were committing something horrendous for demanding Jesus the Son's blood.[49]

However, Hebrews 9:16–26 teaches the importance of Christ's death, explaining why he had to die by relating it to the ability to execute a "last will and testament."

- *How does this simple illustration prove why Christ had to die in order to become the King-Priest mediator of the new means of relating with God?*

THE BACKSTORY

- *Read Exodus 24:3–8. Here we see the first covenant confirmed between Yahweh and his people. Our lesson shows that blood is an important component to the ratification of the covenantal relationship between God and people. Why do you suppose this is? What is it about blood that is so important?*

- *Now compare this passage in Exodus 24:8 to the ones in Luke 22:20 and 1 Corinthians 11:25. What is similar or different?*

- *What does all of this tell you about forgiveness of sin and how it "only comes through an outpouring of blood" (Hebrews 9:22)?*

In Hebrews 9:23, the writer says heavenly realities required something better than the blood of animals to be purified. While that blood cleansed the earthly tabernacle, making it fit for interactions between God and his people, the cleansing of the heavenly realities required a "superior sacrifice." Hebrews 9:24 makes it clear that the "true sanctuary" is God's presence, before which Christ appeared and brought the necessary sacrifice on our behalf.

- *What was that sacrifice? In what way is it superior to the previous one, and why was this new one necessary?*

The writer of Hebrews presents a contrast between the old system, where sacrifices needed to be offered "year after year," and what the Messiah, Jesus Christ, performed: He "did not need to repeatedly offer himself year after year" (v. 25).

- *First of all, why was it necessary for the sacrifices of animals to be offered in this way, "year after year"? What does this yearly performance tell you about the nature and effectiveness of this old blood?*

- *Now, why do you suppose the sacrifice of Jesus did not need to be repeatedly offered each year? What does it tell you about the nature of this blood and its effectiveness for the forgiveness of sins?*

SHARE GOD'S HEART

"Every human being is appointed to die once," the writer explains, "and then to face God's judgment" (v. 27). Many have taken this verse as an implicit exhortation for our need to experience God's heart *today* and not wait to make that decision to follow Jesus—for at the time of death it is too late.

- *What should this passage do for our engagement with people we know with the gospel? How should it motivate you to share the heart of God with someone in your own life?*

One day, Christ will return to bring with him a very special gift for those who are his children. However, whereas the first time he offered the special gift of his blood through his sacrificial death, dealing with our sin, the second time he will bear a different but related gift.

- *What is that gift, that new thing Jesus will bring with him (v. 28)?*

Christ's Eternal Sacrifice

This section of Hebrews reminds us that the old system of living under the law was only a "faint shadow, a crude outline of the reality of the wonderful blessings to come" (10:1).

- *Read Hebrews 10:1–4. Why were the sacrifices offered each year under the old covenant unable to "make our hearts perfect before God" (v. 1)?*

- *Read 10:5–9. As our King-Priest, what did Christ offer instead of the animal sacrifices? What did his sacrifice finally satisfy? What did his willingness to "go and do your will," that is, the will of his Father, ultimately abolish? What did he replace it with instead?*

- *When earthly priests offered sacrifices and carried out so many other priestly duties, they did so while standing. But the heavenly King-Priest Jesus offered himself nailed to a cross, and then after his resurrection from the grave and ascension into heaven, "he sat down on a throne at the right hand of God" (v. 12). What do each of these separate postures (standing vs. nailed and then sitting) illustrate with regards to the different sacrifices offered and their effectiveness?*

EXPERIENCE GOD'S HEART

- *What does it do for you and your experience of the heart of God to know that by Christ's sacrifice, your sins "have been forgiven and forgotten" (v. 18), that another sacrifice is never again needed?*

- *How do you think God would answer the question on your behalf: "Are you guilty?" Is this how God sees you in light of Christ's once-for-all sacrifice? Explain.*

The Power of Christ's Blood

Again, the words of Charles Spurgeon offer a fitting refrain for an exploration of all that the blood of Christ means for us and for our salvation:

> Happy are we who have our title to heavenly blessings guaranteed to us by a Savior who died. But doesn't His blood continue to speak to us? Doesn't it call us to sanctify ourselves unto Him through whom we have been redeemed? Doesn't it call us to "walk in newness of life" (Rom. 6:4), and to motivate us to complete consecration to the Lord? Oh, that the power of Christ's blood might be known and felt in us today![50]

Talking It Out

1. How do you feel about all the Bible's talk about blood sacrifice? Do you think it was necessary, that blood needed to be shed for the forgiveness of sins? Do you feel it is an extreme measure to repair the relationship between God and humanity? Why or why not?

2. Through the ages, many people have offered several views that explain the meaning of Christ's death. Going back to the list of those theories above, which one do you think Hebrews most supports? Why?

3. Hebrews reminds us that everyone is appointed to die once, and then they face God's judgment. With whom in your life should you feel motivated to share God's gospel-heart in light of this sobering warning? Take time to pray for them, for their reception of the gospel, and for your own courage to share it.

4. Consider all that has been "forgiven and forgotten" through the once-for-all sacrifice of our King-Priest Jesus. What is one sin that you are especially grateful has been dealt with once and for all through Jesus' sacrifice, and why?

LESSON 9

Jesus, Our Confidence before God

(10:19–39)

There is a remarkable illustration of the confidence we have in Christ to access and approach God. It comes from the movie *Anna and the King*, staring Jodi Foster and Chow Yun-Fat. Foster plays a British schoolteacher, Anna, who attends to the children of the king of Siam, King Mongkut, played by Chow. In a striking scene, Anna's son gets into a fight with the king's son in the middle of class. King Mongkut's young daughter runs to fetch her papa to intervene, and this is where things become magical.

The camera pans to King Mongkut's throne room, where a number of people are gathered to attend to diplomatic, business, and governmental affairs. They are silent and prostrate before the king seated high on his throne, no doubt regulated by a whole host of implied customs and explicit rules about how one approaches and accesses the king. Yet all of a sudden, the doors to the chamber fly open, and the king's little girl runs down the red carpet and past the people paying homage to her father. She ascends the stairs and whispers something into the king's ear. To which the king immediately stands up, runs past the attendants and dignitaries, and rushes through the doors and out to the schoolhouse to respond to the heart's desires and cares of his little girl.

That's the kind of relationship we have with God—the kind of *confidence* we have in Christ as well as access to approach God as his children, coming close to him with open hearts after having been cleansed from our sins and freed from any sort of accusation. This intimate relationship with and access to God beckons us to reflect this same encouragement and love to others, gathering together as believers to celebrate this relationship and encouraging others to persevere. It also makes persisting in sin all the more repugnant—for we have tasted of the utmost goodness of the Lord and experienced the fullness of his heart.

This lesson reassures us of our access to the throne and heart of God, filling us with confidence to approach him while convicting us of continued willful sin. It also exhorts us to be bold and courageous in our faith, persevering until the day Christ appears when we receive the fullness of his promises!

Bold Assurance

The writer of Hebrews reveals that, because of the blood of Jesus, God "welcomes us to come into the most holy sanctuary in the heavenly realm—boldly and without hesitation" (10:19).

- *Is this how you experience God's heart—coming to him boldly and without hesitation? Why or why not?*

SHARE GOD'S HEART

- *What have you personally experienced by being "in God's family because of the blood of Jesus"?*

- *Who do you know who needs what God's family offers, and how can you share this aspect of God's heart with them?*

The writer of Hebrews now draws an analogy between the veil being torn in two and Jesus' body torn open as signs of our new access to God (10:20). Once again, we need to return to the Old Testament to get some background on this veil so we can better understand the writer's point here.

- *Use a Bible dictionary or encyclopedia (see www.biblestudytools.com) and research what the Old Testament veil was in the tabernacle and later in the temple of the Lord. What was its purpose, and how did it function?*

- *Why might it be important that it has been "torn in two" (v. 20)?*

- *What does that mean for your experience of the heart of God?*

Matthew 27:51 reminds us that when Jesus gave his last breath on the cross, giving up his spirit to death, "At that moment the veil in the Holy of Holies was torn in two from the top to the bottom."

- *How does the tearing of the veil in two point to Jesus' better-than sacrifice? What all do we receive thanks to the veil being torn in two because "Jesus' body was torn open" (Hebrews 10:20–22)?*

- *The writer of Hebrews exhorts us to "come closer to God and approach him with an open heart, fully convinced that nothing will keep us at a distance from him" (10:22). Why is this true, that we can come closer to God and approach him with a confident, open heart?*

- *How do you think this looks practically, and how can you apply this revelation-insight to your own life?*

Another way of translating "we come closer to God and approach him" (v. 22) is "draw near to God" or "offer a true sacrifice." "The Hebrew verbs 'to draw near' (*lehitkarev*) and 'to offer a sacrifice' (*lehakriv*) are nearly identical, and both are taken from the same root word."[51]

- *How can you in your own walk with God come close to him and offer a true sacrifice? Compare Romans 12:1–2.*

- *How do you suppose such a close walk would benefit your life?*

- *Each of us has our own unique besetting sins or the memories of past sins that continue to accuse our consciences. What are those accusations that your conscience continues to replay?*

- *What remedy should Hebrews 10:22 offer your heart in order to silence those accusations once and for all?*

EXPERIENCE GOD'S HEART

Hebrews 10:23 reminds us that "God always keeps his promises!" Scripture is filled with such promises: specific ones given to people like Joshua when Yahweh promised him "I will be with you wherever you go!" (Joshua 1:9); general ones given to his people, such as when Jesus promised, "Never forget that I am with you every day, even to the completion of this age" (Matthew 28:20).

- *What are the promises you have most clung to during the highs and lows of life? Which one or two stand out the most, and why?*

- *Read Hebrews 10:24. Consider the exhortation it gives. What do you suppose are the sorts of "acts of compassion" and "beautiful works as expressions of love" that reflect the heart of God for the sake of the body and the gospel of Christ? Make a list of some of those acts and expressions, especially the ones you find specifically in Scripture.*

- *Why do you suppose believers would "pull away and neglect meeting together, as some have formed the habit of doing" (v. 25)?*

- *If you are among those who have stopped gathering with fellow Christians, why is this so? What would need to happen for you to reverse course?*

- *Do you know another believer who has purposely stayed away from church or other Christian gatherings? What can you do to help this person continue in the faith and rejoin engagement within the body of Christ?*

Another Warning

The writer of Hebrews transitions from an encouraging word about our confidence in Christ to boldly approach and access God to an exhortation that warns us against continuing "to persist in deliberate sin after we have known and received the truth" (v. 26). There is an important distinction between *persisting in deliberate* sin and merely *continuing* to sin.

The Greek word here is *hekousios*, which carries with it the connotation of willing participation in an action; it's an act done with a clear, sober mind and careful, deliberate steps.[52] This seems to mean a person who has embraced a lifestyle that is clearly contrary to our life in Christ and is living a rebellious life against the gospel, bearing flesh-fruit instead of Spirit-fruit.

- *How might this look practically, to persist in deliberate sin, and what sorts of things might the writer of Hebrews have in mind? Give an example or two.*

- *In what way does a person who "[continues] to persist in deliberate sin after we have known and received the truth" have "contempt for God's Son" and "scorns the blood of the new covenant" (vv. 26, 29)? What is promised such a person in this passage?*

- *Why do you suppose judgment might or might not be warranted?*

Hebrews 10:26–31 is a particularly troublesome one, putting fear into the hearts of many—and for good reason—while leading to fire-and-brimstone sermons that might have erred more on the side of judgment than mercy. The commentator Matthew Henry offers some sound insight, especially for verses 30–31:

> Of this destruction God gives some notorious sinners, while on earth, a fearful foreboding in their consciences, with despair of being able to endure or to escape it. But what punishment can be sorer than to die without mercy? We answer, to die by mercy, by the mercy and grace which they have despised. How dreadful is the case, when not only the justice of God, but his abused grace and mercy call for vengeance! All this does not in the least mean that any souls who sorrow for sin will be shut out from mercy, or that any will be refused the benefit of Christ's sacrifice, who are willing to accept these blessings. Him that cometh unto Christ, he will in no wise cast out.[53]

- *Consider this again: "How dreadful is the case, when not only the justice of God, but his abused grace and mercy call for vengeance!" How might Henry's insight inform your understanding of what the writer of Hebrews is warning against? How should you heed it as you walk with God?*

- *Hebrews 10:31 says, "It is the most terrifying thing of all to come under the judgment of the Living God!" These are strong words. What do you think about them? Have you experienced this truth or witnessed it in someone's life? If so, what happened? If not, can you think of a biblical character who underwent divine judgment? Jot down your thoughts about their experience of this fearful side of God.*

- *In 10:32–34, the writer catalogues all that the audience had gone through and endured for their faith. What does he list?*

- *Christians throughout the world still endure hardships for the content and practice of their faith. What have you heard about their sufferings?*

- *Are you prepared to undergo persecution for your faith? Explain.*

Part of the writer's exhortation is to persevere and endure until we "receive the promise in full"—that is, our eternal reward when "the One who is appearing will come without delay" (vv. 36–37).

- *What do you personally long to experience on that day that Jesus returns?*

- *What do you need to do to help yourself endure and persevere in your faith until his appearing?*

- *Consider Hebrews 10:39 again: "But we are certainly not those who are held back by fear and perish; we are among those who have faith and experience true life!" How can you demonstrate the truth of this verse in your own life, that you are "among those who have faith and experience true life" contrasted from those held back by fear and perishing?*

Full Access

Do you fully realize that you have been granted full access to the throne room of God, that you can have confidence to approach him with boldness, without the hinderance of the veil and without the fear of conscience? Let us continue to gather in his presence as a believing community, encouraging others and cultivating the habit of doing so, while persevering in the faith to keep ourselves from sin and enduring under the weight of suffering and persecution—being confident that "the One who is appearing will come without delay!"

Talking It Out

1. Do you believe most people, whether Christian or not, are aware of or believe the truth of the matter that God "welcomes us to come into the most holy sanctuary in the heavenly realm—boldly and without hesitation" (10:19)? Why or why not? If not, what might be standing in the way of their leaning fully into this revelation-truth?

2. What is one creative way you can encourage others and motivate them this week "toward acts of compassion, doing beautiful works as expressions of love" (v. 24)?

3. Consider again the warning offered in 10:26 against persisting in deliberate sin in light of knowing and receiving the truth of Christ. Are there any such sins in your own life, where you are a willing participant in such actions, doing so with a clear mind and taking deliberate steps? Take time to examine your heart, asking the Spirit to search and know it, to reveal deliberate sin within, and then confess it with a spirit of repentance.

4. Persecution and hardship look different for different people. What have you endured for your faith in Jesus Christ? How can you ensure that you "don't lose your bold, courageous faith" (v. 35)?

5. What do you need in your daily Christian walk to not lose your bold, courageous faith? How can those in your community supply this need for one another?

LESSON 10

Jesus, Faith's Fullness

(11:1–12:2)

Babe Ruth, Michael Jordan, Serena Williams.

Harriet Tubman, Neil Armstrong, Martin Luther King.

George Washington, Abraham Lincoln, George W. Bush.

Most of these names would be recognizable as a Who's Who in American sports and scientific exploration, social activism, and leadership. Showcasing talent and tenacity, character, and moral fortitude, these are some of the many people who have shaped our nation. It is a Hall of Fame with examples that have provided inspiration for millions over the decades.

As Christians, we could offer our own Hall of Fame of those heroes of the faith who have offered us inspiring examples for living a Christlike life. Ignatius of Antioch offers us a beautiful image of martyrdom. Saint Patrick sowed the seeds of the gospel among the unreached pagan people of Ireland. Martin Luther stood up against the abuses of church leadership and stood for salvation by grace through faith alone. Jonathan Edwards drew people into great devotion to God and piety through revival. The late Billy Graham was one of the great evangelistic preachers of our day.

The Bible has a similar Hall of Faith that has also inspired believers for millennia, showcasing what it means to have an active faith that moves beyond mere intellectual assent to an idea and onto an active faith full of hope, confidence, and conviction.

From Abraham to Joseph, Moses to Rahab, the judges to the prophets—Hebrews exhorts us to be people of faith who claim a passionate confidence, a firm conviction beyond our own because it rests in the character of God, the sure foundation of our faith.

These men and women lived with bold confidence full of fiery passion and a firm assurance, for they each had a radical encounter with the heart of God, resting in his strength and Spirit. This Who's Who listing of the heroes of our faith offers us inspiration for our own experience of God. It also offers us guidance, showing us what it means to be a person of faith and how it looks to put it into action.

Unlike those true heroes who still "lived in hope without receiving the fullness of what was promised them," God has invited each of us "to live in something better than what they had—faith's fullness" (11:39–40). May you live and lean into that fullness this day.

The Power of Bold Faith

Perhaps nowhere is there a better definition and explanation of faith in the New Testament than in the sermon-letter of Hebrews: "Faith brings our hopes into reality and becomes the foundation needed to acquire the things we long for. It is all the evidence required to prove what is still unseen" (11:1). This is a far cry from the traditional understanding of faith. The word for *faith* here is the Greek *pistis*, which does carry with it the sense of belief and firm persuasion but also assurance and firm conviction.[54]

Biblical faith moves beyond mere intellectual assent to an idea. Instead, it claims a passionate confidence, a firm conviction beyond our own because it rests in the character of God, the sure foundation of our faith. Part of practicing faith is persevering in it despite living in a world that refuses to acknowledge God and opposes the church.[55]

- *How is this definition of faith in Hebrews similar to or different from your understanding?*

- *How have you heard faith defined before, whether from friends or in popular culture? How similar or different is it compared to the definition above in Hebrews 11:1?*

- *Does the Hebrews' description of faith fit with your personal faith commitment to God? Explain.*

Consult a Bible dictionary for a definition of the word *faith*. A good online resource would be https://www.biblestudytools.com/dictionaries/bakers-evangelical-dictionary/faith.html.

- *Based on Hebrews 11:1 and the rest of chapter 11, in addition to the helpful definition offered by the dictionary, how would you define faith using your own words?*

The Hall of Faith

After describing faith itself, Hebrews goes on to give us one of the most beautiful and encouraging sections of Scripture. Often called the Hall of Faith, Hebrews 11:4–39 reminds us of many individuals, some named and others not, who lived by faith and why that matters.

Abel

The first believer mentioned is Abel, who was also the victim of the first recorded murder in Scripture. The evil perpetrated against him was committed by his own brother, Cain, and it concerned an offering to God (Genesis 4:1–16).

Many Jewish scholars believe it was a lamb that Abel sacrificed to God. Sheep were not used for food prior to the great flood

(Genesis 1:29), only for sacrifice. Abel had his heart set on the coming sacrifice, confessed his sin, and brought the first and best of his flock as a sacrifice in faith. Abel acknowledged that he was worthy of death because of his sin and chose a sacrifice that was acceptable to God.

Cain's heart and character, however, were not right with God (Proverbs 15:8). Some commentators believe Cain picked inferior portions of produce (no mention of firstfruits) to offer to God, much like trying to please God with good works without faith. The curse of sin and death, however, could not be broken by a product of the curse.[56]

- *Compare and contrast the faith between Cain and Abel. Why was one expression received by God over the other? What can you learn about faith from this episode?*

Enoch

Hebrews 11:6 says, "Without faith living within us it would be impossible to please God." In this context, Enoch is commended as one who pleased God; his was a life committed to bringing God pleasure. He didn't just live; he also "walked with God" (Genesis 5:21–24). The writer of Hebrews still reflects Habakkuk 2:3–4, which he quoted in the previous lesson (10:37–38), where God reveals his displeasure with those who pull back on their commitment to him. Enoch stands as one committed to Yahweh and thus pleased him.

- *Why do you suppose this is the case, that it is not possible to please God unless faith lives within us, unless we exercise faith? What is it about faith that leads to God's pleasure?*

- *What does it imply about God that "he rewards the faith of those who passionately seek him" (Hebrews 11:6)?*

Noah

This theme of pleasing God is then connected with obedience in the story of Noah, who was the first among these faithful examples to respond in faith to a word from Yahweh; he responded with "reverent obedience" or "in holy fear" to the Word of God, and thus was saved (Hebrews 11:7).

- *When was a time you similarly followed in Noah's steps by "[stepping] out in reverent obedience" (v. 7)? What was that like? What happened, and how did you experience the heart of God in the midst of it?*

Abraham

God called Abram at the age of fifty to follow him. The God of Glory appeared to Abram and spoke with him (Acts 7:2–5). God's appearance to Abram was sudden and without warning. Abram had no burning bush to inspire him, no tablets of stone to guide him, and no ark of the covenant as a centerpiece of worship. Neither did Abram have a temple to worship in, a Bible to read, or a priest to counsel him. Nor did Abram have a pastor to pray for him or a prophet to prophesy to him. But Abram did have a divine encounter.

Leaving all that was familiar to him displayed an incredible act of faith on Abram's part. He was told to go into an unknown land, which would result in the seven-fold blessing of Genesis 12:2–3. At the great tree of Moreh, God taught Abram to walk by faith, not by sight (vv. 5–7). And this continued for the rest of Abraham's life.

- *What aspects of Abraham's life of faith does the writer of Hebrews emphasize (Hebrews 11:8–10, 17–19)?*

- *What do these verses tell us about the quality and extent of Abraham's faith?*

Consider reading through Genesis 12–22, or at least skimming through large parts of it, an incredible narrative of most of Abraham's life.

- *In your reading of Genesis 12–22, what did you learn about the nature of faith in the life of Abraham?*

- *How well do you think Abraham exercised his faith? Where do you think he lacked faith, and how did it turn out? Where do you see him exhibiting it the most, and what was the result?*

- *How might Abraham's life of faith inspire your own exercise of it?*

WORD WEALTH

A new revelation will always bring a new test. Although Hebrews 11:17 states that "when he was put to the test he offered up Isaac," there is no indication that Abraham knew he was being tested during the ordeal in Genesis 22.

> The word for "tested" is most commonly translated "proved." The purpose of God's tests [is] not so that we will fail, but that we will prove that we are faithful. The Midrash shows that the word for "tested" [in Genesis 22] is derived etymologically from a word that means "[elevated] banner," like a flag flying high above a ship or a victory banner elevated over an army. This means that God elevated Abraham and made him great by testing—test upon test, greatness after greatness. He does the same thing today with the spiritual seed of Abraham. [57]

We all want Abraham's faith, but do we want Abraham's trial to perfect our faith? "Tests are God's vote of confidence in our future. The budding qualities of Christlikeness are brought forth in every test of our faith. Someday, you may call a 'blessing' what you once called a 'burden.'"[58]

- *What do you learn from Hebrews 11:17–19 about what Abraham believed God could do for him in the midst of his trial?*

- *How has your own faith been "proved" and elevated like a banner through testing?*

Sarah

Of Abraham's wife Sarah, the writer of Hebrews reveals something important: "Sarah's faith embraced God's miracle power to conceive even though she was barren and was past the age of childbearing, for the authority of her faith rested in the One who made the promise, and she tapped into his faithfulness" (11:11).

- *What can we learn from Sarah's faith in God's miracle power to conceive?*

- *How can you apply it to those moments when you long for God to unfold his plan to you?*

EXPERIENCE GOD'S HEART

- *When was a time in your life when you were longing for something—a job or other provisions, a child of your own or for a friend? How did you lean on God in faith to provide during that time? How did he manifest his will to you?*

This lesson paints a remarkable picture of the heroes of our faith "still clinging to their faith" when they died. Although they had received promises from Yahweh, they had not yet been realized—which is an allusion to possession of the promised land, the multitude of descendants, and the blessings of all nations through Abraham.

- *How do you suppose it looks to still cling to your faith, even unto death, like the heroes of the Bible? How might it look to live this way as you wait to receive all that God has promised you—living your life as one who belongs to another realm?*

- *Consider 11:14–16 and what it means to your life personally. What is all that you have left behind by fixing your hope on the heaven-realm promise? Do you ever feel tempted to "go back," to change course? Why or why not? What can you do to continue "longing for the appearing of a heavenly city" (v. 14)?*

Moses

- *In Hebrews 11:23–29, the story of Moses centers around several action verbs: faith prompted, faith enabled, faith stirred, faith opened. Explain how each of these action verbs were connected to his life of faith—which really began with the faith expressed by his own parents.*

- *How might these insights into Moses' faith inform your own expression of faith?*

More of Faith's Heroes

This Hall of Faith crescendos with a flyover accounting of faith in ancient Israel from the time of Rahab and all she did to help the Hebrews spy out the promised land in preparation for entering it, to the time of the judges, and into the monarchy of Israel.

- *Along with Rahab, the writer lists six names: Gideon, Barak, Samson, Jephthah, David, and Samuel. Using your Old Testament, pick one exercise of faith from the life of these seven individuals to illustrate how "through faith's power they conquered kingdoms and established true justice" (11:33).*

After chronicling the incredibly positive feats of faith, stretching from Adam to Abraham, Noah to Rahab, and on to the judges and kings, the writer switches to a long list illustrating faith expressed through "great atrocities" (v. 35).

- *Who have you known who has had great faith through hardship?*

- *Have you endured something akin to "great atrocities" through clinging to and being enabled by faith? Explain.*

In large measure, the "great atrocities" listed in 11:35–38 reflect persecution, enduring torture and death, living courageously, and paying the consequences. Faith sustained these heroes and informed their experience of God's heart through it all. The same can be said of the persecuted church across the world—ordinary people who continue to express their faith and live boldly for God's glory and kingdom. Spend time praying for these present day heroes, men and women for whom what was said of these past heroes also applies: "The world was not even worthy of them, not realizing who they were" (v. 38).

Although these heroes were "commended for their faith, yet they lived in hope without receiving the fullness of what was promised them" (v. 39). God bore witness to their faith in him and faithfulness in living for his glory, yet they didn't attain the fullness of that faith.

- *What was "the fullness of what was promised them" (v. 39) that you yourself have experienced in faith?*

- *In what way has God "invited [you] to live in something better than what they had" (v. 40)?*

The Great Cloud of Witnesses

The writer of Hebrews describes those faithful heroes in chapter 11 as a great cloud of countless men and women of God who encircle us with their examples of how to exhibit great faith in Yahweh.

- *Why do you think he connects this cloud of "great witnesses" to letting go of every sin that pierces and entangles us? What about their witness should help us "run life's marathon race with passion and determination" (12:1)?*

- *What do you think it means that Christ both "birthed faith" and "leads us forward into faith's perfection" (12:2)?*

- *In the midst of life's trials and daily grind, what does it look like practically each and every day to "focus our attention and expectation onto Jesus" (v. 2)?*

- *How might it look in your own life to take this command seriously and obey it every day?*

SHARE GOD'S HEART

Being a witness of faith involves not just our living out the faith but also our professing the faith to others. Professing can come in a host of forms: conversation, internet posts, emails, acts of service, and works of art, to name but a few. And professing can also involve explaining the faith, defending it from claims against it, teaching it, singing about it, and most of all living it out. We're not responsible for the fruit of our profession; God is. But we are responsible for sharing the faith with others.

- *In what forms have you professed the Christian faith to others?*

- *Are there any forms you haven't tried but would like to? If so, what are they? Commit this week or next to try a new way of professing the faith.*

Lives That Keep on Giving

"Jesus is given to the world," Henri Nouwen wrote. Continuing, he said:

> He was chosen, blessed, and broken to be given. Jesus' life and death are a life and death for others....As God's beloved children we have to believe that our little lives, when lived as God's chosen and blessed children, are broken to be given to others. We too have to become bread for the world. When we live our brokenness under the blessing, our lives will continue

> to bear fruit from generation to generation. That is the story of the saints—they died, but they continue to be alive in the hearts of those who live after them—and this can be our story too.[59]

May the examples of faith offered in Hebrews 11 spur us on toward offering others the same example of faith, bearing witness to Christ and bearing his Spirit-inspired fruit from generation to generation.

Talking It Out

1. Describe a time in your own life when you clearly exhibited faith in a tough situation. What was that like? What happened? What did you learn—especially about God and your experience of his heart in faith?

2. Is it hard for you to have faith? Explain.

3. One of the most famous chapters in Hebrews is the "Hall of Faith" of chapter 11, which catalogues some of the faithful people of God who had a firm assurance in him, resting in his character. Whom from "these great witnesses who encircle us like clouds" (12:1) do you most resonate with? Why?

4. Now think outside the Bible: Whose faith journey, whether from history or your own life, do you most resonate with and why?

LESSON 11

Jesus, Entrance into God's Presence

(12:3–29)

Anyone who has spent any time at a skill—be it running, writing, dancing, or drawing—knows that endurance through discipline is one of the keys to success. Runners discipline themselves by enduring miles of training and the ups and downs of competition. Same for dancers, logging in hours upon hours on the dance floor with exacting discipline in order to perfect their art for perhaps several minutes in a competition or a performance. And any artist knows persisting through millions of words or thousands of brush strokes while also suffering stacks of rejections from publishers and critics is the only hope for disciplining their fingers and producing a harvest of work. Something similar could be said of our life with God.

The writer of Hebrews draws upon this concept of endurance when it comes to fully entering God's presence, comparing our own spiritual journey initially to that of a runner when exploring how to stand up underneath life's pressures—whether of our own making or not (12:1–2). From unemployment to failing a class, divorce to persecution, we must learn to view all of it through the lens of our training in experiencing God's heart. But while training in such activities as sports comes from a demanding coach, training in the Christian life is from a loving Father.

In Hebrews 12, the writer draws an analogy between accepting the training and discipline of God as a child accepts and welcomes correction from a loving father. We are invited to endure God's correction and discipline, for "it will produce a transformation of character, bringing a harvest of righteousness and peace to those who yield to it" (v. 11). And we are invited to experience this loving presence of God in our lives in a new way: the Zion-realm, an unshakable kingdom that demands our purest worship and absolute surrender.

So how do we endure this life in faith? Not through reading variations of *Chicken Soup for the Soul*, not through repeating self-help affirmations while looking in the mirror, not even through the outside pressure of peers and recovery-group accountability. The author draws our attention to one person: Jesus, exhorting us to consider what he endured, to embrace God's correction, to listen to God when he speaks to us, and to enter fully into his presence with the full assurance of faith.

Enduring with Discipline

The writer of Hebrews asks us to "consider carefully how Jesus faced such intense opposition from sinners" (12:3).

- *Thinking back to the four Gospels, what are some ways in which Jesus Christ was tried by his own circumstances, including by the people who confronted him and even those to whom he ministered?*

- *What does Jesus' experience on the cross tell us about what he endured from others?*

We are invited to look to Jesus, especially his endurance of the cross, in our own day-to-day walk so that we "won't become worn down and cave in under life's pressures" (v. 3). The Greek word here is *eklyomenoi*, which means to "faint" or "give up."[60] These believers were experiencing an intense wearing down and weariness of their very souls so that they wanted to give in to such troubles and quit their race. The weight they bore probably likely included persecution as well as the emotional toil of life's often daily pressures.

- *How does looking to Jesus keep us from becoming faint and worn down or hold us back from wanting to give up under life's pressures?*

Here the writer urges us to focus our attention on Jesus whenever we become faint or want to give up under the many trials and pressures we face, enduring them as we discipline ourselves to run the race with patience and perseverance.

- *Have you ever become faint and worn down or wanted to give up under life's pressures? What happened? How did you experience God during this season, and how did looking to Jesus get you through?*

- *The writer makes an interesting remark as he exhorts his audience to discipline themselves and endure their own marathon race of life: "You have not yet reached the point of sweating blood in your opposition to sin" (v. 4). What do you suppose this means as it relates to disciplining ourselves and enduring both the temptations and consequences of sin?*

- *Consider Proverbs 3:11–12, the passage the writer quotes in our lesson on enduring discipline in experiencing God's heart. Also reread Hebrews 12:5–6. What do both passages encourage as they relate to enduring the discipline of God?*

- *What have you learned about the Lord's discipline in our life?*

- *The writer exhorts us to "fully embrace" and "welcome" God's correction and discipline. Why are we encouraged to do this? What do you think these actions look like when God's correction and discipline come our way?*

- *Consider a time when you were corrected and disciplined by God's loving hand. Did you embrace and welcome it or resist and despise it? What was the result?*

- *What have you learned about God through his correction and disciplining work in your life?*

SHARE GOD'S HEART

- *Do you know anyone right now who is experiencing God's correcting, disciplining hand? How might this passage be an encouragement to them in their experience of God's heart in this way?*

- *According to the writer, what is the point of God's discipline? What does it produce (Hebrews 12:6, 8, 10–11)?*

The writer seems to connect the ideas of prayer and worship to enduring the discipline of the Lord and disciplining ourselves to run life's marathon race well, teaching in verses 12–13, "Be made strong even in your weakness by lifting up your tired hands *in prayer and worship*. And strengthen your weak knees."

- *Why do you suppose worship and prayer are connected to endurance and discipline in this way? How is it that both help us "be made strong even in your weakness" and "keep walking forward on God's paths"?*

Although verses 14–17 may seem disconnected from the exhortations on discipline, they continue a vital component to our spiritual walk that links endurance and struggle.

- *What two things does the writer of Hebrews connect to our endurance in running life's marathon race well in Christ? Why do you suppose both are vital, and how might they be connected to Christ's teachings on the Greatest Commandments (see Matthew 22:34–40)?*

- *What is a "root of bitterness" (Hebrews 12:15)? Why is it so toxic to not only one's life and spiritual walk but also (and perhaps especially) to the body of Christ?*

- *Have you witnessed the poisonous effects of such a bitter root in others or in the church? Tell about what you witnessed and what the outcome was.*

THE BACKSTORY

Read Genesis 27:1–28:9, reminding yourself of Esau's story. In it, we see that Esau had the right to his father Isaac's blessing because he was the firstborn. This inheritance would have included property from land to slaves to all the animals and fruits of the land. Yet he easily and quickly gave it away for a meal, representing someone who missed out on all the blessings attached to their rightful inheritance for a shortsighted, momentary craving.

- *How is Esau's story about carelessly giving up his blessing connected to running life's marathon race with endurance while also engaging immorality?*

- *In what way might people nowadays follow Esau in the same path, missing out on the fruits of our honored status as children of God and the precious blessings of the gospel while continuing to sin against God and neighbor?*

Entering into God's Presence

In Hebrews 12:18–21, the writer draws from events revealed in Exodus 19–20 and Deuteronomy 4–5. Although Sinai isn't mentioned specifically here, Israel's experience of God on the mountain from their desert wanderings is certainly the backstory to what the writer wants to teach.

- *What do you notice about Israel's encounters with God at the mountain?*

- *What from that experience does the writer bring into the Hebrews passage?*

- *How did the people and Moses respond to that encounter of God on Mount Sinai?*

- *How do you imagine you would have felt if you had to encounter God the way Israel did at Sinai? What might you have thought about God and his heart through that encounter?*

- *The writer contrasts that encounter at Sinai to the one we have in Christ. How have we encountered him instead?*

- *Similarly, several aspects of Israel's encounter with Yahweh at Mount Sinai are balanced with several more aspects of how we encounter the heart of God in the Zion-realm (Hebrews 12:22–29) and the benefits we receive. List those here.*

- *What do these truths invoke in you, and how do they explain our experience of God's heart under the new covenant?*

EXPERIENCE GOD'S HEART

In contrast to the old way on Mount Sinai, the writer of Hebrews reveals, "We have already come near to God in a totally different realm, the Zion-realm" (12:22). Another word for *Zion-realm* is "Mount Zion," which is not a literal mountain but an obvious metaphor for the realm of God's manifest presence. Mount Zion was once a Jebusite stronghold conquered by David who made it the capital for his kingdom. This is inside the walls of present-day Jerusalem. In both the Old and New Testaments, Zion is more than a geographical reality. Zion is also referred to as the place of God's dwelling. God's people are called "Zion maidens" or "people of Zion." It is the heavenly realm where God is most manifest.[61]

- *Do you look forward to experiencing the fullness of God in the heavenly city? Why?*

WORD WEALTH

The Greek word for "church" in 12:23 is *ekklēsia*, and it is commonly used for church in the New Testament. However, *ekklēsia* means more than a church meeting, for it signified in Greek culture the governing assembly that had the authority to make decisions for the entire city.[62] With regard to this passage, it represents the gathering or assembly of God's people.

- *What does it mean to you that, along with perhaps billions of other names, your name is also inscribed in the heavenly registry?*

"And we have come before God who judges all," the writer of Hebrews reveals in 12:23, "and who lives among the spirits of the righteous who have been made perfect in his eyes!" There is a strong theme of the vindication of God's people in the Hebrew Scriptures, and that probably forms a backdrop here. Read Psalm 9:7–12, which express this theme.

Unlike the Mount Sinai experience in the wilderness where the newly freed Hebrew slaves experienced a strong sense of God's judgment and warning, in our coming to Mount Zion we find vindication, forgiveness, and perfection by God's grace!

- *Do you experience God like on Mount Sinai or on Mount Zion? Explain.*

- *We are exhorted to "make very sure that you never refuse to listen to God when he speaks" (Hebrews 12:25). How do you suppose this looks practically, first to refuse to listen to God's words and second to put yourself in a posture of active listening, hearing his heavenly counsel?*

- *In the end, the Lord wants to remind us that he is shaking the systems of the world, rocking our old order "so only what is unshakeable will remain" (v. 27). What old systems and old orders do you find God shaking away in this day? How about in your life?*

- *What do you suppose God wants to remain instead—not only in our world and churches but also in your own life?*

Toward Victory

In his book *The Imitation of Christ*, the second bestselling book next to the Bible, the medieval German mystic Thomas à Kempis offers some apt closing words about enduring God's discipline and entering into his presence:

> The man who will suffer only as much as seems good to him, who will accept suffering only from those from whom he is pleased to accept it, is not truly patient.... For with God nothing that is suffered for his sake, no matter how small, can pass without reward. Be prepared for the fight, then, if you wish to gain the victory. Without struggle you cannot obtain the crown of patience, and if you refuse to suffer, you are refusing the crown. But if you desire to be crowned, fight bravely and bear up patiently. Without labor there is no rest, and without fighting, no victory.[63]

Talking It Out

1. How would you rate yourself when it comes to "sweating blood in your opposition to sin" (12:4)? What do you think you need to do differently or what resources might be helpful in order to "consider carefully how Jesus faced such intense opposition from sinners" (v. 3)?

2. Why do parents discipline their children? If you are a parent, what do you like or dislike about correcting your own children? What are your goals? How has the practice worked out with your children? Now relate your own experience as a parent to God's as your heavenly Father. Imagine how he would answer these questions in relation to maturing you. What do you think he would say?

3. Have you ever found yourself in the position of Esau, "becoming careless about God's blessings" (v. 16)? If so, what has sidetracked you from enduring and disciplining yourself to run life's marathon race?

4. What does it mean to you that your entrance into God's presence was made possible by Christ's blood and that you "have been made perfect in his eyes" and the better message of forgiveness continues to be spoken over you (v. 23)?

5. The writer exhorts us to always listen to God. How do you do that? How does he speak to you? And what from your life do you think he wants you to "lay down…in absolute surrender" to him (v. 28)?

LESSON 12

Jesus, Living a Better Way in His Light

(13:1–25)

Every great literary work closes with a great ending. Whether Tiny Tim's "God bless us, Every One!" refrain from Charles Dickens' *A Christmas Carol* or *Gone with the Wind*'s "After all, tomorrow is another day" proverb or the revelation that "on the top of the Forest a little boy and his Bear will always be playing" in *The House at Pooh Corner*—all of it serves as a denouement, a validation, a sigh that things will be all right.

Like every great work, each book in the Bible often ends in a way that offers the reader one final bit of exhortation or command or insight into the heart of God—whether the final blessing Jacob gave his sons in Genesis or the Great Commission of Matthew's Gospel or the great "I am coming soon" declaration closing out the book of Revelation. The book of Hebrews is no different, offering us a similar ending as a way to capstone everything that has been taught and revealed in this magnificent book.

All throughout his work, the writer of Hebrews has made the argument that Jesus is *better than*—the angels, the priesthood, the temple sacrifices, and more. Well, he has one final "better than" to offer as he ends his book: Jesus is the better *way*. He is better than a love for self, and we are to love fellow believers and those who are suffering. He is better than money, and we must guard against obsessing over it by being content with what God has given us. He is better than the religious "walls" we tend to erect around God and his heart. He is better than a go-it-alone spirituality, for he has given us leaders and examples to follow.

We discover and experience and live that way by living in his light. When we do, we will experience the fullness of "the God who brought us peace by raising from the dead our Lord Jesus Christ so that he would be the Great Shepherd of his flock," working perfection within us "by the power of the blood of the eternal covenant" to give us all that we need to fulfill our destiny. His better-than way expresses through us "all that is excellent and pleasing to him through your life-union with Jesus the Anointed One who is to receive all glory forever" (Hebrews 13:20–21).

Let us choose that better-than way, every day.

Live Pleasing to God

The writer of Hebrews ends his exploration of our better-than King-Priest by reminding us of his better way—the foundation of which is love.

- *List all the ways from this final chapter of Hebrews in which we are encouraged to keep loving one another as brothers and sisters in Christ.*

- *Describe a time when you experienced the heart of God through another believer loving you well. What was that like, and how did you experience God's heart through their own love for you?*

SHARE GOD'S HEART

- *How might it look in your life to "make room in your heart to love every believer" (13:1)? Make a plan for making this room at least once this week, showing hospitality and suffering along with those who suffer in order to share the heart of God.*

The book of Hebrews is the better-than book, showcasing how Jesus is better than anything else in all the universe, including his way of living. Jesus' way is better than our culture's way, and in no better place do we see this than the area of marriage and sexuality. The writer highlights this in 13:4, but also read what Jesus himself says about matters of marriage in Matthew 19:1–9.

- *Compare and contrast how living in Jesus' light by honoring the sanctity of marriage and vowing to stay pure is better than living in the darkness of the world. Why is Jesus' way better than the way of the world? How does God judge the world's way in contrast to his own?*

- *Consider your personal relationships in light of the writer's exhortation to "Honor the sanctity of marriage and keep your vows of purity to one another" (Hebrews 13:4). How are you at following this command to "honor"? Where do you need to grow in honoring the sanctity of marriage, whether single or married? Now, how can you plan to make this "honoring" more intentional?*

- *On a scale of 1 to 10, honestly assess how obsessed or content you are with money. Where do you fall on this spectrum, where ten is severely obsessed and one is fully content? If you tend toward the obsessed end of the spectrum, what do you struggle with the most when it comes to money? Or if content, why are you content, and how did you reach this state of contentment? Explain. Are there still areas where you need to work on being content with what you have?*

EXPERIENCE GOD'S HEART

- *What do you suppose might be the link between our obsession or contentment with money and our experience of God's heart, which the writer reveals in Hebrews 13:5–6?*

- *What does it mean to you that God has promised "I will never leave you, never! And I will not loosen my grip on your life!" (v. 5)? Do you believe it? Have you personally experienced it? Explain.*

- *Why does it matter that we know deep down that "the Lord is for me and I will never be afraid of what people may do to me" (v. 6)? What should this mean for our daily walk in life, especially when trouble hits and life turns sour?*

- *Who do you know who needs to hear both of these words of encouragement, that the Lord will never leave us and that he is for us? Now share this aspect of God's heart with them this week.*

- *Why do you suppose the writer urges us, "Don't forget the example of your spiritual leaders who have spoken God's messages to you, take a close look at how their lives ended, and then follow their walk of faith" (v. 7)? Why do their examples matter, what they said, and how they lived?*

In Hebrews 13:8, the writer emphasizes the immutability of Jesus Christ. *Immutability* means unchangeable, and in Scripture, when applied to God, immutability has to do with his unchangeable nature (God will always remain fully God, no matter what) and such things as his consistent faithfulness, goodness, and truthfulness. Everything else in the universe changes, but God does not. This is why he is our unshakeable Rock. We can always count on him no matter what.

Look up the following passages and jot down what you discover about God's immutability.

Numbers 23:19

1 Samuel 15:29

Psalm 102:25–27

Proverbs 19:21

Isaiah 14:24–27

Isaiah 46:9–11

Malachi 3:6

Hebrews 6:17–18

James 1:17

- *How does embracing the truth of Christ's immutability help guard us from being led "astray with all sorts of novel and exotic teachings" (Hebrews 13:9)?*

Early on in the life of the church, there was a group of Jewish believers who wanted to hold on to Jewish ceremonial and religious practices, even forcing converted gentiles to embrace them. The apostle Paul confronted them in the book of Galatians, the so-called Judaizers. Paul referred to them as "false 'brothers' [who] had been secretly smuggled into the church meetings. They were sent to spy on the wonderful freedom that we have in Jesus Christ. Their agenda was to bring us back into the bondage of religion"

(Galatians 2:4). There is a sense in which the same risk of crisis is evident in the book of Hebrews, where the major themes point to a group of Jewish Christians who felt a pull back to Judaism.

Although most in today's church are not perpetuating Jewish practices per se, there is still a danger of erecting religious "walls" and clinging to rituals of past religious systems.

- *What sorts of such walls do people in the church put up nowadays?*

- *How might it look instead to "arise and join [Jesus Christ] outside the religious 'walls' and bear his disgrace" (Hebrews 13:13), eschewing religious and ritualistic trappings?*

- *Why is it crucial to rest our security and identification in Jesus and his new covenant alone and not in religious ritual and systems?*

- *What do you suppose it means to "offer up to God a steady stream of praise sacrifices" (13:15)? How is this both connected to and contrasted from offering up "a steady stream of blood sacrifices" (v. 15)?*

- *According to the writer of Hebrews, what are the "true sacrifices that delight God's heart" (v. 16)? Give some examples and consider how you might be able to engage in such true sacrifices.*

- *Who are the spiritual leaders God has placed in your life? How can you show your appreciation to them for keeping watch over your soul and "make their work a pleasure and not a heavy burden" (v. 17)?*

- *If you are a leader, what does it mean to you that you "will have to give an account to God for [your] work" (v. 17) watching over the souls of those God has entrusted to you? How should this realization shape your leadership?*

Apostolic Blessing

The writer offers a concluding blessing:

> May the God who brought us peace by raising from the dead our Lord Jesus Christ so that he would be the Great Shepherd of his flock; and by the power of the blood of the eternal covenant may he work perfection into every part of you giving you all that you need to fulfill your destiny. And may he express through you all that is excellent and pleasing to him through your life-union with Jesus the Anointed One who is to receive all glory forever! Amen! (vv. 20–21)

Several things are highlighted in this prayer:

- the peace we have through Jesus' resurrection, who is our Great Shepherd;
- God's eternal covenant with us, forged in the blood of Christ;

- the Lord's work of perfection on each of our parts, leading to all we need to fulfill our destiny in Christ;
- God's desire to show forth through us and our lives all that is excellent and pleasing, thanks to our life-union with Jesus.

- *Consider each of these areas, meditating on what they mean to you, what you've received in light of them, what you've been called to because of them—spending time praying for their application in your life and praising the Lord for their gifts.*

Conclusion

Toward the end of his matchless letter, the writer of Hebrews urges us "to let your spirits flow through this message of love" (v. 22).

- *What from that message of love have you learned, or what has impacted you the most?*

Talking It Out

1. Do you feel the modern church regularly follows the exhortation to "No matter what, make room in your heart to love every believer" (12:1), across all gender, ethnical, and national lines? How should the church change to better obey God's call on our lives—including you and your community?

2. Do you know deep down that the Lord "will never leave you, never! And [he] will not loosen [his] grip on your life"? Explain.

3. Instead of offering blood sacrifices, we offer praise sacrifices. List examples of all the ways in which we can offer such praise sacrifices. Now spend time doing just that, choosing one and using it as an offering to God.

4. How do you think it looks as believers to "continue to live with a clear conscience" and "live honorably in all that we do" (13:18)? How might that look in your own life, as an individual and as a community of believers in our world?

Endnotes

1 "About The Passion Translation," *The Passion Translation: The New Testament with Psalms, Proverbs, and Song of Songs* (Savage, MN: BroadStreet Publishing Group, 2017), iv.
2 William Barclay, as quoted in George H. Guthrie, *The NIV Application Commentary: Hebrews* (Grand Rapids, MI: Zondervan, 1998), 19.
3 "Introduction," Hebrews, The Passion Translation, 605.
4 "Introduction," Hebrews, The Passion Translation, 605–606.
5 For more on the various authorship options and the pros and cons for each, see Donald Guthrie, *New Testament Introduction*, 4th ed. (Downers Grove, IL: InterVarsity Press, 1990), 668–82; H. Wayne House, *Chronological and Background Charts of the New Testament* (Grand Rapids, MI: Zondervan, 1982), 140–44.
6 "Introduction," Hebrews, The Passion Translation, 606.
7 Philip Edgcumbe Hughes, *A Commentary on the Epistle to the Hebrews* (Grand Rapids, MI: Wm. B. Eerdmans, 1977), 30.
8 "Introduction," Hebrews, The Passion Translation, 606.
9 Emil Shürer, *A History of the Jewish People in the Time of Jesus Christ*, as quoted by Merrill F. Unger, *The New Unger's Bible Dictionary*, ed. R. K. Harrison (Chicago: Moody Press, 1988), s.v. "Pharisees."
10 House, *Chronological and Background Charts of the New Testament*, 74.
11 For more information on the various Jewish groups mentioned here, see House, *Chronological and Background Charts of the New Testament*, "Jewish Sects of the First Century," 73–75; Unger, *The New Unger's Bible Dictionary*, s.vv. "Essenes," "Herodians," "Pharisees," "Sadducee," and "Zealot"; Merrill C. Tenney, *New Testament Survey*, revised ed. (Grand Rapids, MI: Wm. B. Eerdmans, 1961), 105–112.
12 "Introduction," Hebrews, The Passion Translation, 606.
13 "Introduction," Hebrews, The Passion Translation, 606.
14 N. T. Wright, *Simply Christian* (New York: HarperOne, 2006), 140.
15 Hebrews 1:1, note "a," TPT.
16 Hebrews 1:2, note "c," TPT.
17 Thomas Hewitt, *The Epistle to the Hebrews: An Introduction and Commentary*, Tyndale New Testament Commentaries, reprint ed. (Grand Rapids, MI: Wm. B. Eerdmans, 1981), 41–42.
18 Hebrews 1:4, note "a," TPT.
19 Hebrews 1:12, note "a," TPT.
20 Hebrews 2:4, note "i," TPT.
21 Hebrews 2:4, note "j," TPT.
22 Eugene Peterson, *A Long Obedience in the Same Direction: Discipleship in an Instant Society*, revised ed. (Downers Grove, IL: InterVarsity Press, 2000), 132–33.
23 Hebrews 3:1, note "k," TPT.
24 Hebrews 3:1, note "a," TPT.
25 Hebrews 3:1, note "a," TPT.
26 Hebrews 3:5, note "d," TPT.
27 Hebrews 3:11, note "a," TPT.
28 Hebrews 4:3, note "a," TPT.
29 Hebrews 4:12, note "j," TPT.
30 Genesis 14:18, note "d," TPT.
31 Matthew 26:39, note "a," TPT.
32 Hebrews 5:7, note "b," TPT.
33 Hebrews 5:8, note "d," TPT.

34 Hebrews 5:10, note "e," TPT.
35 Hebrews 5:12, note "h," TPT.
36 Hebrews 6:4, note "f," TPT.
37 The spiritual disciplines include such habitual practices as prayer, study, simplicity, submission, guidance, meditation, journaling, solitude, silence, confession, forgiveness, service, sacrifice, evangelism, apologetics, celebration, worship, and fellowship. For more on what these are, reasons for practicing them, and how to turn them into habits, see Richard J. Foster, *Celebration of Discipline: The Path to Spiritual Growth* (San Francisco: Harper & Row, 2018); William D. Watkins, *The Transforming Habits of a Growing Christian* (Minneapolis MN: Bethany House, 2004); Donald S. Whitney, *Spiritual Disciplines for the Christian Life*, revised ed. (Colorado Springs, CO: NavPress, 2014); and Dallas Willard, *The Spirit of the Disciplines: Understanding How God Changes Lives* (New York: Harper Collins, 1988).
38 Guthrie, *Hebrews*, 253.
39 Don Richardson, *Eternity in Their Hearts* (Ventura, CA: Regal Books, 1981), 7.
40 Unger, *The New Unger's Bible Dictionary*, s.v. "Melchizedek."
41 For more on the priesthood in the Old Testament, see Unger, *The New Unger's Bible Dictionary*, s.vv. "Aaron," "Levites," and "Priesthood, Hebrew."
42 Hebrews 7:16, note "a," TPT.
43 Oswald Becker, "*egguos*," in *The New International Dictionary of New Testament Theology*, vol. 1, ed. Colin Brown (Grand Rapids, MI: Zondervan, 1975), 372.
44 Robert G. Gromacki, *Stand Bold in Grace: An Exposition of Hebrews* (Grand Rapids, MI: Baker Book House, 1984), 130.
45 Hebrews 9:10, note "a," TPT.
46 Matthew Henry, *Matthew Henry Commentary on the Whole Bible (Concise),* https://www.biblestudytools.com/commentaries/matthew-henry-concise/hebrews/8.html.
47 Charles Spurgeon, as quoted in *Evening by Evening: The Devotions of Charles Spurgeon* (Grand Rapids: Zondervan, 2010), Kindle Locations 9142–58.
48 To learn more about the various theories of salvation that have been proposed, see Norman L. Geisler, *Systematic Theology, Volume 3* (Bloomington, MN: Bethany House, 2004), ch. 8.
49 Christian theologian Donald MacLeod answers this charge in his article "Divine Child Abuse?" The Gospel Coalition, August 13, 2014, https://www.thegospelcoalition.org/article/divine-child-abuse/.
50 Spurgeon, as quoted in *Evening by Evening*, Kindle Locations 9142–58.
51 Hebrews 10:22, note "g," TPT.
52 Guthrie, *Hebrews*, 355.
53 Henry, *Matthew Henry Commentary on the Whole Bible (Concise),* https://www.biblestudytools.com/commentaries/matthew-henry-concise/hebrews/10.html.
54 See Gromacki, *Stand Bold in Grace*, 182–83; Hewitt, *The Epistle to the Hebrews*, 171.
55 "Introduction," Hebrews, The Passion Translation, 607.
56 See Brian Simmons and Candice Simmons, *The Image Maker: Dust and Glory* (Savage, MN: BroadStreet Publishing Group, 2019), 107–110.
57 Genesis 22:1, note "a," TPT.
58 Genesis 22:1, note "a," TPT.
59 Henri Nouwen, *Bread for the Journey* (New York: HarperOne), Kindle Location 2543.
60 Guthrie, *Hebrews*, 400.
61 Hebrews 12:22, note "c," TPT.
62 Hebrews 12:22, note "g," TPT.
63 Thomas á Kempis, *The Imitation of Christ* (public domain), III.19.